I0666698

THE RED KETTLE

Begonia B. Joan

Moonstruck Ink Publishing

Paperback ISBN: 979-8-218-13123-4
Library of Congress Number: 2023901986
Filed with the United States Copyrights Office on 02/09/2023
Case #1-12224698391

1st paperback edition: February 2023
2nd edition: October 2024

Creative consultant: Megan Bailey
Cover art by: Emilie Joan Spinner
Illustrations by: Phoebe McCaffrey

Printed by Kindle Direct Publishing in the USA

Moonstruck Ink Publishing, LLC
Bristol, RI 02809

moonstruckink.com

Dedicated to Mabel,
my corgi-familiar,
who sat by me as
I wrote nearly every word.

The Red Kettle
Tree of Fate Chronicles Book One

Begonia B. Joan

Moonstruck Ink Publishing LLC

Table of Contents

Foreword

There came a point where the kettle inside me screamed and would not be silenced. Channeling my fiery passion into my writing was my only reprieve. All my life, I've dreamt of being an author, sharing my stories with others, and building my own fantastical worlds. Then when my inner kettle screamed, it all unfolded; the plot, meaning, and characters seemed to be channeled from a higher power.

I wrote this book as my way of coping with a world that left me crippled with anxious rage. My only wish is for you, the reader, to suspend your beliefs, preconceived notions, and attachments to what has always been and open yourself up to the reality of how fantastical life truly can be.

May the kettle within all of you scream when the time is right; may you feel no fear even as its distorting steam of emotions blinds you; and may you be courageous when using your voice to speak up for any injustices you see.

Because it is you, each individual that takes the time to read these words, that can make a difference — please don't ever believe otherwise.

PART ONE:
ROOT

I. Truth

The rain landed in heavy globular drops. Its ferocious velocity produced a ricocheted mist, rendering my hand-me-down truck's windshield wipers nearly useless. Personally, weather like this often made life feel teetering on the edge of meaningful and insignificant.

After a particularly grueling night waiting on Manchester's finest, all I wanted was to burrow under my warmest blanket, knit with love from my late grandmother, with my mutt warming my feet.

To escape from the world for just a little.

"Good luck with the early-morning crowd," I muttered to Robin, the server who had come to relieve me from my shift.

"Thanks, love. Hopefully, that table of creeps didn't get to you too much." The petite brunette kindly said as she pulled her hair back into a food-service-friendly ponytail.

"Not too much." My reply was as lackluster as my spirit.

Hanging up her dripping coat in the staff area, she pulled a clear plastic container out of her bag. "Hey wait, do you want to take any of this home with you?" Robin asked sweetly. "My boyfriend is a vegetarian like you; he made this *incredible* veggie-pot pie last night."

Having not eaten for the duration of my shift, the sight of food not fried and heavily processed roused my stomach to attention. Leaving the haven of my home into the terrors of modern society, especially going to work, caused me such immense anxiety that my stomach could no longer function normally. Though usually, by the time I'm leaving my hellhole of a job, my unease has dissipated and hunger roars through me.

"No thanks." I managed a weak half-smile at my coworker.

"My mom ordered Thai for us tonight."

"Okay, well, just let me know if you ever want to try some," Robin grinned, a warmth glinting in her eyes. "I could always bring it over, and we can hang out somewhere besides the seediest establishment in town."

I laughed once, drily.

"Yeah. Maybe soon." I dipped my head in farewell, my lips a thin line as I made my way toward the exit.

Probably not soon…if ever….

Finally clocking out, my heart ached for home.

The crisp nighttime air hit me seconds before the rain as I stepped outside the fine-dining establishment *"Hank's 'All You Can Eat, All the Time' Diner."* Its neon sign cast the flooding parking lot and surrounding buildings in a dull pink glow.

Working the graveyard shift, from eight p.m. to three a.m., was a punishment from my manager, who did not take the rejection of his unwanted advances well. Perhaps because I ended said rejection with a quick slap across his smug, greasy face. Regardless, he had since only scheduled me for the shifts that no other servers wanted.

My ancient car rumbled awake as I peeled off my soaked jacket, shivering slightly. After attempting to wring out my hair, to no avail, I pulled back my frizzy mane and then rubbed my hands together, willing them to warm as the heater sputtered on.

The radio faded in and out, as it always did when it stormed, so I shut it off altogether. The radio was hardly listenable anyway, constantly playing music that capitalized on how catchy a song can be.

Instead, rain consumed my senses as it transported me back to lazy Sunday mornings when my family was still together. The last one we spent with each other was similar to this night, with heavy, violent

4

precipitation and strong wind gusts that made the outside seem like another world.

As that final stormy morning flooded my memory, an all-too-familiar dull ache formed in my chest. I allowed nostalgia to swallow me whole, just for the drive home.

~*~

The smell of maple syrup and bacon woke my brother, Onyx, and me up from our beds that morning. We opened our bedroom doors, which were directly across from one another, at the same time.

"Morning, kiddo," Onyx said with a yawn and a stretch.

He gave me a sleepy, half-hearted grin before shoving me to the side and racing me down the stairs. It was a childhood ritual he was determined to continue throughout our lives as it ended in us either belly-laughing or play-fighting. Both outcomes brought us joy.

It had been raining throughout the night and had only intensified with the new day, with gale-force winds keeping everyone hunkered inside their homes. Luckily for my family, we genuinely enjoyed each other's company.

Sundays were typically spent together. Instead of going on our usual walk to the botanical garden down the street, we brought out old board games and gathered our candles.

Selene, my angelic mother, was whisking up banana pancakes and frying bacon in a way that only she could with effortless grace. Meanwhile, my father, Jasper, picked out records for us to enjoy.

Whatever my parents did, they made an art form out of it, seeming to create the most beautiful things out of the mundane. For an ordinary family, it would just be a pancake breakfast on a rainy Sunday. Yet, for parents, it was a symphony of senses, an experience for our little tribe to bond and relish in the love and contentment of our quaint lives.

Before cooking, my mom lit the candles, casting the open living room and kitchen in a cozy, orange glow. She sang as she added spices to the pancake mix — a warm blend of cinnamon and cloves that felt like a hug to my tastebuds. As the bacon sizzled and filled our home with its delicious, fatty aroma, my father narrowed his options.

"Shall we have Etta James or Nina Simone serenade us on this fine, gloomy morning?" He asked Onyx, who was the self-proclaimed music snob of the family.

My brother looked up from the book he was currently devouring and said with little hesitation, "Nina Simone. Could you skip ahead to Lilac Wine? Amber loves that song."

I rolled my eyes but still gave him a smirk. Though he was dark and brooding in the way some musicians are, Onyx was a romantic like our parents, and his current girlfriend had him utterly enthralled. Truthfully, he often made me wonder if the deep, sensitive hearts we inherited from them were a blessing or a curse.

That particular Sunday was exceptionally peaceful and heart-warming. It was almost as if a higher power knew it would become one of my fondest, most cherished memories.

~*~

When I arrived home, my mother was still awake, reading peacefully in my dad's old forest-green armchair. Her elbows rested on the armrest's red flannel patches, sewn on to cover the spots worn down with use.

"Why are you still up?" I asked while tending to the stir-fry leftovers she set aside for me and my overzealous pup, Belladonna. After popping my food into the microwave, I approached her chair and kissed her head.

"Just wanted to make sure you got home safe during the storm." She spoke gently after brushing her brown-gray speckled waves behind her ear and then reaching for my hand.

My mother always spoke as if she had infinite amounts of time — never seeming rushed or frantic. In my adolescence, it often tested my thin patience. Though as I've aged, each drawn-out syllable has become a lifeline of stability and familiarity.

"Thanks for saving me some. I can't stomach the shit they serve there. Everything is fried at least three times; I swear anyone who comes in has the risk of going into cardiac arrest." I spoke, exhaustion oozing with each word.

With a kind nod from my mom and a loving exchange of goodnights, I grabbed the steaming plate of leftovers and headed up to my 'den,' which was more of a nest. My family, especially my mother, always told me I acted like a cat, slinking away into hiding only to come out for food and water days later.

"Better to be in my room reading and listening to music than selling drugs or killing people," was my typical response.

My den was originally the location of my father's art studio. My mother had surprised him for his birthday one year with a renovation to the house that was his space and his alone. She worked on it for months in secret, though she suspected he knew all along.

Our previously unused, spacious attic was now my father's artistic haven. The joy and love on his long, scruffy face when my mother revealed that magical, artistic space for him was a memory my five-year-old brain clung to dearly.

That was, after all, how the two crossed paths and fell in love.

He was a young handsome street artist who set up tables with his sculptures and paintings of vivid colors and utopian, abstract concepts anywhere he could. She was a fresh-faced, beautiful admirer of the arts at the same festival, her heart as open as her mind.

My mother always told us that they found each other through the gift of appreciating the beauty in life. My father would say that he found something he didn't even know was lost.

Sadly, after my father and brother vanished in a freak accident over two years ago, his art studio was no longer his and his alone. It became the last semblance of thread that tethered me to them.

Neither my mom nor I saw their corpses since the cops had no bodies to identify. The only thing present at the accident was a car on fire and no one around for miles.

The lack of proof never sat well with me, and because of that, I held onto the hope that they weren't gone. Perhaps it was my way of coping with death, holding onto the possibility that it was all a mistake and they were simply lost somewhere far from home.

Going through the first stages of grief— denial and anger— I got stuck in a never-ending cycle between the two.

The first night they were gone, sleeping in my room resulted in night terrors of massive flames engulfing my home. I was running through the house, trying to save all my family members and animals, but couldn't find any of them. When I jolted awake, covered in sweat, I ran across the hall where my brother had slept nearly every night of my eighteen years of living.

Ripping open his door only reminded me of what was ripped away from me. I completely broke down; the sobs erupting from me came from deep inside my soul. My broken, aching soul that had just lost the two most important men in my life in a single day.

From that night on, barricading myself in my dad's studio was my only option, uncaring about how insane or unhealthy it was.

When I was in his studio, surrounded by his art, it felt like his essence was still with me. Like he could still communicate with me through the colorful brushstrokes of his old masterpieces.

Nonetheless, I'd greet him and my brother each time I passed by our old family photos hanging just outside the door to the attic.

My mother questioned that ritual, and occasionally still does, fretting that I may be coping unhealthily with the tragedy. Though each worry from her was met with assurance from me that keeping their memory alive was my only intention. Even though, truthfully, I believed that by acting like they were still there, they would be again.

"Hi, Dad... Hey, Onyx. Rough shift tonight."

With Bella on my heels, I walked up the short stairs to my bedroom, where relaxation could finally find me. I flipped the switch and took a deep centering breath. Seeing the familiar artwork of my father illuminated, along with our eclectic mix of furniture and art scattered throughout my room, immediately soothed my burnt-out nervous system.

Moseying in, my favorite burnt-orange, cushioned window seat beckoned me to enjoy my late-night, early-morning dinner. It was nestled in front of a floor-to-ceiling stained glass window, depicting a meadow filled with flowers of all colors, shapes, and sizes. Sitting crossed-legged on the bench, I stuffed my face with spicy noodles and vegetables.

Nostalgia kept me in its grip as fond childhood memories attached to this nook surfaced. The worn-down, lumpy stuffing reminded me of the hours spent lounging on that cushion, watching my father create his art.

He always managed to put on a show for me — twirling around, making funny voices, splattering paint everywhere but the canvas. The two of us would laugh until tears formed in my father's eyes, and I could hardly breathe.

He had a soft spot for me since glimpses of a young Selene would shine through in moments of joy, laughter, or admiration. Looking at me and my wild, curly hair, he would shake his head with a smile, *"You're so much like your mother, Kyanie, my sweet little Honeybee."*

His deep voice echoed in my mind, and a small smile cracked at the corner of my lips before a shiver ran through me. The cold autumn rain had left a deep chill that I could not resolve without fully submerging myself in a hot bath.

Wasting no time, I shuffled into the adjoined tiled room.

So consumed with his artistic vision, my father would often spend endless days in his studio. For that reason, he added a bathroom to his private, creative domain. In it, he put a glorious clawfoot tub that he had encountered by pure luck at an estate sale. Though the washroom was small, there still managed to be just enough room to have a toilet, sink, and that magical tub.

Turning on the faucet, I peeled off my sweaty, food-stained uniform and took a second to gaze in the mirror. As a small child, I would often turn the studio bathroom's three-pane mirror in on itself, producing infinite images when looked at just the right angle.

Leaning on the porcelain sink in all my glory, I turned the two outer mirrors to face each other. Once perfectly aligned, I poked my head in to see endless images of myself.

Mirrors seem more like portals to other dimensions or a parallel universe version of ourselves than reflective glass.

My hazel eyes stared back hollowly, and I noted the dark, puffy circles beneath them. I shifted my gaze to the infinite images of my curly-maned, naked self mirroring every move.

How strange it is that this is me...And this "me" is the vessel that I operate on Earth. I touched my face and then tucked a curl behind my ear. *Who am I when the vessel, this meat sack of blood and bones, is gone?*

The faces of my brother and father popped into my head, and I wished this mirror truly was a portal to bring me back to the time when life felt normal. When my heart was whole.

After the tub had sufficiently filled with water hot enough to make a dragon blush, I lit three candles and slunk into the water.

With only the glow from the candles and my thoughts present, the day's stress began to melt away. Candlelight danced along the tiled walls before I submerged my entire body, head included, under the steaming water.

Being underwater immediately soothed my weary soul.

As liquid silence enveloped me, I pushed my arms against the tub's walls, firmly holding myself at the bottom. For a moment, the water and I were perfectly still, both anticipating a reaction from the other. The separation between me, the water, and the bathtub had dissolved. At that moment, we were all one.

It wasn't until my lungs screamed for air that I finally resurfaced. My voluminous hair now slicked down, only my nose and eyes remained above the surface as I let the tub cocoon me with warm, gentle support.

Droplets from the faucet caused beautiful, circular patterns on the surface of my bath. A trance-like state took over my bodily senses as the connectedness between myself, the water, and the rippling effects of outside influences became all-consuming.

I've always craved water when emotions or reality overwhelmed my soul. Whether that was a dip in the ocean or a half-hour-long shower, I've needed to feel the element encompassing my vessel to cleanse the emotional burden from my body.

My recent shift at work had gotten under my skin after one of my last tables was a group of not-so-nice but little-too-friendly men. They had come from a nearby bar, and I could feel their drunken eyes watching my every move from the second they entered the diner. They eyed me hungrily and went as far as to ask what I was doing when my shift ended.

"Frankly, that's none of your concern." I snapped at them with a saccharine smile before slapping their check on the table and walking away in a huff. Rounding the corner to the employee-only area, I could no longer fight the tears stinging my eyes.

I had almost become numb to these sorts of interactions at my job. Almost. I lived in a small New England town with even smaller-minded people, so stuck in their colonial ways that they couldn't even see how backward they were living.

After staying in the water for what felt like an eternity of pure bliss, my fingers looked more like tan raisins than my skin. Unplugging the tub, I immediately felt the pull of water down the pipe. Never rushing to finish my time in the water, I sat in my porcelain clawfoot throne until it had completely drained.

Upon getting out and wrapping myself in a plush periwinkle towel, I walked over to the sink to put the mirrors, which were still turned in on themselves, back into place.

With a small face towel in hand to wipe away the steam, I heard a low voice, almost quieter than a whisper.

"Look..."

My head shot up, eyes bulging, trying to find the source of the voice I had just heard in the quaint, seemingly empty, candlelit bathroom. I took the towel and vigorously cleaned my ears, thinking I must have had water in them, causing me to hear things. The physical and emotional exhaustion had also caught up to me, considering it must have been past four in the morning.

As I reached to wipe the left panel, an impulse to look at the never-ending versions of myself one more time before putting the panels back to normal struck.

"Look at me…."

This time the quiet voice did not startle me.

I leaned forward, loose curls hanging and dripping with bathwater into the sink. Gazing down at the endless reflections, I expected only to see myself looking back.

Within the infinite reflections was something strange that hadn't been there before. A soft golden light behind my left shoulder had me straining in confusion before whipping my head around to see no such glow.

Moving my hand in front of it then shifting my body position to see if it was a trick of the candlelight creating this orb did nothing to debunk the anomaly. The more I focused on it, the stronger the light glowed. Rubbing my eyes in confusion, it began changing shape.

Suddenly, as if a switch had been flipped, the small candlelit bathroom was filled with a blazing white light. I gasped and instinctively covered my eyes to shield them from the newfound brightness.

"Kyanie, can you hear me?"

The faint disembodied voice from earlier spoke again— louder and more profound than before. With my sight adjusted to the exceptionally well-lit bathroom, I looked around wildly for the source of the sound.

"My sweet Honeybee, look in the mirror."

My blood ran cold, and my stomach dropped. The only person who ever called me that was my father.

What a sick joke my mind is playing on me....

My jaw hung agape, and my head shook in disbelief before I leaned onto the porcelain sink again to take one last look. I first saw myself, curly hair falling damply on my shoulders, eyes wide with shock, and hands tightly clutching my towel.

Then, to my disbelief, behind my left shoulder was a hazy outline of my father, glowing a soft golden hue. My jaw dropped even further as I struggled to understand what I was seeing.

"Dad?... Is that you?" I questioned, feeling foolish for even saying it. That familiar deep ache in my heart throbbed as I fought back tears and the urge to jump through the mirror to hold my father.

"Yes... I don't have a lot of time. I need you to listen to me very carefully, my Honeybee." He said with a smile, his deep voice sounding like it was traveling through water before reaching me.

I dabbed the growing tears and moved my wet hair behind my ears, hanging on every word. Any fear had dissipated entirely, only to be replaced with immense, longing love.

"Truth is on its way out... Listen to no one but your inner voice, as all answers are inside you... Remember the Earth Mother... Ground yourself down to Her before you try rising... Never forget that love is a powerful force greater than fear...." At the end of '*fear*,' the bright light was extinguished, and my dad's misty anomaly was gone.

My head suddenly felt heavy, as if full of cement. Before I could process anything, my vision blurred, and I collapsed on the checkered-tile floor.

~*~

Bella's incessant barking and clawing at the door awoke me.

With no indication of how much time had passed besides the melting candle wax, I slowly sat up, head pounding, to let in my concerned canine.

"Belladonna, the strangest thing just happened," I began while stroking her tan, white, and black coat, letting her lick my face and head, where I'm sure she could sense my pain was stemming. "I don't know if I can make sense of it. I saw Dad, and… it felt so real… but now it feels like a dream."

Bella listened to me with her loving eyes, one glacial-blue and one mud-brown, before giving me a lick and a nudge, telling me in her way that all would be well.

Feeling exhaustion's final blow, I decided to shake off the phenomena and contemplate it more in the morning when I wasn't fighting off sleep by the second. With Bella happily by my side, I blew out the remaining candles and left the bathroom.

Walking over to my vanity dresser to grab something for my slumber, I couldn't help looking at my exhausted reflection again, then at the smiling faces framing the mirror.

Simpler, happier times surrounded me. Homecoming photos from old friend groups, family pictures taken in the garden, and numerous other moments of laughter, love, and good company were frozen in time, impenetrable to the changeability of life.

Focusing on a picture of our family vacation at the Grand Canyon, my eyes landed on Onyx in his *Pink Floyd: Dark Side of the Moon'* t-shirt. Despite having all his vintage band shirts as options, that one remained my favorite.

Finishing my nightly routine at 4:42 am, I wearily got into my cozy, quilted bed with Bella asleep at the foot. My bedside lamp, a stained glass shade that cast the room in subtle rainbow hues and was another lucky antique purchase by my father, was the only source of light left. Reaching to turn it off, I saw my dark leather journal.

'truth is coming… listen to my inner self… ground to the Earth…love is more powerful than fear….' Safely immortalizing my father's words in my journal, I turned off the light and fell into a deep slumber.

II. Illusion

A massive open field filled with stars and darkness encircled me. Three full moons illuminated the sky, bathing the wildflowers that lay dormant around me in the pale light. A behemoth-sized barn owl was perched in a nearby tree, its black eyes staring deep into my core.

I was myself, yet lacking a physical body, like a wisp in the wind just witnessing this moment in time. The moons seemed to look down on me, in whatever form I was, and shone their celestial radiance even brighter. Their moonlight turned into a dazzling white iridescent blaze, consuming me and the field just before I awoke.

Opening my eyes, an aching pain in my head that felt like my brain had been jostled around on an amusement park ride thrummed my temples. Slowly, a hazy, distant memory of last night came to me.

I shot up in bed, looking around to see if Bella had given up trying to wake me— she had. My legs slid off the bed before I put on my dad's old slippers to shield my feet from the cold wooden floors.

The rain continued throughout the night, with unrelenting winds making it hard to want to leave the house at all.

Descending into the kitchen, I found a plate of fruit and pastries waiting for me, but my dog and mother were nowhere to be seen. I grabbed a handful of strawberries and a cinnamon danish, putting them on a blue, yellow, and orange Moroccan-designed plate before walking over to the stove to put water on for tea.

The red kettle, which the women in my family passed down for generations, was metal with a wooden handle. Its bright crimson shade stood out starkly from the tans, whites, and occasional pastel greens that adorned our kitchen. Large dark wood beams lined the ceiling, making the space inviting and warm, and matched the wood butcher block that was dead center in the room.

Putting the kettle on the stove and igniting the gas, I went to grab my favorite handmade mug from the local farmers' market. At that moment, my mother appeared in the front doorway, parallel to the kitchen's arched entryway.

Belladonna was leashed beside her, no doubt returning from a walk in the garden. She promptly bounded up to me with a wet, wagging tail, muddy paws, and a tired smile on her maw.

My mother removed her long, soaked raincoat and mud-caked boots in the doorway before striding in her thick wool socks over to the kitchen where I had just put the kettle on. The chill, damp autumn air came into the house along with the two, and knowing my mom, she was craving a hot drink more than anything.

"Do you want some tea? I can add more water if you'd like." I said, glancing at her and noting a distant look in her eyes.

Seeming to extinguish the thoughts plaguing her, she said with a smile, "That would be lovely."

"How was your walk in the garden besides wet and freezing?" I asked with a slight smile, looking to meet her cocoa-brown gaze again to decipher what was going on inside her mind.

We had built such a strong relationship of nonverbal communication, especially after our family of four was reduced to two. She could surely sense my probing eyes.

"Peaceful as always." She gently spoke, meeting my gaze to say nothing was wrong besides the chill she caught from walking in the abrasive autumn wind. Even with the elements seemingly working against her daily rituals, I knew she had found peace within the storm.

The dull ache in my head flared up, causing me to wince in

pain and immediately catch my mother's worried stare.

"The weirdest thing happened to me last night," I began to explain, knowing there was nothing too outlandish to share with her.

My mother stopped preparing her loose-leaf tea and gave me her full attention.

"I took a bath before bed, and when I got out...." Words suddenly became very difficult. "...I saw Dad or his ghost. Or a vision of him, I don't know." My mother's face was calm as she listened to my every word, not passing any judgment on the ludicrous statement I had just made.

"He told me that the truth is on the way out. That I should listen to my gut and stay grounded to the Earth. And..." I rubbed my head which was still throbbing slightly, and finished, "Love is more powerful than fear."

Still, she said nothing, not revealing anything that was going on behind those rich brown eyes but nodded along, giving me the leeway to keep rambling.

"I know it sounds nuts, but it was so real, Mom. He called me Honeybee and... and I know it was him. In some strange form, like a misty illusion or an apparition." I heaved a sigh and gave her a look that pled, *'Please don't think I'm crazy.'*

Selene laughed softly before replying. "I knew he would find a way back to us."

I blinked back at her, "What are you saying? Dad, or his ghost, is...?" Words once again failed me. I leaned against the wooden kitchen island and looked at my mother, desperately trying to make sense of what she said so casually.

A gentle sigh came from her mouth and another slight smile, "Why don't you take a seat," she said as she pulled out the stool next to her, "I suppose it's time we have a talk."

As soon as she finished, the red kettle I had forgotten about entirely let out a loud, high-pitched scream and caused me to jump.

My mother chuckled softly, then said almost to herself, "Ah, the divine timing of it all," as I went over to the stove and turned off the burner.

A piercing whistling lingered in the air.

I went to fill both of our readied teacups with hot water as my mother mused and said, "Have I ever told you about the history behind this kettle?"

Irritated at the change in conversation topic, I hastily shook my head and filled our mugs with water.

"My mother's mother, and her mother before that, and her mother before that, would share this wisdom over tea with the women in our family. It's about the truth." She paused, looking at me, holding in her gaze the importance of what she was about to say.

"Truth is much like a boiling kettle. Once it has started whistling, the steam spewing out of the spout cannot be contained. Though you can remove the kettle from heat and seemingly stop the whistling, the water has boiled, and the steam cannot be suppressed. Truth operates in the same way; once it starts slipping out, there's nothing one can do to prevent it fully escaping, just like the steam from a kettle." She finished talking by blowing on the scalding tea and gazing questioningly at me, reading my face to see if her metaphor had sunk in.

"Okay, but you can take it off the heat and leave the kettle alone until it cools. Then the steam is gone." I retorted, still slightly annoyed and now a bit confused about the relevance of this analogy.

"You were always so quick to argue." My mother said with a

tut and a smile wide enough to crinkle her eyes. "This is true. However, the function of a kettle is to boil water. Even if you let it cool or the kettle doesn't scream, steam will escape. Then one day, that kettle will scream with the force of all the steam that hadn't been released." Blowing softly on her tea, she finished shutting down my snarky comment, "In time, the truth will always surface. Like a kettle put on to boil will steam and scream when it's ready." She concluded with a wink.

Seeing me furrow my brows and then suddenly connect the dots to what my father's apparition said last night, my mother chuckled softly.

"Okay, okay, so last night dad's ghost came to me and told me about the truth coming out, and now you're passing down generations of wisdom that teaches the same thing and...." I emphasized each word, piecing the lesson together with each syllable but still missing what *'the truth'* really was.

"And I feel like there's more you have to say about what happened last night," I spoke definitively and straightened my back, hardening my gaze slightly.

Again, my mother's sweet, gentle smile met me as she said, "Of course I do, but what would I be teaching you if I spelled everything out for you? You are a quick and brilliant young woman— I want to ensure your mind gets enough exercise." Another wink and a gentle blow. "Firstly, you must understand that I cannot tell you everything you need right now. Rather I can only say enough to enlighten your path so that you may start your journey."

"Um...okay, are you going to speak in riddles and metaphors the entire time like a troll guarding a bridge? Or can you talk to me like a human being, mother-to-daughter style?" My attitude was tangible at this point, as my patience was as thin as it was in my adolescence.

She exhaled, then reached for my hand and squeezed.

"I wish I could tell you everything and more," adding another squeeze for emphasis, "but it's simply not safe. Nor will it be beneficial for you in the long run. So bear with me as I navigate this."

Meeting her eyes, I could almost see everything she ached to say and accepted that the whole truth would be revealed in time.

"You see, your father and brother were seekers of truth. As you probably remember, they spent a great deal of time going to the library and researching various topics." She finally took a hummingbird-sized sip and grinned genuinely. "Your father was always interested in...unusual beliefs. From the first day I met him, he craved going as deeply as possible when learning something new. That's a trait he certainly passed on to Onyx."

I nodded in agreement, thinking fondly of their studies and the "unusual" topics they would relay to me. They would speak of magick, mystical creatures, and otherworldly powers far too complicated for our human minds to wrap around.

"These studies were risky for them and even riskier to share with others." Her warm eyes sharpened with seriousness as if she could see the memories within my head. "Because they shared too much, they exposed themselves to the Trine of Power: The Solar Lord, his Guardians of the Order, and the Machine."

I knew of the Solar Lord, as nearly everyone did. Thankfully, my family never worshipped or adhered to his strict, organized religion and moral code. Though the others I was hearing of for the first time.

"The...Machine? What kind of machine? And guardians of what order?" My brows were knit with confusion, though I accepted they'd likely remain that way for the rest of the day.

"The Machine is not a singular object. It is an entire hidden system that operates to control the human population. It's not obvious to most, but those who ask too many questions and learn about the Old Ways can see right through their Veil of illusion." My mother hesitated as if she was already giving me too much information.

I clung to every word like the last drops of water in a desert.

"The Trine of Power is nefarious. It's like a dark beast that prowls below the murky waters of our existence. It preys on faith and hope, giving false information to believe in and further diluting the truth of life." She set her teacup down beside her and leaned forward with her elbows on her knees. "Your father and brother did not die in a car accident, as I know you know. They left this reality not by physically dying— they had to flee and escape the persecution of the Guardians of the Order."

My jaw, heart, and stomach plummeted. *I knew it; I always felt deep in my bones that they weren't truly dead.*

"And before you ask questions, this was not an ordinary type of fleeing where they went into hiding somewhere. No, they *ascended*." She barely whispered, hoping perhaps speaking quietly would mask the loaded claims she was making.

"Where did they go? What do you mean they ascended?" Immediately the questions poured from me as I was incapable of holding back any longer. "Why was the car burned? Did you know they were leaving before it happened? Why didn't you say anything while I spent months sobbing hysterically over their passing?"

Reaching out to grab my hand again, she doused the fire building inside me and cooed, "My girl, I'm sorry I had to let you feel those emotions." Stroking the back of my hand with her calloused thumb, she continued, "You must know it wasn't safe to tell you this. I had no idea if your eye would open, and it's never the job of another to do that for someone. You had to reach this point on your own. Just like your father and brother did before they were sold out."

As if a match was lit on gasoline, my inner fire blazed.

"They were sold out?! How do you... do you know who did it?" I sputtered as rage consumed my thoughts.

They were ripped from my life because someone betrayed them.

"I have my suspicions." She took a deep breath. "Listen carefully now; I've shared more than enough and need to finish. Now that you know part of the truth, you must not talk about it to anyone unless they do so first, or you can trust without a doubt that they are not Guardians of the Order. These soldiers of The Machine will stop at nothing to please their righteous Solar Lord— you are more valuable to them dead than alive."

She paused and lowered her voice, "The most dangerous thing about the Guardians is that some don't even know they're members. They go around, mindlessly doing the bidding of a corrupted head of power."

I felt her words seep into every pore of my being. What should have been a shocking revelation was hardly even a surprise to me. As if part of me knew this *'truth'* all along, and I was simply hearing it aloud for the first time.

The questions within me screamed to be asked, but instead, I tried to digest what had been revealed quietly.

"How will I know if someone is a Guardian?" I had to let that one slip— I'd never been the best judge of character and needed specifics on what to look out for to steer clear.

"That can be tricky, love. They often look completely normal, able to disguise the vile hatred in their hearts to blend in with everyone else." Her lip curled towards a snarl as she continued. "There are certain, rather boisterous, Guardians that choose to wear their emblem with pride.

"It's a symbol, usually on a badge, of a twelve-pointed sun with an X in the middle and a vertical line bisecting the center. It's one of the oldest depictions of the Trine of Power, made to trick people into pious submission. They claim it shows our connection to their mighty Solar Lord, but anyone with their eye open will see it shows severance."

My mother heaved a sigh as if the weight of all she had exposed was now on her back. Though she pressed on, her voice hardly a whisper. "They want people to be separated. From one another. From themselves; mind, body, soul. There is strength in unity, and that strength threatens their Order— their Trine of Power." Her mouth pressed in a thin line, and I knew she could not speak anymore on the subject.

"Trine of Power," I unintentionally mimicked back to her, shaking my head slowly before her other words sunk in. "Wait, why do you keep saying 'eye'? What do you mean open my 'eye'? Both of them are open right now." My brows knit as I looked at her, hoping she could spare me just one more answer.

"Well, we have normal eyes to look with and take in our environment. But our other eye, our *hidden* eye, lies in the middle of our forehead, and it helps us truly see. What our normal eyes would never notice, our hidden eye feels. It's our connection to something bigger than ourselves. I believe yours is peeking— you'll know when it's fully opened. Nothing in your reality will look the same." She tapped my forehead and smiled.

I took her hand and squeezed, taking in her appearance as I never had before.

Her tan-olive skin resulted from numerous ancestral lineages blending into a single human. She'd often joke that she was a mongrel of a person; mixed with so many different breeds, she didn't know what to call herself. In truth, she took characteristics from all over the world to create a beautifully bewitching, unique, multi-racial being.

We had the same hair— an untamed, frizzy mess of brunette and golden waves. Our eyes were also nearly identical, though hers were a warm brown while mine were hazel. Her face was aged through the smile lines by her eyes and mouth, showing a life filled with laughter and happiness.

She wore a thick-stitched tan sweater that had robust wooden buttons with intricate designs. Her blue denim pants, and every pair she owned, were stained with paint, dirt, or whatever other creative pursuits she was immersed in at the time.

I then spent the most time memorizing my mother's delicate, slender hands with fingernails always miraculously long and pointed. She was a crafter at heart, so her hands were her most valuable asset. Silver rings with colorful jewels adorned half her fingers. However, her emerald engagement ring from Jasper seemed to sparkle the brightest.

"So now that I know this 'truth,' what do I do?" My stream of consciousness slipped out, and the words I spoke genuinely sunk in.

"That is for you to decide for yourself. Many people know the system that rules our world yet continue a normal life of complacency. Others hope to ascend and leave behind this realm of chaos and corruption. The choice is yours to make." With that, she rose from the kitchen island, signifying our conversation was over.

"I'm going to take a hot shower; the autumn chill has lingered in my aging bones." She gave me one last squeeze on the shoulder. "I know you'll do what's right." With a final wink, I watched my mother disappear down the hallway.

I was left in the kitchen with a full cup of tea, a heavy heart, and a concerned pup who could sense how this conversation had permanently altered my life path.

III. Complacency

That afternoon I had plans to meet my two closest remaining friends, Rosemary and Adelaide, at our favorite cafe. They had been my friends long enough to assume I'd arrive late, but today was certainly later than usual.

In the wake of the talk with my mother, my mind could not stop reeling, picking apart everything she said and contemplating everything about the world around me.

"Well, look who finally decided to grace us with her presence." Rosemary gave me a mocking bow and a cheeky smile before patting the open booth next to her. "You've just walked in at the height of a rousing debate." She flipped her lilac hair over her shoulder and motioned to our companion to continue.

"All I said was that I wonder if Luke will propose this weekend. Now Rose is going off about how monogamous, heteronormative marriages are part of a corrupt system that keeps women subservient and owned by men." Addie threw her hands up in exasperation. "We don't need to turn *everything* into an argument."

I let out a low chuckle knowing all too well that my two best friends could not be more different. More often than not, any extended amount of time spent alone between the two ended with one huffing away.

Rosemary moved to our hometown when we were five. Her family came from a devoutly religious, rural town. Anyone who did not conform to their Solar Lord and his laws was outcasted or persecuted.

Her mother refused to adhere to their rules, and though her father tried to oppress her into drudgery— she refused. She refused until she fled for the north, where he would never find her or her daughters again. Her mom packed up their station wagon, fastened Rose and her younger sister in the back, and finally escaped their alcoholic father, never turning back.

As for Adelaide, her family was born and bred in our hometown. They all lived perfectly normal lives of complacency and had no desire to do more with their time on Earth than work, spend money, procreate, and die.

While Rosemary's entire existence seemed to contradict the expected norms of our society, coming from a single mom, only ever preferring the company of women, and changing her hair color every month, Adelaide was the poster child of a perfectly pious female.

Addie's long brunette hair was always down and flawlessly curled. She wore the same makeup daily— mascara, pastel pink blush, and lipgloss. Her freckles littered her nose and big blue eyes, creating the innocently charming "girl next door" look.

In addition to her conventional beauty, Addie was quiet, gentle, and a true romantic at heart. I knew someday she would indeed marry a man who could give her the simple life she desired for herself — and not much more.

"You know, Rose, marriage can be very freeing for women. Once they lock down a man, they can live the remainder of their lives as housewives! Free to do whatever they please within the confines of suburbia." I returned the cheeky smile she had given me, knowing she could see through my attempts to rile them up again.

Rosemary's green eyes glinted mischievously as she sarcastically agreed. "Ah yes, the complete and utter joys of suburbia!" Her southern accent resurfaced. "My oh my, all my little heart desires is a husband, two kids, a dog, and a white picket fence." She crossed her hands over her heart. "Well, if I had all that, I could die happier than a pig who escaped the slaughterhouse!"

I snorted in response, though Addie was not amused.

"I never make fun of you guys like you do me." She took a sip of her latte. "I don't think tearing down my friends is funny."

"Aw, Addie, come on, we're not trying to tear you down! Just wake you up and reconsider your life, that's all." Knowing she had pushed one-too-many buttons but being too stubborn to apologize, she reached out for her hand. "My dear sweet Adelaide, will you ever forgive me for believing that what you want is patriarchal nonsense?"

"I don't accept that apology, Rosemary. Try again." She rejected her outstretched hand and sank further into her side of the booth, crossing her arms over her chest. Though Addie was kind and gentle, she became a stonewall of emotions once she was irked.

Rose rolled her eyes and loosed a sigh. "I'm sorry, I don't support the institution of marriage. Can we please agree to disagree and change the topic to why our lovely friend here decided to show up almost an hour late to our cafe date?"

Seeming to accept that, or perhaps knowing she wouldn't get a better apology, Addie turned to me. "You could have let us know if you were busy. What took you so long?"

I shifted in discomfort, remembering the life-changing information my mother had told me and how it wasn't safe to share.

My throat became tight as I fumbled for an excuse. "I...uh...I got into a pretty intense talk with my mom. Family stuff, you know?" My friends had learned at this point that bringing up my family was a conversation no one wanted to have.

"Agh, speaking of family... my mom's new boy toy is arguably worse than the last one." Rose was truly a ringmaster of discussion—

it was no wonder why she was the captain of our high school's debate team.

"This one's name is Mark," Rose sneered at his name and tore off a bite of her muffin before popping it into her mouth. "He calls her 'baby cakes' and shows her affection by buying her crap she doesn't need. Yesterday he brought her three different *As Seen on TV* kitchen supplies because he genuinely thought that's what every woman truly wants."

Addie, who just wanted to have a relaxing midday latte with her friends and perhaps divulge some gossip, pressed. "Is he at least cuter than the last one? I remember you saying he had a toupee and fake teeth." She giggled as she was undoubtedly picturing this heinous bald and toothless ex-lover of Rosemary's mother.

"Eh, it depends on what you define as cute." Ripping off a bigger muffin bite, she continued chewing obnoxiously. "Because honestly, I find this half-eaten muffin cuter than most men I've seen in my lifetime. Though, my mom is always prattling on about how handsome he is. I think it's just because he's more than ten years her junior, and she's enjoying having the devotion of an actual boy-toy."

Grateful that the attention was entirely off me, I added, "How long have they been seeing each other? I thought the last one... what was his name... John?" Rose nodded in confirmation. "I thought John was living at your house a few weeks ago?"

"Yeah, he was, but he got weird." Wiping the crumbs off her face and then hands, she leaned forward as if she was about to tell some pipping hot gossip. "He started preaching to her about this 'males only' club he just joined— telling her he had certain rules that she had to abide by....It reminded her of my dad, so she threw his stuff out on the lawn and told him never to talk to her again." Rose sat upright in her chair and huffed a laugh. "Man, I love that crazy bitch."

My stomach turned.

Was he a Guardian of the Order? If this random lover of Rosemary's mom is involved, how many others are there in our quaint town?

"Did he say what the name of the club was?" My palms were suddenly clammy, and I tried my best to keep a level voice.

"Either I can't remember, or he never told us… We'll go with the latter for my sake." Rose washed down her food with a sip of black tea. "He would go on about 'protecting the order' or 'keeping the order' or something along those lines. He'd tell her of her womanly duties and what he expected from her— he wanted her to be nothing more than a submissive housewife who catered to his every whim." I knew the eye roll she did was entirely involuntary. "*Pig.*" She shook her head, plopped one last bite of muffin into her mouth, and sighed.

"You know my dad and brother are members of a 'males-only' club," Adelaide said with the casualty of someone blissfully unaware. "They attend meetings almost every week but never try to berate my mom about her 'womanly duties.' In fact, they barely talk to either of us at all."

Rosemary had a devilish smile, showing whose advocate she was about to play. "Well, does your mother adhere to their rules without needing to be reprimanded? If your family prays to the Solar Lord, I'd bet she's already in pious servitude to their desires." She took another drink of her tea with a raised eyebrow at our stunned friend.

"I…I never questioned… My mom always reassures me we're a happy family. I thought, or think, we have a normal household. Like all married couples sleep in separate bedrooms and hardly speak to one another. I assumed love fizzled out after the honeymoon phase, and instead, there's more of an indifferent fondness." Addie began chewing her inner lip, a telltale of when she was getting flustered.

"Oh, you no doubt have a 'normal household.' I'm sure your parents got married, had your brother and you a few years in, and are now looking forward to retiring. Probably move somewhere warm. Or maybe they'll just have a timeshare in that warm and sunny place so they can stay close to you and Carl." Rose's flame had been stoked, and there was no holding back. "They'll stick around, watch you guys pop out children of your own, and eventually die as very happy and fulfilled grandparents."

I watched the tears form in Addie's eyes as she rapidly blinked them away. "What's so wrong with that? Why do you have to be so cruel and cynical about everything?"

"There's nothing wrong with it, and, may I remind *you*, that's what I'd call normal. There's nothing wrong with it if you want to spend your life as a useless puppet for the human race to continue. To live mindlessly in a world that you barely understand."

Rose's green eyes turned sharp, like daggers would actually come out of them. "I'm 'cruel and cynical' because I see our world for what it is. The only memory of my biological father is the look of pure evil in his eyes as he screamed at my mom for the last time. I'm cruel and cynical because I came from a man who would rather have seen my mother weep than laugh. Who would have beaten the gay out of me had he known when I was that young."

If her eyes were daggers, then her words were pure venom.

I wasn't sure what to say, and every time I opened my mouth to diffuse the situation, I found myself staring blankly at my two closest friends.

Addie, also at a loss for words, looked down and started

getting her things together. "I'm sorry you've never lived in a stable, happy home as I have." She blinked away more tears and arose from the table. "I'm going away with Luke for the weekend, so I'll see you guys next week." She walked out of the cafe and did not turn back.

Both of us sat there in silence for a heartbeat more.

"Did she really just call her family a *happy home.*" Rosemary gawked, taking a final swig of her tea. "Maybe I am cruel and cynical, but at least I'm not delusional."

"Hey, come on, she doesn't know any better. She's been taught one way of living her entire existence and can't fathom anything outside that box." I took my first sip from the herbal tea my friends had ordered for me, which had turned lukewarm at best by now. "I feel sorry for her."

Rosemary, whose fire was harder to cool than mine was, shot back up in her seat. "I don't feel sorry for her. Pity would be a closer feeling, but no— she's not a child, and it's not our job to teach her to be better. I'm sick of being surrounded by ignorant privilege." She also started gathering her things together, needing to take a cool-down walk as she often did after getting riled up in conversation.

I had hardly had any of my tea and certainly wouldn't now that it was unpleasantly cool.

"Mind if I join you for a stroll in the garden?" I asked, knowing she would never turn down a companion whose ear she could talk off.

IV. Connections

The local botanical garden was a little more than a mile from the cafe. Since the rain had stopped and a hazy overcast took place, we decided to walk and enjoy the eerie ambiance October gave our quaint town.

We walked in comfortable silence, busy mulling over different conversations in our heads, with only the dull crunch of fallen, soggy leaves to disturb the quiet.

The truth that my mother revealed echoed through my consciousness alongside the rippling effects of my family's death.

If only I had known they didn't truly die.. .

Being voted the yearbook's "Social Butterfly" in my senior year of high school had become a bitter irony between myself and the universe. The version of myself that my classmates knew was dead and buried next to my father and brother's empty coffins.

Light-hearted mingling, laughing at seemingly endless inside jokes, and finding things in common with almost everyone I encountered was my norm.

In an act of reverse metamorphosis, depression took my inner butterfly, reduced it to goo, and left a dark, empty chrysalis of grief. My friendly demeanor shifted into that of a cold recluse. Conversations became short, blunt, and avoided entirely if possible.

Truthfully, I always felt more like a chameleon than a butterfly — changing my colors and personality to blend in with whoever and whatever people wanted me to be. Shifting my face, continuously morphing into the most charismatic, likable version of myself, made no difference to the people who flocked to my warm energy like moths to a porch light.

That is, until the glow within me faded.

No one saw me in that light, or even remotely normal again, shortly after my high school graduation. Considering it was a week before the accident, it was the last time my family was seen all together in public.

Afterward, I could no longer stand being around people with whom I only had surface-level conversations. Perhaps it was being worn down by all the people I had to talk to and accept grievances from at the wake and funeral. Or the fact that my soul felt more vacant than it ever was before.

It was always the same questions about how I was doing and how my mom was holding up. As if anyone truly cared to understand the immense pain and emptiness we both felt in our hearts.

No longer going to any social events and successfully pushing away nearly everyone close in my life besides my mother, Rosemary, and Adelaide, I spent most of my free time at the botanical garden. Being surrounded by greenery consistently breathed life into my spirit, resetting my emotional and mental state without fail.

My father made it a point to expose us to as much nature as possible, as often as possible. We would take strolls through the garden or nearby forests at least once a week.

My mother was always in charge of food, often packing a full picnic basket to enjoy in the wildflower field. Meanwhile, my brother unfailingly brought his harmonica or signature acoustic guitar, carrying a tune wherever we went.

Even with the bittersweet memories from the past that haunted me, I had cultivated a consistent sense of inner peace inside the garden's perimeters.

Entering its dark iron gates, we first passed by a gazebo used for countless weddings and parties, a handful of which I'd attended. There were three walking paths from the gazebo— the one to the left led to a temperate forest with maple, oak, and ash more like giants than trees. In contrast, the right one went to an elaborate flower garden with a labyrinth of roses and dahlias that exploded with rich hues in the spring and summertime. Lastly, the path dead-center went to an herb garden and medicinal greenhouse. Between all the paths lay sprawling fields and hills filled with wildflowers, plants, trees, and people enjoying the natural beauty.

That day we went left, immersing ourselves with the giants and hiding away in the cool forest.

"Hey, Rose, I need to talk to you about something." I met her eyes, hoping she would see the seriousness in mine. "Something that you can't repeat to anyone...like not a single soul." I stopped walking, feeling the lump in my throat resurface.

"Oh great, you know I love having deadly serious conversations." She smirked but saw my solemn face. "What's up?"

"Last night after work I...I saw my dad. Or a vision of him, at least. He told me about the truth coming out."

Rose had stopped walking to look at me directly, with no hint of sarcasm on her face, just intent on listening.

"When I woke up today, I told my mom about it, and...this is where I need you to solemnly swear you won't repeat this to anyone." My voice dropped to a whisper.

"Cross my heart and hope to die." She did indeed cross her heart, then stuck out her pinky to solemnly swear as we had since we were kids.

"My mom told me that my father and brother didn't die. They

had to flee...to escape through *'ascending.'* She said they knew too much, which posed a threat to certain people, so they were sold out to Guardians of the Order. To or by whom I'm not sure, she didn't say."

Rose made no move to interject.

"Now I feel like I need to go...somewhere. I need to find more answers and possibly even my family. I feel...I feel like something has just been unlocked inside me, and now I can't return to normal life. Whatever normal is for me anyway." I heaved a sigh. "My mom told me not to tell this to anyone unless I trusted them without a doubt, and you're the only person I thought to turn to. I needed to talk about this because I feel like I'm on the brink of going crazy." I met her gaze and sighed again, showing I had little left to say.

She gently grabbed my hand, showing a softness that hardly anyone saw. "Is that all?" Rosemary questioned, a small smile tugging at the corner of her full lips. "Well, I can assure you you're not going crazy! I've heard stories like this— people going missing under mysterious circumstances— but I never wanted to bring it up because I know how sensitive you can be on the subject."

She looped her arm through mine and turned us back towards the gates. "Sounds like we need to take a trip to the library."

~*~

I hadn't been to our local library in easily three years. The last time I came with Onyx, who desperately tried to find one specific book that seemed to have vanished from all library and bookstore shelves. I now wondered what magical, occult text he was searching for and wished I had paid better attention to his ramblings.

Luckily, Rosemary's girlfriend, Poppy, worked part-time at the library. The two got together not long after my family's separation; by now, I considered her one of my few friends.

"Did you have a specific title you were looking for?" Poppy's high-pitched, chipper voice asked us.

"No, but is there a section of occult books? Books that are likely on a list to be banned or destroyed?" I inquired, feeling awkward for asking in such a way. Truthfully, I had no idea what I was looking for other than that it was dangerous enough to separate families.

Rosemary laughed and put her elbows on the help desk, "What she means to say is, do you have books on spirituality? Different belief systems and texts on the Old Ways?"

The Old Ways. My mother had mentioned that, but I didn't say anything about it to Rose.... How much does she already know on the subject?

"Ah, I see. We used to have an extensive occult section, but a few years ago, some people broke in and cleared the shelves of anything involving religion. Even some fantasy and fiction rows got ransacked. We replaced some of them, but not even close to all." Poppy smiled politely and emerged from the desk. "Let me show you what we do have."

I only ever saw Poppy wearing dresses, and today was no different. She wore a mid-length olive dress with pink flowers embroidered up the sides. Its green hue paired naturally with her tan skin and jet-black hair, cut just above her shoulders.

Poppy had an air about her that was consistently calm and gracefully feminine. Any time I'd compliment her on the matter, she'd credit her father for teaching her about mindfulness from a young age.

He was a Tibetan monk who fell in love with her mother while she was visiting distant relatives in Nepal. A military unit pillaged his monastery, and he was fleeing persecution. Hoping to make a new life for himself, the two met in passing at an open market. Her father took that as a sign from the divine that he had found his destiny— he was not wrong. They came to America a year later when her mother became pregnant with Poppy.

We followed her down to the lower level, to the furthest back corner of the building. She stopped before a sad, half-empty shelf.

"Well, this is our selection!" The upbeat attitude of her voice did not match the dark, vacant section of the library we had reached.

"Thanks, babe. I think the two of us can handle rummaging through all of this," she made a sweeping motion towards the shelf, "if you want to go back to work."

Poppy giggled softly and pecked Rose's cheek. "You know where to find me if you need help." She gave me a warm, friendly smile and vanished up the stairs.

I took in the barren shelf in its entirety. There were maybe, *maybe*, twelve books. "I can take half and skim through them if you want to do the same?" I suggested to Rosemary, who had already started reading the bindings for titles.

"No need. A handful of these books are exclusively about the Solar Lord... his early years, how he came to power...." Rose traced her finger down their spines. "Oh, interesting, this one is about the Earth before he came into it." She pulled it out and threw it down on a nearby table.

I went to the opposite end of the row and examined the few bindings in front of me. One thick, black book with silver lettering caught my eye.

"Numerology: The Language of the Universe," I read quietly aloud as I pulled it off the shelf. *"Written by Nikola Vaughn."*

As if saying his name triggered a memory deep inside me, I felt incredibly drawn to this text. Holding it close to my chest, I looked at the other small handful of books.

'Angels & Demons, Occult Practices, Mystical Beings & Places'

I grabbed them all and brought them to the table where Rose had begun reading about our world before the Solar Lord took over.

We spent the next hour or so quietly consumed by the sparse spiritual texts we had successfully gotten our hands on. Rose became entirely enthralled with her book, doing far more than skimming.

As I read about otherworldly beings accompanying us here on Earth, whether angels, demons, fairies, or elves, the more I read, the more I felt déjà vu. The same feeling I had when my mother revealed the partial truth— as if I'd known it the entire time. Like a part of me, deep within my vessel, holds 'the truth' to everything.

I wanted to take notes on the books and asked to borrow Rose's library card to bring them home. My next best step seemed to be locking myself in my room, with papers and books sprawled across my bed. I would spend hours, days even, delving into the studies my family had researched for years.

As Poppy scanned our stack of five books upon our departure, she paused, tilting her head to the side questioningly as she eyed the last one in the pile.

"Nikola Vaughn…That name is so familiar…." She tapped her finger on the cover. "Vaughn…Oh! Professor Vaughn! He used to teach at the university." Her voice squeaked in excitement at her discovery.

A connection clicked into place inside me.

My father went to school at the local university. What a coincidence I felt so called to a book written by a former professor from my father's school.

I thanked Poppy repeatedly for her help, and Rose gave her a cheeky remark about being the sexiest librarian to grace this town before we left to walk home.

41

The overcast from earlier blended with the dusk sky to cast a warm golden-orange hue over everything.

"Want to spend the night reading in total silence with one another? I'll make popcorn and cookies to sustain us." I gave Rose a childish smile, hoping she'd accept my slumber-party offer.

"Not tonight, Kya," She returned my sweet smile. "As fun as a silent sleepover would be…I have plans with Poppy once she gets out of work. We're staying in and watching one of her favorite vintage movies. She specially ordered it to the library so we could watch it." A coy smile appeared on her lips that I only saw her make when talking about her beloved. "She's so cute renting movies instead of illegally downloading them as I would."

A soft chuckle escaped both our lips.

Their dynamic sometimes reminded me of a fox and rabbit in love. Rose, the cunning and mischievous fox, forgoes all her naughty ways to be the lover and protector of the soft, innocent rabbit.

We parted ways and made tentative plans to meet in the morning to share what we had learned from our research.

V. Questions

Walking through my front door, immediately, my nostrils and tastebuds rejoiced. My mother was baking something warm with fall spices that made me want to curl up in my dad's armchair and read down here rather than in my tower.

I entered the kitchen as she pulled a perfectly golden pie from the oven. The delicate lattice top crust glittered with chunks of sugar, and bits of gooey, caramelized filling escaped through the cracks.

Sniffing the air obnoxiously, I approached my mom, "Mmm, is that apple?" I questioned and set my small pile of books on the kitchen island.

"It is! What a nose you have on you." She replied kindly before eyeing the pile beside me. "What do you have there?"

"Rose and I went to the library to research…some of the things you told me about…." As I answered her, I saw the look of concern on her face and hesitated. "I didn't really tell her anything you said, just, you know, the gist."

She said nothing and inspected the books further, pausing at the one about numerology. "Did you know that this author was an old professor of your father's?" My mother's eyes met mine, and I could have sworn I saw a glint.

"Not really. Poppy mentioned he used to teach at the university, but I wasn't sure if he was one of dad's teachers." I replied vaguely, hoping my mother would fill in the gaps.

"He's a mathematician and a brilliant one at that. Your father was never very good at math, so he got a lot of outside tutoring from Professor Vaughn, who seemed to have taken a liking to him." She flipped open the cover and started filing through the chapters. "They stayed in close touch for years. He came to our wedding and was actually at your first birthday party."

"Did they have a falling out?" I wondered, considering I had no memory of this man ever being present in my life.

"No, nothing like that. Professor Vaughn started veering off the approved curriculum, teaching things that were not the norm. The university finally fired him when he hosted a seminar after school hours, going in-depth about numerology and how to communicate with higher beings through numbers."

"Did anyone hear from him after he was fired? I'm sure Dad would have reached out to see how he was doing." I pried, digging for as many answers as my mother would let surface.

"He did…" Trepidation crept into her voice. "I think I have his address written down somewhere if you'd like to go ask him some of your burning questions." She turned away and started rummaging for their address book in a drawer.

I watched my mother pull out an old blue book, no bigger than her hand, and promptly flip to the page I needed. She ripped it out briskly and handed it to me.

"The top is his permanent address; he only uses it for legal purposes. The bottom is his vacation cabin, which has become his home. He hardly gives it out to anyone, so you must exercise caution when you go. Announce that you know Jasper Redferne before even giving him your name, then wait until you're inside to talk to him about what you want to know."

I could see the worry in her eyes, likely from the fear that Guardians would get word of my quest before I even got to Professor Vaughn. I opened my mouth to comfort her, but she interjected.

"Before you leave, you should understand how important it is to remain below the radar. Turn off your phone— it's the easiest way they can track you." Selene motioned to the pile of books. "I understand your need for answers, but you never know where Guardian-eyes are watching. It probably wasn't the smartest move to check out a stack of occult books from the local library. But, to be fair, I did not warn you against it and would have likely done the same thing." She grabbed my hand with loving ferocity. "I know your life journey is already underway, and I want to prepare you as best as I can before you actually depart." A knowing sadness glazed over her face.

Tears started forming in my eyes before I could even think to respond. "I love you so much, Mom." Squeezing her hand with the same loving ferocity she just did mine. "You're my everything, and I can't imagine where or who I would be if I had lost you too." Lifting my chin, I filled my lungs with a deep breath. "I will get answers, and I'm going to free us, all of humanity, from the monster of the Machine, the tyranny of the Guardians— the entire Trine of Power."

"I'll be praying to Goddess that you're successful, my beautiful, brave-hearted Kyanie. But for now, why don't you enjoy dinner and a slice of apple pie with your loving mother? You can leave first thing in the morning rather than right now like you're thinking of doing." Her smile was sweeter than the freshly baked pastry we would shortly eat.

So I did. We spent the evening by the fireplace, eating, laughing, and talking without a care in the world. As if we were the only two beings on Earth— minus Bella, who sat curled at my feet the entire time.

I went to bed early that night, not mentally bogged down from the worry of my new life's journey, but with a full belly and a heart freshly warmed by my mother's love.

~*~

Arising with the sun, I wasted no time getting on the road. Truthfully, I had hardly slept because of a recurring nightmare that followed me from sleep to wake.

In the dream, I was running through the most extensive, elaborate library, looking for the same book Onyx had searched for years ago. Every row I ran down burst into flames until only one section remained unscathed— a single black book sitting by itself amidst the fire.

It was thick and heavy, bound in dark leather with foreign writing on the cover. Though unable to read it, I knew it was of the utmost importance that I held onto it with my life.

Before I could turn to escape the burning library, a cold, clawed hand grabbed my shoulder and spun me around. Behind me stood a man in a dark suit; his bald head was lumpy, with lizard-like horns accentuating his angular, slightly green face. I was about to scream when he smiled, showing off small, razor-sharp teeth.

"Silly girl…" The man hissed. *"You will never have the answers you seek…You are nothing but a cog in the Machine."* His smile broadened as he ripped the book from my hands and shoved me into the flames.

I could still smell the sulfur on his breath and feel the clammy claws that dug into my shoulder when I shot up in bed.

Following a cold rinse to cleanse myself of the nightmare, I hurried through my morning routine, grabbing a banana and granola bar for breakfast on the road.

~*~

Professor Vaughn's cabin was a few towns over, so I decided to take Bella on the journey with me, promising her we would go for a hike in the woods on the way home.

There was a spectacular sunrise that morning. Bursts of rose, crimson-orange, and gold painted the sky before the overcast from yesterday crept in again, absorbing all the colors in a dull gray fog.

The drive went by quickly enough, likely because my thoughts and the smoldering questions I wanted to ask were consuming me. In what felt like no time, I pulled up to the given address, a giant wooden gate displaying the house number— 1999.

I ignored the multiple *'No Trespassing'* signs, and to my surprise, the chained gate's padlock was unlocked, opening with little effort. I crept onto the property, taking in the overgrown, disheveled yard filled with old cars and scraps of metal before parking beside a tire-less van.

If I hadn't seen the light in the front window and the smoke coming from the chimney, I would have assumed this place had been abandoned for years.

An uneasy feeling crept into my stomach. Bella and I approached the front metal-screened door with equal trepidation.

Now is no time for doubt.

I encouraged myself before knocking.

Immediately I heard rummaging inside as if my knock had startled something awake. Before I could think twice about leaving, two bulging blue-gray eyes stared at me from inside the cabin.

"Who are you? I don't entertain solicitors, can't you read?" With irritation in his voice, he pointed to a small sign next to the door, *'Any solicitors will be met with a gun to the head.'*

Swallowing my fear, I calmly stated. "I'm Jasper Redferne's daughter. I was hoping I could talk to you about him."

His eyes opened impossibly wider as he mumbled, "Jasper...". With haste, he unlocked the door and hurried Bella and me inside.

If his yard would leave me to believe his property was abandoned, then the inside of his cabin would be my final confirmation. It was a quaint, one-bedroom house with an open floor plan that blended the kitchen and living space into one large room. However, I could hardly notice anything about the professor's home besides the chaotic mess of scattered texts. Books, stray papers, old newspapers, journals— all kinds of reading material strewn over the floor and every surface in the cabin.

"I apologize for the disorder; I haven't had company in years…." His voice was deep and groggy, and I wondered when the last time he spoke aloud to another human was.

Perhaps he's spent the last few years in silent isolation.

"Oh, it's totally fine." I gave a weak smile and further absorbed what was around me, looking for a book or newspaper clipping to catch my eye. "I did come unannounced, to be fair."

"That you did…." He huffed in agreement. "My condolences about your father and brother, by the way. I know it was some time ago, but I always regretted not attending the funeral." A sadness reached his voice.

I ignored the lump in my throat that inevitably formed when someone brought up my family and focused on why I came here in the first place.

"Thank you. Honestly, my father would have hated the funeral; everyone was so formal and stuffy. I know he would have preferred getting cremated and having his ashes thrown into the wind while everyone who knew him celebrated his life by getting rip-roaring drunk."

A genuine smile grew on both our faces as we remembered my outrageous and lovable father.

"I was hoping you could tell me about what you taught him, Professor Vaughn. About numerology?"

"Call me Nikola. I'm not a professor anymore." He said tersely, with a tinge of resentment marking his words. "What was your name again? Last I saw you, you were only a year old." He sauntered over to the kitchen counter, piled high with books on astrophysics, and grabbed a red-clay mug, taking a swig of unknown liquid.

"My name is Kyanie or Kya for short." My eyes narrowed warily at the sight.

"Alright, Kya, how much time do you have…, and how much do you really want to know?" His stark white hair and long shabby beard matched the lunacy in his piercing eyes.

Bella sat dutifully next to me, cautiously watching the interaction, unsure whether this mad-scientist-looking man was trustworthy.

"I have nearly all day…Tell me everything you can." I shuffled some papers off a nearby chair and sat down, motioning for my dog to lie at my feet as I took out a notebook and pen.

~*~

Nikola spent the next few hours explaining numerology basics and how numbers are the cosmos' way of communicating with us on Earth. How each number carries a unique frequency or energy and seeing repeating numbers is like following a path carefully illuminated by the universe. How sacred geometry is the gateway to our 'galactic DNA'.

"Did you notice my address? One-nine-nine-nine. The beginning of an ending. I've heard repeating numbers in threes often called 'angel numbers.'" His eye-roll was slight but did not go unnoticed. "Whatever you want to refer to it as…When you see the same number repeatedly— take note of it. It's an angel or a cosmic being contacting you and showing you their support."

"So ones represent beginnings, and nines are endings?" I noted aloud while writing it down.

"Yes, yes, more or less. You're starting to get it. Don't think; *feel* into the number. That's where the true meaning lies." He twirled the bottom of his beard around his equally mangy fingernail, contemplating his next lesson for me.

"Starting at the beginning of all numbers is zero. A perfect egg. A womb. It holds all that is and will be, just like the Void of darkness. It's where we all came from and will all return to someday. Following that is one— a strong pillar to structure the creation of matter. It is the number of manifestation and calling in that which you desire."

A bell chimed inside me, connecting what he taught me to my inner truths. "Is that why people wish when it's 11:11?"

His gravelly laugh warmed me. "I suppose so. Having four repeating numbers is certainly a potent cosmic blessing. So it would make sense that people make wishes when they see a clean slate for manifesting at one-one-one-one."

My notebook became a collection of numbers and letters scribbled frantically on its pages. I wanted to absorb everything, to learn all I could about the things that the Trine of Power worked so hard to keep hidden.

"Now to continue… Two's hold the vibration of the numerical expressions that came before it. It holds the Void of zero with the creation and structure of one to create duality. The masculine and feminine. The energy that comes from two powerful beings joining forces into a truly blessed union.

"Don't be surprised if you see two's everywhere you turn as soon as you enter a new relationship. The universe is confirming the necessity of you two coming together." I felt my midsection turn at the thought of romance.

I had no desire to take this ascension journey with anyone— it was one I *needed* to handle alone. Yet, the walls I built after my father and brother left started to feel like a prison, keeping me locked away from feeling anything for anyone.

If I wanted to find answers, the stonewalls I had built around my heart had to be dismantled. How could I someday free humanity from suffering under the guise of 'the Solar Lord's wishes' if I couldn't even free myself from the shackles of grief and my depression?

He elaborated as if he could see the far-off look in my eyes and sense those walls around my heart. "Remember that every encounter with another being is a form of 'relationship.' A soul contract, connecting your timelines to bring about a certain lesson for all parties involved. Whether briefly or long-term, every energy exchange makes a difference in your soul's journey."

The spark of lunacy returned to his eyes as he veered off the topic of two's and delved into the idea that our souls have a contract they've come to Earth to fulfill.

Zoning in and out of his ramblings, I quickly glanced at a wall clock to check the time—*1:11 p.m.*

I've been here for three hours, and he's only on two's....

Interrupting his monologue, I pointed. "Look, it's 1:11!"

A joyous look spread across his haggard and worn face. "What a cosmic gift! The date is a blessing as well! October 10th, 2030. Ten-ten-twenty-thirty. One-zero-one-zero-two-zero-three-zero. One-one-two-three. Something is starting. A journey is beginning. The first steps are being taken today." His tone shifted into something robotic as if his voice was no longer his to use.

"Your family disappeared on June 28th, 2028. Zero-six-two-eight-two-zero-two-eight. Three twos. The difference between eight and two is six. Six-six-six." The stark white of his hair matched the bulging white of his eyes as they rolled back into his head.

"Change is afoot and has been since that day. You will lose your grounding if you don't focus on the goal ahead. Their disappearance was not in vain: this is your destiny on Earth." His once deep and gravelly voice was now mechanic, sounding like a voice recording rather than a human being I was in the presence of.

I arose from my seated position, Bella already ready to run out the door at one wave of my hand. My heart pounded in my ears, and I wasn't sure if I should flee or soak up every word this mad numerologist spewed.

"Do not fear me or these synchronicities. Your father appeared to you between 3:33 and 4:44 a.m. the other night— he told me so. You have taken well to the path he started clearing for you. The numbers…The signs are everywhere. Watch for the signs."

His jaw was slack, and his head hung limply, supported by his white beard. Slowly he straightened his neck, the consciousness in his eyes returning along with his sanity.

I stood there like a doe in headlights, unable to speak. My knuckles were white from gripping my notebook as if I'd need to use it as a weapon.

"My apologies, Kyanie. Sometimes when I get lost in the numbers, Moses comes in." He mumbled while scratching his head, his hand disappearing in his cloud of hair.

I felt the urge to mimic his movement.

"He's my higher self— the self that is connected to the other Realms and is thus all-knowing." He elaborated after seeing my confused expression.

It felt like lightning struck me right between the eyes. I stepped back and couldn't help the gasp that escaped me. "What did you say? About other Realms?"

Another low laugh rumbled in his throat. This time it warmed me differently— anger roiled in my gut.

Do not patronize me... I threatened in my head, not daring to say it out loud. Though coming here for answers, I couldn't help but feel anger at this man for holding the information I needed.

"Ah, I forgot your eye is just opening... You've only just begun learning your basic numbers...." He grumbled and heaved a sigh. "Put simply, this existence is divided into three Realms. We live as humans on Earth in the Logic Realm, where the Solar Lord, Lacius, and the laws of man govern us."

He traced the air as if drawing out these different planes of existence and the beings that ruled them. "Below Earth is the Basal Realm, ruled by the Dark Goddess, and above is the Ethereal Realm with the Cosmic Goddess as its crowned head. They're all separated by the Veil— shielding humans from the truth of this multidimensional experience."

Before Nikola finished talking, I had taken my seat again and feverishly jotted down this reality-altering information.

He pointed to my notebook. "Now, you better guard that information with your life, little lady. I hope you're aware of the target you have on you now that you've started digging for answers. You're lucky I've removed my life so far from the grid that no one could have tracked you here."

Indeed his cabin was down a long dirt road, with nothing but potholes and trees for miles. At first, I thought he was just a self-isolated hermit who had lost touch with reality in the numbers he studied. Now I saw that he was *so* aware of our reality that he was hiding from the ever-present scrutiny of the Trine of Power.

"Yes, I'm aware of the dangers. I may be new to all this, but I think my father and brother instilled a lot of this knowledge in me without directly teaching it. I always felt there was more to this existence. Always felt that my missing family was still with me— still watching us but unable to be here fully." I spoke calmly, still piecing together my reality.

"Good." He mumbled in approval before clearing his throat. "Shall I go on with the lesson? I believe we left off at two's...." I nodded, giving him leeway to begin his ramblings once again. "I'll try to keep it brief...." Nikola smirked, knowing that was likely not going to happen.

"The number three has always been revered as a sacred number, and interestingly enough, the triangle is the strongest shape. Threes are excellent reminders that we are never alone; we are constantly uplifted and supported by other-dimensional beings." He touched his pointer fingers and thumbs together. "As if you are the tip of the triangle held up by the cosmos...."

"Fours carry a similar energy, though rather than support, it's more of divine protection. Fours can represent structure and safety. Think of it like a spiritual box, creating boundaries around your precious spirit.... Fives are a personal favorite of mine." Nikola cracked a half smile as he continued his prattled teachings. "Five is the pentacle— the symbol of magick and the elements used to create it. It represents change, transition, and the power of transmutation...."

Taking a short break for another swig from his mug, he cleared his throat loudly before carrying on. "Sixes, after following the number five, remind us to stay grounded and centered on Earth. They can also represent our Earthly desires and serve as a warning not to let our vices take control…."

I eyed the mug beside him, eyebrows raising subconsciously.

"Sevens have such a happy, jovial energy— they're often associated with luck. Think of them as angelic blessings, directly from the cosmos to you." He smiled warmly, and I returned the gesture.

"We've come to eights! The infinite number, with its never-ending-loop formation, symbolizes the continuous changeability of life. Not to mention the strength it takes to stand firm and tall amidst cosmic chaos…. Finally, we've reached the nines— the culmination of hard work, the completion of a cycle to welcome in the new…."

Try as he might to be brief, he finished my introductory numerology lesson more than an hour later. I took sufficient notes on the 'energetic frequency' of each number and held onto my notebook as if it were the most valuable object in my possession. I knew I'd be referring back to these scrawls while learning how to decode the numbers and, thus, the reality around me.

'0: Void, womb, start & end of life/ 1: beginnings, creation, blessings underway/ 2: companionship, unity, duality/ 3: angels, otherworldly support, divinity/ 4: protection, safety, structure/ 5: change, transmutation, magical creation/ 6: grounding, staying centered, desires/ 7: angelic blessing, cosmic energy, spiritual luck/ 8: strength, cycles of life, staying centered through change/ 9: endings, culmination, completion of a cycle.'

"Thank you so much for all this information, Nikola. I know it can be dangerous for you to do so…." He waved off my concern with another swig from his mug.

"I take thank you's in the form of never speaking of this interaction to anyone," he smiled sarcastically, "Or checks made out to *'CASH.'*"

I laughed at his comment, knowing I would share this information with Rosemary as soon as possible. Then we exchanged goodbyes, and as he walked Bella and me out, I took in his ramshackle cabin one last time.

"Hey, why was your gate unlocked?" I pondered aloud as we stood in his threshold.

"Typically, it's always locked, but this morning Moses told me I'd have a guest that would need me for their destiny." The right corner of his tugged upward, "I doubted him, but he's proven once again that he's never wrong."

"What a coincidence," I smirked.

"There is no such thing as coincidence. Everything is cosmically, divinely guided." He raised his eyebrows and gave me a worn, wise smile before closing his door, locking it firmly from inside.

Walking to my truck, I couldn't help but wonder what exactly drove him to live here. Getting fired from the university undoubtedly played a part, but living so far away from anyone or anything made me reconsider true loneliness. The self-induced isolation I felt in my den paled in comparison to Professor Vaughn's living arrangements.

As my truck bobbed down the uneven dirt road, seeing his towering gate grow smaller behind me, I swore never to let the Trine of Power drive me into hiding.

I will never lock myself away. The truth will free me— it will free us all.

VI. Spark

I kept my promise to my loyal canine companion and stopped by a small state park we had passed on the drive up. The answers Nikola had given me swam in my head, consuming me to the point of nearly missing the turn into the parking lot.

Parking my truck, I glanced at the time: *3:33 p.m.* A small laugh of disbelief escaped my lips as I reached for my notebook to check what the energy of three's meant.

"Truly divine, magical number. Angelic blessings." I skimmed, my smile growing wider at the thought of my father and brother watching over me.

Bella leaped out the door, tail wagging and mismatched eyes glowing with excitement. I grabbed my small bag to hold my keys and rummaged for my phone, turning it on for the first time since leaving my home.

"What happened to the library-find-debriefing we talked about??? So much to tell you. Call me when you get this."

I scrolled by the first text from Rosemary out of several, along with a handful of missed calls. Her last message was not as polite and contained a handful of obscenities.

I started us along a walking path before returning Rose's calls. The phone only rang once before she picked up, her fire roaring from my lack of response all day.

"Where have you been? I was about to file a missing person report." I laughed though I knew she was dead serious.

As I was about to explain myself, Rose pressed on. "Did you temporarily drop off the face of the Earth? My texts and calls stopped going through this morning, and I thought something bad happened...." I heard the genuine fear in her voice as she trailed off.

Guilt with a hint of regret ate at my insides, and I felt my laugh upon answering was in poor taste.

"I'm sorry I blanked on our debriefing date. Last night when I got home, my mom saw the stack of books and gave me the address of that old college professor Poppy mentioned." I could sense her unyielding irritation through the phone.

"Oh, I blanked." She mockingly mumbled as I continued.

"He was like a mad numerologist, and his property looked like it hadn't been maintained in years...." A tug at my gut told me to save the details for an in-person conversation.

"Anyways, I'm sorry again about forgetting. I'll be home in a few hours. Do you want to come over for a *brief* debrief?" I inflected, widely grinning, knowing Rose was rolling her eyes at my pun— a classic testament to our friendship. "Then maybe homemade popcorn and a movie?"

"Hmm, I suppose I accept your apology and will consider your invitation for this evening on two conditions." Her words were tinged with mock formality.

"What do you desire, m'lady?" I imitated her tone.

"Firstly, I'd like to have homemade kettle corn."

"Done."

"Secondly, I'd like to request that when you come to me with life-changing, possibly life-*threatening* information, don't even think about bailing on me without warning afterward. Next time, I will not hesitate to proclaim that you're missing to the world... or at least to the local news."

I smiled into the phone, eternally grateful I had someone like

Rose who cared about me with loving fierceness.

"Done."

~*~

Dusk had begun painting the sky by the time I returned home. I spent the entire drive taking in all the numbers around me— from license plates, street signs, and addresses. Though I swore I wouldn't end up like him, I understood more why Nikola locked himself away. This world could be so overwhelming.

My mother was home, happily concocting a vegetable soup like a witch over her cauldron. The scent of garlic, onion, paprika, and chili filled the air, warming me from the inside.

Bella whined to me nearly the entire drive back about being hungry, so I quickly got her dinner while mine was simmering.

"You left early this morning." My mother implored, looking over her shoulder and watching me place Bella's cobalt food bowl on the floor. "Checking in with your worrying mother would have been appreciated, you know." She said, turning back to her edible masterpiece.

I breathed a laugh, remembering one of Rosemary's more obscene messages. "I do know, and I'm sorry. If it's any consolation, I got into hot water with Rose today over my disappearance."

My mother chuckled knowingly. "Well then, I'll assume I don't need to scold you further."

"Speak of the devil…." I smiled and shook my head as I heard Rose pull into the driveway.

Her music was notoriously on full volume in her already noisy car. The very same station wagon her mother drove across state lines and was nearly twice as old as us by this point.

"I hope you don't mind if she stays over. We're having a movie

59

night, and I promised some homemade kettle corn." I walked over to face my mother, smiling sweetly. "If I could borrow your culinary skills for a tad longer this evening." I batted my eyelashes and hugged her around the shoulders.

She patted my arms and returned my sugary smile. "How could I deny my other daughter the joy of my kettle corn?"

"Hellooooo." Rosemary crooned from the doorway, immediately removing her shoes and lime-green windbreaker. "Smells divine in here, Selene; you are truly an artist of the senses."

She sauntered into the kitchen. Her purple hair was tied in a topknot on her head, and she was wearing her infamous overalls she had spent years covering in patches, with a long-sleeve black-and-white striped shirt underneath.

I observed the two swap greetings, feeling my once sunken heart beat a bit fuller as we all settled in for the evening.

~*~

The three of us sat around our circular dining table, a bouquet of marigolds in the center and glowing warmly in the candlelight.

"So, miss Kyanie, why don't you share what you learned today?" Rose queried while dipping a chunk of sourdough in the hearty soup my mother had prepared.

My mind became swamped with numbers and lessons from the universe transmitted by Nikola. I got a brief flash of the old professor's eyes rolling to the back of his head as 'Moses' took over and confirmed my dad and brother were in a different Realm.

I knew that of all the people in the world, the two of them would be the ones I could talk to about what Nikola had taught me that day. Yet the trepidation in my stomach couldn't be ignored.

Luckily I had taken a large bite of bread and soup when she asked me and bought myself an extra second to filter through what I wanted to say.

"Quite a lot," I replied.

Smooth Kya....

They both sat quietly eating, waiting for me to elaborate on why I had been off the grid for all daylight today.

"Professor Vaughn...er Nikola, as he prefers to be called, went through all the details of numerology and what each number... symbolizes." Stuttering and unsure of what to say, I took a centering breath and let whatever was meant to be shared come through.

"How the universe uses numbers and other 'signs' to talk to us, to point us in the right direction for our soul's path. There's sacred geometry everywhere, in the petals of a flower and the repeating patterns on pinecones....."

"What other signs are there besides numbers and geometry?" Rose questioned in between bites, the crunch of sourdough lingering in the air.

"He didn't specify much. He told me my gut would tell me when it's a 'sign'...." I could feel what I wanted to say bubbling in my throat. "Nikola also told me about the other Realms."

My mother put her spoon down, her brown eyes firmly on me. "Oh, he did? What did he teach you?" A hint of worry in her voice.

"He was surprisingly brief regarding the subject: All he told me was what the three Realms were and who governed them. I already knew of the Solar Lord, obviously." Rose snorted. "But he taught me that the Dark Goddess resides in the Basal Realm and the Cosmic Goddess is in the Ethereal Realm...with Dad and Onyx."

I chewed the inside of my lip and locked to them both to say something, anything after my revelation.

"I see." My mother's lips became a thin line as she no-doubt contemplated what would happen now that I was uncovering the truth.

"Well, I'll be damned...." Was all Rosemary managed before slurping down the rest of her soup from the bowl. "This is an excellent segue into my findings. If I may?" She wiped her mouth on a napkin and her hands on her overalls.

I nodded in approval and felt relief that I didn't have to continue faltering over my words.

Clearing her throat, she began her monologue.

"In the dawn of creation on Earth...." Rose began theatrically. "There was nothing but darkness: a darkness that was the beginning and end of everything— the Void. This Void wanted to create life, so it had a daughter from the ocean. This daughter would later be referred to as the Dark Goddess. It was only the Dark Goddess on the planet for years, creating and stimulating the life for which the Void had made space. She created the natural world we see around us, pulling mountains from the sea and growing rainforests as tall as skyscrapers with a flick of her hand.

"One day, the Dark Goddess prayed in her favorite garden, saying she was lonely and wanted company. So the Void gave her a sister— the Cosmic Goddess. The two ruled over the Earth for hundreds of thousands of years. The Dark Goddess sustained the flora, and the Cosmic Goddess created the fauna that would walk amongst them. The two developed a world of magick, with mythical creatures and strange animals that would someday evolve into the birds and reptiles we see now.

"Eventually, the Cosmic Goddess wanted to create humans to

act as stewards of the Earth so the two could rest. The Dark Goddess was hesitant but supported her sister. It wasn't long before humans lived with unicorns, dragons, and all the other magick this planet had to offer. For thousands of years, creation lived in harmony— attuned to the Earth Mother and living in accordance with the Dark and Cosmic Goddesses." She paused, taking an exasperated sigh.

"Then the Solar Lord appeared. The two sisters did not pray to the Void for him and were initially confused about his creation, though they soon learned that man made him. Nonetheless, they welcomed him as a brother, and the three resided over the Earth together...briefly...." Rose's lip curled into a snarl.

"Until the Solar Lord hatched his plan to sever the world into three Realms and separate the Three Divine Rulers. He claimed it would help the humans behave— to threaten eternal damnation in the dark pits of the Basal Realm while also bribing them with the offer of infinite bliss and happiness in the Ethereal Realm. Since the Dark Goddess had been the firstborn of the Void, she was sent down to light the way in the Basal Realm. The Cosmic Goddess, stricken with grief at losing her sister, declared she would rule over the Ethereal Realm, overseeing all three Realms from above."

Rosemary's speech had wholly enraptured us.

"Not long after the Earth was severed, and the Solar Lord's world came into being, the first twelve Guardians of the Order were handpicked. Their purpose was, and still is, to uphold their Lord's 'wishes' across the globe, making constrictive and suppressive laws, always claiming righteousness as motivation for obeying. Meanwhile, Lacius, the Solar Lord's nemesis, rose to power as the portrait of pure evil in the Logical Realm, bringing fear to the masses.

"Soon after that, the Guardians of the Order, with the Solar

Lord's blessing, created the Machine." Another exasperated sigh escaped Rose's mouth. "My understanding is that the Machine was born from greed, and its only purpose is to degrade, develop, and dominate the Earth."

Shaking her head, she continued.

"The combined power of the Solar Lord, his Guardians, and the Machine was unstoppable. Many humans did not adhere to their new world order, fighting as long as possible to hold onto their Goddesses. Unfortunately, the Guardians claimed the Dark and Cosmic Goddesses had abandoned them, leaving them feeling like they had no choice but to conform." Rosemary's rage was visible as her green eyes turned sharp. "The Guardians also made quick work burning and destroying any evidence of the Old Ways."

The Old Ways... The ways of the Goddesses: The original ways of life here on Earth.

"With the Goddesses out of the picture and a new world ruled by the Solar Lord, the Trine of Power worked diligently to claw its way into every facet of human life. In this 'new world,' women were treated like cattle— their main purpose was to serve men through domestic labor and breeding. Over the next few hundred years, women's rights were stripped away and degraded just as the Earth was treated in the same manner by men in power. Our beautiful flora and fauna, made with love by the Goddesses, were now seen as resources to exploit. To degrade and use for capital gain." She spat out her words like poison.

"The most egregious part of it all is how deeply the claws of piety and drudgery went into the subconscious mind of humans. How those claws left a scar that would cause humans to police themselves through shame and guilt, with no need for the Guardians to 'uphold the laws'— though they still did and continue today."

Heaving a sigh to calm the rage boiling in her being, Rose commenced. "This brings us to the present. A world ruled by the Machine, defended by the Guardians of the Order, and headed by the Solar Lord. A world designed for people to consume and gain as much as possible, climbing an unending ladder to the top, regardless of the consequences. Until the day death knocks at their door and makes them beg for forgiveness so that they may taste the ecstatic splendor of the Ethereal Realm or be engulfed by the icy-hot flames of eternal damnation in the Basal Realm.

"Little do people know that such ecstatic bliss was here on Earth, and it was their Solar Lord who took it away from them. Instead, everyone walks around, distracted, ignorant, and numbed to the inner workings of our reality, either completely unaware or uncaring of the true evil that runs the world. Acting as complacent drones for the Machine to thrive while our planet is decimated in the name of greed." Rose huffed.

"So that's how I learned that everything we've ever been taught is complete bullshit." She concluded, giving a twisted smile. "Do you have any wine in the house? I need a drink."

VII. Smolder

"Tell me, Mom, how much of that did you already know?" I asked, refilling my glass and topping off my mother's and Rosemary's.

Alcohol never appealed to me much; I had other vices that I much rather preferred. Though tonight I felt the need to drink as a way of joining us all together. As if this would be the last night I could hang around my kitchen table, gabbing and relishing in the company of my two favorite women in the world.

"Most of it." My mother swirled the burgundy liquid around her glass and took a small sip. "The Old Ways were stories passed down through the women in our family. I never knew how or why the Goddesses stepped down and allowed the Solar Lord to take over— I should have guessed it was not their choice to forgo all they created." She shook her head, gray and brown waves falling on her shoulders.

"And you knew about the Realms?" I queried.

A slow nod.

"Who do you think taught your father about them?"

I scoffed, the wine in my system making me unable to hold anything back. "So everyone in the family knew 'the truth' except me? I feel like my whole life has been a lie—."

"Stop right there before you start spinning your narrative. We kept the truth from you to protect you." My mother's voice was sharp as she firmly held up a hand. "I told your father years before you and Onyx were born and made him swear to hide it from both of you. I've had to play a role your entire life to keep you safe. Be quiet, respectful, and overall keep to myself, never making any close friends of my own for fear that they would betray us if they knew we believed in the Old

Ways." A saddened pain marked her words.

"And you couldn't trust me, your flesh and blood, to keep it a secret?" The deep anger I had felt earlier smoldered in my veins alongside the alcohol. "You didn't think I'd want to know how our reality is a corrupt illusion?"

"Kyanie…" Her harsh tone had melted away into a coo. "I knew you would find the truth in your own time, and when you'd find it… you'd be leaving me to complete your soul's life purpose."

My heart ached.

Rosemary sat with her eyebrows raised, lips pursed together as if using all her willpower to refrain from interrupting.

"I could feel from the moment you were born that you would stir up trouble in the absolute best way possible. When I heard your first cries, I knew thousands would hear your voice. You had come here to demand freedom and justice and would stop at nothing to see it through."

"Mom, I'll never leave you…." My anger fizzled out to be replaced by adoration.

"But you will. And that's okay." She reached across the table for my hand. "So for now, let's put on a movie, and I'll make us some kettle corn."

~*~

We finished the bottle of wine, pairing it exquisitely with sea salt caramel corn and an old French film. As soon as my mother chose that black-and-white movie to watch, I knew she did so to feel her love, Jasper, with her. With us. My parents regularly watched it, each time reminiscing on their honeymoon in Paris.

We all fell asleep in the living room, though my mother snuck off to her bed at some point during the night. Upon waking, I saw

Rose's bun, now resembling a bird's nest made of lavender. Then I registered Bella's weight on my feet and sat up to pet her, only to quickly go back down because of a throbbing pain in my head.

The sun had just begun rising through the dark orange curtains, casting the living room in a warm hue. Groaning, I rolled over to check the time on the stove through the kitchen archway.

5:55 a.m.

Rubbing the sleep from my eyes, a hoarse croak of a chuckle escaped my throat. Laying back down, I gathered my mental strength to recall what Nikola had taught me about fives.

"Change. Transition. Five is the pentacle— the symbol of magick and the elements used to create it." The old professor's husky voice clattered in my head.

As I closed my eyes to get a few more hours of sleep, something stirring in my gut.

Enjoy this rest— today is a day of change.

Little more than an hour had passed when I arose for the second time, feeling a restlessness in my bones.

Rosemary was still in a deep slumber as I shuffled to the kitchen to put on hot water for tea.

As I stood at the sink, filling the kettle with water, my eyes drifted out the window above it. My mother was sitting in the sun, a book in hand and morning coffee on the table beside her. We shared a love of basking in the sun's early morning rays and listening to the symphony of birds that accompanied it. Since the rain and overcast had finally cleared after days of only gray weather, seeing blue skies and sunshine felt like a blessing.

After putting the kettle on— that red kettle, which meant so much more to me than a means to drink tea— I walked over to the back door to let Bella out and visit my mother in the sunshine. Upon stepping outside and looking upwards, I spotted a red-tailed hawk circling our home.

The trees in our backyard were bursting with golden, burgundy, and orange hues. Set ablaze with color before they withered into brown, crinkled versions of themselves that littered the ground with a satisfying *crunch*.

The wild cats my mother regularly left food for were sitting beside her chair. One was white with gray spots and yellow eyes, lounging on my mother's right side, the other black with piercing green eyes, sitting upright on her left.

Onyx had grown rather fond of the black one in the last year he was home. Not coincidentally, he had started seeing Amber, and she had a black cat that was eerily similar.

Looking at those chartreuse orbs, I thought of the first time Amber came to our house. It was a temperate and sunny summer day, with a warm breeze flowing through our backyard's oak and maple trees. The entire family, animals included, gathered around our long teak table, sharing stories and laughter over an assortment of fruit.

Amber was petite with ochre-brown skin and jet-black hair. The first thing I noticed about her were her eyes, so brown they looked black, beneath full lashes. She looked like she was capable of holding such darkness— as if her eyes were indeed windows to the dark depths of her soul.

She blended into our family so naturally that we quickly understood why Onyx was enamored. As soon as Amber saw that feral black cat, she crooned and got to her knees. The cat approached her immediately, showing her a friendliness none of us had ever seen before in the animal.

"She's enchanting, isn't she?" Onyx swooned.

His hazel eyes, greener than my own, focused intently on her and the pastel yellow sundress she wore. I don't think his eyes left her for one second on that sunny summer day.

My brother was right. She was undoubtedly enchanting, as I still think about her every time that black cat with green eyes meets my gaze.

"Morning." My mother said kindly without opening her eyes. Evidently, she was too busy enjoying the rays of light as much as the cats basking next to her.

"Any plans for the day?" She asked after I mumbled a good morning back and took the seat next to her.

"Well, it's a Friday, so I'll be working the graveyard shift at Hank's." As I spoke, something tugged inside me— *my last shift.*

I couldn't keep working there after all I had learned. I was preparing to leave home, possibly forever. I would go there tonight, give them the last bit of my labor, then square up the rest of my earnings before quitting.

My mom tutted in reply, unaware of everything buzzing in my head. "I don't understand why you've chosen to stay at that job so long — all it does is suck the life out of you."

"I'm not sure why I have either." *A slight lie.*

Years ago, I planned to quit Hank's before going to college with dreams of spreading my wings out of the confines of my hometown. I dreamed of studying in far-off lands, immersing myself in more exotic and fascinating cultures than my own. However, the tragedy clipped my wings and left me desperately clutching onto any twig of normalcy from my old life. Sadly, Hank's was a part of that.

My logical-thinking brain could not understand why I subjected myself to the mistreatment and often screamed at me to quit, to find *any* other job. The customers were rude or dismissive more often than not, and my boss was even worse— a narcissistic, misogynistic pig.

A flutter of excitement for finally leaving it behind warmed my lower stomach.

Suddenly the scream of the kettle, accompanied by Rosemary's shriek of anger from being awoken, interrupted my thoughts. Chuckling softly at her dramatized wailing, I hurried inside to remove the kettle from the heat and soothe my storm of a friend.

"Who puts hot water on full heat and then goes outside without a care?" Rosemary's groggy voice told me everything about how she was feeling internally. "Some of us were sleeping."

She removed the elastic from her nest of lilac hair, allowing it to fall upon her shoulders in a tangled mess of waves.

"Since you're up now, care for a cup of tea?" I smirked as Rose took a seat at the counter and promptly put her head down, rubbing her temples.

She merely groaned in response.

I prepared a blend of black tea and loose herbs that my mother would make to alleviate headaches. On mornings like this, it was also a sure-fire hangover cure.

Pouring the steaming water into our mugs, I watched as swirls of tawny brown leaked from the tea strainer.

Hopefully, this will cleanse the excess wine in our systems.

Suddenly, dull guilt formed in my stomach as Adelaide's sweet face came into my mind. She loved wine arguably more than all three of us combined. I could have easily invited her over, considering she lived in the house closest to ours.

Our neighborhood was the largest, oldest suburb in town.

However, it was still far from the cookie-cutter neighborhoods we'd see in the cities and towns adjacent to us. Each house had ample yard space, and a thick stretch of forest enclosed the community's borders, giving each family a sense of privacy and rural seclusion.

So even though Adelaide's home was the closest to mine and still within walking distance, we were separated by my long, dirt driveway and the densest set of trees in the area.

I knew she would have enjoyed sitting around my kitchen table, cackling with laughter at old embarrassing stories while we all engorged ourselves with wine.

"Hey, how would you feel about getting breakfast with Addie?" I asked, setting Rose's mug down carefully near her heavily-knotted head.

She lifted it only enough to take a sip. Once the piping-hot liquid hit her tongue, her eyes rolled back, and she sighed happily.

"This is why I barely drink...," she muttered. "Sorry, what did you ask? This tea just brought me back to life." Another blissful sip by the look on her face.

"Care to join me for breakfast with Addie?" I coaxed, unsure how she felt after their quarrel the other day.

"Depends. Shall we be going to Hank's?" Rose looked up at me, smiling sarcastically. "Or our usual spot where she rudely walked out on us the other day?"

"I suppose the cafe. Unless you're both up for taking a trip out of town to get a decent meal?"

Rose weighed her options while swirling around the dark brown liquid. "I'll pass. We both probably want space from each other, and frankly, I'm already feeling like a grump, so it wouldn't take much from her to send me on a tangent."

"Fair enough." I knew it was for the best— especially considering my inner voice beckoned to have a heart-to-heart with my oldest friend without risking another heated discussion.

The two of us sat and drank our elixirs of life in silence, with nothing but the song of birds to distract me from my thoughts. A raven's caw blared above the chatter of little birds, seeming to come from right above the kitchen sink window.

Would today be my last day wasting away at the only job I've ever had? Am I feeling called to see Addie because I know I'll be saying goodbye? Where am I even supposed to go to begin this journey?

Once again, questions that I didn't have the answers to plagued me.

Time will tell….

VIII. Scorch

Around mid-morning, I parked my truck outside Addie's childhood home. Laying on my horn to signal my arrival, I silently apologized to her mother, Mary, for disturbing the peace she so carefully tried to instill in her household.

However, I wouldn't have to arrive so obnoxiously if Addie's brother and father weren't nearly impossible to be around.

Cain, her older brother, was the same age as Onyx. Our parents had hoped they would get along, so all four of us could spend time together, though my brother was adamant in his disdain for him.

Onyx was a sensitive soul who would much rather be an observer in this lifetime. In contrast, Cain was a showman— a loud, boisterous athlete who had no shame in public humiliation. Though he was conventionally attractive, and most girls in my class drooled over the thought of him, he always gave me an uneasy feeling. As if I had no idea what he was truly capable of.

Roman, their father, was even worse. He came from a long line of military men and treated his family with as much love and affection as a sergeant would his troops.

I often thought that's why Addie was such a romantic— always seeking the warm embrace of men who would hold her as delicately as the flower she was inside. She was constantly seeking it because she did not have that with the men she shared a home with, not even close.

Honestly, I felt sorry for her. Adelaide was a kind and gentle soul, though too sensitive and naive, like a lamb walking alone in the woods at nightfall.

Since we were infants, we had grown up alongside one another, experiencing the world for the first time together. We'd been through it all— first days of school, first kisses, first heartbreaks, first deaths…. We'd braved the storms of life together, and I could count on her to be there when needed and vice versa.

That said, I always felt a barrier between us. Whereas Rosemary and I had no secrets from each other, knowing the inner depths of each other's souls, Addie kept her heart and soul guarded.

In hindsight, she grew up in a house with two potential Guardians, so perhaps part of her knew she wasn't safe to express herself fully. She wasn't safe exploring the inner workings of her mind and spirit while being carefully monitored by the males in her life.

I was about to lay on my horn again when Adelaide emerged from her red brick home, wearing a long ivory dress and a thick burgundy sweater. Her perfectly done curls bounced with each step toward my shabby, old truck.

She almost perfectly contrasted me with the simple black leggings, forest green sweatshirt, and brown worn-leather combat boots I had opted to wear.

Her smile warmed me every time I saw it, and this morning was no exception. "Thanks for inviting me to breakfast. I'm glad we could do this before I go away with Luke." Addie's grin grew wider after she mentioned his name.

"Me too," I managed to say with a weak smile while pulling out of her driveway.

"He's planned an entire romantic weekend for the two of us — we're going to a cabin in the woods, complete with a fireplace, hot tub, and star gazing deck." She swooned. "I'm so lucky."

The grimace on my face was uncontrollable, even as I saw the love in her doe eyes. Luke made her happy, but I never trusted him. He was close friends with her brother, and Cain was surprisingly in full support of them getting together.

I always thought that was bizarre. Perhaps because the few friends my brother did have were firmly sworn off by him. He warned them not to even look my way for too long, or they'd get a swift punch to their lower regions.

My chest twisted in nostalgia, missing the security my brother gave me. Though he was a sensitive soul, he was also fiercely protective of our family and me.

"Where's the cabin?" I half-heartedly asked, trying my best to seem interested.

"I'm not sure he didn't give me much detail. All I know is it's out of state, surrounded by forest for nearly twenty miles." She spoke nonchalantly, picking at her nails as she did so.

My head whipped to look at her as a bad feeling took up residency in my gut. "Adelaide." My voice dripped with worry. "Find out where the cabin is and tell me before you leave, okay?"

"Luke said it's a surprise, and he can't tell me in case I try looking up the cabin beforehand." Her smile unfaltering. "He knows me so well."

"*Adelaide.*" I gasped, making no effort to hide my fear for her. "You can't just go with a guy to another state without knowing any information. Especially somewhere you likely won't have any service."

"Oh, relax, Kya. It's not just some guy; he's my boyfriend. We've been together for over a year now. When are you going to trust him?" Addie's usually peppy voice cracked slightly at the end.

I knew she wanted my approval of their relationship; she had since they started dating. Yet I could not ignore the distrust that stemmed from my inner voice screaming '*Snake!*' every time his icy blue eyes met mine.

I sighed. "Forgive me if I worry about you," I had for as long as I could remember. "You have such a soft and trusting heart. I just… know the dangers of having a caring soul… I want you to be careful. Stay alert and aware, and don't let love blind you like it usually does." I fumbled, keeping my eyes dead-set on the road to avoid her gaze.

"Like it usually does? What's that supposed to mean?" The hurt in her voice was unmistakable.

"Well…" *No going back now.* "You've seen your fair share of heartbreaks. Not to mention, your brother and father have been…less than kind to you for your entire life. Yet you still adore them." I choked on my words, not wanting to hurt my dear friend but unable to bite my tongue any longer.

"They've belittled and patronized you, made you feel like you need a man to do everything for you. Planted ideas in your head that you're this '*pious little princess,*'" I nearly gagged, quoting an actual nickname her father called her, "who's incapable of being a strong, free-thinking, independent woman." I briefly took my eyes off the road to look at her, though she did not meet my gaze. "When in reality, you are capable of so much more. Which I know you know because I've reminded you that for years."

Addie pursed her lips, and her beautiful doe-eyes darted everywhere but at me. "Look, my father and brother are a little traditional and can be rough around the edges, but…they love me. They want me to be happy and in love. To find a nice, caring husband who will care for me as they have."

She hardly blinked, eyes unwavering on the road ahead. "My father and brother have protected me all my life, keeping the evils of

77

this world at bay for me and my mother's sake."

I balked, blinking rapidly at what she said, my jaw agape.

'Keeping the evils of this world at bay.' Oh, they were Guardians of the Order, no doubt about it. They had fed her tales of heroic justice, painting this 'club' they participated in as a group of moral superheroes, protecting the innocent... How could I tell her they were keeping 'the evils at bay' because they were part of the system that governed it? That they were cogs in the Trine of Power's ploy for total control.

I couldn't bring myself to shatter her reality. Even if I attempted to tell her the truth, her ears would likely remain closed. Adelaide was rooted in her ways of living. No matter how much I could try to warn her of the true evils afoot, she would not leave the comforts and conveniences of the life she's always known.

We sat in silence for a moment before pulling up to the cafe— I had suddenly lost my appetite. Nonetheless, we walked in and sat in our preferred booth, hardly saying a word to one another.

Addie and I had been friends for so long it wasn't uncommon for us to be in comfortable silence, though this morning was different. I searched my brain for some neutral topic of discussion for us to have a friendly chat over baked goods.

"I'm working at Hank's tonight." I blurted, aching to break the tension. Though as soon as the words came out, I hoped my plan to quit and fully commit to my journey for truth wouldn't come tumbling from my mouth.

Her big robin's-egg-blue eyes peeled away from the menu she was intently scanning. "I figured. You've worked almost every Friday for years at that...diner." She hesitated, the word '*shithole*' on the tip of her tongue from years of me exclusively referring to my job as such.

I nodded in agreement, falling short on something else to say on the subject that didn't involve me leaving behind everything I'd ever known.

"How's college going?" I inquired, steering the conversation away from myself and towards a subject Addie would commandeer. She loved gossiping about the 'fashion fails' she saw around campus and seemed to care more about the social aspects than academia.

"Pretty good!" She squeaked. "I'm taking a pretty interesting journalism class and thinking of adding it as a minor." The corners of her mouth tugged upward. "I could see myself working at a fashion magazine, starting as an intern and slowly climbing the corporate ladder to someday be CEO." A dreamy look came over her face.

Part of me envied the life Adelaide lived. She had always been a dreamer, though I never thought she dug deep enough to discover what she *truly* yearned for. Instead, Addie had dreams of upper-middle-class normalcy. A successful career, a loving husband, and eventually two beautiful children— one boy and one girl, as she would always say— were all she wanted. It was a simple life that wouldn't require much free thinking or individuality.

The tiny bit of me that envied her also craved the stability of 'normal.' *Normalcy and its predictable repetitions are strangely comforting once you've devoted your life to selling your labor as a functioning member of society. To be a numbed, oppressed, working piece to fit perfectly into the Machine's puzzle....*

"Do you think you'd want to take some classes sometime soon, Kya?" Addie's kind voice asked, interrupting my internal musings. "We could take one together!"

"Er, probably not soon...." *Definitely not soon or ever.*

"How come?" *A simple question.*

"I just don't have the time for it." *An outright lie that Adelaide would be able to see through in a second.*

79

"Well, that's the good thing about the community college! There are lots of class options for full and part-time students." She spoke as if she had just been hired as a recruiter, with a painted smile. "It's easy to make time for the right studies. Didn't Onyx take some night classes after he graduated?"

I tensed. *He had, briefly, before pursuing different studies....*

"He did," I said shortly, still unable to talk about my brother without feeling a lump.

Sensing my discomfort, Addie's face and voice softened. "I'm sorry I wasn't trying to make you upset. I thought it would be a nice sentiment to follow in your brother's footsteps."

Hah, if she only knew....

"No, I know. It's okay. I just have trouble hearing his name." I lowered my eyes, chalking it up to grief to deflect the sea of words aching to be free.

"I understand and would be the same if I lost Cain or my dad," she mused sympathetically.

My mouth thinned as I nodded slowly.

"Hey, do you ever wonder what life would have been like if our brothers were as close as we were?" Her attempt to change the dialogue caused me to retreat further into myself.

We entertained the thoughts of *'what if'* numerous times throughout the years, concluding that our brothers could not have been more different if they tried.

"Yup, and it never would have happened. They're about as similar as day and night." My tone was sharp, uninterested in entertaining this illusion at all.

"Oh, come on, they must have had something in common." She implored playfully, always loving to create fantasies in her mind.

"No. I seriously doubt that." Annoyance rose in my voice as I was getting pushed to the point of no return for the second time that morning.

"Why?" Addie chuckled, her face slightly perplexed.

"Are you that detached from reality, Adelaide?" I snapped. "My brother was a quiet, dorky musician. Your brother was an *actual* bully, who made it a game to knock the book out of Onyx's hand any time he caught him reading…which was *often*."

Addie was taken aback, lips parted as if she would defend Cain, though no defense came out.

My inner flame was stoked, and I felt the bridge I was about to burn start to quake.

"Your brother borders on actual evil. He preys on the innocent, especially women, to fuel the vile power trip that your wicked, misogynistic father instilled in him." I spat, no longer caring about hurting her feelings.

A distant memory of Cain cornering me in their kitchen during a sleepover— our last one at her house— came to the surface. The way he placed his long, muscled arm on the counter next to me to ensure I could not walk away easily. The way he crooned and tried wooing me with insincere compliments. Saying he loved my hair even though I had previously overheard him calling me a troll-doll for it. The way that I knew he was only trying to get me into his bed to piss off my brother royally.

I tried shoving the memory away though it only stoked my fire more. If today was one of the last times I'd see Addie before my departure, I might as well go out with a bang— a scorching bomb of truth, to be specific.

"Don't you wonder why I won't step foot in your home

anymore? Being around your brother, let alone your father, unnerves me to my core. I'm on edge whenever I'm in their presence, worrying that they'll either insult or degrade me. Honestly, Adelaide, I have no *idea* how you grew up in the household you did and still managed to come out a decent human." I felt like I was breathing fire. Like the scathing words I said were hurled at her alongside invisible flames, directly attacking her heart.

I couldn't stop. Not when I already felt the immense guilt from seeing her teary-eyed expression as I ripped into her reality and left it in shreds.

"That 'club' your father and brother belong to is called the Guardians of the Order. Their sole objective is to keep people subordinate, compliant, and scared. They feed on the submissive fear of the brainwashed masses to keep 'the order,' which involves distracting everyone from the real evils that rule our society."

I could hardly breathe; the words flowing out of my throat came straight from the fire in my gut.

"The Solar Lord you and your family pray to has been one of the greatest facades in history— masking the dark, wickedness of humanity with elite and holy patriarchy. And…." I sighed to steady my breath. "I believe the Solar Lord and his Guardians caused my family's disappearance."

Addie's face was a contorted mix of sadness and anger as she searched for a response to my rage.

"I'm sorry, I… I don't know what to say. I'm not sure how many times I can tell you I'm sorry for your losses, but I hardly think displacing your anger at my family and our religion will help you get over their deaths." Tears fell on her freckled cheeks. "I know you miss your father and brother, but you don't have to tear mine down to make you feel better." Adelaide's perfectly-glossed lips quivered.

My rampage wasn't over. Not yet.

"You know what? I'd rather have lost my dad and brother than be *cursed* with the ones you have." I concluded, leaning as far back in my seat as possible and keeping my face unmoving as a stone.

The final blow.

I'm unsure what overcame me during this conversation, but it felt like eighteen years of friendship had just been blown to smithereens. Like I was an angry dragon who had burned down an innocent village in my blinding rage.

Addie just sat there, shaking her head with tears fully flowing. "I miss the Kyanie I knew when we were kids. Not this cynical *bitch*." She returned my verbal poison.

Her last syllable struck me in the heart. I felt remorse over what I said and the irreversible damage I had done to this friendship.

"I miss her too." My mouth turned downward as I sighed dejectedly. Honestly, I had become a different person. And soon, I would be a new and different person all over again.

"Look, Addie, you know how much I love you. You are kind, thoughtful, and sweet. But for years, I've tried waking you up. To show you how strong and capable you are. To show you that only *you* can give you the love you truly deserve. That you are the one you've been waiting for…." I reached for her hand to give her a loving squeeze, to which she hesitantly met mine, "there will never be a knight in shining armor coming to rescue you. You have to rescue yourself."

"Yeah, I know that," Addie whispered before wiping her nose with her free hand. "And I love you too, Kya," She added softly.

"I'm sorry for what I said. You didn't deserve that… You don't deserve to get spoken to like that by anyone, especially a friend." I couldn't leave us like this; I had to repair the bridge I destroyed so hate wouldn't linger.

"I know I don't." Addie sniffled and reached for her phone. "I'm going to call Luke to come and pick me up. We're leaving in a few hours anyway."

"Wait, Adelaide, let me explain…." Panic ran through me at the thought of losing one of the last people I held close to me.

I would tell her everything. Tell her why I believed they caused my family's disappearance, why I harbored so much anger towards the Machine and its Guardians.

"I don't need to hear it right now. I find it ironic that you claim my family has been unkind to me, yet you and Rose take any chance to bash me and my life." She arose, snatching her bag from the cushioned booth. "Thanks for the breakfast invite. Once again, I'm sorry for what happened to your family, and I really, *truly*, pray you can get over it soon."

"Please listen to me. There's so much you don't know…." I pleaded, my face remorseful.

"Clearly. But unlike you and Rose, I'd rather live in blissful ignorance than cynical insanity." With that, she turned on her heels and flipped her chestnut curls over her shoulder.

This time Adelaide only glanced back once when she reached the door to give me a look of loving, sympathetic pity.

~*~

I ended up eating two muffins by myself that morning. Unable to decide between chocolate or fruit and bothered by my conversation with Addie, I treated myself to both. Sitting alone in the booth where Addie, Rose, and I had shared numerous conversations, debates, and laughs, I contemplated the road ahead.

Surely I had to leave behind any desire for 'normalcy' if I was serious about my journey to find the truth. Perhaps my fiery rage, burning one of the last bridges to everyday life, was my inner flame, ensuring I couldn't go back now. I had learned too much; I could start seeing through the cracks in our society and how utterly distracted everyone was from what was happening.

I didn't intend to hurt Adelaide, let alone destroy my lifelong friendship with her, but I realized it would happen someday. Our life paths were going separate ways and had been for quite some time now.

Finishing my second muffin, I made peace with my guilt and sent Addie a silent prayer for love and protection. Both of which I knew she prayed to her Solar Lord for daily. Instead of the patriarch, I asked the Goddesses to watch over her from above and below.

Hank's was the only other bridge left to burn, and I would make a show of it. The thought of telling off my pig of a boss, Dominic, with no repercussions left me nearly giddy. The symbolic fire I would leave in my wake would be a pyromaniac's dream.

IX. Ashes

When I returned home after breakfast, Rosemary was sleeping on our emerald-green couch. However, she awoke immediately from Bella's barking greeting.

Joining her in the living room, I told her everything I said to Adelaide, sparing no details. Upon finishing, she just smirked, her eyebrows raised.

"I'm impressed, Kya. Clearly, you've picked up everything I know about verbal dueling." Rose leaned over to the dark wood side table where she had put her elixir from earlier and took a sip. "What a shame she's too stubborn to see what a helpless sheep she is," she added after grimacing at the cold tea. "If she weren't so adamantly stuck in her ways, I would care more to wake her up."

"You don't think I went too far?" I questioned, feeling a trace of that regret in my gut.

"Maybe a little, but it's not like she made it easier for herself. Her blind faith in the men in her life has always clouded her. Even with you saying this corrupt system was the cause of the greatest tragedy in your lifetime, it still wasn't enough to turn her head away from the illusion. She'll likely die holding onto the belief that everything in life is good and true because her father, brother, and Lord command it." She shrugged and put her mug down, "Can't say we didn't try to open her eye."

Suddenly my mother appeared in the kitchen archway. "What's this I hear about Adelaide?"

I repeated my story, keeping it more succinct this time out of fear that my mother would admonish me for being so harsh. Rather, she sat there silently, with a knowing look as if she had gone through the same.

"Then she said she'd pray for me before walking out of the cafe for Luke to pick her up." I heaved a sigh, waiting for the reprimand from my mother.

"Well, Kyanie, there was definitely a gentler way you could have handled that…," She tutted once. "Poor Adelaide, she was always such a sweet, sensitive soul. I'll keep her in my prayers to the Goddesses." My mother closed her eyes and took a deep breath before continuing. "I'm sorry she reacted so badly. I should have warned you about trying to open other people's eyes. Every human has a unique experience on this planet. More often than not, they're not open to their reality shattering. Only those who have begun seeing through the facade are receptive to learning the truth."

She strode over and put a hand on my shoulder. "You're starting to understand that this is a journey you must take alone." Those warm, rich, umber eyes met mine with seriousness. "You can never go back to the life you once knew."

Though I realized this on my own, hearing it from my mother's mouth confirmed it further. Glancing at Rosemary, who sat beside me with her jaw slightly agape, I knew that this was probably the last time I'd see her sitting on my couch.

I took a breath, appreciating every last bit of this moment, and mentally painted a picture. My two favorite women in the world—at least that would never change.

~*~

The rest of my day was spent sleeping, restoring my energy for my final shift in hell. When I awoke from my 'short power nap,' the sky was completely dark, and I was alone in my living room.

Rosemary had initially joined me in my nap. Having reacted more severely to her hangover than I did, she claimed sleep was the only reprieve from her splitting headache.

When I opened my eyes and did not see her tangled mess of lilac hair, my heart sank at the thought of not saying a proper goodbye. Luckily, she was never the type to vanish without a word, so she left a note where her head had laid.

"Stop by my house before work. Have a gift for you and your travels. P.S. Please burn this note after you read it for dramatic effect."

I chuckled and walked over to our stone fireplace, grabbing a match. While the flames engulfed Rosemary's scrawled letter, I mulled over how fire had been following me— beginning with the burning car that changed my life forever. From all the fires started by severing my cords to 'normal' reality, I began to truly embody the phoenix. As if the metaphorical ashes of my father and brother were the essence I needed to start my new life, to fulfill my destiny on Earth.

The small piece of paper burned quickly, and when I arose from my kneeling position by the hearth, I saw the time on the stove.

5:55 p.m. For the second time today. Okay, Universe, I get it; change is very much happening…. That meant I had little less than two hours to get ready for work, for the final pyre to be lit.

I spent that last bit of time in my room, packing a bag with the necessities for my upcoming travel. Aiming to pack light, I struggled to decide what was truly needed considering I had no idea where my end destination was.

All the wilderness skills my father instilled in me taught me to be prepared. The importance of wearing layers, warm socks, and a good jacket to keep the elements out could be a matter of life or death.

I thanked him in the Ethereal Realm for taking our family

camping at least twice a year. He taught us that we could survive in the woods with the proper preparation and knowledge.

A handful of socks and underwear, one pair of hiking pants, one pair of jeans, one pair of shorts, one pair of sweatpants, one long sleeve shirt for layering, one thick sweater, my two favorite band t-shirts of Onyx's, and an insulated windbreaker filled my backpack. After my clothes were packed, I stuffed the pockets with small necessities. My Swiss army knife, gifted to me by my parents on one of their wedding anniversary trips to Switzerland, my Dad's old compass, a first aid kit, a chunk of flint for fire-starting, and a bundle of cords finally completed my inventory.

For the third time that evening, I plopped onto my bed, questioning how I could leave without having a destination. *How can I prepare for something if I have yet to learn what it is? All I know is that I'm aiming to ascend into the Ethereal Realm, which is certainly easier said than done.*

Suddenly, my free time before work was over. I threw on my last clean uniform, which I noted was very fitting, and grabbed my backpack to stow in my truck.

I hurried out of the house, kissing my mother on the cheek and a promise to come home before leaving for real.

"You better," she said, accompanied by one of her winks.

Luckily, Rosemary's house was on my route to Hank's, so I quickly ran up to the door and called for her.

It only took one holler for her to throw open her green front door with a wise grin. Clearly, she had been well-rested and was no longer feeling as if her *'brain were being split by an ax,'* as she described.

"I see you found my letter. I hope you followed the directions as written." She leaned on the doorframe with a smirk. "So you've come for your gift?"

I laughed softly at her theatrics. "Yes, I have and did not manage my time well, so I only have a few minutes before I need to get to the worst place on Earth."

Rosemary returned my chuckle. "Straight to the point! She wastes no time...." She pulled the book she checked out from the library and a small sheath from behind her back.

"Originally, I was just going to give you this." Rose placed the worn-leather sheath in my hand. "It's a pocket knife I stole from my biological father the day we left. I was young and scared and thought he would hurt my mother with it. I want you to have it."

"Rosemary, I don't think I can accept this." I faltered, turning over the sheath to see a symbol imprinted in the leather. The sign of the Guardians— a twelve-pointed sun with a bisected X in the center — just as my mother had described

"Do you realize...." I started.

"It's the mark of the Guardians of the Order. I figured you could show them you have connections if they endangered you." Her knowing smile indicated that she had thought this through. "I have no use for it besides a painful memory." She shrugged.

"And this," she held up the thick book, "I thought would both inform and entertain you along your journey. Before you say anything, I bought it from the library through connections of my own." Rose smiled in the manner she only did when Poppy was on her mind.

"Didn't you give my mother and me a thorough report on this?" I questioned, grabbing the book by its spine and taking in its name for the first time— '*The Original Religion: Discovering the Old Ways of Earth.*'

"I highlighted the most important information, what I thought would be most beneficial to you. But there are hundreds of pages of historical context that I didn't mention for the sake of time and my sanity." Rose breathed a laugh though her eyes stayed locked on the book. "I sped-read through it in a day, and honestly, my world changed forever. There's still so much to learn that the Trine of Power has hidden. You... trust me when I say you'll want to read it too."

Her green eyes, like pools of emeralds in the dim lighting, met mine with that familiar loving fierceness. I could feel tears and the lump in my throat start to form before anxiety tugged at my gut and told me I would be late.

"Rosemary, I can't thank you enough for this. For everything you've done for me in our friendship. I...I wouldn't be who I am today without you." A single tear rolled down my left cheek. "In recent years, as I grew colder to society and everyone in this town, my love for you stayed warm in my heart. You... your friendship kept me from freezing over completely into a heartless wench." We both laughed, tears flowing from me and Rosemary's eyes growing mistier.

"Shocking to hear that the heartless wench prevented a frozen heart in another." She smirked, though the humor faded back into the ferocity of her love. "Kyanie, you are the best friend I've ever known. As utterly pissed as I am that you're leaving, I know you have to, that you're *meant* to... and I'm honored that I could be a part of your life."

She took a step toward me and embraced me fully in her long, slender arms. Rosemary had always been taller than me, so when she hugged me, she completely cocooned herself around me, resting her head on the top of my mane.

We exchanged *'I love you's,'* promises to see one another again, and many tears— a proper goodbye to a true friend.

As I drove away, the reality of my journey became all the more real. *Now it's time for the final pyre.*

X. Release

I clocked into my shift less than five minutes late and prayed Dom wasn't in the diner to chew me out. The other servers informed me he would come in later tonight as he had 'other business' to attend to, to which I heaved a sigh of relief.

Friday's were consistently busy at the diner, with an eclectic mix of people of the night. Young bar-goers, truck drivers passing through, and an assortment of strange, nocturnal characters always seemed to appear.

My first tables weren't terrible. One was a couple too intoxicated and occupied with each other that they hardly cared about the service. Another was a single older man who regularly ordered one cup of black coffee while he read his book. The others were a blend of young people preparing for a long night on the town and hungry travelers who couldn't resist the 24/7 appeal of this fine establishment.

Hours flew by, and I was halfway through my last shift before I knew it. Nearly every check I ran for my tables included repeating numbers, 5's and 6's being the most recurring, further confirming my need for leaving.

I decided to take a quick break and eat the snack stashed in my bag, as I always did to avoid the wretched food we served. We didn't have much at home, so an apple was all to hold me over. Luckily, it was exceptionally crisp and juicy, so every chomp felt nourishing and energizing.

As I took my final bites of the bright red skin, the back employee door opened, and my heart dropped. In strode my boss wearing one of his signature brightly colored polos, which tightly hugged his bulging stomach, and brown khakis that I swore he had numerous, identical pairs of. His face was turned downward, showing the staff what kind of mood he'd be in for his visit.

I hurriedly finished my apple so he wouldn't catch me and make me his first victim of verbal abuse for the evening. Tossing the core in the garbage, I was heading to check in on my table when I rounded a corner right into him.

Dom's balding head reflected the fluorescent lights above us as he sneered down at me.

"Thought you could slack off while the boss wasn't here, eh?" His crooked smile was threatening, like a predator taking in his prey. "It's nearly midnight. You know we get a wave of bar crawlers around this time, so why on Earth are you hiding in a corner?"

"I wasn't hiding; I was about to check table three. So if you don't mind…." I shouldered my way past him and refused to look back even as I felt his gaze burning into the back of my skull.

I will keep my temper in check until my shift ends… Or until my smoldering inner fire simply must be released….

Thankfully he didn't come up to me again for a good hour. Through the staff, specifically another server Clarissa, I learned he had just come from a date that went horribly. Likely because of his vile views on women, though I couldn't be sure.

I had successfully avoided him, giving all my energy and attention to my current tables, filled with men from the bar down the road. One table I paid no mind— they were happily eating, sobering up, and chatting with themselves about the sports game broadcasted that night. However, for the other, my guard stayed up firmly.

I tensed the moment their familiar faces walked in. Immediately, the memory of them hounding me about what I was doing when my shift ended a few nights ago resurfaced. I could still feel the tears I fought so hard to hold in while storming away from their egoic game of cat and mouse.

They saw me and the fear in my eyes as soon as they walked in the door— all four of them with a near-identical sneer. As if they came back hoping I would be here and have to serve them again.

I asked Clarissa if she would take them for me, my voice slightly shaking as I did.

"Sorry, love, Dom said I can head out once my last table pays." She answered over her shoulder while walking back to the kitchen with an armful of dirty plates. Her auburn hair was tied back tightly to show the entirety of her soft face. "Normally, I wouldn't mind staying, but I've got a sitter at home. Tomas said he's no longer helping with Gabriella, so I'm all on my own." Clarissa's sapphire eyes were full of motherly pain.

My heart ached for her struggles.

"No worries, I'm sorry to hear that. You should go home to your kid. I can handle these brutes a second time." I responded, more so comforting myself than her.

After she disappeared behind the swinging kitchen door, I took a centering breath. Slapping on the biggest, most hospitable smile possible, I approached their table.

"Welcome back. Can I get you guys anything to drink to start?" I swallowed all my trepidation at being too friendly and kept my grin plastered.

"We've had plenty, sweet cheeks." The man in the far left corner said with a hungry grin, his long, greasy black hair hanging limply.

"Why don't you bring us a round of water for the table." The

94

one sitting closest to me on the right interjected. His face was kinder, his slight smile more genuine than predatory, as he looked up at me through his raggedy brown locks.

I nodded and turned on my heels, my smile unwavering until they could only see the back of me. At that moment, the front doorbell chimed, and I glanced back from the drink station to see a head of bright orange hair saunter into the diner.

It was a tall young man, no older than thirty. He had an angular face with hair the color of flame, so bright it seemed to glow beneath the harsh diner lighting, and eyes the richest, most piercing shade of green I had ever seen. Even standing over ten feet away, I was mesmerized by the deep shamrock hue.

Smiling politely at the new patron, I motioned for him to choose any open table. He returned a half-smile and nodded before sitting at a small table in the corner by the window, only one away from the heckling men.

He wore fine clothes— a dark, forest green velvet jacket, brown-corduroy pants, and shiny leather boots. His regal-looking coat had embroidered vines and leaves along the arms and collar.

Shifting my focus to serving, I dropped the check off at my other table of mostly-sober men before returning with their waters.

"Ready to order?" I asked sweetly, my cheeks hurting from the fake smile I forced.

"We're definitely hungry." The man with oil black hair answered. "But I don't see you on the menu anywhere." He drawled, voice still tinged with the alcohol in his system.

I struggled for composure and felt my nostrils flare but managed to keep a service-smile. "Sounds like you need more time then," I responded sharply before walking away to my new guest.

95

He appeared to have been watching rather than perusing the menu and did not attempt to hide the fact. His sharp gaze remained on me, then the brutes' table, then back to me.

"How are ya this fine evenin'?" He asked with a foreign accent before I even had the chance to greet him.

Taken aback, I retorted. "You know that's usually my job to do the welcoming." Softening my tone, I answered. "I'm good, though a bit on edge. Thanks for asking."

"That bunch of blokes botherin' ya?" His voice was an alluring blend of Gaelic descent, and I hung onto every syllable.

"A bit, but... it's not just them, I...." Shaking my head, I changed the subject. "How about you? Are you passing through?"

His smile was easy and charming as he replied. "Just a weary traveler searchin' for a hot meal and good company." He put his elbow on the table and propped himself on his hand. "I believe I've found what I'm lookin' for."

Those deep, green orbs were unmoving from my face.

I felt my cheeks heat and looked down at my pad and pen. "Are you ready to order something warm to eat then?" I asked, my hospitable smile turning coy.

"You'll have to forgive me, your beauty has taken my full attention, and I haven't even glanced at the menu yet." His voice was like silk, soothing and melting me in my core.

"I'll give you a minute to decide...." Blushing, I smirked though it quickly faded as the brutes beckoned me over.

"Hey, sweet cheeks, if you're done flirting, we'd like to get some grub." Oil slick's voice jeered from behind me.

Trying my best to look unfazed, I took their order and hurried it to the kitchen staff, begging them to make it as quickly as possible.

Returning to the dining room, I watched one of my three final tables leave. A whoosh of panic coursed through my veins at the realization that I was nearly alone with these men, save for the fire-haired traveler.

Glancing at the corner of the room, I saw his piercing eyes were still watching my every move with cat-like curiosity.

"Ready to order?" I asked sweetly as I approached him, my smile just as saccharine as my words.

"I am, but I'd like to ask ya somethin' first." An impudent grin spread across his face. "What's a girl like you doin' working in a roadside diner durin' the wee hours of the night?"

"Well, I…" I'm not sure what about him made me want to be completely open and honest, but I felt him dismantle the stonewalls inside me with every word he spoke.

"I've worked here for years; it's not the *worst* job ever. Honestly, the most insufferable part is my boss, who's made it his mission to make me miserable by giving me the worst shifts."

"And why would he do that?" He pressed inquisitively.

"After I turned eighteen, he tried making a move on me and asked me to go to his place after work. He didn't take well to my rejection… or the slap that came with it."

He guffawed with laughter. I smirked in response.

In my peripheral, I saw the brutes turn toward us and did my best to ignore the daggers they were sending my way.

"You've got a fire inside ya. I'd love to see more of it." His eyes glinted with mischief, and he glanced at the men behind me. "I say you shouldn't have to put up with that sort of lot."

Usually, being hit on by a lone, strange man during the graveyard shift made my stomach turn. But now, I felt enraptured by the attention of this handsome traveler.

Suddenly, as if me bringing up my rejection summoned him, Dom barked from the kitchen. "Food's up!" I could see his scowl, which had somehow deepened throughout the evening.

"I'll be right back to take your order, sorry…." I turned to leave, but he grabbed my wrist.

"Do you ever want to leave this Realm? To escape from the horrors of man and see the Ethereal?" His face was solemn.

My blood ran cold at the mention of the Realms. I snatched my hand out of his grip, then stared back at him blankly, unable to form words, before I hurried over to the kitchen.

Dom snapped at me as I started filling my arms with plates of assorted meat and fried food. "You've only got two tables, yet I had to stop doing inventory to get you to do your job. Didn't you hear the bell? Or were you too busy hitting on the customers to notice?"

"I didn't hear the bell: It must be broken," I said as calmly as possible. It was true; I hadn't heard anything besides the banter of the orange-haired man.

My head was reeling at the strangeness of it all.

Who is this alluring traveler? He hasn't mentioned where he came from, only that he was passing through, and I don't even know his name.

"Idiot girl…" He mumbled under his breath. "I'll bring some of these over and apologize to those fine men for the completely unnecessary wait caused by your daftness."

A match was lit within.

I swallowed my anger and followed him to the table, my hospitable smile growing weaker with each step.

'Do you ever want to leave this Realm… To escape the horrors of man…,' echoed on a loop in my head.

Dom put on his best managerial attitude as he hand-delivered their meals. "My apologies, gentlemen. You know how women can be — they get so distracted by pretty things that their brains shut off."

"It's about time." Oil slick grumbled, and the bald man who sat across from him snickered.

The man closest to me on the left, who looked the most military out of the bunch with buzzed-blonde hair and a large, broad build, smiled slyly. "No need to be sorry. I can't blame her for wanting attention to feel as sexy as she is."

He concluded his comment with a swift slap on my rear.

I gasped in surprise and stepped back.

"How dare—."

Heat rising inside me, the match met with kindling.

"Hey, watch it. If anyone has a claim on this broad, it's me." Dom snarled dominantly.

"Excuse me?"

The kindling blazed.

"Get in line, boys. I've been trying to hit that for years— I'm not sure if she's a prude or a dyke." Dom spat, and the men laughed as if I weren't standing next to him, hearing this slander with my ears. As if I'd stand there like a defenseless doe as these misogynistic hunters hurled their attacks.

This is it. My inner voice cheered. *Go off!*

"Alright, I've had enough!" Ripping off my half apron and throwing it and my notepad on the grimy floor, I was ready to burn *'Hank's All You Can Eat, All the Time Diner'* to the ground.

"You are all despicable, horrid excuses for human beings. I wouldn't touch any of you with a fifty-foot pole. And you—." I turned my fierce gaze to look at Dom in his rodent-like eyes. "You are a loathsome sexual predator who tried grooming me the moment I started working here my senior year of high school. I can't wait for karma to come and knock you on your ass— you deserve a life with love as polluted and toxic as you are."

My words were like a raging fire that grew with each breath.

They all balked at me, unsure if they were amused or terrified.

"I'm not working here for another second." I stormed to the back office to retrieve my last check, yelling over my shoulder. "I QUIT!"

Having worked there for so long, I knew exactly where my check would be and made quick work grabbing it. I felt so enraged, like the heat inside me would start an actual fire.

Dom followed me to the back. "What was that stunt? Get back out there and finish your shift." He said with as much domineering conviction as he could.

I felt the urge to leave him with another slap but restrained myself. "Didn't you hear me? I quit." I seethed.

"You still have tables you can't just leave—."

"Watch me," I said through gritted teeth as I pushed past him to leave through the back employee door.

Just as I was about to clock out and walk out the door, Dom ambushed me from behind, wrapping an arm around my stomach and grabbing my throat. "I've been waiting years for this...." He whispered, his lips making contact with my ear as he did so.

I didn't hesitate for a second before letting out the loudest, most bloodcurdling scream I could muster and sending my elbow right to his groin. Then I bolted through the exit.

When I turned back to ensure he hadn't followed me, the kitchen staff was on my heels. The smell of smoke hit me as flames escaped from the back kitchen window.

My eyes were wide, adrenaline pumping through my blood when I noticed a figure leaning against the neighboring brick building, smoking a cigarette and watching me intently. It didn't take long for me to recognize who the mysterious stranger was.

Before I knew it, I was holding the pocketknife Rosemary had gifted me and hurtling for the fire-haired traveler.

PART TWO:
SACRAL

XI. Liberation

"Was that your doing? Who are you? Some traveling pyromaniac?" I shrieked, flailing the knife Rosemary gave me toward the ever-growing flames. "And what do you know about the Realms?"

He took a slow drag with his back to the bricks of the rundown laundromat. His charming face suddenly became more irritating than attractive.

Only the crackling of the growing fire and an unkindness of ravens squawking in a nearby tree hung between us for a moment.

"Right, well, nice to meet ya, tough gal. Name's Pyter, and no, that wasn't me— your fiery nature must've been the spark." He winked, blowing the smoke out like a sultry dragon.

My heart was racing so hard I swore he must have heard it, but I kept my chin high and held my weapon like a knight wielding a sword.

"Cut the charm. Where did you come from? Tell me what you know of the Realms." I demanded.

Another low chuckle sent my blood pumping. "What a sharp and inquisitive mind you have. If you must know, I've come from Miami to visit Salem for Halloween. Then I'm headin' west indefinitely. My destination is Mount Hope in Washington." He raised his eyebrows and dipped his head down, speaking quietly. "I know of a tree there— the Tree of Fate— that can bring one to the Ethereal Realm."

My shock was interrupted by the brutes' hollers as they ran out the front door. Hidden from view in the shadows, I watched them pile into a black SUV and peel away.

Dom followed suit, yelling obscenities into his phone and clutching a wad of cash he nearly burned to save.

I became overwhelmingly aware of the building burning beside me, feeling somewhat, somehow, responsible. The anger I felt— the anger I've been feeling— has been burning through my body, leaving metaphorical ashes in my wake. Now those ashes were real.

Logically thinking, I assumed the grease trap, which hadn't been cleaned in years, was a likely suspect. *Though what was the spark?* The sheer coincidence of it all baffled me.

"There is no such thing as coincidence. Everything is cosmically, divinely guided." Nikola's most impactful lesson resounded as I watched the flames engulf the tacky dining room I had spent years despising.

Turning my attention back to Pyter, I tightened the grip on my knife and held it up to his face, which was nearly a foot taller than me.

"Where did you hear of this tree? And how did you plan on getting to it? I don't see a car here for you." Motioning to the parking lot, which only held my truck and Dom's, I narrowed my eyes.

"After years of being a nomad, I've learned how to trust the path of travel. I'm sure I'll find a way. Perhaps a beautiful young woman, who clearly is going through some breakdown— or breakthrough if you'd prefer it—..." he smirked, "would be willing to be a travel partner." He concluded with a fiendish smile.

My face was a contorted mix of shock, confusion, and anger. "You think I will agree to travel with you across the country when we met less than an hour ago?"

"Stranger things have happened, wouldn't you agree?" His emerald eyes glanced at Hank's. "All I know is you just quit your job, and now that job is burning to the ground. So either *you* are the traveling pyromaniac, or you've lived in this small town, working at this depressing job, for far too long, and you're finally leaving... hopefully for good."

His lips met the cigarette once more as he watched me struggle for a response.

"You don't even know me...."

"No, but I'd like to," A wicked smirk spread across his smoking lips. "So I have a deal for you— accompany me on my journey, and I will ensure you reach the Tree of Fate."

I chewed my lip as I grappled with my inner voice.

On the one hand, he claimed to have vital information about getting to the Ethereal Realm. He knew of Mount Hope and this magick tree I never even knew existed.... It would also be safer for me to travel with a male. Considering how dangerous it could be for a lone female to be caught by Guardians on a quest to expose the truth and dismantle the Trine of Power.... Then again, he is a total stranger. He could have easily made all of this up to get my attention, possibly to sell me out to the Guardians....

"I would like to find this tree...I need to find it if it brings me to the Ethereal Realm. So, I am willing to travel with you if you can help me ascend. However, if I don't trust you or your word for even a second, I'll throw you out of my truck so fast that your charming face will do nothing to help you." I eyed him warily and tried to look as threatening as possible.

"You think my face is charming?" He smiled smugly, smoke swirling around him.

I rolled my eyes. "Was that all you got from what I just said?"

"Of course not. You also agreed to be my travel companion." Pyter took a final drag and flicked the butt onto the pavement. I scowled at the sight of the litter. "So, before we begin our journey together, may I know your name?"

A wry laugh escaped my lips, realizing that I had just agreed to a cross-country trip with someone who didn't even know my name.

"My name is Kyanie. I go by Kya, though." I spoke slowly, lowering my knife.

"*Kyanie.*" He crooned, grinning from ear to ear. "I rather like the feel of your name on my tongue."

I grimaced and rolled my eyes again in response.

The blaring horn and flashing red lights of a firetruck interrupted my witty comeback and obscene gesture.

"Should we stay and see how this turns out? Or would you rather leave unknowing if your red-hot-resignation burned this sad, outdated diner to the ground?"

Pyter looked positively feral, and part of me was fearful of the deal I had just made. However, another part of me tingled with butterflies while standing on the edge of the unknown.

An excited buzz to explore, to live again, flittered through me.

I laughed and shook my head, some curls falling in front of my face. Turning to see the incoming truck, I decided on the latter.

"Do you have a place to stay for the night?" I absolutely could not bring him home— doing so would result in my mother giving me a proper smack upside the head.

What would she say if she knew I had just agreed to drive to the west coast with a total stranger?

"There's a motel with vacancy a few blocks away. Before you extend your kindness, I will happily walk. I love a good nighttime stroll." Pyter finally leaned off from the bricks.

"I'd like to leave at dawn," I said firmly, my eyes meeting his.

"Then shall mote it be, m'lady." He gave me a slight bow and one final wink before sauntering down the street— away from the pyre

107

of my old life.

~*~

When I arrived home a little after one in the morning and saw Bella waiting by the front door for me, I decided that she would accompany me on my journey. She was more than a dog to me— she was my soul mate.

I got her at a shelter almost two years before my family's disappearance and, truthfully, would not have survived the heartache without her.

From the moment I saw Belladonna's mix-matched eyes, one so blue it looked white and the other a warm, comforting brown, I knew she was the one. She was a mutt of a few different breeds— though her coat, face, and demeanor reminded me of my father's German Shepherd that passed when I was a young girl. In contrast, her overall build was short and stocky, genetically dominated by her notable Cardigan Welsh Corgi lineage.

Bella was perfectly imperfect to me. The love we shared would surely surpass any challenges we would encounter in our ascension journey.

After a few hours of restless sleep, the first birds began their serenades. Upon getting out of bed, my canine shot up with zest as if she knew we were about to embark on the adventure of a lifetime.

I mentally thanked past-me for packing a bag and loading my truck, helping me avoid fumbling in the early morning light for my necessities.

The two of us barreled down the stairs and went straight to my mother's room. She was still fast asleep with the curtains drawn completely, keeping her in a cocoon of darkness. I motioned for Bella to wait in the doorway as I snuck into bed with her, burrowing under the thick quilt to feel her body heat.

My mother stirred and wrapped her arm around me. It was muscle memory from all the nights, childhood until now, that I cuddled into her bed, yearning for a mother's love to soothe my heartaches and pain.

"I'm leaving," I whispered, clinging to her tighter.

She opened her eyes and pulled me closer in response, so our foreheads were touching. Our gaze met, and a knowing love was all that was between us.

A tear fell down my cheek: My mother wiped it away and took my face in her warm hands.

"I've been waiting for this moment for your entire life." Her voice was hoarse with sleep. "You are meant to do incredible things for this Earth— for the Realms. You are my strong, fearless warrior-daughter, and I am proud of you beyond words."

A few more tears fell as she kissed my forehead.

"I love you endlessly, Kyanie. From this lifetime to the next and all others beyond that." Her loving words were cemented in my heart— locked in a box of golden steel that could never be broken.

"I love you." I choked, fighting back the urge to start sobbing and abandon my journey.

We held each other for a handful of heartbeats, reconnecting to when we were one. I arose when I knew any longer would only cause me pain.

"I will see you again. Promise." I said from the doorway before Bella and I descended the stairs, then out the front door.

~*~

My voice echoed the entire drive to the only motel in town.
'You can't just go with a guy to another state without knowing any

information.' One of the last conversations I had with Addie — what a hypocrite. Am I a naive fool like her, believing the charming words of men?

I had a pit in my stomach and was obsessively picking at my nails when I pulled into the parking lot, narrowly avoiding a dastardly pothole. In that instant, a red-tailed hawk swooped overhead, flashing its speckled underwing and glowing amber tail feathers.

Pyter was standing outside wearing a different, but still lavish-looking, velvet jacket with fur lining the collar and cuffs. It was a similar color, a vibrant forest green, but lacked the delicate embroidery like the one from last night. He had a small knapsack that looked like it could hardly fit more than one other outfit and a toothbrush.

How could he possibly be traveling across the country like that? The pit in my stomach only continued to grow. *Maybe I'd get all the information on getting to the Tree and then ditch him....* I debated while parking the car.

Pyter gave me a welcoming grin when I unlocked the doors.

His eyebrows raised. "You've brought a dog?"

Bella was eyeing him, a low growl of uncertainty coming from her throat.

"Her name is Belladonna. Anywhere I go, she does too." I answered definitively, stroking her black-tan coat to soothe her defensive instincts.

"I'm not quite sure if pets can get into the Ethereal Realm." Pyter rubbed his chin before shrugging and throwing his simple backpack into my truck.

"Anywhere I go, she does too," I repeated firmly. "If I can ascend, so can she. Besides, her soul is purer and more deserving of the Ethereal than ours."

Pyter's smile and the look he gave me were new, not feline or charming, but a warm expression that spread to his eyes.

"Ya make an excellent point. It's clear your heart is as deep as the ocean, and this dog has a special place in it."

I grimaced but gave him a slight smile in agreement as I motioned for Bella to climb into the back seat. He was right; my deep-feeling heart was always one of my dominant attributes.

When I loved, I did it with all my being. Emotions didn't come and go like a breeze for me— they were tsunamis born from that deep ocean heart of mine. Waves of love and fear, happiness and sorrow, crashed on the shore of my existence, moving me to experience the entire range of human emotion fully.

Now the emotion that was overtaking me was anxiety-fueled dread. The uncertainty of what I was embarking on and the awareness that I had put my blind faith in an utter stranger left me feeling sick to my stomach.

"So, what's our route of travel?" I asked, pushing my worries down, though the pit of apprehension still lingered.

Pyter pulled out a map from his coat pocket. "It's quite simple — we follow 95 south down the east coast until we hit 40 west and take that straight to Los Angeles." He spoke with his hands, tracing the thin lines that represented our route with enthusiasm. "Once we get to L.A., it's a straight shot up the west coast on Route 101 to Mount Hope in Olympic Park."

My brows furrowed, looking at the map. "Why don't we go across the northern part of the country? Or go diagonally to get to L.A.? This 'simple' route seems long-winded."

He gave me a knowing smile.

"You want to get to the Tree of Fate, yes?"

I nodded.

"Then this is the route we must take. Getting to the Tree

111

requires a journey of another kind. We're not simply *taking a road trip to Mount Hope*; we are preparing our souls for the possibility of ascension." His voice was throaty, full of desire for our end destination, and his eyes glinted with excitement.

"How long have you been preparing for this?" I questioned—determined to learn as much as possible about my new travel partner, the Tree, and the Realms.

His eyebrows raised slightly. "Eh, hard to say. In theory, one could say their entire life is spent preparing to leave this earthly plane." Pyter shrugged. "But I suppose it's only been a few months."

"What were you doing in Miami then? If you've been preparing for this for months, why didn't you go from Miami to Los Angeles? Why go up north only to go back down again?" I narrowed my eyes as I began to see holes in his story.

"I do love your inquisitive brain, Kyanie." Pyter smiled cheekily. "I mentioned before I was going to spend Halloween, my favorite night of the year, in Salem with some old friends. Until then, I was vacationing, enjoying the perks of this Logical Realm— basking in the sun, swimming in the ocean, partying with the most beautiful women money can buy....." He winked.

I scowled. "Oh great, you're a misogynistic creep, just like those men at the diner last night."

He laughed heartily. "Quite the contrary, dear. I love women; I *worship* women. From the beautiful curves of your bodies to how ya think and view the world. Everythin' that women create is pure magick." Pyter had a distant, dreamy look on his face.

"You realize I don't believe any of the ass-kissing that's coming out of your mouth, right?" I kept my words curt and icy.

Another hearty laugh escaped his lips.

"Why would ya? I'm a complete stranger, after all. Though, perhaps your trust is something I will earn."

I stared back at him, mentally filing through snarky comments to retort. "We'll see about that."

The red-tailed hawk screeched overhead, circling the motel before disappearing above the trees. Pulling out of my parking spot, I exited the pothole-ridden lot, heading to the highway and towards my liberation.

XII. Clarity

"There's something you should know about my truck." I turned down the music, interrupting the slightly uncomfortable lack of conversation that hung between us for the last five minutes of driving.

Pyter took his eyes away from the window he had been gazing contemplatively out of. "Go on."

"It doesn't do well going long distances. Or driving when it's too hot. So we'll have to do short spurts of driving if we want to make it to Washington." I patted my steering wheel, reminiscing on the times my truck broke down in the middle of nowhere, and I had to call either Onyx, my dad, or Adam, my ex, to rescue me.

My truck was, after all, a hand-me-down from my father to my brother, then to me. Though it had cost me more in repairs than the vehicle was worth, the value it held to me now was priceless.

"Well, that certainly extends our journey." He spoke slowly while pulling out the map again. "It shouldn't make too much of a difference, though. Let me plan our route in more detail…."

"Can you drive?" The thought struck me so suddenly that it slipped out almost immediately as it came.

"I can." Pyter chuckled softly. "Though my license is more than likely expired."

"So you can't drive. I'm not risking getting pulled over while you have an expired driver's license." Annoyance laced my words as I thought of making this cross-country journey as the sole driver.

"Nothing to worry about there. I have connections that one could say put me above the law." A half-smile danced on his lips.

My stomach turned at the possibility that these 'connections' were, in fact, Guardians of the Order.

Keep your friends close and your enemies closer. Though I hate to admit it, I need his companionship to reach the Tree and ascend.

Once again, I swallowed my trepidation, turned up my CD of *"The 70's Greatest Hits"* that I took from my father, and focused on the drive ahead of me.

~*~

An hour or two had passed, with us making small talk and commentary on the sights we passed before we stopped for gas.

Pyter offered to pay and pump for the first tank, oozing with his gratitude for allowing him to journey with me, to which I could not contain my eye rolls.

After using the restroom myself and discovering I had started my monthly bleed, I took Bella over to a small patch of grass. It was surrounded by maple and oak trees exploding with fiery hues— a trademark to the east coast autumns I've adored all my life. A gust of wind caused an autumnal tornado of fallen leaves to encircle me. I closed my eyes and relished the warmth of the sun's rays.

Just as my insides shed each month, the trees shed their leaves each year: Shedding the old and creating space for the new. The cycles of death and rebirth....

"Ready to hit the road, ladies?" Pyter approached, grinning.

"I suppose so," I replied while finishing my leg stretches, feeling discomfort growing in my lower back.

"I can drive the final leg for today, considering I know where we can camp tonight. You can go over the route and see what ya think." Pyter spoke kindly, with no exaggerated charm or feline curiosity in his words or face.

"Okay, that works for me." I reached into my pocket to hand over the keys. "But if I don't like how you're driving for even a split

115

second, then I revoke all your driving privileges for the rest of the trip." Raising my chin, I dropped the keys in his outstretched hand.

"I would expect nothin' less." He dipped his head respectfully before motioning for us to lead the way back to our trusty steed.

~*~

I had skimmed over Pyter's travel plan, going through one to two states each day and making camp where he circled on the map, relatively quickly. The rest of the drive was spent delving into the book Rosemary had gifted me, soon learning why I needed to read it myself.

"Did you know that for 2.5 billion years, all life on Earth existed in the female-like womb of the ocean? That all life came from an asexually reproducing, single-celled organism born from said womb? So that means we all came from a female source, without needing a male to 'fertilize' life on Earth for billions of years." I proclaimed, only a handful of pages into the dense read.

He glanced at me, eyebrows raised and that familiar cheeky smile. "I did, actually. I used to love a woman who was adamant that the Earth was, or is, female and only created males for more genetic diversity…which backfired horribly."

"Huh, you don't say," I responded shortly, slightly irritated that he already knew of this revelation I had only just learned.

Pyter simply nodded, eyes transfixed on the road ahead of him. I swore a shadow passed his eyes, like the ghost of this woman was now haunting his mind.

~*~

The sun had begun its descent in the clear sky, leaving behind an ombre of blue to orange hues, by the time we pulled off the highway to make camp for the night.

Using the last bit of daylight, I jotted down some repeating numbers I had spotted on the drive. A small handful of ones and twos appeared, which made sense, considering today was the first day of my journey with Pyter. However, it was the number of sixes that stuck with me. Countless license plates, billboards, and road signs were littered with repeating sixes. Based on Nikola's numerology lesson, six represents grounding, creating, and getting focused and centered.

Noted; stay calm and stay centered.

On top of the numbers I was deciphering, my mind was swimming with all I had read. How the Earth began with matriarchal clans, worshipping the Goddess, female sexuality, and the cycles of the Earth. Humans participated in ecstatic dance circles that connected humanity to a cosmic serpent of life-force energy for hundreds of thousands of years.

It wasn't until the rise of the Solar Lord that there was a severance in the physical and spiritual bridge of human existence, causing humans to believe they are separate from the divine and the Earth. Instead of a cohesive understanding that we all came from the Dark and Cosmic Goddesses to be stewards of the Earth and share in the magic of existence, a system based on fear and control took power.

The book was closed on my lap as I sat brooding out the window, picking apart the society around me. Painful cramps in my lower stomach caused me to retreat inward while physically drawing my knees up to my chest in reprieve. Lost in my mind, I thought about how this shift in belief systems changed humanity forever.

"Anyone there?" Pyter's voice broke through my contemplation. "Earth to Kyanie." He snapped his fingers at me.

I whipped my head to face him. "Don't snap your fingers at me like I'm some pet. Don't even snap your fingers at Bella." Her head perked up from the backseat where she had been peacefully resting.

"My my, someone's sulking got the best of them. What did you read now? Something about the Solar Lord and his dastardly patriarchy?"

There was enough mocking in his tone that cold rage surged as I replied curtly. "I'm not in the mood to talk right now."

Better to take a moment to digest than have anger conduct my tongue.

"So be it…." Pyter answered coolly, deflecting my icy anger. "Welcome to your home for the evening."

I hadn't even noticed that we had arrived at a quaint state park, with only a handful of cars joining my truck in the parking lot.

My vow of silence continued as I got Bella and my camping gear out of the car. The exhaustion from only a few hours of sleep the night before finally hit me, along with a wave of nearly-debilitating cramps. Hunger joined the fatigue a few steps into the wooded area. Combined with my bleed, my energy levels were at a low.

"Can you set up the tent while I make us dinner?" I spoke only out of necessity, with exasperation oozing from me.

"Happily." Pyter winked.

I had a box of dry food rations that I had kept in my backseat from years of being wilderness-trained by my father. Packs of freeze-dried food, canned dog food for Bella, boxes of pasta, and a few cans of soup were all that separated us from going to bed hungry.

Making a mental note to buy food tomorrow, I walked back to the site with lentil soup, instant mashed potatoes, and dog food. Amazingly, Pyter had already pitched the tent and was tending to a blazing fire a few feet to the right of it.

Out of my peripheral, a bushy red and white tail darted behind a tree into the darkness— a fox was surveying our site, looking for food to swipe.

Bella bounded to me, gleefully unaware of the critter lurking in the shadows. I prepared her dinner on the red-painted picnic table before starting ours.

"You made camp quickly. I couldn't have been gone for more than five minutes." I commented to Pyter, who was dutifully tending his fire.

His eyes did not move away from the flames. "I've got years of experience living off the land; these things come second nature to me at this point."

Accepting his answer and perhaps too tired to question further, I prepared our meal over my small propane burner in comfortable silence.

The crackle of fire and crickets chirping filled the air as the night sky took hold, a dark and rich navy blue speckled with stars.

After we had all eaten and practically licked our plates clean, we sat around the fire, watching the flames dance. Visuals of ecstatic dance worshipping came to me. Deep within my core, I felt the pull to get up and swirl around the flames, embodying the fluid, yet sporadic, movement of fire.

Suddenly, the face of Adam came into my mind. His effortless, charming smile, dazzling blue-green eyes, and sandy-blonde hair made me— and almost every other girl in my high school— swoon. Adam could have had anyone, but he chose me. He had loved me.

He was my last and only real relationship, my high school sweetheart I thought I'd be with forever. That is until the Trine of Power destroyed my family and sense of self.

In an act to feel something, *anything*, besides pain and grief, I cheated on Adam with one of his friends. We ended on relatively bad terms, hurling swears and insults at each other between fits of tears.

For a while, I blamed his friend for preying on me in my vulnerable state. Though, with time, I've taken accountability for being reckless with someone else's heart.

Truthfully, he had every right to be upset— I was a shattered version of who I was when we got together. I stopped trying. Stopped caring.

Not even the half a dozen one-time lovers I briefly entertained after our split was enough for me to forget about the heartache. My fleeting pleasure could never mask the pain I knew I'd caused him and ultimately brought upon myself.

My heart felt a pang of remorse, so I wrapped my arms around my midsection for comfort and buried my feet under Bella's warm body lying beneath me. Tearing my burning eyes away from the flames, I saw Pyter staring intently at me.

"What's plaguing you?" He asked with such sincere concern that I felt my inner walls crumble down.

"Just an old relationship and some lingering regrets." I tried my best to be vague and aloof.

"What do you regret?" Pyter tilted his head slightly, like an animal discovering something new.

I heaved a sigh. *Where to start?*

"I regret letting grief consume me. The last words between us were angry, cruel, and wholly untrue. I regret how cold I let my heart become." Tears started forming in the corners of my eyes, and I swallowed, focusing on steadying my breath.

"Grief is a monster that few can tackle on their own. Did you lose someone close to ya?" His brows were knit tightly with concern and intent listening.

"My father and brother. They…they were in a car accident.

We never even saw their bodies. They just…vanished." I wasn't sure if I would tell him my belief that the Trine of Power was the cause of their disappearance. Maybe in time. Maybe with trust.

"And your old lover? He didn't know how to handle ya in your grief-stricken state, did he?" Those piercing green eyes burned through me as if he could see my thoughts, my memories of a not-so-distant past.

"Adam did his best. Truly he did." I kept my eyes on the fire as I spoke. "He was a good guy with a good heart, and I loved him so much sometimes I felt like my heart would implode." I half-smiled, reminiscing on the love we shared.

"But?" Pyter pressed.

My smile faded. "The monster of grief had me in its grip. I felt like he couldn't understand me anymore. Like he couldn't handle the storm of emotions that erupted from me seemingly without cause….Truthfully, he had demons of his own that clashed with mine. Adam grew up in a household run by a strict father who wanted nothing from his son but a football star— which is what he got. Any show of emotion was ignored or condemned, so I can't blame him for not knowing how to handle me and my mood swings." I sighed, feeling all the suppressed emotions behind our breakup float up to the surface of my heart.

My eyes remained fixed on the fire. I couldn't bring myself to see Pyter's eyes boring into my soul as such a vulnerable part of me was shown. However, once again, something about him beckoned me to lay bare completely.

"It also didn't help that I had this recurring dream of us. I would be swimming in a vast ocean, towards this beautiful iridescent-white light on the horizon. I felt so much love and peace coming from it— I knew I had to reach it at all costs. But every time I checked to see if Adam was behind me, he was farther away. Standing on the shore with arms full of rocks, screaming he couldn't or would drown. I would cry for him, begging him to drop the stones, but I would continue floating farther away. Towards this blazing source of light and love where I knew my heartache would ease.

"He never stepped foot in the water, so I took it as a sign that I was drifting away from him. That he couldn't go where I was being pulled to." I cleared my throat and finally met his gaze.

"It sounds like your destiny has been beckonin' ya for quite some time. Can I be frank?" Pyter leaned forward, a smirk growing.

I nodded, stray curls loosely hanging in front of me.

"If someone can't handle ya while you're a raging a storm of pain and sorrow, they don't deserve ya when you're a calm meadow of peace and love. Truthfully, I don't think he deserved ya at all." His voice was throaty, low, and full of earnest meaning.

Color rose to my cheeks, and I offered a slight smile, tucking the curls behind my ear. "Thank you for that."

"Any time." He bowed his head respectfully. "Just know that I can weather any storm ya throw at me. I've had my fair share of passionate relationships, and what can I say? I love a fiery woman." His eyes glinted with mischief.

I snorted. "Good to know. Thanks." My words were blunt once again, indicating no desire for anything more than a travel partner.

~*~

Though exhaustion claimed my body, I struggled to fall asleep that first night on the road. My overactive mental state prevented my nervous system from calming fully. Luckily Bella slept between us,

122

acting as a furry barrier between this stranger and me.

Pyter didn't bring anything to rest on or with, so I offered him a spare blanket I kept in my truck. It baffled me how he quickly fell asleep on the hard, lumpy ground with only a thin fleece blanket for comfort and warmth. I— in my plush sleeping bag atop a foam pad— could hardly relax my mind enough for sleep to carry me into the next day of travel.

Instead, I tossed and turned, grappling with my inner voice.

Maybe I should leave and keep driving. I have the route I need to take mapped out for me.... Though I would have to ditch my tent so I wouldn't wake him...And who knows how light a sleeper he is....

The thought of abandoning this stranger, who was slowly becoming a companion, to do the rest of this journey solo was appealing. He was strange; that was certain. His accent was vague and foreign, and he had not mentioned where he originated.

There were still so many questions and uncertainties surrounding Pyter, but he hadn't done anything to make me mistrust him. At least not yet. It went against everything in my being to trust his word, and still, something in him called to me. Like he was the catalyst I needed to propel me onto my journey. If it weren't for Pyter and the sheer luck-timing of him coming to the diner, I wouldn't have had a clue where or how to get to the Ethereal Realm.

I was grateful for his knowledge. Though I hated that traveling with a male was safer, I was grateful for that too.

In the stillness of the night, I let myself admit that Pyter aroused something inside. Not lust per se, but a deep, primal urge to be wild and free.

Just know I can weather any storm ya throw at me.' His voice reverberated in my head. His deep, alluring voice both soothed and stoked my inner flame. As if he was an enormous stone hearth that could hold my fire, no matter the size or intensity, and would never falter as I changed with the wind.

Finally feeling at ease within my head and body, sleep found its way to me for a night of uninterrupted slumber.

~*~

Pyter was not in the tent when I opened my eyes that morning.

I shot upright, with Bella doing the same, and rummaged around me, looking for my phone to check the time. Thanks to my mother's warning, my cell service was off to prevent Guardians from tracking me along my ascension journey. Now the device was simply a portable, digital clock to me.

7:13 a.m. The sun had risen over an hour ago.

Emerging from the tent, I let my canine go before me and found Pyter reading the book Rosemary gave me while a pot of water boiled next to him.

He was no longer in his fine, forest green jacket. Instead, he wore a plain white t-shirt and dark jeans, looking more normal than not with bare, freckled arms corded with muscle. His orange hair was slightly disheveled from sleep, resembling a small campfire.

"Mornin', sunshine." Pyter looked up, and that familiar cheeky grin greeted me. His eyes trailed along my sleep-ridden face, surely imprinted with lines from my pillow and covered by stray hairs that did not stay in my plait overnight.

Mumbling a greeting, I rubbed my eyes and took a deep breath of pine-scented air.

Mornings were my favorite part of camping. I adored waking up with the sun and birds, smelling the crisp, fresh air with hints of dew and dirt, and feeling like I was rising alongside the Earth.

Though there was a quiet and scattered symphony of birds this morning, all I could hear was a squawking raven perched in the tree that hung over the tent. It stopped its call long enough to watch me intently as I approached my companion.

I sat across from Pyter at the picnic table and noticed he was nearly halfway through the behemoth of a book.

"Read anything interesting?" I threw him a smirk, which he caught and grinned in response.

"Quite a bit, though I must say there are some historical inaccuracies." He thumbed through the pages.

"Oh really? I had no idea you were such a historian." I raised my eyebrows in mock surprise.

A low chuckle came from his throat. "I've seen and learned a lot during my time here on Earth. All I'll say is the section about the Solar Lord's rise to power isn't *exactly* how it happened."

"What, did you have an eye witness to attest?" I joked, turning the burner off to calm the boiling water.

The corner of his mouth drew upwards, "Something like that...." Pyter continued rifling through the pages before drawing his attention to the hot water. "Please tell me ya have coffee."

I shook my head. "Only black tea, I'm afraid."

Pyter slumped, looking so utterly sad and defeated I had to stifle my laugh. "I worried you'd say that. It sounds like we need to make a stop for resources as soon as possible."

"*Resources*." I mimicked. "You sound like an alien."

"Maybe I am." He winked and his face flashed of mystery.

I shrugged and smiled. "That would explain a lot. After all, stranger things have happened." I returned his wink and strolled away to retrieve tea and breakfast for all three of us.

125

~*~

It didn't take long to eat our breakfast of plain oatmeal, pack up the site, and hit the road.

I offered to drive the first half of the day until we stopped for food and 'resources' and secretly hoped he would insist on driving all day. All I wanted was to continue reading and learning about the Realms, the Solar Lord, and the Machine. Alas, the lack of coffee seemed to seriously dampen Pyter's energy levels— he hardly made a cheeky comment for the remainder of our time at the site.

"So, where were you born?" I asked soon after getting in the car and starting our drive for the day.

His emerald eyes had a haze over them all morning like he was so deep in thought he could barely see what was in front of him.

Pyter had his head propped on his large, wide hand, resting on the door armrest. His hands looked incredibly strong, with protruding veins flowing from his forearm. I wondered what labor he'd done throughout his life to gain such defined muscle in his appendages.

His lips turned upward slightly as he turned to me. "Do you ask because my accent is so strange and alluring?"

I breathed a laugh through my nose. "I ask because all I know about you is that you love feisty women and just came from Miami ogling over them."

A deep belly laugh came from Pyter. "Ogling over them? Is that all you think I did?" His smile turned hungry, and I broke his gaze, fixing mine on the road.

"Watch your tongue, or it'll be begging for rides from lonely truckers on the side of the highway." I snapped, willing my words to be as icy as possible to mask the heat imagining what else he'd done.

"I'll be good, m'lady, I swear." Pyter's eyes gave away the

naughtiness he felt within. "I was born on the west coast of the U.K. and traveled around Ireland a lot durin' my early years. Finally left as a teenager to venture into the great unknown. I've seen all the continents and been to too many countries to count by now."

"And your parents?" I questioned, hoping to get as much information as possible.

Pyter shifted uncomfortably. "They were never in my life. I practically raised myself."

"I'm sorry to hear that. It must have been difficult for you to parent yourself." I couldn't help the look of concern I had on my face.

Pyter, obviously taking note of my sympathy, grinned widely. "No need to be sorry. I've been through a lot, but I wouldn't change anythin'... Well, maybe one thing, but that's a story for another time." He concluded with a smirk.

I looked away from him to immediately notice the car in front of us with a license plate that read LC-6616.

Stay centered, stay focused, and stay grounded.

I decided then to get off on the next exit in search of a grocery store. Pyter would be elated to get a cup of hot coffee for his shift, and I was antsy to delve deeper into The Original Religion.

With every page I read, the world that was once so structured and sound dissipated. As if society had been built under the guise that everyone would stay asleep, unaware of the truths that the Trine of Power worked so assiduously to hide.

XIII. Opening

The following two days of driving were relatively uneventful.

After we stopped for groceries, I became so consumed with my reading that we had crossed through two more states in what felt like the blink of an eye.

By the time we arrived in North Carolina to make camp for the third night, I had read over half of the book. Becoming so enraged with it by the end, I snapped it shut and huffed so loudly that Pyter laughed.

He parked and turned off the engine, prepared to give me his full attention. "Yes?"

"I can't believe everything I wasn't taught in school. I feel like history books only showed the story from one perspective." I chewed on my bottom lip angrily. "Our entire 'modern' society was built with slavery, genocide, and the attempted erasure of indigenous ways of living and belief systems. This horrible rotten root has taken form in the food we eat, the media we see, and the systems we unknowingly rely on to maintain 'normal.' All of it combined convinces us to keep consuming until the day we kick the bucket...."

I looked out the window, hoping to find clarity in my haze of anger, then sighed. "Millions of people have died at the hands of the Guardians of the Order. All for the sake of what? So the Machine can eventually consume every last green tree, every breath of fresh air, every soul? Is ultimate domination and compliance the end goal?" My voice had taken on a shrill tone, as it usually does when I got passionate about something.

Pyter smiled that irritatingly-charming smile and said. "Ah, so you're awakenin' to the horrors of the Machine. Most humans turn a blind eye to inconvenient truths— hardly ever lookin' evil straight on."

I turned to him.

"And you're not like most humans because you see the evil and do nothing about it?" I questioned with agitation.

"That's not what makes me different from most humans, dear Kyanie." Pyter winked.

"So enlighten me. I'm tired of feeling like I'm only getting the half-truth. From you. From society. From my family...." The last slipped from my subconscious.

"Why do ya feel your kin hid information from ya? It sounds like it's not me and my past that you're angry with." He questioned, effectively steering the conversation away from himself.

"They were trying to keep me safe. I know they had good intentions, but I think it made me resent them." I shook my head, suddenly wanting to take back everything and piece the stonewall back up inside me.

Calling for Bella, I hopped out of the truck before he had a chance to respond.

Our campsite for the night was nothing special. In fact, it was just a pull-off on a dirt road surrounded by a handful of dogwood and cherry trees. The small rock fire-pit was my priority as the sun descended and left behind baby blue, sea-foam green, and lavender streaks in the darkening sky.

Pyter took it upon himself to pitch the tent and gather our dinner for the evening. After being on the road together for three days, we developed an understanding of nonverbal communication.

I would take the morning drive until we stopped for gas at midday, and then we'd switch off. Pyter would drive until we reached our destination, and we'd divvy up our responsibilities based on what I felt like doing.

Everything was always my decision to make. Pyter never argued my choices or prodded when words seemed to fail me. Honestly, he was a respectful gentleman, and though I would never admit it to him, he had gained some of my trust in those first few days.

As my kindling took and the tiny flicker of fire grew, I looked up to see Pyter putting the last stake in our tent.

The wind had picked up within the last half hour, and a slight change in the air indicated we might be dealing with some turbulent weather for the evening.

His probing eyes caught mine as I contemplated how best to prepare for a windy, rainy night.

"Do ya still have feelings for him?" Pyter asked with a smirk from the other side of my swelling flames.

"Who?" I questioned, poking the fire and his aloofness.

"Right," he chuckled, "your old lover; I believe it was Adam."

I smiled, watching him fidget with his hands for the first time.

Most of my lingering feelings were successfully, though temporarily, buried amidst the random lovers that followed the month after our ending.

"No," I declared, sacrificing my fire poker to the flames.

"That's good— means you're not livin' in the past." Pyter grinned, then turned away and began cooking our evening meal.

~*~

The rain came down with unrelenting force shortly after we had eaten and cleaned up our dinner.

Hearing the first sizzling drop onto the fire, followed by a handful more with increasing velocity, I knew it would be a long evening of weathering out this storm.

I woke up twice in the middle of the night.

Firstly from an incredibly vivid dream involving me swimming in a moonlit lake with three enormous moons above me and the Goliath-sized barn owl watching me intently from a massive redwood tree. I jolted myself awake when the bird took to the air and flew straight at my head, the turbulent winds outside echoing its flight.

Second to the all-too-real feeling of water leaking into the corners of my tent.

"Shit." I shot up and grabbed at the end of my sleeping bag, feeling dampness building on the edges.

The rain had not let up in hours, and though we had put an extra tarp over our shelter, the equally unrelenting winds caused water to fly from every direction.

Pyter rolled over sleepily, unfazed by the raging storm.

"Shall we sleep in the car then?" His voice was groggy and deep, slumber laced in every word.

"There's hardly enough room for me to lie comfortably in there. Let alone you and Bella."

"The dog can sleep in the back. Ya take the front, and I'll stay here, anchor down our shelter." He smiled lazily.

For a moment, I looked at him and fought the urge to move some of his stray, fire-colored locks from his eyes. To take his face in my hands, gently running my thumb over his full lips, then shaking him and screaming, *'What's the catch?! What is wrong with you?!'*

My eyes narrowed, brows knit together in confusion, as I asked, "Why would you choose to sleep in here when you were the one to suggest sleeping in the car?"

"I'm not bothered by the storm. I actually find it quite

131

soothing to be out in the elements during turbulent weather." He laid his head down flat, closing his eyes as if he would fall right back asleep. "You're the one who woke me up with your obscenity, so it's clear ya don't feel the same about rain as I do."

"So you also find it soothing to wake up wet?"

He chuckled, eyes remaining closed. "I believe there are only a few more hours before sunrise, and I've hardly gotten damp at this point, so I think I'll be okay."

"Suit yourself." I shrugged and gathered my things as succinctly as possible before darting through the rain to my steed.

Slamming the door shut and laying out my sleeping bag across the front seat, I looked at my canine in the back.

"Bella, there's something about him I can't quite place... It's driving me wild." I spoke to her, though primarily to myself. "I'll figure it out soon...." I mused as sleep took me for the third and final time that night.

~*~

Miraculously the sky had cleared by sunrise. Bright pink and ruby-colored, fluffy clouds littered the sky as I cracked my eyes open. The morning went by quickly, with the excitement of finally heading west fueling my inner fire.

Pyter didn't complain as he took down the tent and shook off the puddles of water that sat around the base. He hardly spoke at all, though his smirk was always lingering.

"Ready to head west, partner?" I smiled, handing him a mug of steaming coffee.

That lingering smile widened. Pyter's face turned to pure bliss as he took the first sip. "I've never been more ready for anythin'."

I laughed and rolled my eyes before climbing into the driver's seat and turning on the engine.

I wonder what this day of driving will hold. I mused, assuming it would be as uneventful as the days prior.

~*~

How foolish of me to presume. We were nearly an hour from our destination, a state park just west of Memphis, when my truck sputtered, lurched, and began making a terrible, loud sound.

Pyter was driving and immediately turned off the radio to listen intently. "Do you hear that?"

"Obviously." I snapped. "Pull over."

I sighed exasperatedly and rubbed my hands on my face while Pyter parked us on the side of the main road in a ghost-of-a-town.

Great, my car decides to have trouble while we're driving through the middle of nowhere.

He shut off the engine and looked at me with wide, wondering eyes. "Are ya handy with your vehicle? Or shall I find us a mechanic?"

"All I know is how to change my tires and my oil. My dad was good with this stuff, and either he or my brother would usually take care of my truck when it did this." I ran my hands through my hair.

"It's done this before?" His eyebrows raised.

"Once or twice…possibly closer to five other times." I smiled weakly, realizing how pathetic it was that I couldn't even name what was wrong with my truck.

Pyter breathed a laugh. "Let me go walk and find a mechanic then. You stay here with your vicious guard-dog." He patted Bella goodbye, and I noted how she leaned into his hand.

When had they bonded?

I watched Pyter saunter down the cracked pavement road until he was a blip among rundown buildings.

133

Pulling out *'The Original Religion,'* which had now become my enchiridion of Earth-Goddess-based truth, I disappeared into the text.

~*~

"It all started in the Garden. Here in the Garden of Paradise, it has been told that woman created evil, that She defied Her Solar Lord for the sake of transcendent knowledge and freedom. Here, She was successfully tempted by the Cosmic Serpent to forsake all of humanity and curse all Her descendants with suffering.

By defying Her Lord, She condemns Herself to a life of patriarchal confinement— to be subservient to Man as Wife, to belong to Him and His will for Her body.

It is taught that women created evil through disobedience in the Garden of Paradise. She was untamed and in need of control.

It is taught that the Solar Lord is the primordial being who created universal laws that shall be obeyed with little questioning.

It is taught that because She was wild, untamed, and free, She is evil— for she cannot be controlled, and that poses a threat.

Wild women have been demonized for centuries because they are too dangerous to the Order when they stand in their power....."

Pyter tapped on the window, startling me out of my reading daze so abruptly that I jumped and caused Bella to bark awake from her power nap. I leaned over the driver's seat to unlock the door.

"I have good and bad news. Which'll it be first?" Pyter climbed in, the smell of fresh autumn air following him.

"Bad."

"Bad news is we can't get your truck fixed until the morning. The local mechanic is closed for the day, and no amount of sweet-talking would make him budge." He smiled, and I imagined him attempting to croon an old, stoic, southern man.

I laughed softly. "And the good news?"

"Good news is I got us a room at a motel for the night, and there's a bar right next door! So dinner and drinks are on me this evening." He grinned, holding out his hands as if the good and bad news lay on his palms.

"Does this motel room have two beds? If not, I'll happily sleep in the car again with Bella…." I began to protest.

"Not to worry, my dear. I got us two beds and made sure they allowed pets inside." He beamed, seeming to be very satisfied with himself.

Hearing her name, Bella's pointed ears popped up from the back. She smiled at me as if she understood and was elated that we'd be sleeping on a real bed tonight.

"Okay, well…thank you. For finding a mechanic and figuring out our sleeping arrangement. I, uh, appreciate all you've done so far on the trip." I sucked in my cheeks, worrying that any ounce of extra kindness would give him the wrong impression.

"You're welcome, Kyanie. Helping you helps me too." His shamrock orbs fixated on my face.

"So, how far is this motel?" I asked, blushing, looking down the road to avoid meeting his gaze.

XIV. Awareness

We had settled into our dingy accommodations just as the night sky won its battle with dusk.

There were indeed two beds with comforters of varying shades of tan in geometric patterns. The carpet was mocha brown, dappled with blue and green flecks, reminding me of how the floor of my childhood home looked after my fifth birthday party, where the theme was 'glitter.'

"Would ya like the honor of showering first?" Pyter asked while plopping down onto the nearest bed, leaving the one closest to the bathroom open for me.

I hadn't even realized how badly I needed to cleanse until he asked. Then I became all too aware of the dirt under my fingernails and nodded in response.

Within twenty minutes, the scolding hot water had cleaned every nook and cranny on my body. The pastel-pink-tiled bathroom had filled with steam so thick that I had to crack the small window above the toilet to dissipate it. Noticing the fogged-up mirror right before I exited, I decided to leave a note.

"Enjoy," I smirked, feeling the kitten-like playfulness seen often from Pyter.

"It's all yours," I said, striding out of the bathroom, firmly clutching the rough gray towel around my chest and letting my wet hair hang loosely around my shoulders.

Pyter looked up from the farming magazine he had discovered on one of the bedside tables. His gaze lingered on my exposed skin, slowly tracing them up my bare legs and hovering where my collarbone jutted out.

I felt myself heat under his stare and warned, "Watch it."

He threw his hands up, smiling naughtily as he vanished into the bathroom.

Perhaps alcohol would finally reveal the secrets of Pyter that I was dying to unearth. I wondered where this night would lead us as I dressed in my only pair of faded jeans and Onyx's Led Zeppelin t-shirt.

~*~

As one could imagine, the bar was even dingier than the motel. Old news clippings, faded photographs, and several fluorescent signs decorated the decaying wooden walls. Only three other patrons, all middle-aged men that kept their backs to us as we entered, sat at the rustic bar.

There were two high-top tables with bar stools; one against a wall with a glowing fluorescent sign beside it and the other in the dead center of the room. Starting toward the table against the wall, Pyter stopped me, grabbing my arm gently.

I looked down at his velvet sleeve adorned with embroidered vines. It was the jacket he wore the night he came to the diner.

He leaned in and asked, "What'll ya like to drink? I'll go get the first round."

"Surprise me," I replied, smirking and breaking loose from his grip to get settled.

With my back to the wall, my eyes scanned the news articles floating around me. *"Award-Winning Pie Breaks Record at State Fair... World's Largest Knife Store Expands Selection... Local Man Single-Handedly Saves Neighbor's Farm Animals from Fire...."*

A small red fabric between articles caught my attention, and my breath stopped. The Guardians of the Order's symbol was

137

embroidered on a patch and sewn onto a little flag, sitting proudly among the local memorabilia.

I reached for the pocketknife from Rosemary to ensure it was safely in my boot.

"What's got ya on edge?" Pyter asked, placing two stout glasses with a dark brown liquid on the table.

I grimaced. "Whiskey?"

"*Whiskey*." He crooned, taking a small sip and smiling as broadly as he did when drinking coffee first thing in the morning.

Before I could protest, he continued. "You said to surprise you, so I thought I'd order my favorite drink. It reminds me of home." Another sip. "In the winters, the wind chill is so violent ya can hardly step outside without catchin' a cold; nothing'll warm ya from the inside like a glass of whiskey."

"But you realize drinking alcohol in freezing temperatures only increases your chance of freezing to death? Because the booze has thinned your blood?" I asked with my eyebrows raised, nervously swirling my drink around the crystal-clear glass.

"You try telling that to a proper Irishman." Pyter breathed out a laugh, "It's also a good thing we're not in freezing temperatures, so there's no reason ya shouldn't enjoy this fine liquor with me." He held up his drink, motioning for me to do the same.

Keeping the disdain on my face, I raised the glass to my lips and tipped it back. The amber liquid burned its way down my throat as I tried to hold my composure. It did indeed warm my insides and immediately gave me a slight buzz.

"So, what was botherin' ya when I came over?" Pyter asked earnestly, lowering his voice so only I could hear it.

"I'm just a little worried about the Guardians of the Order.

Their mark is over there on the wall." I whispered, nodding my head towards the fabric.

"You have nothing to worry about, dear. I told ya I have connections, so nothing and no one will harm ya. You have my word." His emerald eyes were fierce, blazing like a tumultuous ocean current beneath the neon-blue light on the wall above us.

"You realize that makes me not want to trust you, right? Because I have no idea who or what these connections are and, in case you haven't noticed, I'm kind of on a quest to dismantle the entire Trine of Pow—."

Pyter clamped his broad hand over my mouth, causing me to look at him wide-eyed and furiously.

"This is not somethin' ya should talk about in public. Ya never know where Guardian-ears are listening. Especially in a small town like this." His voice was tinged with warning. "I want ya to trust me. Believe me when I say you are safe with me because my loyalty does not lie with the Trine of Power. Only with myself… and now you." He uncovered my mouth and looked around to ensure we hadn't caught the attention of the three men at the bar.

Clearing his throat, Pyter spoke loudly. "One grilled cheese comin' up, my love." He smiled and winked before walking to the bar and ordering us something to eat.

I stared back at him with my jaw agape and my eyebrows knit in confused anger. He perhaps was right to quiet me, but to do so by covering my mouth was just a tad too disrespectful for my liking.

Taking a slightly larger sip, I willed the alcohol to give me the brazenness I desired to throw back at him.

"If you ever put your hand on my mouth like that again, you'll be losing a finger," I said sweetly as he sat back on his barstool.

"Noted." He responded with a smile before sipping his precious drink. "I hope a grilled cheese will satisfy because it's the only thing without meat that they serve here."

"That sounds great, actually." I offered him a meek smile of gratitude. "Thanks for making sure I'd have something to eat."

"Of course." Pyter dipped his head down as if he was tipping an invisible hat.

"So," I began, hoping to dig deeper into the mystery of Pyter. "Would you rather live by the mountains or the ocean?"

"The ocean, quite obviously." He answered quickly.

"Why's that?"

"Well, the ocean to me is freedom, changeability. It's wild and uncontrollable yet can also be calm and soothing." He took a small sip. "Being on the ocean makes me feel like anything is possible."

"Huh," I said, leaning back. "I feel the same."

"Perhaps we should abandon this quest to the Tree then. Why don't you run away with me, and I'll find a beautiful, remote island for us to relax and enjoy the Logical Realm." His eyes turned carnivorous, "I'd love to see you in a barely there bikini, baring your skin to the sun on a white-sanded beach…."

I scowled, then swiftly kicked him under the table, causing him to guffaw heartily.

"Kidding! But I do believe we have more in common than ya think, dear Kyanie." He replied with a wicked smile.

"Hmph, we'll see about that," I thrummed my fingers on the table, thinking of another question. "What brings you joy?"

"Mmm, diggin' a little deeper this time," he raised his eyebrows. "I'm a simple man; sitting with my back against a tree with a good drink, book, and company is all I need."

Memories of the garden and the joyous times I had spent there flooded my mind. Sitting alone between my favorite oak trees, reading with Rosemary and Adelaide in comfortable silence, and picnics with my family were all sources of my happiness.

"What are your biggest fears?" I deflected, refusing to admit another common trait.

"I'm not afraid of anything. Well, more so, I'm afraid of nothing." My contorted look caused him to chuckle.

"Oblivion, Kyanie. I fear slipping into oblivion where I will never be heard from or seen again." Pyter added grimly.

"So you're afraid of death?"

He shook his head. "No, not death because death is not the end. Bein' permanently erased from consciousness, from the Void, *that* is the end." He took a large swig of his whiskey. "And you?"

"Well, dolls give me the heebie-jeebies, but that seems pretty lame compared to you... So I'll say losing everyone I love."

Pyter sputtered, "I'll drink to that."

He raised his glass and tipped his head back, finishing his first drink. Then he followed up with a series of questions of his own, to which I answered and rapid-fired some back.

The two of us thoroughly interrogated one another on topics ranging from favorite desserts to what happens to the soul after death. Pyter, surprisingly, made me belly-laugh when he revealed his 'shameful' past of Irish Step Dancing.

He was about to get up for another round when the hot plates of fried food appeared. I hadn't realized how hungry I was until the smell of salty french fries hit my nose.

There will be no survivors of this meal.

While clearing my plate of the last extra crispy fries, the front door opened, and two young men meandered in.

They appeared to be motorcyclists, with black leather jackets donning their posses emblem of a skull with a snake wrapped around it and through the eyeholes on the back. Both had bushy beards and long, dark hair.

It didn't take long for them to notice me staring, and though I looked away as quickly as possible, I could feel them assessing Pyter and me— clearly not from around here.

I finished my meal with a final swig of whiskey, washing down the salty food with the burn of liquor.

"Satisfied?" Pyter asked with a slight chuckle as he picked at the remains of his burger and fries.

"Very," I responded, hearing a change in my voice from the growing intoxication in my veins.

"Mind if I step out for a cigarette?" He said as he got up from our table, grabbing his jacket.

"I do," I blurted. "You can't leave me alone in here." Whiskey permeated each syllable.

He looked at me patronizingly as he smoothly slipped the velvet garment over his toned shoulders. "What because of those two blokes? No one will bother ya. Let me get ya another drink to settle your nerves."

Pyter walked over to the bar before I could protest. Outrage burned through me as he ordered another two glasses of whiskey, making friends with the two young men. My lips pursed as I watched him walk back with an arrogant pep in his step.

"You don't want to drink this with your new buddies?" I asked as snidely as I could.

Pyter breathed a laugh, shaking his head with amusement.

"Oh, relax. I told them you're my fiancé, and we had car troubles, so we're only passing through. I made sure they paid us no mind."

"I'm your what?" I spat, nearly knocking over my second whiskey as I lurched forward.

"Calm down, dear. You're practically invisible to those blokes now that they think I have a claim over ya. So, if you'll excuse me, I'd like to go smoke my cigarette in peace." He said with charm though not a drip of his honey-soaked words soothed my growing, fiery anger.

"Claim over me?" I seethed, wanting to reach around the table and take him by the neck out of that seedy bar.

"Here, this'll sell them." In no time, he walked around and gave me a quick but forceful kiss goodbye.

I balked back at him, seriously debating causing a scene and telling him to sleep in the car.

"*Enjoy.*" He spoke sensually, eyeing the second drink he had given me before swaggering out the door.

The mirror.

Suddenly I was alone, ragingly mad, and feeling so glaringly out of place that I fought the urge to cry.

My breathing unsteady, I grabbed the glass and downed half of the amber liquor, immediately regretting my decision. It didn't burn as badly as the first drink though it hit my stomach with force.

Reaching across the table, I took a swig of the water Pyter had ordered with our food.

"Not normally a whiskey kinda gal?" An unfamiliar, southern voice said at the end of the table.

I swallowed, anxiety pulsing, as the two men smiled at me.

"No," I replied shortly.

Slowly, I reached for the knife in my boot, praying the

movement would go undetected.

"We're just here to keep ya company while yer fancy little boyfriend gets some air." The other male said with a stronger accent while leaning onto the end of the table.

I noticed he was slightly broader and taller than the other.

"He's my fiancé." I quickly corrected, hoping my face didn't reveal the blatant lie.

"That's funny. I don't see a ring or nothin'." The taller man said while looking at my bare left hand.

Shit.

My right hand wrapped around the pocketknife as I nonchalantly looked at my empty ring finger.

"I must have left it in the motel." Shrugging, I inched the knife under my thigh.

"Better be careful, little lady." The shorter one, whom I noticed donned a scar below his right eye, stepped forward to lean on the table like his friend. "Someone could steal it right from yer room. Or even steal you from your *fiancé*." He inflected mockingly.

Shifting back against the wall, I aimed to create as much space as possible between the two men and me. My stomach twisted, and my throat parched as I saw their carnivorous expressions.

"I don't think either of those things will happen." I managed to say calmly.

"And why not?" Scar asked with humor in his tone.

"Because we have…connections," I answered vaguely but with enough confidence to convince them not to mess with me further.

They both chuckled lowly.

"We've got connections of our own, sweetie." The tall man sneered and grabbed the empty stool next to me. In doing so, he flashed the butt of a handgun tucked into the waist of his denim pants.

I scooted my stool back on impulse, hitting the wall behind me and causing the knife to slip out from under my leg. The blade clanged down my seat before landing on the splintered, wooden floor with a definitive thud.

Shit. Shit. Shit.

Panic spread to every nerve in my body as the tall man looked down to see what had fallen. He grabbed the knife by the blade before noticing the sheath with the Guardian's symbol face-up.

"Well, look what we've got here." He threw them down on the table and eyed me with predatory focus.

"Our lucky night to find a Handmaiden of the Guardians." Scar rounded the table to sit on Pyter's stool.

"We ain't part of that Order nonsense." His tall companion said, displaying a set of jagged, yellowed teeth.

"Why not?" I asked calmly, unwilling to show any drop of fear even as my blood thrummed in my ears, my heart pounding.

"Too many rules with 'em. We like to do things…a different way." Scar shrugged and mimicked his friend's wicked expression.

"We call us the Sons of Havoc, and we take it upon ourselves to keep the balance." The tall man said boastfully. "And for reference, sweetie. We make the Guardians look like a bunch of lil' girls havin' a tea party."

I snatched the blade and sheath, then jumped off my stool.

"Good to know. Now I'll just be seeing myself out to check on my friend…er, boyfriend… agh…*fiancé.*" Stammering, I struggled to keep my balance. The whiskey hit me entirely, and my vision blurred, causing me to steady myself on the stool.

"Aw, come on now, don't leave so soon." Scar snickered from

across the table.

"You can barely stand. Let us take care of you while yer… all alone in here." The tall one had gotten close enough to hook his arm around my waist.

I pushed him off with as much force as I could muster without sending myself flying backward. "Don't touch me." I snarled, feeling like a wild dog backed into a corner.

Raising the pocketknife to the tall one's neck, I circled him and started towards the door.

"Hey, what's going on over there?" The bartender hollered from across the room.

"Just messin' around, Billy. No need to worry." Scar shouted back. I caught his ravenous stare and felt panic fully set in.

There is no knight in shining armor to rescue me. I have to save myself….

I had just eyed out my path of exit when Pyter reentered.

"What the—." He seethed, immediately noticing me threatening one of his new buddies while the other sat with his hands up and a look of pure guilt on his face.

Wasting no time, I ran past Pyter and out the exit.

"Screw this!" Shouting over my shoulder as Pyter looked from me to the men with a building rage in his shamrock eyes.

As soon as the cool nighttime air hit me, so did the unease in my stomach. I made two steps towards the motel before emptying my stomach on the side of the decrepit bar.

Between wretches, I could hear men shouting from inside.

"Kyanie?!" Pyter burst out the front door.

I was still heaving when he approached me, laying a tentative hand on my back.

"Are you okay?" He asked gently.

Wiping the corner of my mouth with the back of my hand, I finally took a breath. Slowly I straightened and looked at Pyter with fury replacing my unease.

"I told you not to leave me." I spat.

He looked ashamed but said nothing.

"Why don't men understand how utterly terrifying it can be as a lone, young woman? I told you not to leave me, and instead of listening to me, you took the word of some random chums in a seedy bar." I let the verbal poison flow from my deep, raging inner fire.

"You took it upon yourself to metaphorically *piss* all over me, to mark your territory and make me seem invisible instead of making me feel safe. Well, do you know what they told me? They're not part of the Guardians, and they make them look like little girls in pink tutus." My words slurred, but I paid no mind.

Pyter listened with concern in his eyes.

"They said it was their lucky night to find a Maiden of the Guardians or whatever. They looked at me like a slab of meat for them to devour." I scowled.

"I shouldn't have left ya——." Pyter began.

"I don't want to hear it. I'm walking back to the room and going to bed. Stay and drink the night away for all I care." I pushed his arm off me and stomped away.

"Let me at least make sure you get in safely." He said from behind me: I did not turn around to ensure he was there.

Swiftly unlocking the door to our room, I slammed it shut before he could step a foot inside, if he were even behind me to do so.

Belladonna, who had been sleeping on the bed closest to the door, was immediately up and sniffing my hands. Her tail wagging, she licked me vigorously as if she knew exactly what had happened. From being cornered by strange men to throwing up my dinner on the side of the building, it was certainly an eventful evening.

I sat on the bed near the bathroom, stroking Bella's ears and head next to me, and mused. "I hate how some men make me feel."

Her icy-blue eye met mine deeply, and she licked my hand.

I shook my head and heaved a sigh. "It's you and me until the end, baby girl."

She blinked at me with a knowing look before I laid back on the drab comforter. Closing my eyes, I willed the room to stop moving to sleep off this nightmare-of-a-night.

~*~

Pyter was not in the room when the morning sun awoke me. I had fallen asleep without changing out of my clothes or brushing my teeth— the faint taste of vomit being an indicator of the latter.

My head throbbed slightly from the excess whiskey in my system as I meandered into the bathroom. After scrubbing my teeth with vigor, I turned on the shower for a quick rinse. I wanted to cleanse last night from my body further and was unsure when the next time would be that we'd have access to hot, running water.

Peeling back the faded-mint green curtain, I immersed myself in the scalding stream. For I'm not sure how long, I stood there and let the water wash away my anger. The water poured over my head, consuming me in a blanket of steam.

It's not Pyter's fault that those guys were scumbags…

But it is his fault that he left me inside after I explicitly said not to.

Though I suppose I could have gone out with him if I was so nervous about being alone…. I shook my head, water droplets flying off my nose. *No. I won't blame myself.* I vowed and then finished lathering my body.

I just hope things aren't weird between Pyter and me today: My final thought upon exiting my shower.

Thankfully he hadn't returned when I emerged from the bathroom wrapped in the same slightly damp towel from last night. I quickly got dressed in my favorite sweatpants and comforting black hoodie.

Passing by the window, panic struck me. My truck was not parked outside our door as we left it.

What if that bastard ditched me?

I went to find my phone but quickly realized I didn't have Pyter's number— I hadn't even seen him use a cellular device of his own. Not to mention that using my phone could be a beacon for the Guardians to find us.

Breathe....

I reminded myself to calm my nerves.

He probably went to the mechanic.

I checked the time — *9:33 am.*

Three times three is nine, so break it down to 3333... angels. My angels are with me, and I am not alone, being abandoned by Pyter. All is well.

A sudden pain in my head caused me to sit back down on the bed, so I switched on the television seeking a distraction as I waited and prayed for Pyter to come back.

News, commercials for pharmaceuticals that caused more harm than good, infomercials for gadgets that no one really needs, and countless chain-food advertisements were nearly all I could find. Finally settling on the local weather channel, I watched with dazed interest as the beautiful, perfectly done weather woman pointed to an incoming warm front with zest.

Roughly half an hour passed when Pyter finally opened the door, tentatively peaking in with a bundle of multi-colored wildflowers.

"Morning." He smiled weakly at me.

I grabbed the remote next to me and clicked the television off as he entered.

"Did you go to the mechanic?" I asked flatly.

He closed the door behind him. "I went as soon as they opened so we could get on the road early. If you want, I brought some tea and baked goods from a local bakery." He said, putting a white paper bag and one disposable cup on the table between the two beds.

"The flowers I picked myself." Another weak smile as he placed the small bouquet beside the bag.

My stomach growled as if on cue.

"Did you sleep in here last night?" I asked, eyeing a blueberry muffin inside the paper bag, sparkling with chunks of raw sugar.

"No, I thought I'd give you some space, so I slept in the truck." He said while observing me intently. "It was surprisingly comfortable." Pyter shrugged.

Before I could respond, he exhaled loudly.

"I shouldn't have left ya after you asked me not to… or kissed ya as a way to hide you from their prying eyes." He shook his head and looked down at his hands. "I hate that I made ya feel unsafe."

I eyed him suspiciously.

"Maybe I overreacted a little bit, but to kiss me as a way of marking me as your own... that was violating. I felt like a pawn in a war that I can't fight myself for fear of the worst becoming a reality...."

He looked at me imploringly, waiting for my forgiveness.

"And you'll have to do a lot more buttering up before I forgive you for leaving me like a piece of bait." I finally responded, biting into the muffin to conclude.

Pyter chuckled ever-so-softly, that familiar glint returning to his eyes. "What if I ask your permission before leaving you like a piece of bait?"

He saw my unamused expression, then bowed his head.

"I will gladly do anythin' you ask of me, Kyanie." He purred my name like a satisfied cat.

"Great. Then you can drive for the full day today." I responded sweetly, licking the sugar off my fingers.

He eyed my mouth as I did so, then bowed, smirking slightly.

"So shall it be."

XV. Expansion

Pyter didn't complain once when I made him drive until we reached our campsite. So he drove all the next day as well. A little bit because I wanted him to think I was still holding a grudge from the night at the bar, but mainly so I could continue reading.

Regardless, another three days of driving passed, blurring into one long montage of desert ecosystems. Thankfully, the conversation between us flowed naturally and consistently when it was my turn to drive again, making travel go by quickly.

Dilapidated ghost towns were broken up with spurts of familiar restaurants and chain stores to remind me of our capitalism-run society. The highways blended into one long stretch of trash-filled pavement, each vehicle housing a depressed, lost soul.

Every time we stopped for gas, I made Pyter pump it. Interacting with strangers who seemed to morph into the same being, all with the same downcast face and blank stare in their eyes, left me feeling depression creep back up my spine. If they weren't staring at their devices, they were scowling at the world around them, judging anything abnormal.

Going into the small gas stations, with fluorescent lights blazing down, sleazy humans eyeing me as if I were for sale, and walls of brightly colored junk food all made me feel glaringly out of place.

Perhaps it was all the truth I was learning through 'The Original Religion,' or maybe my other eye was fully opening. Still, I had begun to feel like an alien trying their best to be human and failing miserably.

By then, I had nearly finished the book, learning the horrors of tyrannical, multinational corporations. They prey on an oppressed, primarily female, labor force to keep them working like soulless cogs in their wealth-producing Machine.

Women get paid pennies to work in hazardous factory conditions. At the same time, millions of dollars flood the pockets of the select few, almost entirely all-male, people in power. They sit comfortably in their mansions, surrounded by gobs of money they could never spend in a single lifetime, maybe several, as their laborers suffer and starve.

Further, women's manual labor is enslaved and manipulated, just as their reproductive system is controlled through politics and domestication. Women have been forcibly turned into glorified cattle to breed and work for the repressive Machine. Until the Trine of Power's devastating effects eventually kills them because the politics of death, not life, rule our reality. This creates masses of disposable souls who can be governed via their bodily choices and labor to benefit society's elites.

Those in power have effectively kept humanity distracted and ignorant. Any repressed anger towards the Machine killing our Earth gets funneled into militarizing ordinary people, fueling the Guardians of the Order. All of which strengthens the Trine of Power while consistently weakening humanity's power and divine autonomy.

Clearly, no one in the Logical Realm is genuinely free as long as women cannot make their own choices regarding sexuality, reproduction, and labor....

I had just finished reading all this and more when Pyter parked the car for the evening and eyed me knowingly.

"What's got you riled up this time?" He asked earnestly.

I huffed. "I feel like I'm housing the rage of centuries-long persecutions of the feminine, and I'm just...." I shook my head slowly, trying to find the words. "So angry that I lived in blissful ignorance for

153

most of my life and that… that most people on Earth are doing just the same. And no one seems to care enough even to try to change.

"In less than four thousand years, a new world order took power, taking control of *all* the money and resources on the planet. Then they convinced everyone that *this* is how we should live— like brainless, soulless bodies. All they want us to do is consume garbage food and trash media, poisoning ourselves and our Earth Mother with the toxins of the Machine until we die."

I looked at him, chewing my lip.

"Right, that's a lot of rage you're holdin', and rightfully so. But can I give ya some advice?" Pyter turned in the driver's seat to face me straight-on.

My lips pursed. "Sure," I responded.

"Don't let it get to you. If ya let your rage against the Machine burn too hotly, you'll only get consumed by the flames. Keep learnin' the truth but establish an emotional boundary, so ya don't lose your inner peace." He spoke gently.

I snorted. "I haven't known true inner peace since my father and brother left."

"I see." His eyebrows raised as he paused for a moment. "We should change that… and I believe I've got somethin' to help."

Pyter reached into the back, giving Bella a quick head pat before putting his backpack on the seat between us.

"I wasn't sure where ya would stand on them, so I wanted to wait for the right moment…." He concluded by pulling out a small jar with an ivory-tan powder.

"Is that heroin?" I gawked.

Pyter belly-laughed. "No, no, no, I would never introduce ya to such a harmful drug. This," he said, holding up the jar to my eye level, "is powdered psilocybin mushrooms."

I stared back at him with my jaw hanging loosely in disbelief.

"Why is it powdered? Do we snort it?" I asked.

Another deep laugh came from Pyter. "No, we'd put it in tea after our dinner."

He looked at me, smiling kindly. "I, of course, won't make you do anything you don't want to. But, in my experience, psychedelics and the desert at night go together beautifully. Given that it's our last night in the desert before we get into California, I think it's the perfect evening for them."

I closed my mouth and chewed the inside of my cheek.

The month before Onyx left, he went on and on about the transformation he went through after trying mushrooms with Amber on the beach… I suppose they wouldn't be that dangerous if he recommended them to his little sister….

"Okay, I'll give them a try….You said they'll help me find peace?" I asked with uncertainty surely painted on my face.

"Mhm." Pyter nodded. "These will show you exactly what you need to see for your soul to grow."

It sounded too good to be true, and I knew it wouldn't be as simple as he made it seem.

"Okay…." I said with hesitation.

"Great!" Pyter clapped his hands on the jar. "I'll get dinner started to get the *fun-gi* going." He winked cheekily.

I rolled my eyes at the bad pun and prayed to Goddess that this wasn't a bad idea.

~*~

Anxiety rumbled in my veins from the moment we got out of the truck to when I barely finished eating our spaghetti dinner around the fire that I had made.

155

The final hours of light had left us with the most spectacular sunset I had seen thus far. The entire atmosphere took on a golden hue, with hints of blazing orange and ruby surrounding fluffy, lilac, and salmon-colored clouds. Even the breathtaking sky, which looked like the Goddesses themselves painted it out of love and light, could not calm my churning stomach or clammy, fidgeting hands.

"I've never done any psychedelics," I said, setting my empty plate down for Bella to lick clean.

"I figured that much," Pyter responded after taking his final bites of dinner. "There's nothin' to worry about— I'm here to calm ya down if it becomes too much."

His attempt to reassure me only gave me more doubts.

"How do I even know those are mushrooms? That could very well be a lethal dose of some random drug you've stashed, waiting for the ideal time to dump my dead—."

"Stop." He put up a hand. "Dear Kyanie, if I wanted to harm ya, I would've done so when we were in the middle of the country with no civilization to find your body."

My heart thudded, and I swallowed loudly.

Pyter sighed. "Please relax. I promise ya there's nothing to be nervous about." He looked at me, eyes blazing in the fire's glow, before taking our plates away and preparing water for tea.

I tore my gaze away from him and focused on the dancing flames in front of me. After a few breaths, I made mental notes of our environment as the darkness crept in. The tent and truck were less than ten feet from the fire, where a downed telephone pole served as our bench. Besides that, jagged rocks, cacti of varying heights and shapes, and dusty, red-tinted dirt were all that surrounded us.

Just breathe.

156

I reminded myself before taking a series of long, deep breaths. *Inhale for five… Exhale for eight….*

The roaring in my veins had quieted, and I looked up to see the first handful of stars emerge for the night. All the clouds had dissipated and left behind an expansive midnight blue sky with only a sliver of the moon and the emerging stars to adorn it.

"Ready?" Pyter asked with a tentative smile while handing me my preferred mug.

I exhaled loudly. "Okay."

"I mixed it with chamomile tea and lots of honey, so hopefully, the taste isn't too bad for ya. Though I'll warn that there's certainly a distinct earthy flavor that can't be masked."

With that, he took a steadying breath and had his first sip.

"*Divine.*" He sighed contentedly.

Unsure I'd have the same reaction, I mimicked his movement and let the steaming tea go past my lips and down my throat.

At first, I only tasted the chamomile and honey, sweet and floral, but then a new flavor hit my receptors. Dirt was the first thing that came to mind. Then as the three blended into a swirling potion of nature's bounty, a comforting warmth like a liquid hug from the Earth Mother herself was all I could taste.

The honey from the flowers from the dirt that housed all three. The soil that holds every tree and flower in place, as well as the ever-reaching mycelium networks that balance the energies of life and death itself. My inner voice ruminated philosophically.

"*Wow.*" I breathed. Letting the experience take me over, I finished my mushroom tea in four rather large sips.

Pyter raised his eyebrows and smiled. "Well, I'm glad that bit went smoothly. Now we wait."

~*~

Less than an hour had passed of Pyter and I sitting in silence by the fire when a new sensation spread throughout my body. It started at the back of my neck and felt like someone was pouring liquid light down my spine. Slowly it seeped into my muscles, then my bones, and settled in every vessel of my being.

An overwhelming sense of happiness encompassed me.

I didn't want to talk to Pyter about what I was feeling. In fact, I didn't want to speak at all; I wished to quietly melt into this warm energy of pure love that began building in my core.

Smiling so widely and genuinely, I noticed Pyter look at me from the corner of my eye. But he didn't ask what I was thinking or feeling. Instead, he just smiled to himself and returned his focus to the flames, allowing me my own unique experience.

Thoughts of my family and all the nights we had spent around a campfire came. Though no sadness or grief plagued me as I pictured my dad and brother making music with Onyx's acoustic guitar while my mother and I roasted marshmallows.

I felt only immense love.

The ache that usually came when I thought of the two didn't.

Suddenly I became acutely aware of the shared love between my family and me. Though their ascension took them from us physically, that love never disappeared.

My love for my brother grew when I knew I would never hear him tuning his instruments again.

My love for my father grew when I knew I would never see him mixing his paints in his studio again.

My love for my mother had grown since I left her, and I realized I might never smell her cooking upon entering our beloved home again.

None of it saddened me. All I felt was love.

I basked in the liquid love that pumped through my veins and watched the flames twirl, flicker, and crackle. Truthfully, I'm not sure how long I watched the fire before finally tearing my eyes away and re-examining my surroundings.

The dull orange glow illuminated only a small area of the expansive desert we called home for the night. The cacti and desert flora took on new shapes, appearing as oblong, humanoid creatures lurking in the shadows. Looking at them, I could have sworn I felt them looking back. The desert seemed just as aware of my heightened sense of reality as I was of everything around me.

I stared at a particular three-pronged shadow until my vision fully adjusted, and a pair of eyes stared back at me.

A ghostly white face and pitch-black eyes watched me from atop the cactus. It was a barn owl— just like the one I had seen in my dreams for the past month.

I tilted my head to the left, and the bird mimicked my action. Smiling, I tilted my head to the right, and it did the same. We watched each other for a series of breaths, both as curious as the other.

Suddenly, the bird's wings opened, scaring from the cactus over my head, and it vanished into the shadows. As I watched its flight above me, the air whooshed from my lungs.

The most incredible night sky display I had ever beheld glistened above me. The few stars I saw earlier were nothing compared to the dazzling array of constellations that were out now. The Milky Way was visible, like a glittery belt accessorizing a sequined sky that sparkled with every inch.

Have I never truly seen the night sky before now?

I could hardly tear my eyes away from it— I didn't want to miss a second of this grand reveal. Though eventually, the dropping temperature had me retrieving my sleeping bag.

As I walked the less-than-ten feet to the tent, I became incredibly aware of the bones and muscles in my legs that propelled me forward. Then I felt every bone and muscle within my feet as they connected with the Earth below me.

The synergy between my bare feet and the Earth jolted something within me awake. I saw flash images of the Native Apache people who lived off this land for thousands of years before colonization decimated the Old Ways of being— the original, indigenous ways.

My heart grew heavy from the pain and devastation I imagined these people going through. The horror of watching strangers from a foreign land come in with brute force and pillage, destroy, and degrade the people and the land they worshiped.

Not only were their homes and villages destroyed, but the land they stewarded and worked alongside as equals was never the same. The trauma inflicted by colonizers had soaked into the Earth along with the bloodshed and could never be allayed or erased.

Tears began flowing from my eyes as the heartache of Native Americans became my own. I knelt on the dirt in the shadows next to the tent and repented.

"I'm so sorry for the pain that my ancestors caused. I'm so sorry that entitled, egoistic men in power stole your land. I'm so sorry that you've had to live through the genocide of your people and continue to watch the Machine degrade the Earth." I sobbed quietly to the land. "I promise to do everything in my power to make it right. To do what I can to decolonize myself and those around me. I'll leave this land forever if it means making amends for the horrors of this country's bloody past."

My tears fell on the dusty ground as I wept for Mother Earth's pain and the indigenous communities that suffered alongside Her.

"I will make it right. I will make it all right." I gasped between sobs. Suddenly, a slight breeze rustled through my hair.

Thank you, my child. I love you....

The Earth Mother whispered in the wind.

"Thank you for giving me life," I replied aloud. "For opening my eye to the truth."

Bella's wet nose touching my hand startled me out of my sobbing. She looked at me lovingly, her dark brown eye and icy blue eye locked on me firmly. My love for her transformed my tears of pain into joy. I wrapped my arms around her, nuzzling into her warm fur.

Finally, with Bella dutifully by my side, I retrieved my sleeping bag and set it down on the ground next to our bench.

Pyter had been in the same spot where I left him, only now he was lying flat against the old telephone pole, watching the stars.

He picked up his head slightly.

"How are ya feelin'?" He asked gently.

I smiled, wondering if tears still littered my cheeks.

"Good," I said with a hoarse voice.

"Good." He returned my smile and lowered his head.

I laid down flat on my sleeping bag, looking at the magnificent sky once again.

"Hey, Pyter?"

"Yes, Kyanie?"

"What do you think the meaning of life is?"

He chuckled lowly before inhaling contemplatively.

"To love," Pyter answered confidently. "To live fully is to love fully."

I sighed deeply in response, smiling to myself and the universe. As I drifted into oneness with the cosmos, each glittering star felt like a distant relative.

Three exceptionally bright stars caught my attention and held it for quite some time. They burned more brilliantly than all the stars around them, with a faint orangey hue differentiating them from the others. Suddenly the Cosmic Goddess came to mind, and I felt her presence looking down on me.

Come to me....

She called from the stars.

The waning crescent moon shone on my face, bathing me in the silvery moonlight.

With one hand lazily petting Bella's head, which was lying by my hip, and the other on my heart, I let the stars consume me and pull my soul into the ethers.

~*~

That night I slept on the ground, unable to tear my eyes away from the dazzling galaxy above until sleep forced them closed.

I awoke soon after dawn began to stir from its slumber. Bella and I had spooned for body heat by the fire embers as Pyter slept a respectful distance away on the wooden pole.

He looked uncomfortable, with his arm acting as a pillow.

Why would he choose to sleep out here instead of in the tent where he would have had ample room to stretch out?

I sat up slowly and felt a dull pounding in between my eyes. Rubbing it mindfully, everything I felt and saw last night flooded my inner sight.

Looking around at the cacti and desert flora that were once sentient, aware beings watching me back, the feeling of their spirit lingered from last night. Even as the stars had begun vanishing from the returning light, I could still feel their presence as well. A newfound interconnectedness had taken residency in my soul.

My vision also seemed to have shifted— everything took on a vibrancy as if I saw entirely new colors.

I looked at Pyter sleeping soundly and mentally thanked him for helping me expand my reality. For showing me what I didn't even realize was lost, hidden right in front of me.

Life is just a series of actions and reactions. By choosing one course, we effectively steer our life away from all other options. If he hadn't come into Hank's, mentioned the Realms, and invited me on this journey to the Tree of Fate, where would my life path have taken me?

As the sun peaked its first golden rays over the horizon, I looked at Pyter with a warm feeling growing in my chest.

~*~

The days following our desert trip felt wholly different from all the others prior. I told Pyter briefly of my breakthrough regarding the grief of my family but certainly didn't include the newfound love and appreciation for him.

"Did you notice colors looked more vibrant after your first experience with psychedelics?" I asked excitedly with wide eyes watching the red and orange terrain pass us. "I swear everything looks like it's glowing now."

Pyter breathed a laugh through his nose.

"I always say that psychedelics open the door to our true reality... A reality so colorful and vibrant that most humans can hardly see it." He glanced at me. "To answer your question, though, yes, I did notice a difference in my vision after first encounterin' the incredible, world-altering psilocybin mushroom." He concluded cheerily.

To me, my vision change felt more profound than seeing more vibrant colors. I could now see the world with such acute clarity. Every time we passed by a large corporation, I could practically see the corruption beneath its polished, marketed exterior.

Passing through Los Angeles, in particular, my heart grew heavy as the vastly divergent social classes became glaringly apparent to me. Not to mention the heart-breaking amount of trash I saw littering the side of the highway and main roads.

Some of the wealthiest people in the world lived here, residing in some of the most expensive real estates in the nation. Yet they shared this area with people who lived under tarps, rummaged through mountains of garbage for resources, and slept on cardboard boxes with newspapers for blankets. People who fall victim to drugs and painkillers to escape their debilitating suffering caused by a disconnected world.

All the money that lay dormant in the bank accounts of mega-rich celebrities, CEOs, and politicians, while people begged for spare change to feed themselves made me sick with anger.

"Do you understand why we had to travel this course to reach the Tree of Fate?" Pyter asked, interrupting my current inner raging over wealth distribution.

"Does it have anything to do with the numerology behind 101?" I responded, having given it some thought a few days ago while looking ahead at our travel route.

"Nothin' gets by you." Pyter winked from the passenger seat. "Though there's a little more to it." He took out a pen along with our worn-down map. "Right, ya see, the route starts in Los Angeles, where the Machine works tirelessly below the surface to create and control the media of the masses." He drew a large one beside it on the map. "It's the focal point of the Logic Realm, hidden beneath the glitz-and-glamour of celebrities and Hollywood itself."

Next, he drew a large zero next to the border of northern California and Oregon. "Along the way is an energetic void where anythin' is possible. Think of it as the highway between the Logic and the Ethereal Realms in which good and evil have equal sway. The Veil is incredibly thin here. I wouldn't be surprised if we started seeing mystical creatures, especially in the forests."

"What kind of creatures?" I asked, smiling, imagining the fantastical beings I once loved reading about in my childhood.

"Dragons, fairies, elves,… you name it. Even elusive creatures like phookas could manifest. Remember that anything is possible there." Pyter mused as I beamed with excitement. "I should also include not to believe everything you see. Evil has a funny way of disguising itself as something harmless so never, ever accept food or drinks from any strange creatures in the woods." His voice took on a sharper tone, as it did when he broached a grave topic.

"Okay, noted." I nodded. "What about the second one?" I tore my eyes from the highway to glance at the map quickly.

Pyter marked a large one beside the top of Washington state. "Last but certainly not least is our end destination— the Tree of Fate and the Ethereal Realm. The final leg will likely be the most difficult part of our journey: we'll have to hike Mount Hope nearly to its peak."

"And what about the Basal Realm?" I questioned.

"What about it?" Pyter looked at me with confusion.

"Well, you said we start in LA, representing the Logic Realm, and go towards the Ethereal Realm in Olympic, but where does that leave the Basal Realm?"

Pyter shifted in his seat and took a moment to gather his words. "Technically, all Realms are simultaneously happening in the same place in time. Though the Basal Realm is around and below us at all times, no matter where we go." His energy seemed to draw inward, so I didn't press for more information on the subject.

Focusing my attention back on the highway, I saw a semi-trailer with *(800) 888- 8888* in front of me.

Without checking my notebook, I recalled the energy of eights — strength, determination, and understanding of the cycles of life through the infinite loops of the number.

I could sense something looming on the horizon of our journey aside from our final destination.

Something was waiting for me, for us.

XVI. Integration

Before I knew it, we had been on the road for two weeks and were closing in on Mount Hope.

The further north we drove, the more magical everything appeared. Redwood trees loomed over our route like giants guarding this wild land while, to the west, the Pacific ocean churned with white-tipped waves and covered my truck in its salty spray.

Visuals of dark, grayish horses came to me, made from the waves and froth galloping beside us as we journeyed along the coast, up and up Route 101. Pyter informed me that they were sea kelpies, and as beautiful as they were from afar, they would drown anyone who came on their shores and attempted to ride their waves.

After crossing into Oregon, the flashes of magical creatures only increased tenfold. Soon among the massive fir, yew, and redwood trees, I saw my first dragon— colored to blend in with the deep green moss and wings so enormous I wondered how it could fly between the dense forest with ease. Its face was long and pointed, with sharp teeth protruding from its mouth and glowing yellow eyes that gave away the beast's camouflage.

The dragon flew beside us for nearly five minutes, locking eyes with me as if to say, *"I see you seeing me."*

Fairies were plentiful as well. Every time we made camp for the evening, I caught glimpses of sparkly, tiny, humanoid-beings and heard faint bells from the dark and unknown forests. Though the melodic noises were always tempting, I heeded Pyter's warning and kept a respectful distance between myself and the tricky fae folk.

Patches of wildflowers at night would reveal glowing will-o-the-wisp and pixie parties, while decaying logs served as homes for elves and gnomes. Even some trees looked back at me as ancient druids kept a watchful eye over their sacred land.

It amazed me how all these life forms were hiding in plain sight, usually in nature, and how little most humans knew or even cared about it.

As I sat mulling over the matter, staring at the pouring rain dripping down the window, Pyter informed me that we could stay at his friend's cabin for the night. It was just outside Astoria and, thus, the perfect stopping point before we got into Washington, concluding our journey to Mount Hope. Additionally, the current thunderstorm was forecasted to continue until the next day, making the thought of camping for the evening *very* unappealing.

"Does your friend know we're coming?" I wondered.

Pyter took a hand off the wheel to rub his chin. "No, not exactly, but we've known each other for quite some time, and he knows that I come and go as I please. Surprise visits are nothing out of the ordinary."

"How do you know he'll be able to accommodate us? All of us?" I motioned to Bella, who was sleeping soundly in the back.

"His cabin is massive and in the middle of the woods. There's no shortage of space for us to lay our heads for the night." Pyter glanced away from the road to me. "No need to worry, dear."

Though his words satisfied my pondering, the feeling of dread stirred in my gut.

~*~

Nighttime had fully taken hold of the Earth by the time we pulled down the long, bumpy dirt road that led to Pyter's friend's cabin. The windshield wipers worked feverishly as the heavy, turbulent rain lowered our visibility. I felt genuinely disconnected from the world, with no other houses and not even a single street light for miles.

"What did you say his name was again?" I asked with trepidation over the stranger who was about to house us.

"I didn't... He goes by Sir Shadowmere." Pyter said with equal hesitation as he parked the truck, likely because he knew how I would react to hearing such a name.

"Excuse me? What do you mean he goes by ——." I began, only to cut myself off after taking in the cabin where we would be staying.

Indeed it was massive, at least three stories high, and made entirely of dark, round logs stacked upon each other. The front of the house had only two narrow windows, which bordered the extravagant double-front door with carvings I had yet to decipher. Peeking around the side, I saw only a few windows marking three floors.

Getting out of the truck, with Bella leashed on my belt and my backpack squarely on my shoulders, two massive gargoyle statues guarded the front walkway. Pyter held my large umbrella over all three of us as we started toward the ominous home.

Suddenly, a twig snapping drew my attention to a nearby ash tree. High within the branches, a dark figure mimicked the seated position of the stone gargoyles in front of me. It had shaggy black hair, long, twisted horns, and bulging yellow eyes watching me with alarm.

Pyter, who noticed where my focus had been drawn to, leaned down and explained. "That's a phooka— a mischievous, shape-shifting creature."

I continued to stare at it, feeling like it was trying to tell me something through its gaze.

"Come on." Pyter nudged me forward with his free hand.

I looked again at the phooka and watched in horror as it

turned its head upside-down like some dark, deformed owl, then smiled at me, baring a mouthful of sharp teeth.

Upon reaching the front door, I could finally make out the intricate carvings in the wood. Depictions of war, with gruesome images of decapitation and torture, were etched into the left door. Meanwhile, the right side was littered with vulgar scenes of sex.

The dread I began feeling earlier only solidified into a heavy weight in my gut. I was about to tell Pyter we should leave and sleep in the truck in the expansive woods surrounding us when he loudly knocked three times.

To my surprise, a woman cracked open the door.

A breathtakingly beautiful woman peered at us from behind the etched wood. She had shining golden hair that fell in luxurious waves down to her hips and eyes so blue that they reminded me of a clear summer's day.

She seemed equally surprised to see us and asked in a high-pitched, breathy voice, "Can I help you?"

"I'm an old friend of Shadowmere and was hoping we could take refuge here for the evenin'. We're just weary travelers who've come a long way," he motioned to Bella and me, "And would like nothin' more than a hot meal and some good company." He smiled charmingly.

His words, the *exact* words, from the first night in the diner echoed in my head, and I wondered how often he used that line to get what he wanted. Suppressing my irritated pondering, I made a mental note to bring it up to him once we were alone.

"Oh." The blonde woman said with uncertainty. "Let me go get Sir Shadowmere for you then."

She motioned us inside by fully opening the right door and, in doing so, showed the satin, pastel blue dress she wore that reached the floor and flowed behind her like a gentle stream. Though the dress was loose-fitting, it put her curvy body on display, and I struggled to avoid looking at her nipples which peeked through the sheer fabric. Her lean, bare arms had goosebumps, and I wondered why she only wore a thin garment on this chilly autumn night.

The shimmering fabric disappeared down a dark hallway to the left as I took in the grand entryway where we now stood.

Its walls and floors were all the same shade of dark-stained wood, giving me the feeling of being locked in a wooden chest. A black and red Persian rug was the only thing to break up the shades of umber surrounding us. In the center was a massive staircase that split at the top and led to several hallways and closed doors. A large archway led to a kitchen and dining area to the right of the stairs on the bottom floor. All along the walls were portraits of men of varying paleness, staring down at us with disdain.

"Well, look who it is." A deep voice bellowed.

Bella barked and growled at my side.

We turned to the left to see a tall man with long, slicked-back, jet-black hair approaching us in a perfectly-tailored black satin suit. His facial hair was immaculately clean and symmetrical, as were the rest of his features.

He strode toward us with a dashingly charming smile, and I was mesmerized by his beauty, especially his eyes, which were such a rich blue they looked nearly purple.

He clapped Pyter on the shoulder, standing several inches taller than him. "I was wondering when you'd be stopping by next— you know how I love your visits and the wonderful things you bring me from your travels." His smile curved wickedly as he looked at me.

"Who is this?" He cooed, tilting his head like a curious predator.

"This is Kyanie," Pyter answered shortly.

"Nice to meet you," I said sweetly, sticking out my hand.

Pyter raised his eyebrows in surprise, having not heard such kindness in my tone towards any of the strangers we had encountered thus far.

The man mimicked his expression, then took my hand in his and lightly kissed the back of it. "The pleasure is all mine. You may call me Sir Shadowmere." He said, oozing with seduction.

I pulled my hand back quickly and laughed nervously. "Thank you for letting us visit, Sir Shadowmere," I swallowed my grimace. "I hope you don't mind my dog," I said while bending down, stroking Bella, who had been lowly growling since Shadowmere entered.

He waved a bored hand. "We have some canine and feline companions running around the property. I'm sure you could take her off leash and let her socialize."

I had yet to see any sign of an animal, and my gut screamed not to let Bella out of my sight.

"That's okay. I would prefer if she stayed with me," I answered kindly but definitively.

Shadowmere shrugged and turned to Pyter. "You came at the perfect time, old friend— my Handmaidens are just finishing dinner. Why don't you and your lady freshen up, and I'll have one of them fetch you when it's ready?"

I stiffened at the mention of the Handmaidens and grew more on edge when Shadowmere snapped his fingers at the blonde woman who had greeted us.

"Handmaiden Angelina, go show them to their room."

The woman bowed. "Yes, Sir Shadowmere."

172

Shooting Pyter a wary look, he gave me a half-smile in return, attempting to assuage my obvious discomfort to no avail.

We followed her up the stairs to the first closed door on the left. The room was drab and straightforward, with only a small writing desk and a bed that matched the gray slate walls.

"Thank you, Angelina," Pyter respectfully said while bowing slightly. She curtsied and walked away without another word.

Closing the door behind her, I whipped my head to Pyter. "Where the hell did you take me? Am I a sitting duck in the lair of the Guardians? And what's up with the Handmaidens? Those guys from the bar thought I was one of them—."

Pyter held up a hand. "Firstly, I will kindly ask ya to lower your voice. Second, to answer your questions, yes, we are in the home of a Guardian of the Order— and a very important one at that, so please be on your best, most *respectful* behavior. Lastly, and I apologize for not explaining this to you sooner, the Handmaidens are females chosen to serve the Order." He plopped down onto the bed, which creaked in response.

"What do you mean service them?" I flinched, sensing the misogynistic response that was to come.

"They act as maids, cooks, and...em, lovers for the Order. They ensure all their basic needs are met, so they don't have to worry about anythin'." Pyter answered.

My eyes widened, and I felt the surge of hot, inner rage begin to build. "So they're essentially enslaved? Held here against their will to fill the role of a dutiful housewife?"

He nodded from side to side, weighing the best response that wouldn't stoke my fire. "I suppose ya could say that… though some come here on their own accord."

I huffed. "I don't believe that. What woman would knowingly give up her freedom and autonomy to live in this dark, depressing cabin in the middle of nowhere?"

Pyter shrugged. "I'm not sure. You'll have to ask them yourself if ya want more answers."

"Maybe I will…." I said before there was a brisk knock on the door, causing Bella to bark in alarm.

Upon opening it, I saw a different female with tightly curled, shoulder-length auburn hair, tawny-brown skin, and bright green eyes reminiscent of Pyter's. Her figure was just as, if not even more so, the perfect image of womanly curves Angelina displayed when welcoming us into their domain.

"Supper is ready." She spoke with a low, sultry tone.

She wore a dress almost identical to the blonde Handmaiden's. But instead of blue, it was a lovely shade of lilac purple, similar to Rosemary's most recent hair color. My heart tinged with longing for my companion, wondering if her hair was still the same shade.

"Thank you. Could you tell me what your name is?" I asked sweetly with a broad, friendly smile on my face.

She puckered her plump lips as if she was uncomfortable saying anything besides what she was ordered to. "Solette."

"Hi, Solette; it's so nice to meet you! I'm Kyanie." I stuck out my hand, to which she looked at me perplexingly.

"Hello, Kyanie. Supper is ready." She said bluntly before turning on her heels to lead us to dinner.

I dropped my backpack next to the doorway, turned to Pyter, brows raised, and motioned for him to follow us.

The three of us walked in silence down the stairs, through the archway and kitchen, which was so starkly white it felt sterile, into the grand dining room. It had a magnificent fireplace, which was so large I could have stood up inside it. An incredibly long dining table made of the same dark wood as the rest of the cabin filled most of the room.

Shadowmere was already sitting at the head of the table, centered with the fireplace that blazed behind him. Upon first glance, it appeared that he was aflame himself.

Pyter went to grab the seat at the other head of the table, but Shadowmere boomed. "Nonsense! Come sit next to me." He said with a feline smile and a wink. "I would love to get to know your little friend here."

My stomach churned, and anxiety coursed through my veins.

Pyter looked at me, pleading to play along.

"Of course," I said, hoping my voice didn't waver.

I started towards the chair on Shadowmere's left, but Bella hesitated, pulling me back towards her. Her hackles were raised as she growled slowly.

Stooping down to her level, I patted her soothingly. "It's okay. We're just going to eat with him, and then we can go to our room."

"Is your canine hungry? Here, allow me." Shadowmere shouted from across the room before snapping his fingers. "Handmaidens." He hollered. "Bring us our dinner along with some for Kyanie's mutt." He looked at me, smiling charmingly.

My lips thinned in a weak smile of gratitude. I continued to the table and sat across from Pyter, coaxing Bella to lie under my chair. Before I could express my thanks, Angelina and Solette, along with another woman trailing behind them, entered the room with arms full of covered silver platters.

My eyes widened with shock as I took in the identity of the

third Handmaiden. There was Adelaide in a matching blush-pink satin dress, holding a platter in one hand and a bowl of slop, which I assumed was for Bella, in the other.

She noticed me simultaneously and looked at me with her doe-eyes full of panic. Her face had lost its rosy disposition, and a hollowness took on her features. Though on the surface, she was just as beautiful as the last time I saw her, with her loosely-curled hair buoyant and voluminous, there was a new gauntness about her.

It took every fiber of willpower not to jump out of my chair and embrace her. To take her away from this horrible cabin I now understood had been Luke's destination for their 'romantic getaway.'

Addie said nothing to me even as she knelt beside my chair and gave Belladonna her dinner.

Then, as if they had rehearsed it, the three Handmaidens uncovered the platters in perfect synchronization. A true feast of an entire roasted duck, seasoned potatoes, steamed carrots, peas, broccoli, and rolls of freshly baked sourdough bread lay before us.

My mouth watered uncontrollably as I waited for the cue from our host to dig in. Pyter eyed me warily, looking as if he had suddenly lost his appetite.

Shadowmere watched me intently as if he could sense the hunger and longing in my stomach. He leaned on the table towards me. "Please, help yourself."

So I did.

~*~

After stuffing my face with multiple servings of every dish besides the duck, I sat in bloated silence and let Pyter fill Shadowmere in on our travels.

Though Shadowmere probed me with questions about my

home and family, I kept all my answers blunt.

"Where are you from?" He queried.

"The Northeast."

"Do you have siblings? Sisters, perhaps?"

"A brother."

"What do you do for work?"

"Waitressing."

I had barely spoken a complete sentence during the entire meal. Finally, Angelina and Solette began clearing our plates to make room for dessert, likely as extravagant as dinner, leaving Addie alone to service us.

I cleared my throat. "That was delicious, though I don't think I have any stomach for dessert. Would you excuse me so I could go shower, Sir?" I asked respectfully, quelling my natural insubordination.

Shadowmere swirled a burgundy liquid around his crystal chalice, annoyance at my excusal tinging his features. "First, I'd like you to answer something." He took a sip of the dark liquid. "What color dress would you like? Green? Or perhaps a cheery yellow?"

I blinked rapidly back at him, jaw hanging as I struggled for composure. "Neither. I don't want any dress from you, especially one that objectifies my body and turns me into a life-size doll for you to play with as you please." My tone turned biting; my words became my only line of venomous defense.

Shadowmere's expression turned carnivorous. "But I so badly want to play with you."

Pyter and Adelaide both watched me in alarm, on edge for what might come hurtling out of my mouth.

I rose from my chair, tugging Bella up with me, and concluded icily. "The feeling is not mutual. Please tell me where I can find the bathroom so I can shower and go to bed."

Shadowmere snarled, baring his teeth and true colors. "Fine." He snapped his fingers. "Handmaiden Adelaide, bring her to the shower."

With a wave of his hand, he dismissed Addie and me.

The two of us walked up and to the right of the grand staircase in silence until we reached a large, black-and-white-tiled bathroom with a shower big enough to bathe six people at once.

I quickly shut the door behind us and grabbed Addie's hands, lowering my voice to just above a whisper.

"Are you okay? Have they hurt you?"

She shook her head, eyes getting misty. "I'm fine."

"You're clearly not fine. Where the hell is Luke? When I see him, I'm going to rip his——."

"He left me. Dropped me off here, trading me like livestock in exchange for a 'gift' from Sir Shadowmere." She chewed her lip nervously. "I shouldn't say too much—— there are cameras everywhere, always watching and listening."

Looking around the bathroom, I was horrified to see a minuscule lens in the corner.

"Come with us. We can sneak out tonight, and they'll have no idea." I pleaded.

Addie continued shaking her head. "You don't understand what these men are capable of. Nine intelligent, highly *aggressive* men live in this cabin. Even if you don't see them—— they're there. Watching and waiting for their… turns with us." She looked down at the floor, and the pain in her features broke my heart.

I gripped her hands tighter. "That's all the more reason for you to leave."

"They threatened my family, Kyanie. They told me if I ever left without their permission, they would kill my mother and bring her head to me as a present." She choked.

Words failed me. I ran through scenarios of us safely escaping in the middle of the night but came up empty.

"I'm getting Pyter. We're leaving now." I said definitively, ignoring Addie's quiet protests.

Ripping open the door, I nearly collided with a tall, broad-shouldered man with buzzed hair and a snide look on his round face.

"Excuse me." I dipped my head respectfully as I quickly shouldered past him, not waiting to see how the interaction would end.

Bella and I bolted to the bedroom, grabbing my backpack before hurrying down the stairs back to the dining room that had been emptied while Adelaide and I conversed. I went back through the kitchen, where Angelina and Solette were dutifully cleaning the dishes.

"Where are Pyter and Shadowmere?"

Angelina turned to me, hands still scrubbing a pan coated with charred spices. "They retreated to Sir's study for an evening brandy and cigar."

"You shouldn't barge in. Females aren't allowed in his wing." Solette deep voice warned.

"His wing is across the entryway, yes?" I asked.

Neither answered, but their glances gave me all the information I needed.

The low vibrations of males conversing led me into the darkened hallway where Shadowmere first appeared. I passed by a handful of open bedrooms with men of varying, muscled builds working out or reading at the small, uniform desks. Each room was adorned with various shining weapons— from bows to pocket-sized daggers to guns to full-length swords and spears.

Fear fueled every muscle in my body as I made my way down the hallway as quickly and quietly as possible.

Finally, at the very end of the corridor, two double doors were partially cracked open. The dull orange glow of a fire lit a sliver of the carpeted floor. As I approached, I could make out walls lined with books from top to bottom and plush furniture surrounding the fireplace.

"She's not for you." Pyter's voice snapped.

I crept as close to the door as possible while keeping Bella and me hidden in the shadows.

"Shall I remind you that the Solar Lord ordered you to leave her with me? Now you're telling me that you're actually *helping* this arrogant little bitch to the Tree because you've caught feelings for her?!" Shadowmere's voice rose. "Pathetic *weakling*." He spat. "I should report you so you can rot for eternity in the Basal Realm with your body and old lover."

"And shall I remind *you*," Pyter said with deadly calmness, "that I answer to no one? The Solar Lord and his men are well aware of who I am and what I do— I am chaos incarnate. Though I may have struck a deal with your Lord, I never guarantee success. She's got more free will in her bones than any human I've ever met. So unfortunately for you and your Lord, she cannot be subdued."

'I am chaos incarnate.' My stomach dropped at the realization that I genuinely had no idea who or what, Pyter was.

Bella barked, and I turned, gasping as I came face to face with another broad-shouldered man with long brown hair and tattoos covering his arms.

He promptly pushed the door with vigor, shoving us into the

study, and hollered. "Look what I found snooping."

Shadowmere stood up, the fire casting his features in a hellish, red hue. "Tsk tsk, my Handmaidens know better than to allow a female into the west wing. I suppose I'll have to punish them later...."

"No!" I shouted impulsively. "Don't punish them. They told me not to come down here, and I did it anyway."

"My, my, well, perhaps I'll have to show you what we do to disobedient females." He nodded to a group of males, which I hadn't noticed were split between the two sides of the door behind me. They all eyed me hungrily, and one shut the double doors with a firm *click*.

"If you lay a finger on her, I promise you'll regret it." Pyter snarled, standing quickly, so he was in between Shadowmere and myself.

"Or what? You may be thousands of years old, but you're still greatly outnumbered here." Shadowmere said with the same lethal composure that Pyter spoke with earlier.

Thousands of years old?! My eyes widened at the revelation.

"If you harm her, you'll have hell to pay. The Solar Lord isn't the only divine being with sway and power in this Realm." With each word, Pyter inched closer to me.

I stood frozen in anticipation while scanning the room for any escape besides the double doors behind me, where four very tall and strong-looking men surrounded me.

One slightly cracked window directly beside Shadowmere, but I would have to cross the room and avoid all the brutes. Even if I reached the window successfully, I would waste time opening it further, then hoisting Bella out of it. I also can't tell if there's a screen—.

Suddenly, several screams broke out behind me. I whipped around to see the men on their knees, clutching their heads in pain.

"What are you doing?" Shadowmere seethed.

"I'm boilin' their blood— it was already so hot with rage. That's mild compared to what I'll do to ya if you touch her." Pyter spoke through his teeth: I had never heard such fury from him before.

"Whose side are you on?" Shadowmere shouted.

Thunder rumbled outside, and lightning flashed through the slightly cracked open window.

"Mine," Pyter said with a maniacal grin before snapping his fingers. At the sound of his *snap*, the fireplace erupted, dousing everything within reach of it, including Shadowmere, in flames.

Pyter turned to me, eyes wide. "RUN!"

I didn't hesitate for a second before ripping open the double doors, bolting out of them, and then out the main entrance into the storm-ridden dark of the night.

"Don't let her escape!" Shadowmere screamed behind me.

With Bella still leashed at my side, the two of us ran as fast as our legs could take us away from the cabin.

Rain pelted my face, and panic surged as I turned to see five shadows barreling after us.

The storm had swallowed the moon and stars, leaving no light to guide me as we ran blindly through the unfamiliar forest. Twigs snapped beneath my boots while thorny vines wrapped around my legs, snagging on my damp pants.

My breathing was ragged and uneven as I ran faster than I ever had before. My heartbeat hitched in my throat while the rain came down with unforgiving intensity, soaking my hair and clothes.

I darted through the forest, ducking below thick, low-hanging branches and jumping over protruding roots. The dark figures kept up with us, and one began closing on my right.

Hardly able to see the ground in front of me, I veered left, and my foot fell through a patch of damp leaves, getting caught under a root and causing me to tumble down an incline.

Bella yelped as she was yanked to the ground, rolling beside me. We fell down the slope, with thorns tearing my clothes and exposed skin and a jagged rock colliding with the side of my head.

Finally, we stopped falling, and as I lay on the damp leaves and moss, I felt blood dripping down the side of my face and small, stinging cuts covering my arms and legs. My blood mixed with the precipitation, leaving me in a wet heap of pain, fear and adrenaline.

Slowly I lifted my head to check on Bella. Pure terror coursed through me at the sight of her front paw bending the opposite way while she whimpered in pain.

My vision spotted, and I felt myself verging on the edge of consciousness when five cloaked figures surrounded us.

I laid my head down, accepting defeat, as reality faded away from me and the darkness took hold.

XVII. Intuition

I was witnessing the complete and utter destruction of planet Earth. Ocean waves churned into massive tsunamis and drowned all civilizations on the coasts. Earthquakes crumbled skyscrapers like sandcastles. Extreme heat scorched the land and killed all the crops. Riots with dumpsters ablaze as people voiced nay screamed their anger, their unrest.

Knock, knock, knock.

A faint tapping roused me from my unconsciousness.

I cracked my eyes open only to be slammed with shooting pain on the right side of my head. Lifting my hand tentatively, I saw several bandages on my arm and felt one wrapped around my forehead.

Steadily I took in my surroundings, and to my bewilderment, I was lying in a lush, four-post-canopy bed in a bedroom fit for royalty. At the foot of the bed was a black marble fireplace with a fire dutifully aflame. To my left, next to the door, was an ornate vanity and matching armoire with vines and flowers carved into the white-painted wood. To my right, a massive window reached from floor to ceiling with dark purple velvet curtains parted slightly and a simple yet regal writing desk that matched the rest of the furniture.

Knock, knock.

The door creaked open carefully.

"Hello?" Came a soft-spoken voice.

Slowly a head of nearly white, platinum blonde hair poked in, followed by a sheer, floral-patterned dress. A young woman entered fully and smiled upon seeing me awake, staring back at her.

"You're up! Wonderful!" She squeaked. "I'm so relieved my

elixir worked. I tried a new herbal combination and wasn't sure how they would blend, but here you are— proof that it was a successful experiment!"

Her smile lifted her cheeks, which were rosy and full of life.

Every aspect of this female was alive— from how she talked to the flow of her dress to the way her long, platinum hair framed her beautiful, youthful face. She was spring embodied.

Memories of the cabin flooded me, and I shot up, panic striking my nerves. "Belladonna! Have you seen my dog?" I gasped.

"Yes, no need to worry. We started healing her as soon as we got you two back here. I have her broken paw wrapped in a bandage and splinted, and I've been checking on her every hour to give her some bone-healing medicine I whipped up fresh last night." She floated towards me, smiling warmly, before gently touching the bed near my left arm. "Are you hungry?"

I nodded, an empty aching forming in my belly.

"Great! It's midday, so we're about to sit for lunch. Why don't you take a few moments and meet us in the dining room? It's down the stairs to the left." She motioned towards the open door.

"Uh, okay," I mumbled as my consciousness returned.

"Lovely." The corners of her warm, brown eyes crinkled from her wide smile. "There are spare clothes in the armoire. Please help yourself." She turned on her heels and flitted out the door like a butterfly on a gentle breeze.

As I sat up fully, questions flooded my inner voice.

Who was that? Where am I? Where's Bella? What day is it? My eyes crunched shut as I grimaced in pain. *I suppose I won't get any answers by sitting here in bed....*

I gathered my strength and hobbled over to the wardrobe,

noting a throbbing ache in my left ankle from my tumble downhill.

There were numerous floor-length dresses of varying colors, patterns, and fabrics on hangers, along with a single pair of black leggings next to a thick-stitched crimson sweater on the bottom shelf of the armoire. The decision of what to wear was easy.

As I pulled the sweater over my head, it got caught on a small twig that had wrapped itself within my frizzy curls. The urge to take a steaming hot shower or bath flooded my senses.

I noticed my backpack resting on the chair by the writing desk and riffled through it, seeing if I had lost anything in my descent. '*The Original Religion*' was tucked safely on the bottom, along with the knife and my compass. Most of my clothes were still there, minus a pair of socks and my jeans.

The only item missing was my phone, which had hardly been used since leaving my home. I was so consumed with either driving, reading, or setting up camp each night that the technology had lost its value to me. And now I had truly lost it.

Meandering out of the bedroom into a long hallway, I counted ten rooms on the same side as mine and five across the way. A broad staircase sat in the dead center of the floor, splitting up the ten rooms into two clusters of five.

The interior was wooden like Shadowmere's cabin, but instead of being dark-stained and depressing, it was naturally cozy and inviting. The walls were lined with beautiful paintings of landscapes, from snowy mountaintops to pristine beach sunsets. Meanwhile, light fixtures shaped like lotus flowers, each with a rose-shaped silver candle holder below it, illuminated the space.

As my foot stepped onto the blue-and-green, ornate rug at the bottom of the stairs, I glanced both ways and saw two identical archways: one leading to a gray-stone kitchen and the other to a dining room. The latter had a window so massive I couldn't see where it started or ended.

I tentatively made my way toward the dining room where, at one of the longest tables I had ever seen, the white-haired woman was sitting with four other women. The realization that I had hardly been around other females since leaving home hit me. Instantly, I felt relief, even as they all turned to watch me enter.

Spring-embodied perked her head up.

"I'm so glad you're joining us!" She chirped.

"Thank you for..." I trailed off upon entering the room. "Wow." I breathed while taking in the entirely-glass wall that encompassed the dining area.

In addition to the long, wooden dining table that sat at least fifteen people, a crescent-shaped bench with a circular table was tucked into the rounded front end of the room. Outside the enormous windows, I could see gray skies unloading sheets of rain on an expansive garden, with dense forest glooming on the edges.

"Isn't the breakfast nook so lovely? It's the perfect spot to sit in the morning and watch the wildlife with a warm mug and a good book." She mused before shaking her head. "Where are my manners? My name is Gardenia; what's yours?"

"Kyanie, but you can call me——."

"Kya." A dark-haired woman said from the head of the table before lifting her gaze.

My eyes widened as I took in a familiar face.

"Amber?" I asked incredulously.

"Long time no see, kiddo." Amber's deep, dark eyes met mine, and she winked. "Take a seat. We have much to discuss."

~*~

We were each served a colorful salad and a bowl of steaming soup by a kind-faced woman with dark brown hair worn short and tight to her head. She beamed with pride as she set down the dishes and boasted that she had flavored the soup with new spices and herbs in honor of my visit.

I sat beside a fire-haired woman, who informed me her name was Fiadh, spelled with a silent "-DH" at the end. She had shoulder-length hair, jade-colored eyes, and freckles covering her ivory complexion. Within the first few moments of meeting her, she made me laugh heartily— something I had barely done in weeks.

Each woman introduced themselves as I took turns between the warm, seasoned vegetables and crisp, refreshing salad.

Directly across from me and next to Gardenia was Larimar, who went by Mar. If Gardenia was spring-embodied, then she was summer. Her sun-kissed skin, bright blue eyes, faint freckles on the bridge of her nose, and sandy-blonde hair looked as if the ocean was her stylist.

Next to Fiadh was Celeste, with a mane of dark, tightly-curled hair and feline features to match. Her mahogany eyes observed me as she puffed on a jewel-encrusted cigarette holder. She wore shades of tan and brown, giving off the energy of a wise, old tree while simultaneously being a cautious lioness waiting to strike.

"So, what is this place?" I finally asked after they finished their introductions.

Amber cleared her throat and tucked a straight, jet-black strand behind her ear. "This is our coven— Daughters of the Wild. We are all witches here."

I raised my eyebrows. "Oh…er…." I stammered, taking it in.

"Witches actually exist in the Logical Realm?"

"Of course," Amber smiled wickedly. "A witch is someone who has reclaimed their innate power and learned that they have everything they need inside themselves. A witch practices magick, utilizing the ever-present energies on Earth to call in a desired outcome." Her words were factual and fierce as she gracefully spoke with her hands.

"For centuries, witches were revered for their healing and spiritual abilities. That is until the infamous witch hunts resulted in the burning of upwards of nine *million* people, at least eighty percent of that number being women." She stated with a snarl. "The Solar Lord and his Guardians *attempted* to erase witches from history, but instead of cowering in fear, we grew smarter and stronger in the shadows."

"My great-great-great-grandmother created our coven over a century ago when the Guardians started to grow in numbers and cement the Trine of Power's tyranny." Gardenia chimed in. "She warded it to be hidden from view by anyone with evil in their hearts, so it's a haven for witches and truth seekers."

I nodded along. "And what are Daughters of the Wild?"

"We're a sect of magick practitioners that worship the Goddesses and the natural world. We take an oath to protect our sacred Earth Mother and all her creatures." Fiadh answered beside me while heroically placing a hand on her flannel-covered heart.

"Not all witches are Daughters of the Wild, though all of us here are." Amber declared while picking at the salad in front of her. "Witches can range greatly in spiritual beliefs, especially the deities they worship."

"How long have you been a witch?" I asked her, thinking back to all the tidbits of wisdom she would bestow on me in passing when

189

she was with Onyx.

She chuckled softly. "My entire life, love. I'm not sure if you know this, but I'm a Native Apache. I grew up living off the land in peace; it always came naturally to me to live alongside nature in harmony. From the moment I could walk, I would wander into the wilderness to make spells and potions with mud and twigs."

"Even her birth chart is in the shape of a pentagram." Spoke Celeste, who hadn't said a word since her brief introduction.

"Her what is shaped like a what?" My eyebrows knit together.

Celeste took a slow drag. "A birth chart is a map of the sky from the moment your soul emerged on Earth. Think of it like a blueprint to understand why you behave, communicate, and love the way you do." She talked with her hands, smoke swirling around her fingertips. "A pentagram is the ultimate symbol of magick. Each point represents an element— air, fire, water, earth, and spirit." She drew out a five-pointed star in the air. "Symbols are incredibly potent and hold a *lot* of power."

"So basically, what she's telling you is that I was born to be a witch. Magick is written in the stars for me," Amber concluded, smirking at Celeste, who rolled her eyes in response.

I swallowed a mouthful of salad and turned to her. "So, how did you end up here? I had no idea you even left the East Coast."

"It's a long story, but I suppose you have the time." Amber sighed and waved her hand. "I spent my childhood with my tribe in Arizona until I was about eleven. Then the Guardians came, pillaging and burning our homes to the ground, and doing other heinous, *unspeakable* things." She closed her eyes in anger and sighed before continuing, "My parents moved us to the Pacific Northwest, where they felt we could safely hide away in the dense forests." A look of sadness flashed in her dark eyes. "Unfortunately, Guardians are everywhere, and they found us within a few years. They...they kidnapped my mother from a grocery store parking lot, dismembered her, and dropped her severed hand on our doorstep as a warning that we would be next." She exhaled a deep, sorrowful breath.

I listened earnestly, feeling my eyes growing misty with anger from the shared pain caused by the Guardians' bloodlust.

"Luckily, before my father and I fled to the East Coast, I befriended Gardenia, and she showed me this coven. Saying goodbye to her and this magical haven hurt almost as bad as losing my mother, but I knew I would be back."

I glanced to Gardenia, whose mouth tugged into a half-smile.

"Then I arrived in Massachusetts for my high school career and met your angel-of-a-brother." Amber's lips curved sweetly. "To glaze over all the sappy love talk, I fell for him hard and fast and opened up in ways I never had before. I told him all the truths I had learned about society and the Trine of Power, and he took to it almost a little too much. Onyx dove head-first into truth-seeking, knowing no bounds. Despite my warnings not to, he and your father ventured into the desert for a Native-held conference on plant medicine and the transformative power of psychedelics."

She shook her head glumly. "It was on their way back that the Guardians got word of them, so they staged the accident, lighting their car on fire and fleeing to the Tree of Fate on foot."

I stared at her intently, "How do you know all of this?"

Amber tilted her head to the side and shrugged. "I have a handful of familiars, both animal and other-worldly, so I have eyes and ears all over the place. When Onyx left for that trip, I to tried to warn them that a Native gathering of that size would draw the attention of

Guardians for miles, like a moth to a flame, but he was too stubborn. So I sent my phooka to watch over them. Indigenous peoples are the biggest threat to the Trine of Power because we are living, *breathing* proof that another way of life exists. Coexisting in harmony with the Earth is how humans originally lived for thousands of years."

"So, was it your phooka I saw outside of Shadowmere's cabin?" I questioned, piecing everything together.

"Mhm." She smirked and nodded. "This brings us to the end of my story. After Onyx's disappearance, I put wards of protection around my father and gave him the location of an abandoned, off-grid homestead to live away from the Guardians' eyes. Then I journeyed back to the only place that ever truly felt like home— this coven." She reached out and grabbed Gardenia's hand. "I was less than an hour from here when that bastard Shadowmere found me at a gas station. If my intuition weren't as sharp as a dagger, I would have fallen for his charming bullshit. He tried every angle to make me agree to come with him and be one of his Handmaidens. After my verbal deflections failed, my knee met his groin, and I got in my car as fast as I could."

I laughed in surprise, though I knew the feeling of terror at that moment was anything but funny.

"Truthfully, I seriously debated living in a cave in Arizona after my mom died to reconnect with my land and heritage. But I figured I was no help to the planet as a cave-dwelling hermit. So here I am." She held her hands up. "I arrived here thinking it would only be a stopping point before I went to the Tree to ascend myself," she smirked. "But I soon discovered I was exactly where I'm meant to be." Amber looked around at the group of women with love in her eyes.

"And thank Goddess she did." Drawled Mar, who had been silently devouring her lunch while we all conversed. "Our coven was incomplete without her— since Amber arrived, we've been a strong unit of thirteen witches."

"The witch's number," Fiadh said with a wink.

I had just taken my final slurp of soup when a loud *MEOWWW* sounded in the dining area.

At first glance, it was a shadow moving along the base of the archway, but as it neared the head of the table, I recognized the feline.

"Sounds like my sweet baby Lacius wants to say hello!" Amber crooned as she swept the pitch-black animal into her lap, blending in thoroughly with the long-sleeve, black chiffon dress she was wearing. Only its golden yellow eyes could be seen.

"Wait, Lacius? Like The Solar Lord's evil nemesis? Do you guys worship him?" I questioned, feeling uneasy and unaware.

Nearly all five witches rolled their eyes.

Amber sighed. "No, love," she said kindly. "There are some who believe in him, witches and magick practitioners who perform rituals in his honor, practicing blood magick to receive their wildest dreams and desires… But truthfully, the idea that witches worship Lacius was part of the Solar Lord's deception. To label witches as evil hell-bringers and thus justify the burnings brought upon them."

"I see." I nodded, burning anger growing in my gut. "Sounds like throughout the Solar Lord's reign, he's worked *very* hard to eradicate witches…."

"It's because we can't be controlled." Came Mar's alluring drawl. "Guardians of the Order have worked for thousands of years to control every single aspect of the feminine— physically, mentally, romantically, reproductively, spiritually….agh!" She rolled her eyes and shook her head. "Witches, and Daughters of the Wild especially, threaten them because we cannot be tamed or subdued into following their rules and falling victim to their manipulations." She concluded by pursing her lips and shrugging.

Though her voice was slow and lazy, the power behind her words sank into my chest like a blast of truth.

Biting my lip, I shook my head. "I can't believe how much I was blind to before...."

"But not anymore." Spoke Amber, her dark eyes locked on me firmly. "I'm not quite sure what your plan is from here, Kya, but we're here to help."

"Your dog is healing well!" Gardenia chimed in. "In a few days, she'll be able to walk normally again."

"Wait, what's the date?" I asked with no concept of time.

"It's October 28th, only three days away from my birthday," Amber said, smirking.

Gardenia rolled her eyes jokingly while maintaining her warm smile. "Yes, which is also Samhain! How exciting you'll be here to celebrate with us."

"Sah-ween?" I said with eyebrows knit in confusion.

"Most humans call it Halloween." Stated Celeste, who had replaced her jade cigarette holder with a nail file and was attentively grooming her claws.

I nodded. "Oh." Guilt suddenly ate at my insides as I thought of Bella, alone and scared, in a strange new house. "Where is my dog? Can I go see her?"

~*~

Amber and Gardenia took it upon themselves to give me a proper home tour on our way to the third floor, where Bella was resting. We first went to the far back of the dining room and turned left, entering a massive common space with plentiful, plush couches and small coffee tables scattered throughout. Multiple rugs covered the hardwood floors, centering around clusters of sofas and tables. Two roaring fireplaces on opposing ends made the room incredibly toasty for such an ample space.

The harmonic melody of a harp came from the far corner. A woman with light brown skin and straight black hair sat playing with her eyes closed, her head moving in tandem with the music she plucked. Her full lips were plumped in a pout of concentration, and she wore a long-sleeved periwinkle dress that flowed effortlessly with her movement.

Next to her was a dark-complexioned dancer, moving fluidly and gracefully. The bright green leotard they wore clung tightly to their muscled torso and showed off their toned legs. They moved as if they were the strings being played, writhing to the music with such controlled poise I couldn't help but stare in admiration.

Amber cleared her throat. "I hate to interrupt such beautiful, musical magick, but I wanted to introduce you to Kyanie. She'll be staying here for a few days to heal and rest."

I smiled and waved meekly, feeling meek in front of these incredibly talented witches.

"I'm Leanan, but call me Lea." Said the harpist with a faint Hispanic accent as her delicate hand shook mine.

The dancer stuck their hand out toward me. "Nice to meet you. My name's Iris," they smiled softly, catching their breath.

I nodded and shook their slender hand.

Beholding the grand, stringed instrument before me, I turned to Lea. "You play beautifully. I hope to hear more."

Iris chuckled. "Be careful what you wish for. She hardly ever stops playing her instruments."

Lea shrugged. "Music is the way my soul speaks. Without it, I would be a mute."

I thanked them again and apologized for the intrusion before Gardenia took the lead toward the kitchen.

The floor and walls were made of round, gray stones, broken up by large wooden pillars and beams. Another roaring fireplace blazed and warmed the quaint space, which I imagined got quite cold without it. Two closed doors sat at opposite sides of the room. Shelves filled with jars of spices and other dried goods took up an entire wall. I inhaled deeply to appreciate all the aromas.

There I officially met Juno, the woman who served us lunch.

"Thank you for cooking! It was delicious." I praised.

Juno, who hadn't stopped her food preparations for my introduction, glanced up from the vegetables she was chopping. "You're welcome." She half-smiled. "I cook every meal for the coven, so it's my pleasure... my magick."

A look of pride flashed across her face, which was rosy and gleaming with sweat. She had her long-sleeved white shirt rolled up to her elbows, and various stains blotted both her shirt and the apron tied around her waist.

I wonder how many hours a day she spends in this toasty little kitchen, working diligently to feed and sustain the coven.

"So you put a spell on the food before serving it?" I asked.

Juno breathed a laugh. "Not exactly. While cooking, it's almost like I'm brewing a potion. Or at least that's how it feels to me." She shrugged. "It's not so much that I'm putting a spell on the food but more that I weave each dish with magick and intention, so the food becomes the spell. Does that make sense?"

I nodded in confirmation, reflecting on my mother's cooking

and how she applied a similar method.

We exchanged goodbyes, and as Amber opened the door towards the front of the room, Juno hollered. "Dinner is six o'clock every night— don't be late!"

I turned to the doorway and was surprised to see a stone spiral staircase leading into the darkness. Small, circular windows lined the ascent, along with more rose-shaped candle holders to light the way. We soon came to a closed wooden door, and Amber opened it to show me the hallway of bedrooms before we continued our tour upwards.

Traveling up the spiral staircase, we finally reached the third floor and immediately encountered an ornate, extensive library— floor to ceiling of books, with ladders leaning on the highest shelves. A handful of couches and armchairs were placed about the library, with more in the adjoining study.

Next to the only fireplace, which sat perfectly centered between the two areas, was a desk with a brown-skinned woman writing furiously.

Gardenia had taken the lead and cleared her throat softly to grab the woman's attention. "Ehem, Isha?"

The woman's dark hair, tied in a loose and messy knot atop her head, bobbed as she jolted out of her writing trance.

She adjusted her glasses and looked at me.

"This one is new."

Amber snorted. "You are so astute."

"My name is Kyanie, but call me Kya," I said kindly, sticking out my hand for another greeting.

I admired her burgundy, woven dress with intricate patterns embroidered in gold that wrapped around her fuller figure like it was custom-made for her.

"My name is Ishanvi, but call me Isha." She returned my smile and handshake. "I'm the self-appointed coven librarian, so let me know if there's anything you're looking to read."

"Do you have books that the Guardians otherwise destroyed?" I asked, looking around at the impressive collection.

"You mean this entire library?" Isha chortled.

We made brief small talk, and she invited me to return to dive deeper into all the truths I had yet to learn.

Well aware that I was only beginning to uncover the lies fed to us through societal programming, I knew I was only skimming the surface of how magical this existence could be. No matter how many books I read, I would still know *nothing* in the grand scheme of life.

To conclude our tour, we passed through the study and opened a door into what looked like a home laboratory filled with glass bottles and measuring cups. Bella's bark sounded from the corner.

"Baby girl!" I squealed, seeing her curled up on several blankets, tail wagging gleefully, and mix-matched eyes watching me lovingly.

The guilt bubbling in my gut roared through my veins as I took in my injured pup. I dropped to my knees and laid my head on her as she feverishly licked my hands. The corners of my eyes stung, and I tried, unsuccessfully, to hold in my tears.

How selfish of me to take her on this journey. I should have left her at home with my loving mother, where she would never have hurt herself like this....

"She's been such a trooper." Said Gardenia as she came to crouch by my side. My canine stopped licking me and moved to Gardenia's firm yet gentle hands.

"Luckily, her paw had a clean fracture. With the help of my bone-mending elixir, a handful of other tinctures, and home remedies,

I believe her bone is already fusing back together." She beamed as she scratched Bella's head.

"Gardenia is our coven's healer. Bella is in the best hands with her." Amber said warmly, placing a hand on Gardenia's shoulder.

Gardenia blushed. "I do my best."

"I can't thank you enough for rescuing us both." I straightened, wiping the tears from my face. "I know this is just a stopping point for me, but you've all been so welcoming, I... I feel safer here than I have anywhere in a very long time. I feel like I've found a new home."

"Wait, I want to show you my favorite part of the house," Gardenia interrupted excitedly before leading me through a door on the other side of the room.

"Isn't it the most wondrous thing you've ever seen?" She breathed as we entered a greenhouse exploding with life.

The entirely-glass wall from the dining room continued up the house, creating the perfect space for an indoor greenhouse stocked with thriving herbs, flowers, and various houseplants. In the center of the room stood a spiral staircase, with vines wrapping themselves up the thin, white-painted iron. I peeked down the stairs and saw more plants in a near-identical greenhouse below us.

"It's two stories, so the best part is that my room is right next to it on the first floor." Gardenia beamed.

"And, let's not forget to mention the observatory that's above us. We get some of the best moon views from up there." Said Amber, who was now leaning in the doorway, head motioning up the staircase.

"Wow, I..." I smiled and shook my head in disbelief. "This place feels like a dream. How am I ever supposed to leave?"

"You'll leave when the time is right." Amber shrugged. "But I think you were destined to come here. To learn and grow in ways you never thought possible because, well, I don't think you knew that magick is all around you."

"I had no idea." I scratched my head, feeling another twig tangled in my curls then holding it up to them. "But I do know that I desperately need to bathe."

They both laughed before leading me down the staircase to a bathing room conveniently located right next to my chambers.

The room was all-white, honeycomb tile. It had a shower with multiple heads and a steam-room function, in addition to the longest, deepest clawfoot tub I had ever seen. A diamond-shaped window opened up to the garden outside, still being drenched with rain.

As the porcelain tub filled with steamy, hot water, I carefully removed the small bandages covering my arms and legs. Then slowly, I undid the gauze wrap around my head, examining a nasty gash that already had stitches in it in the mirror.

I sat on the tub's edge in all my glory and digested everything that had happened to me in a matter of weeks.

How much is different since the last time I took a bath and my father appeared to me afterward? I feel wholly changed from the Kyanie that left with anxiety in her gut and fear in her heart.

Shedding years of programming and manipulation from modern society, I was evolving into the version of myself that could face the Trine of Power with unflinching bravery. Because I was stepping into *my* power.

With the help of these witches, I will become the biggest threat to the Order. I will become completely and irrevocably uncontrollable.

Sinking into the tub, with the scalding hot water stinging my cuts, I imagined it was lava to burn away all that no longer served me.

When I emerge from this water, I will be a true phoenix, leaving behind nothing but the ashes of my former life.

Musing internally, I sucked in my breath and fully submerged my head, reveling in the peace that only came to me underwater.

XVIII. Haven

After brewing for what felt like multiple hours, divulging in face masks and body scrubs, and watching rain droplets slide down the window, I finally emerged from the tub feeling revitalized.

I'm not sure if it was the depth of the tub or some enchantment on it, but the water never cooled. It stayed as scalding as it was coming out of the faucet, leaving my skin pink and steaming.

Mar had a collection of bathrobes hanging in the bathing room that she welcomed me to use. I happily chose an ankle-length white, plush one to wrap around my bare shoulders.

Judging by the ever-growing darkness in the house, I assumed it was nearing evening. Though the rainstorm casting everything in a dark gray hue made it hard to gauge the time.

I had just entered my room and closed the door behind me when something shifted out of the corner of my eye. A translucent figure stood in the shadows next to the unlit fireplace; they appeared female, with wild gray hair and a long white dress.

We looked at each other for a moment, both of us sizing the other up. I surprisingly felt no fear as her vacant eyes watched me.

"Hello," I said calmly.

The ghostly female said nothing.

"Were you a member of the coven?" I asked.

Silence.

"Can you tell me your name?"

She simply lifted her skeletal hand, pointing upwards towards the library, before turning into the corner of my room and vanishing into the wall.

A small wall clock hanging above the fireplace informed me of the time. *4:44 p.m.…. My angels are here. I am safe because I am not alone. I am protected because I am never alone.* I mused while putting on the same leggings, sweater from earlier, and pair of moccasin slippers Amber lent me. *I can feel their protection and guidance now more than ever.*

With my hair still damp, I meandered into the hallway and made my way up the stone spiral staircase.

A few steps into my ascent, I paused, hearing faint footsteps in the stairwell. Eyes straining in the darkness, I searched for the source of the footsteps, wishing I had a match to light the wall-candles.

I saw nothing and continued up another handful of steps, only to stop again from hearing the same pitter-patter.

"Who's there?" I asked firmly, squinting at the shadows.

"Don't be alarmed, ma'am," said a high-pitched voice from below. "I'm only heading to my chambers." There in the stairwell, standing less than knee-high on me, was a tiny being.

"What are you?" I breathed.

"My name is Finrod Aktaion, Miss Kyanie, and I am the coven's house brownie." He squeaked.

"And how do you know my name?" My eyebrows were bunched as I tried making out the details of this brownie in the dimly lit stairwell.

Finrod climbed up a handful of steps, stopping when he was nearly eye-level with me. "I am the eyes and ears of this coven, and it is my duty to look after the house. To know exactly what's going on at all times. Especially when new faces arrive."

I could make out his humanoid face with a small, rodent-like nose and whiskers that twitched as he spoke.

"I see. Where are your chambers exactly?" I asked with curiosity, wanting to learn more about this well-mannered creature.

"I live in the attic, ma'am." Finrod dipped his head down as he spoke. I wondered if it was a sign of respect, submission, or perhaps both.

"Can I see it?" The tour Amber and Gardenia gave me did not include the fourth floor.

The brownie perked his ears, which were short yet pointed like a rabbit's. "No, ma'am, you may not."

"Why not?" I asked, crossing my arms.

"Guests are not permitted on the fourth floor without being accompanied by a coven member." Finrod crossed his arms as well. "These are the rules."

"Fiiinnnnn?" Fiadh crooned from the bottom of the stairs. "Did you grab the playing cards from your room yet?"

"I must go now, Miss Kyanie. I don't want to miss my weekly card game with Mistress Fiadh." With that, he scurried up the stairs, disappearing into the shadows.

~*~

The library had become even cozier in the early evening's dim lighting. The wall candles were lit and created a warming atmosphere to contrast the gloomy gray that lingered outside.

Two males sat reading beside each other on a forest-green velvet couch seated next to the fireplace.

"Hi," I whispered, approaching their reading nook.

They both looked up in surprise.

"You must be the guest that's staying with us." Said the male on the left as he moved an umber-colored curl out of his face, and his golden-hazel eyes met mine. His sweater was earth-toned with a swirling pattern that brought out the array of colors in his eyes.

"The one with the dog?" The other questioned, his piercing blue eyes looking at me beneath dense, dark eyebrows knit together. He also wore a thick-stitched sweater though his was solid evergreen.

Together, they looked like a pair of young druids that chose to take on a human form rather than a tree.

"That's right," I answered genially as I sat in the golden corduroy loveseat across from them.

"I'm Kya. What are your names?"

"I'm Eli, and this is Jo." Answered the male in the swirling sweater, his warm smile bringing a glint to his golden eyes.

"You're probably wondering why two males are part of the coven, eh?" Asked Jo with a sly smile.

They were the only males I had seen thus far.

"A little bit," I replied.

"Well, it's this delightful story about how the backward town Eli and I came from tried to burn us at the stake!" Jo began with ironic enthusiasm lacing his words. "And I mean *literally* burn us at the stake."

Eli tutted, "You always give away the most exciting part of the story! Next time I'm telling it."

Jo turned to him. "It's fine. A good story doesn't diminish from a few spoilers.... Anyway," He waved his hand lazily. "Eli and I had decided to be brave and come out to our families about our relationship, which had been going three years strong at that point."

"Closer to four years, but go on." Eli drawled, smiling subtly.

"Ehem, as I was saying, we figured why not come out about our witchcraft as well? Either they would accept us totally as we are, or they wouldn't.... Well, I suppose you can piece together that they didn't accept us at all. In fact, our own families turned us in to the local Guardians, saying we were a major threat to the Order."

I sat there shaking my head in disbelief.

"So in the middle of the night, we were taken from our beds and tied to old telephone poles to be publicly burned alive." Jo sighed dramatically.

"Truthfully, I still don't know how we managed to escape. My best theory is that nearby fairies or elementals loosened our ropes enough for us to wiggle free." Eli interjected.

"Though we didn't make it out unscathed— they had already lit the pyre, and flames were consuming our clothes by the time we got loose. I grabbed Eli, and we ran as fast as possible into the forest where none of the townspeople ever dared to go for fear of the dark unknown." Jo reached for Eli's hand.

"Thankfully, we knew that forest like the back of our hands from years of practicing magick inside it. We made a beeline to our favorite swimming pond and jumped in to fully extinguished the embers." Continued Eli. "We laid low camping for a few days, plotting and theorizing exactly where the rumored coven was and using our bird familiars to scope out the land. By the grace of Goddess, it was only a five-day journey on foot until we arrived at our new home." He concluded by squeezing Jo's hand.

My jaw hung loosely as I digested their story. "I can't believe… I'm so sorry…." I began somberly.

Jo waved his hand. "Agh, don't get all sappy on us!"

"Yeah, we heard that you're witty and full of fire. Don't let our depressing story dampen your flames." Eli continued. "The past is the past, and we wouldn't be living in this *extraordinary* mansion if those terrible things hadn't happened."

"We're big believers that everything does indeed happen for a reason," Jo said with a grin and a reassuring nod.

"Okay…well, I'm still sorry that your families turned you into the Guardians. I…" I stammered. "My vendetta against the Trine of Power is really deepening," Biting my inner lip angrily, I concluded, "and truthfully, I want to see them all burned at the stake."

They both chuckled. "Don't we all." Said Jo.

"So, what brings you to the library?" Questioned Eli, eyeing me curiously.

"Have you two ever seen a ghost here?" I asked, leaning towards them.

Eli breathed a laugh out of his nose. "Which one?"

"Uh, I'm not sure. After I got out of the bath, a woman in a long white dress was in my room. I tried talking with her, but she didn't say anything and only pointed upstairs when I asked her name."

"Sounds like Cornelia. She hasn't appeared here, so she may have been pointing to the fourth floor," pondered Eli.

"Yeah, I think Jude is up there now in ritual." Continued Jo as he leaned in towards me. "If there's anyone you should speak to about ghosts— it's them. They communicate nightly with the dead, and all the house ghosts are quite fond of them."

"Okay, noted. I don't think I've met them yet…." I trailed off as Eli glanced down at his watch.

"Only five minutes until dinner!" He exclaimed. "Sorry, I get so excited before mealtimes, especially dinner. Juno always whips up her best work for our evening meals."

The two of them rose from the couch, clutching a book and their beloved's hand in the other.

"We'll see you down there." Said Jo with a warm smile before they disappeared down the dark staircase.

~*~

When I emerged from the staircase into the kitchen, a wall of spicy aroma immediately greeted me. My mouth began to water instantaneously.

"It smells heavenly in here, Juno." I swooned as she frantically moved around the kitchen.

"Huh? Oh. Thank you, but please wait in the dining room. Too many cooks in the kitchen, you know?" She said as she added last-minute herbs to a plate of stir-fried vegetables after a quick taste.

Juno had changed from her stained-work clothes and put on a cream-colored blouse with pomegranates embroidered and a floor-length, navy blue skirt.

"Of course," I said politely before exiting. I chuckled, realizing that just one other cook in the kitchen was too much for her. She truly preferred to work alone.

As nighttime fell upon the coven, the entire house seemed to shift energy. All the candleholders were lit, casting that familiar, flickering orange glow on the walls and floors and creating an ambiance of comforting warmth.

From across the entryway, I could see the dining table lined with candelabras and nearly every seat filled. In contrast to the intimate lunch with the first five coven members I met, this meal was more of a banquet.

I entered the dining area and smiled shyly, assessing the available chairs. One was next to Amber, who sat regally at the head; the other was at the opposite head, besides Jo and Eli.

I smiled at my two new friends.

"Kya!" Amber called. "Come sit next to me. I want to hear about your travels so far."

I plopped down onto the wooden seat between Amber and Fiadh. The latter wore a large orange and green flannel and an orange knit hat to match. I smiled, noting that she corresponded with the numerous pumpkins scattered decoratively around the house.

Amber put her elbow on the table between us, propping her head up. She had changed out of her dress from earlier and was now wearing a maroon sweater dress with a circle of red, white, yellow, and black in the center.

"I realized while you were in the bath that we hardly let you get a word in at lunch! How rude of us." She puckered her lips with a *pop*. "I am so very curious about how exactly you got here."

Before I could begin my long-winded explanation of seeing my father's apparition and the events that followed, a bell rang, and everyone rose from their seats.

Juno entered, pushing a cart filled with silver platters. I shuddered as the memory of Adelaide carrying a similar platter crossed my mind.

Shaking my head, I reminded myself to stay present and took a few long, deep breaths.

Look at all these beautiful souls that have welcomed me into their sacred home. They're all so vastly different and unique in their ways.

I mused while looking at Mar. Her relaxed state of being flowed into how she dressed— in a loose, cerulean pullover with a single dolphin on the chest and an unkempt top-knot with stray sandy curls surrounding her head like a halo.

Next to her, Gardenia's hair was immaculately braided, cascading down her left side like an icy waterfall. She had changed into a pastel yellow sweater with large, brightly colored flowers and sparkling golden jewelry to make her shimmer more than she did naturally.

"Tonight, my witches, we're having a stir-fried vegetable medley served alongside coconut rice and miso soup. There's crispy sweet-and-sour tofu for my herbivores and spicy fried chicken for my omnivores." Juno announced, placing the serving dishes on the table.

"Goddess, I love this woman..." whispered Fiadh beside me as she eyed the mouth-watering meal before us.

Finrod stood atop a box on the seat beside her, and I finally got a good look at him in the light. A tuft of russet fur stuck up at the top of his head, which resembled a mouse-human hybrid. He wore a white button-down shirt, sporting only two mismatched buttons, with plaid patches on the elbows. His pants, which looked like they were made from old socks, donned matching knee patches. Lastly, in contrast to the rest of his appearance, a fine jade stone hung around his neck on a woven, brown cord of twine.

Juno took her spot at the other head of the table. "Let us all join hands and say our grace."

Linking hands with Amber on my left and Fiadh on my right, I solemnly bowed, mimicking their movements.

"Goddesses Above and Below,
Thank you for the Earth that grew our food.
Thank you for the water that gave us life.
Thank you for the fire that cooked this meal.
Thank you for the wind that brought us together.
May this food nourish, heal, and bless our bodies.
Blessed be."

"Blessed be." The coven responded in unison before we all retook our seats.

"So, Kyanie, please, tell me about your journey," Amber said, wasting no time hearing my story as she scooped a pile of steaming rice onto her plate.

"Well, it started almost a month ago when an apparition of my father came to me and left me with some cryptic messages...." I began, catching the attention of everyone at the table.

Slowly throughout the meal, I told them everything that had happened to me. How the night I quit my job, Pyter appeared, mentioned the Realms, and asked me to accompany him to the Tree of Fate as my old job went up in flames behind us. How charming and alluring he was that I trusted him with my life right off the bat, despite hardly knowing anything about him.

I described the fateful night at the bar, where two Sons of Havoc cornered me and mistook me for a Handmaiden.

"What are the Sons of Havoc, anyway?" I asked the coven before shoving a mouthful of vegetables and rice into my mouth.

"They're essentially a bunch of violent racists that broke off from the Guardians so they could torment and torture anyone they please... meaning people of color, especially women and queers." Hollered Iris from the other side of the table, waving around a piece of chicken aggressively as they spoke. "Their whole bullshit mantra about 'keeping the balance' is just code for 'keeping minorities in fear so they won't rise up and murder all of the bastards in power for creating a system structured around oppression and genocide.'" They snarled before ripping off a piece of skin with their teeth.

"It's a touchy subject," Amber whispered to me.

"*Sorry,*" I mouthed to her.

"Anyway," I cleared my throat, "after that, we spent a few days in the desert, and on the last night... Pyter gave me my first dose of mushrooms." I swallowed before adding hastily, "The fun kind."

211

Gardenia and Mar both raised their eyebrows across from me as Amber asked. "And how was that?"

"It was life-altering… but not in the way I expected. I feel like it opened me up. My other eye had just begun to peek open, but after drinking that mushroom tea… my entire reality shifted. Like my perception of life was changed, so I can never go back to being unaware and asleep."

Amber eyed me and nodded while the handful of witches around me silently ate their meals, listening intently. I told her about the pain and heartache for her people and the tears I shed on her ancestral land.

"How can I make reparations for the damage my ancestors have caused?" I asked earnestly.

Amber leaned back in her chair, a single eyebrow raised. "Well, I suppose dismantling the Machine destroying our sacred land and ending the Solar Lord's reign, along with the Guardian's tyranny, would suffice." She winked. "Fight for our Earth Mother, Kyanie. Get us our land back." She concluded firmly, with a sharpness in her near-black eyes.

I smirked and slowly nodded. "That's the goal."

Celeste poked her head from around Fiadh and Finrod. "So, are you aware that you're a witch?" She asked.

"What?" I asked incredulously after finishing a bite of flavorful vegetables. "Why do you say that?"

"Oh, honey." She laughed. "You spend most of your free time in nature, have communicated with the dead, seen mythical creatures, and are hellbent on overthrowing the Trine of Power, which has persecuted witches for millennia…. Trust me; *you* are a witch," Celeste concluded with a saccharine smile before stabbing a piece of tofu and popping it into her mouth.

"I always saw you as my little witchling sister," Amber added. "Your mother also gave me hearth-witch vibes the moment I saw her kitchen, so I think it might be in your blood." She smirked.

"Maybe it is…." I smiled softly.

"I believe every woman has a witch lying dormant in their blood… waiting for them to remember." Mar mused dreamily from across the table.

I sat there picking at the remains of my meal and mulling over the label— witch. It felt right: To be a witch seemed less about potions and spells and more about coming home to myself through focused, clear intention and awareness.

~*~

After I relayed my story, everyone looked at me with a newfound respect and then shared their horror stories of living in a society run by tyrannical patriarchy.

Surprisingly, we found ourselves in fits of laughter multiple times, finding light in even the darkest memories.

"You know," said Isha from behind me as we carried our empty, dirty plates to the kitchen, "every single person in this coven has gone through trauma of some kind. But none of them have taken it upon themselves to become a hero over it."

I paused and turned around to face her.

"Your courageous fire is inspiring, Kyanie, and I believe in your mission. I believe you will succeed." Isha said definitively.

"Thank you…I hope I do." I stammered, feeling bashful.

"Believe you will, and you will. Remember, you create your reality." Isha stated bluntly before continuing to the kitchen.

I stood there momentarily, digesting the massive truth behind

Isha's words.

I create my reality. I affirmed to myself before Gardenia emerged from the kitchen archway, her smile glowing as brightly as her sweater.

"We're all going to hang out in the common space if you want to join us. We typically end our evenings talking and playing card games by the fire." She leaned in, smiling. "Though, fair warning, Fiadh has a bit of a competitive side and will *absolutely* take advantage of you being a new player."

I chuckled. "Thanks for the invite, but I think I'll turn in early this evening. My head is starting to throb again, and that cloud of a bed is calling my name." I rubbed my temples for emphasis.

"Totally understandable!" She chirped. "Is there anything I can get you? Some tea, perhaps?"

My mouth widened in delight. "Tea would be lovely. Though there is one other teeny favor I wanted to ask of you."

~*~

Gardenia and I carefully transported Bella down the winding staircase and onto a bed of blankets by the fireplace in my room.

I had already received my loose-leaf tea blend consisting of chamomile, lavender, lemongrass, and passionflower— Gardenia's personal "sleepy time potion"— and was watching the swirls of steam float upwards from the hand-sculpted clay mug when she bid me farewell for the night.

"Drink that whole mug, and you should be out like a light." Gardenia winked from the doorway. "Oh, and breakfast is pretty laissez-faire: Juno usually leaves food out for people to pick at until mid-morning so eat whenever you'd like." She sighed happily. "See you tomorrow."

With the warm mug in my hand, I raised it towards her and

214

smiled. "Thank you for everything." I took a sip and couldn't help my eyes rolling to the back of my head. "Especially this tea that will hopefully knock me out within the hour."

Gardenia breathed a laugh. "Sleep tight, Kya," her voice was as mellifluous as a mourning dove's coo.

Suddenly I was alone with my injured pup, and the intrusive thoughts I had successfully silenced all day.

I shuffled over to my thorn-torn backpack and pulled out *'The Original Religion,'* flipping to the final pages I had left to finish.

"It is in the imagination of the Earth, in the dreams of the Earth, that we find our way home.

When we tune into the energies of our evolutionary-revolutionary ecstasy, removing ourselves from the shackles of sexual life repression put on us by the patriarchy, we shall know freedom.

When humanity sees that evil is not in a singular place or thing but instead is that which prevents the evolution of One, we shall know love.

When every woman is free to choose what she wants to do with her body, when she feels safe around men to do so, we shall know bliss.

When we remember the herbal, medical, astronomical, and symbolical knowledge passed down to us from our ancestor's DNA, then we shall know wisdom.

When we acknowledge the atrocities done to the indigenous female by the imperial male, then we shall know forgiveness.

When man relinquishes the desire to mechanize and mass-produce, and reverts to communal living and freely sharing our innate, creative gifts, then we shall know joy.

When we see that we are God, we are Creator, we are the Void, then we shall know truly magical ecstasy.

Only when we go back to the beginning can humanity dream of a better future."

I first closed the book on my lap, then my eyes. Crossing my hands over my heart, I prayed to the Goddess.

I remember. With each beat of my heart, I remember.

XIX. Awakened

Despite the soothing pitter-patter of rain and drinking every last drop of Gardenia's tea, sleep did not come easily to me that night. Not even the pleasure and release from my hands between my legs was enough to lull me into oblivion.

After finishing '*The Original Religion*,' I journaled in detail everything I had experienced and found myself grieving over Pyter. Who he was truly was still a mystery to me, yet I couldn't shake the bond we forged or his voice in my head.

"It's clear your heart is as deep as the ocean...Just know that I can weather any storm you throw at me...I told you I have connections, so nothing and no one will harm you...."

It's as if he knew exactly what I longed to hear... To be seen for everything I am and feel safe in his company....

I tossed and turned relentlessly, grappling with my inner voice, until I finally got out of bed and checked the clock above the unlit fireplace. *1:11 a.m...* I smiled to myself. *It seems like a good time for something new, like a late-night exploration of this magical mansion.*

Bella perked her head up at the sight of me slipping on the moccasins and wrapping the plush white robe around my silver, silken nightdress I had found in the armoire's drawers. I shuffled over to her and knelt, petting her head and lulling her back to sleep.

Then, I grabbed the double candelabra that was lit on my bedside table, preparing to venture into a pitch-black coven.

Indeed all of the lights and candles were dark as I tiptoed down the long hallway, then down the central set of stairs, into the main entryway.

I paused at the bottom of the stairs, on the ornate rug that covered the cold hardwood floors, noticing a faint glow from the kitchen. Slowly approaching the archway, letting the candle glow reveal what may be hidden in the shadows, I saw the door in the back corner was open.

We hadn't opened or even acknowledged the door on my tour of the coven, and I had assumed it was simply a pantry.

Tentatively walking in, dwindling embers in the fireplace produced a faint glow in the otherwise dark room. I pondered how late Juno was in here, tending the hearth and planning tomorrow's meals.

Approaching the back corner, candles still in hand, the open doorway was not lightening in the presence of my flame. Instead, a dark shadow lingered.

I squinted and moved my candles around, casting different shadows within the stone kitchen, but none of my movements caused a change in this black mass.

"You…" A hoarse whisper floated in the air.

"Holder of the flame…."

Suddenly, two eyes, glowing red like the embers in the fireplace, looked at me from within the shadowed doorway.

"What provides light must also endure the burning…." The breathy voice rasped before slinking further into the doorway and disappearing into the darkness.

Immediately I went over to investigate but found only a pantry filled with jars and dried goods.

~*~

Making my way up the stone staircase to the library, I clutched my candelabra tightly, feeling slightly on edge from my encounter with the shadow figure.

218

To my surprise, the library was well-lit, with nearly every candle aflame. The fireplace was roaring and beside it, on the couch where I had met Jo and Eli, were two witches reading silently next to each other.

There sat Celeste, with a book in one hand and her bedazzled cigarette holder in the other, smoke swirling above her head.

The other witch was one of the two I hadn't officially met yet out of the thirteen coven members living here. As I approached them, I prayed it was Jude to ask about the paranormal.

"Someone's up late." Crooned Celeste after taking a rather large puff, watching me curiously as I sat down.

"I don't believe we've met." Interjected the gothic witch next to her. Their hair was black and short, with rich brown eyes outlined thickly with eyeliner that matched the rest of their all-black ensemble. Several silver piercings glinted on their ears, eyebrows, lip, and nostrils.

On the surface, they were dark and a *tad* bit scary, but the moment they smiled and stuck out their hand to me, I could see how warm their heart was.

"I'm Kyanie. Are you Jude?" I asked, shaking their slim hand covered in rings.

"I am." They replied smoothly. "How did you know?"

"I didn't— just really hoped it was you." I breathed a laugh nervously. "Could I ask you about the coven's ghosts?"

Both Jude and Celeste perked their heads up.

"What about them?" Jude asked with a wicked smile.

"Well, earlier today, I saw a female apparition in my room. I tried talking to her, and she pointed upstairs after asking her name. Then I ran into Jo and Eli, and they thought she may have been pointing to the fourth floor where you were." I said, fidgeting with my hands as they both eyed me intensely.

Something about the two of them together put me on edge. Not in a way that I feared them, more so that I could sense that they were both powerful and *'take no shit'* kind of people.

Jude nodded. "Ah, yes, Cornelia. She was one of the original coven members that tragically died from a potion experiment gone wrong. She's pretty shy, but ironically she loves meeting new people and learning their stories."

"Yeah, my first week here, she stood in the corner of my room every night until I finally introduced myself. She didn't say a word but nodded like she understood. Then she vanished, and I've hardly seen her since." Mused Celeste before inhaling.

"I also just saw this strange shadow down in the kitchen. It had glowing red eyes and—."

"A shadow with red eyes?" Celeste interjected, eyebrows raised incredulously as smoke billowed from her lips. "*Ay Dios mío....*" She shook her curly mane.

Jude's eyebrows, on the other hand, were knit together with concern. "I've never seen that spirit here. Perhaps you have an attachment."

My stomach dropped, and my blood ran cold.

"It spoke to me. Intelligently. It… it said, *'What provides light must also endure the burning'*" I swallowed, waiting for their response.

They glanced at each other, sharing a knowing look.

"Follow us." Said Jude firmly.

~*~

They took me up to the fourth floor, passing first through the sky-lit observatory shrouded in stormy, gray clouds.

"Before you leave, you'll have to spend a night sky gazing with

220

me, and I'll read your birth chart," Celeste motioned me to follow her as I ogled at the nocturnal beauty around me.

The observatory was simple yet still incredibly impressive. It was a glass dome with an utterly massive telescope in the dead center of the room. Astrology books, academic papers, and maps of the night sky littered the space.

It reminded me of Nikola's home and his scattered genius. Though this space was more organized chaos, echoing the cosmic law of entropy and our ever-expanding universe.

"And here's where the magick happens," proclaimed Jude. They had a proud smile, their pearly white teeth glowing in the candelabra's light, as they opened the only door in the observatory.

Slowly we entered the space, and a wall of energy hit me, causing my inner eye to throb dully.

"This is our ritual room." Stated Celeste. "We hold circles here four times a cycle— for the new, waxing, waning, and full moons." As she spoke, Jude lit various candles around the room, allowing me to take in more of this magical space.

It was open and spacious, with hardly any furniture besides several tables pushed against the walls. Candles, feathers, divination cards, scrying stones, jars of herbs, and crystals covered every surface. In the center of the room was a large circle encompassing a pentacle. There was only one window— a large, stained-glass circle with a red pentacle inside to match the ring on the hardwood floors.

Celeste eyed me curiously, watching me admire the stained glass dripping with rain that hadn't let up once that day or evening.

"During the full moon, beams of moonlight shine through that window and onto our circle." Celeste took a drag, and I noticed a sweet smell coming from her smoke.

"Is that a cigarette?" I asked.

"Goddess, no. I beat that poison addiction years ago. This," she said, holding up the jewel-encrusted holder. "Is an herbal blend Gardenia helped me create. It's mugwort, lavender, damiana, blue lotus, rose, and sometimes cannabis." She winked. "For those restless nights like tonight."

"Could I try some?"

"Sure," she shrugged casually. "It might be good to open you up before we do our cleansing."

After taking the smoking herbs from her pointed, perfectly manicured fingers, I inhaled deeply. Perhaps a little too deeply.

Instead of blowing out the smoke gracefully and sensually like Celeste, I spluttered and coughed aggressively on the floral, pleasant-tasting smoke. The two witches could not hold in their laughter.

Though as soon as my coughing subsided, a deliciously calm feeling spread throughout my body. Relaxation flowed from the top of my head to the tips of my toes.

"Ready for a cleansing?" Asked Jude, who had been preparing the space diligently.

I smiled slowly and nodded. "Let's do it."

Together the two cast a circle, surrounding us with candles and a ring of salt.

"We call upon the earth of the north, the wind of the east, the fire of the south, and the water of the west to create our cleansing circle." They spoke in unison. "May beings of light come to aid in our magick. So mote it be."

"With this cedar and sage, we clear this space of unwanted energy." Said Jude seriously while waving the smoking bundle in a counter-clockwise circle around herself, then Celeste, and finally me.

"I declare any unwanted spirits attached to Kyanie be purged from her.

May only spirits of the highest good have access to her energy." Spoke Celeste, who had risen from her seated position to draw large circles in the air around me with a clear, crystal wand.

I began to feel happier and lighter as the ritual went on.

Then, moving in the shadows along the far wall, I saw a dark mass. It slunk by the witches, seemingly going unnoticed until it elongated vertically in the corner I was facing. The familiar glowing eyes met mine as I watched a mouth filled with sharp teeth form in the dark mist and slowly widen into a predator-like smile.

I gasped and pointed to the corner, interrupting the ritual. "There it is!"

As soon as the two turned, it vanished into thin air, leaving me pointing at an empty wall.

"I swear it was just there..." I choked out.

"We don't doubt you saw it." Assured Celeste sweetly.

"That was likely the spirit's last appearance, making itself known and seen before we banished it." Said Jude confidently, easing some of my growing fear.

With that, they completed the ritual and closed the circle.

I certainly did feel lighter, though it was hard to distinguish between the cleansing ritual and the effects of smoking Celeste's herbal blend. Still, a small part of me worried that the cleansing ritual did nothing to detach me from the dark mass but instead irritated this shadow being. I did not let myself dwell on the matter too much.

"Thank you for that," I said as we tidied up the ritual room. "It's so powerful to be surrounded by magical women."

"Well, not all of us are women." Interrupted Jude.

"Right, of course. Minus Jo and Eli—."

"And myself and Iris. Both of us are non-binary."

"Could you tell me more about that?"

"Happily!" Said Jude with a broad smile. "Put simply, I do not identify as female or male. Instead of a 'he' or a 'she,' I am a 'they.' Some days more feminine, others more masculine." Still smiling, they shrugged their mouth. "Honestly, some days I wish I could take my tits off, and others I want to show them off to the world like a proud whore." They lifted their chin. "Regardless, I feel empowered every day by my identity of just being Jude and not giving a shit about society's gender norms."

I smiled back, comprehending what it meant to them to identify however they pleased.

"You know," Celeste interjected respectfully, "ancient indigenous cultures acknowledged that there are more than just two genders. Gender identity, as well as sexuality, has always been fluid."

Another bit of history that the Trine of Power tried to erase.

"And Iris is the same?" I asked.

"Well, not entirely. Iris was assigned male at birth but transitioned to a transgender woman. Now they identify as non-binary." They shrugged. "I know it can be a little confusing, but respecting how others want to be referred is the most important thing. Just remember that Iris and I are the only they-bies in the coven." Jude concluded with a smirk.

"Understood. Thanks for explaining that to me." I said kindly before a yawn escaped from my mouth. "On that note, I think it's finally my bedtime."

I thanked them again for the cleansing ritual as they led me out a different door that opened to the stone staircase and a small door on our right.

"That's the attic which doubles as Fin's room." Noted Celeste.

224

"Hardly any of us go in there. Mostly out of respect, but slightly because it's arguably the most *unnerving* room in the house."

I eyed the locked door curiously before descending the stairs and moseying back to my room, candelabra in hand, running out of wick to burn.

~*~

Sunlight burst through the crack in the velvet curtains.

I shot up, adrenaline pumping from a nightmare, and rubbed the sleep from my eyes with agitation before squinting at the clock.

10:10 a.m. My stomach growled as if it read the time and was now roaring for a late-morning breakfast.

I got out of bed and stretched, greeting Bella, who appeared to have been fed already, and quickly noticed a new outfit folded neatly on the bench at the end of my bed. Another pair of black leggings and a mint-green turtleneck sweater.

I wonder if they knew this is my favorite color. Smiling to myself, I pulled the knit top over my head before slipping on the leggings and moccasins I had grown quite fond of.

Slowly meandering into the kitchen, I greeted Juno, who was starting her post-breakfast-cleanup to prepare for her pre-lunch-food-prep.

I helped myself to toast, scrambled eggs, breakfast potatoes, a heaping serving of fruit salad, and a steaming mug of tea before shuffling into the dining room.

The all-glass room was now beaming with natural light as the sunlight made the garden and richly-green forest come to life. The urge to go outside and roll around in the grass like a child beckoned.

Sliding onto the curved bench in the breakfast nook, I joined Fiadh, looking intently out the window with a pair of binoculars.

"Morning." I greeted the fire-haired witch.

She jolted and lowered the binoculars. "Oh, hi, Kya. I didn't even hear you come in. I've been pretty consumed with my wildlife-watching this morning." Fiadh leaned across the round table as if she had a secret to spill. "A fox has been lurking around here the past few days, and this morning I saw it dart behind the shed. I'm hoping to make it my new familiar."

"I've been hearing this word a lot, familiar, what is that?" I questioned while stabbing a little bit of everything onto my fork.

"A familiar is a witch's companion! In traditional lore, it's believed to be a spirit or goblin taking the form of a domesticated animal. But I've learned familiars can be any animal that acts as a messenger between the Realms and the witch in question." She answered cheerily before gazing out the window once more. "I've always felt so connected to the spirit of the fox— nature's stealthy little trickster that's too smart for its own good. Goddess, I would absolutely *love* to have one as a familiar."

I smiled at her in understanding and then turned my attention to the delectable breakfast in front of me.

Stuffing my face with the best morning meal I'd had in weeks, I couldn't tear my eyes away from the shed Fiadh had spotted the fox near. Its door swung loosely open, moving in the wind as if summoning me to come closer and see what was inside. I felt a pull in my gut that I simply had to investigate.

After cleaning my plate of every last crumb and gulping down the perfect-temperature tea, I decided to explore the grounds— starting with that shed. I replaced the moccasins with my trusty old boots, which were placed neatly among the rest of the coven's outdoor shoes by the front door.

Upon opening the door and walking down the front stairs, I admired the large porch with swinging benches hanging on each end.

Reaching the bottom step, I turned around and took in the coven's mansion in its entirety. It looked like a castle out of a Victorian-era fairytale, with towering turrets on both sides and ivy vining up it, encompassing the stone turret almost entirely. I also noted the front door had a sign hanging above it, engraved *'Boaz Jachin.'*

Continuing in the direction of the glass turret towards the small shed nestled in the far corner of the garden, I could almost feel a tangible pull. While standing roughly a yard away, the shed door slowly creaked open further, inviting me in.

Entering the quaint structure, all I saw were gardening supplies: seeds, gloves, hoes, trowels, and empty planters. A long, tall wooden work table with jars, pots, several watering cans, and a mortar and pestle took up one of the walls. Breathing in the earthy aroma of dirt, I felt an inner stillness circulate.

Turning to leave, I noticed something large hidden beneath a white sheet tucked into a corner with rakes of differing sizes. My brows furrowed as I tried making sense of the oblong, oval shape, though I couldn't think of a single gardening or landscaping tool that looked like it. The need to know took me over as I moved the rakes out of the way and tentatively grabbed the sheet, pulling it off to reveal a large, ornate, silver-framed mirror.

For a moment, I stared at my reflection, feeling like I hadn't looked in the mirror in weeks. I smiled, noting that my eyes were no longer distant and dull as they had been the past few years.

"My daughter…."

A ghostly female voice floated in the air.

"Can you see me?"

I squinted my eyes at my reflection, then quickly glanced around the small shed to ensure no other human was there with me.

As I turned back to the mirror, it was no longer my reflection I saw. Instead, the hazy image of a woman with tan-brown skin, long black hair, glowing purple eyes, and a silver crown with an eight-pointed star resting atop her head was watching me.

"Courageous Kyanie, you've done so well." The misty woman said with a smile. *"Someday, your bravery will be celebrated across all the Realms."* Her voice sounded as if she were underwater.

"Who are you?" I asked, brows knit tightly together.

"You shall know who I am in time. Trust me. More importantly, I have a message for you: when all hope is lost, come to me, and you will find it."

The image of the woman faded into nothingness, and I was left staring at myself, jaw agape.

Tentatively I covered the mirror again and made my way out of the small garden shed; eyebrows furrowed tightly.

Deep in thought, decoding the message that this strange apparition gave me, I nearly tripped over a pair of outstretched legs. If not for the bare feet sticking out like a bizarre, flesh-colored flower, I would have mistaken the legs for roots.

"Oof, I'm sorry!" I exclaimed, stopping dead in my tracks and grabbing a close-by branch to avoid falling.

A pair of moss-green eyes peered up from below me with agitation under mousy brown bangs. A young woman, possibly the youngest in the coven, sat against a tree with a closed book beside her. She nearly camouflaged with the tree behind her, her tan suede jacket, similarly-colored corduroy pants, and wavy brown hair mimicking the swirls and whorls of bark.

"Watch where you're walking." She snapped, her pale,

freckled nose crinkling slightly as she spoke.

"Sorry. What are you doing?" I asked.

"Talking to the trees." She replied, closing her eyes and leaning back against the bark.

"And you can hear them?" I tried not to sound skeptical but rather intrigued.

"Only if my mind is quiet." She answered, eyes still closed. "Which is incredibly difficult with you interrupting me."

"I don't think we've met... I'm Kya." I knelt to her level and stuck out a hand, though she didn't see it.

Slowly she peeked an eye open. "I'm Alden." Both eyes opened. "Lovely to meet you." Sarcasm laced her words.

"Do you communicate with the trees often?"

"Every day." She replied with a sigh.

"And you do it by sitting with them and silencing your mind?"

Alden sighed exasperatedly. "Yes, I already answered that. Now is there something you need from me, or do you just like the sound of your own voice?"

I've definitely heard Rosemary ask that exact question.

I snorted and smiled. "I like you."

Alden was taken aback by my response and grimaced, but did not let her sarcastic defenses down. "I'll take that as you just like hearing yourself talk...." She again closed her eyes and leaned back.

Perhaps she knows of the Tree....

Came an inner voice that wasn't necessarily my own.

"Wait! Have you heard of the Tree of Fate?"

Alden's eyebrows lifted before she even cracked her lids open. "I have." Her eyes fully opened again. "What do you want to know?"

"Well, I'm not sure if you've heard from other coven

members, but I ended up here on a journey of ascension to the Tree of Fate. All I know of it is that it's located on Mount Hope and serves as a bridge between Realms."

"Ah, I see." Alden shifted, drawing her legs inwards into a cross-legged position, her barefoot soles resting on her knees. "Have you ever meditated and quieted your mind before?"

"Kind of." Barely.

"Well, the most important part of it, and arguably life, is your breathing. Paying attention to your breath and letting it anchor you to the present moment is the key to a happy and healthy mind, body, and spirit. As thoughts arise, notice them, and breathe them away." Alden took a deep centering breath. "Don't fight the thoughts or try to ignore them because it won't work, and you'll end up riling up your mind again. Notice them, and acknowledge them. Then always come back to your breath." She spoke like a wise old sage trapped in a young woman's body.

I mimicked her position and took a few deep breaths, grounding myself in the present.

"So I should meditate with the Tree when I reach it?"

"Yes, well, sort of. The Tree of Fate is mighty and holds the magick of the Veil separating the Realms, so leaning against the bark may cause intense reactions... I would say sitting near the Tree should suffice." Alden shrugged her shoulders and mouth.

"Now, to ascend, you need to get to a very calm, centered state of being, which will be easy if you practice quieting your mind. Then imagine the feeling of ascending; *truly* feel it. Hold it in your being as if it is real, and it will be.

"When you're in an aligned state, think of your loved ones and the things that bring joy to your life. Gather all those warm and fuzzy feelings into a glowing ball in your heart center and keep it there." She spoke with her eyes closed and her hands crossed over her heart.

She smiled slightly and looked at me. "Once you've gathered all the love and joy in your being into your heart, face the Tree then walk towards the waterfall behind. It won't take long for you to feel the Veil and eventually pass through it." Alden blew a deep breath out of her nose. "And that's all I know about the Tree of Fate."

"Thank you! Where did you learn all of that? Is there a book I can check out of the lib— ?" I began.

"The trees," Alden said, assuming her original position against the bark. "The natural world holds such vast, all-knowing intelligence: It only requires us to shut up and listen."

As if the wind was listening to our conversation, a calm breeze swept through the forest grove, ruffling our wavy manes.

"See." Spoke Alden quietly, eyes once again closed. "It's always there, communicating with us in the most subtle ways. All we need to do is be quiet and remember where we came from."

XX. Liminality

Two days flew by of immersing myself in the coven's way of life, learning more about each witch's unique magick.

After visiting the shed and meeting Alden, I sought out Gardenia amid her daily greenhouse duties to see if she had any answers about the woman in the mirror.

"Hm, I've never seen a figure in that mirror besides my own. It was a family heirloom from my great-great-great-grandmother. She used it to scry and find this magnificent abandoned mansion in the woods for the coven." Gardenia answered while remaining focused on pruning. "Since I'm the only one allowed to use it, I've kept it hidden in my gardening shed because I figured it would be unassuming. But considering you found it on your second morning here… perhaps it's time to change its hiding spot."

Gardenia shifted her attention to misting a blooming purple orchid, so I left her to her responsibilities and went to the library. I spent most of the morning reading book suggestions about witchcraft, the Old Ways, and magick from Isha.

She had casually mentioned that where she grew up, in a rural village in southern India, girls weren't allowed to go to school, let alone learn how to read or write. It wasn't until her mother demanded to her father that they migrate to America that Isha's love of books and learning could blossom fully.

I'll never take my privileges for granted again.

I stopped my studies for a lunch break and then a restorative bird-watching walk through the surrounding forest with Jo, Eli, Jude, and Celeste. The latter, I had surprisingly learned, loved watching birds when she wasn't studying the stars. Day or night, her head was in the sky.

That evening when we returned, I spotted the most impressive fish tank I had ever seen while passing by Mar's open bedroom door. Feeding her fish familiars at the time, she beamed with pride and took me into her room, where she gave me a detailed rundown of her tank.

Mar had just begun raving about the ocean and how it was her only true home throughout her unpredictable, nomadic life when Fiadh passed by the open doorway.

"Fin found this old board game upstairs. Wanna join us?" She asked excitedly, holding up a dusty box.

Mar and I glanced at each other, shrugged, smiled, and then played with Fiadh and Finrod until the dinner bell chimed.

After our evening meal, Celeste invited me to join her in the observatory, where she mapped out my natal chart.

"An Aries sun with an Aquarius moon and a Gemini rising...." She thoughtfully mused as she jotted down the exact degrees and placements of the planets the moment I was born.

"It makes so much sense. You're a fire sign at heart, and all the air in your chart fuels that. But the intriguing part is how balanced it is — you have exactly five masculine and five feminine placements. Plus, you're right on the Pisces and Aries cusp, like you were born to walk the line of opposing energies. Being both fire and water in one." Celeste continued explaining my planetary influences until I could no longer keep my eyes open.

Then, after another night of nightmare-riddled sleep, I had an action-packed, non-stop day in the coven.

Amber invited me to archery practice in the morning, taking me back to where she had made a targeting range. She taught me the hunting tips her father instilled in her, like the importance of a good bow, the right conditions, and patience.

Soon after we had finished, Juno emerged from the forest carrying an armful of thick branches and thin logs. She was responsible for keeping all the fireplaces blazing, and, in between her cooking, she was either foraging for wood or chopping logs.

I offered her my help, and by the time we went inside for lunch, my upper arms were sore and trembling. It felt good to ache, to feel the muscles I had long neglected since my brief high school athletic career.

That evening, Juno prepared a proper-autumn feast for us: Vegetable and meat pies, roasted squash and potatoes, sautéed green beans, a hearty soup, and bread rolls, all made from scratch. I hardly spoke as the physical exhaustion, and ravenous hunger took over, causing me to get second helpings without hesitation.

After we had all engorged ourselves, the entire coven sat around one of the fireplaces in the common room chatting. With Lea lyrically practicing the violin, Iris soon got up and started flowing to the rich, brilliant sound from the strings.

Though I was tired and sore from archery practice and chopping wood, seeing Iris move so freely just looked like it felt *incredible*. It reminded me that dance, amongst other art forms, is universal. Dance transcends language, religion, and cultural background— it's our bodies' natural mode of physical expression.

With encouragement from Gardenia and Fiadh, I joined Iris's flow and let the music move through me. I didn't care how I looked because of how good it felt to move intuitively, stretching the stiffness in my muscles.

When I finally retreated to my chambers for the night, sleep snatched me as soon as my head hit the pillow.

~*~

The nightmares had been plaguing me since Shadowmere's cabin. Each night was more vivid and terrifying and always involved the brutal death of those I loved and cherished most. The morning of Samhain, I awoke screaming, sweat drenching my body and nightgown.

In my dream, the coven went up in a blazing fire, with each member bound at the stake and aflame along the tree line. It was so real; I could smell smoke filling the air and hear each witch's scream of terror. Then I saw Shadowmere holding a burnt match in one hand and Bella's leash in another. I lunged towards him, blind with rage, as he smiled demonically and vanished in a wisp of dark mist.

Sitting up in bed, my hand grasped my heart, willing the beat to regulate. My adrenaline spiked even higher at realizing that Bella was not sleeping soundly in the room with me. Without thinking or changing out of my nightgown, I ripped open the door and barreled down the stairs to the dining area.

Had I not been so distraught, I would have greatly appreciated the decorations strewn about the coven. Carved pumpkins sat at the bottom of the stairs and in every room, with candles burning brightly in each. Fake bats dropped from the tall ceilings with fishing wire. Skeleton hands and figures danced about each doorway, some hanging on the backs of doors like old coats.

Gardenia and Celeste were tucked into the breakfast nook when I came rushing into the room. My hair was wild and tangled from sleep, and sweat stained the front of my satin slip: I surely looked like a mad-woman.

Immediately Gardenia arose, a look of sweet concern on her

235

face. She wore an amethyst sweater with a giant spiderweb stitched in black in the center, and her hair was braided into two long pigtails that went down to her ankle-length black skirt.

"What's wrong, Kyanie?" Gardenia asked as she gently grabbed my hand, tethering me to the present.

"Bella is gone, and I had this nightmare. Well, I've been having a lot of nightmares, but this one…was so real." My words were as scattered as my brain.

"Fiadh has been taking Bella outside around the property each morning to build her strength. I suppose you've been asleep when she usually gets her…." Gardenia trailed off. "Tell us about this nightmare." She motioned for me to sit on the bench between her and Celeste, who shared a look of worry.

I told them about Shadowmere and the visceral image of the coven burning along with each witch. When I finished explaining my nightmare, I nervously chewed my lip, waiting for their explanation with anxiety bubbling through me.

"Huh," Celeste spoke after silently mulling over what I said by picking at the lint pills on her dark purple pashmina. She turned to face me, our eyes meeting. "And you've been having these nightmares since you were at Shadowmere's cabin?"

I nodded.

"My theories are either that you have bad PTSD from the ordeal or," she took a quick sip of coffee for suspense. "By eating the food he offered you, a part of him has burrowed inside you to claim you for his own, and these nightmares are manifestations of that."

Gardenia's lips thinned, and her eyebrows drew together.

"I'm sure I can whip up a cleanse for you…." She began before excusing herself to the greenhouse.

"Do you think my nightmare could be some premonition? Like Shadowmere is tracking me down here?" I asked Celeste, twisting my hands with worry.

She shrugged, not seeming to be too concerned with the matter. "Even if he did track you here, Shadowmere wouldn't be able to see the coven with his own eyes, considering the amount of evil in his being. But I'll let Amber and the other witches know to be on alert. After all, it is Samhain." She winked mischievously. "With the Veil this thin, anything could happen."

~*~

After my cortisol levels had evened out, I stuffed my mouth with pumpkin spice pancakes slathered in butter and doused in maple syrup. Following that, my day consisted of helping decorate the coven and prepare for the festivities.

During lunch, Amber took the opportunity to remind the handful of witches at the table that the theme for her combined birthday and Samhain celebration was a black-and-white masquerade.

"Lucky for you, I have an extra gown and mask you can borrow," Amber said with a sisterly smirk.

Mar, who per usual wasted no time devouring her meal, wiped the remnants of grilled cheese crumbs on her worn-down jeans, then used the sleeve of her orange pumpkin sweatshirt to clean tomato soup off the corner of her mouth.

"How could we possibly forget, Amber." She chuckled lowly. "I'm pretty sure within the last moon cycle, you've helped every single coven member plan their outfit."

Amber smiled coyly. "What can I say? I used to be a part of the theater— designing costumes brings me joy."

I looked at her with a newfound understanding. Her avant-garde fashion sense and how she did not care how others perceived her were some of my favorite qualities about her. She had an undeniable uniqueness, especially now, in brightly-colored, patterned pants and an oversized, black fur coat matching the obsidian feline on her lap.

"What are you wearing tonight?" I asked Alden, who had been quietly reading beside me during the meal, donning a simple black hoodie and leggings to match.

She glanced up from the page, eyebrows raised, and closed the book. "You'll just have to wait and see like the rest of these witches," Alden replied with a coy smile before getting up and bringing her empty plates to the kitchen.

Shifting my focus to the massive window in front of me, the foggy, gray weather outside began to seep into my being. For a split second, I saw a fox in the shadows bordering the garden before a group of corvids in the tree closest to the shed caught my attention. I began to zone out, hyper-fixating on one blackbird that seemed to be focusing on me in return.

Though there was an air of festivity in the coven, I couldn't shake the feeling of fright that had solidly formed in my gut from my most recent hellish nightmare. Suddenly, a piece of bread crust hit me in the nose and broke me from my daze.

"Oi! Earth to Kya," Fiadh called across and down the table. "Want to help me clear the common room to make space for a dance floor?" I smiled both at the request and at her oversized, black t-shirt depicting classic horror movie characters that read *'Monsters Have Feelings Too.'*

Getting up to clean my dishes and assist Fiadh, I glanced back once more at the group of corvids. Unsurprisingly, the same bird was still looking intently in my direction.

~*~

I had just finished moving the furniture in the common room and returned to my chambers when darkness began creeping into the coven. The overcast from earlier had developed into an unrelenting rain which, combined with my increasingly sore muscles, made me want to nap with Belladonna until the dinner bell rang.

Bella's physical state had improved vastly in the last few days, and she was finally able to get onto the bed, where she was tucked into herself sleepily. Seeing her on the plush comforter left me no choice but to climb into bed with her, laying my head on her back legs as I had always done.

My consciousness began drifting away when a quiet knock brought me back to reality.

"Kya?" A soft voice came from the doorway.

"Can I come in?"

I mumbled in approval and sat up.

Gardenia entered, holding a dress bag and a small, round glass jar with a cork. "I brought your outfit for the ball and a detox elixir that I believe will exorcise Shadowmere's hold on you." She carefully placed the dress at the foot of my bed and the bottle on the vanity. "Take it twice a day, morning and night."

My heart was warm and grateful for all the herbal witch had done for me. "Gardenia, I can't thank you enough for every—."

She smiled and shook her head, braided pigtails swaying. "Healing is my purpose. When Amber informed me that her familiar had spotted you at Shadowmere's, I vowed to see you safe." She gracefully sat on the edge of the bed. "All of us here want you to succeed. Truthfully, I think each of us wishes we could be the ones to destroy the Machine and unveil the truth behind the Solar Lord and

239

his Guardians. However, there's also so much healing and transformation that still needs to happen in the Logical Realm."

I grabbed her hand, which had been gently stroking Bella's coat, feeling the unending support from her and the coven. "I won't let you guys down."

~*~

In the dark of Samhain night, the interior of the coven was aglow with warm light from a seemingly infinite amount of candles.

I had gotten dressed for the festivities with less than five minutes to spare before dinner. Having not worn a dress since prom, I felt incredibly awkward in the long, half-white, half-black form-fitting dress given to me for the evening. Though as I placed the bejeweled black mask, with a conjoining sun and moon design, on my face, one of my father's favorite quotes floated into my mind.

'Life begins at the end of your comfort zone.'

As I entered the dining room, I couldn't help but beam at the unique, evidently personalized fashion choices.

Jude and Iris sat beside each other, the former wearing an all-black tuxedo and the other all-white. Jude's mask was devilish, with small horns protruding out the top, while Iris's was pearly and angelic.

Jo and Eli sat across from them and wore eerily similar ensembles— one in a black suit and white tie and the other in a white suit with a black tie. Both with bird-like masks.

While I was admiring Lea's long, white silken dress and glittering lace mask, she turned to the breakfast nook, speaking Spanish to a group of transparent people.

I finally took my seat between Gardenia and Fiadh. The former wore an elegant, long white dress with beaded black lilies and a matching white floral mask. Her outfit complimented her complex braided hairdo, which created a halo of platinum blonde embellished with tiny flower-shaped jewels. Meanwhile, Fiadh's black velvet gown was sleek and sensual, with a plunging neckline that showcased her cleavage and intricate chest tattoo. Her bare arms displayed several other tattoos of nature and wildlife, the biggest of which was a fox that matched the silhouette of her white mask.

Next to the animal-loving witch sat Finrod proudly atop his box, wearing an adorable all-black ensemble with a wolf-like mask.

I smiled and then leaned towards Gardenia. "Who are all those ghosts?" I asked quietly, counting nearly twenty apparitions.

She breathed a laugh through her nose. "Some of them are relatives of Lea that she invited to be our undead orchestra for the party. The others are house ghosts taking advantage of the thin Veil to participate in the fun."

Suddenly the dinner bell chimed, and we all arose, though Amber had not arrived yet. Juno strolled into the room, pushing her meal cart and wearing a black beaded gown with a large ivory bow on the rear that matched her simple creamy white mask.

"On this blessed Samhain and day of birth of one of the most powerful—." Juno began before seeing that Amber was not present. "This witch would be late to her own birthday dinner...."

As if that was her cue, Amber strode into the dining room. She wore a breathtaking, bewitching black lace dress with a long train, loosely hanging bell sleeves, and an ornate, bejeweled mask that looked like a black, sparkly crown. My jaw dropped at the sight of a raven perched on her shoulder, her black cat walking in stride beside her, and phooka tentatively trailing behind.

Amber's crimson lips parted in a smile that dazzled the room as she beheld her fellow witches. "Let us pray and bless this meal!" She bellowed.

She took her usual seat at the head of the table, this evening seated beside Mar, whose white, mermaid-style lace gown complimented hers beautifully. I admired the seashells on her mask and the turquoise jewelry she wore, showing where her heart truly belonged.

"Blessed be." We concluded our usual prayer before feasting on various hand-tossed, steaming pizzas covered in meats and vegetables, with a colorful salad on the side.

The meal was shared with numerous fits of riotous laughter, no doubt fueled by an endless supply of wine. Though I did not drink any because of my newfound aversion to alcohol, the coven's energy was intoxicating.

"So, out of all the meals that Juno could have made you, why pizza?" I asked after catching my breath from a particularly side-splitting joke by Fiadh.

Amber's mouth curved, then she took a slow sip of sparkling white wine and shrugged. "I figured that the unnecessary formality of my masquerade ball birthday party could use some balance. Plus, I selfishly wanted to eat my favorite comfort meal."

I nodded and started mulling over the concept of balance. Celeste, who sat across from me in a black skin-tight, floor-length dress with a feline mask, had mentioned it repeatedly during my birth chart reading. As I sat there wearing a half-white, half-black dress, I began to feel like the embodiment of duality.

You can't have light without darkness; you can't have good without evil. The miracle of life is the encompassing of both, holding space for all that is and all that is not.

My inner voice philosophized just before our meal plates were cleared, and Juno brought out a decadent death-by-chocolate cake, aflame with thirteen candles. To my surprise, all of us, including the dead, sang *'Happy Birthday'* to Amber like one big, eclectic family of truth-seekers and misfits.

~*~

The common space had transformed entirely into a gothic ballroom by the time festivities were in full swing. The undead orchestra played beautifully haunting music with an organ, harp, cello, flute, and two violins while the witches and I spun and pranced throughout the open area. The wine flowed as freely as peoples' dance moves, including the house ghosts, who seemed to glow even brighter with exuberant, festive delight.

I had forgotten how much I loved to dance. How much joy it brought me to let my mind shut off and let the music take hold of my body and soul as I moved to the beat.

Dancing fluidly in a small circle with Isha, whose white dress with black paisley print had utterly mesmerized me, Jude and Iris pulled me aside. They informed me they were both pan and poly-sexual, then asked if I would like to have some 'explorative fun' with them after the party.

"Think about it— you'd be protesting everything the Trine of Power represents. Unlike the mechanical, biological reproductive sex of 'hetero-normies,' queer love is purely pleasurable." Jude, almost successfully, persuaded.

"That's why they work so hard to oppress us; they're jealous of how much fun and pleasure we can have." Iris included tucking a stray hair behind my ear and looking at me keenly.

My flushed cheeks grew even hotter as I politely declined their offer and locked eyes with Alden from across the room. She had consistently stayed on my mind, along with the simple yet imperative lessons she taught me in our brief initial meeting.

I made my way over, moving between writhing bodies and flowing fabrics. She wore the only short evening dress with a checkerboard pattern, a plain yet elegant white mask, and black tights ending in clunky black combat boots.

"I like your outfit," I complimented, leaning into her ear so she could hear me over the music.

Alden smirked. "Thanks, I like yours too. Though I wouldn't have pegged this as your style." She said with a raised eyebrow.

I shrugged. "When the occasion calls for it."

The upbeat music switched pace into a slow waltz, and I extended my hand dramatically.

"Care to share this dance with me?" I asked, knowing the intoxicating environment had something to do with my overly confident behavior.

"I don't dance…." Alden began to object.

"Nonsense! Everyone can move to music— follow my lead." I replied cheerily, grabbing her hand and dragging her into the heart of the dance floor.

Together we swayed and twirled to the melody, hands resting on each other's hips and shoulders. I looked around to see all the witches equally blissed out from the festivities and the ever-flowing alcohol. My smile grew impossibly wide.

"So, what's your story?" I asked after a heartbeat of silence.

Alden's face turned grim, her mouth dejectedly curving as she stared back at me. "It's not really a happy tale to share in passing at a birthday party." She concluded with a caustic smile.

"I'm sorry, I…," I shook my head nervously.

"And what about yours?" Alden questioned, eyeing me intently. "I've found that those who ask for others' stories are often running away from their own." She broke away from me, patting my shoulder as she turned, "Enjoy the party, Kyanie— try living in the present and stop drudging up the past."

Suddenly alone amid the dance floor, Alden's words sunk into me slowly. I found my way to the wall and took a moment to myself.

I can't believe Pyter and Shadowmere are the reason I found this coven. That two deceitful men led me to find the only place I have ever felt safe besides my childhood home....

Several loud bangs abruptly echoed through the room. The music halted, and everyone froze. I glanced at Amber and Gardenia, who looked at each other with puzzlement.

Amber hoisted her gown, revealing a switchblade knife strapped to her thigh. She unsheathed and wielded the weapon in one swift movement.

"Everyone stay here!" Gardenia yelled— the loudest I had ever heard her voice— before the two hurried out of the room.

Without thinking, I followed them, wishing for my pocketknife in hand to back up Amber. I trailed behind them to the entryway, where several more bangs resounded loudly.

Standing in the archway of the dining room they had just passed through, I watched them hesitantly crack open the front door and felt the air whoosh out of my lungs.

There on the porch, dripping with rain, stood Pyter.

XXI. Illumination

The combined effect of shock and festivity-high had me clutching the wooden archway for support.

"Before you cast me out in the storm, please listen. This coven is in danger. Shadowmere and his men are comin' here tonight. Just before midnight, he plans on strikin' a match and burnin' all of this, includin' all of you, to the ground." Pyter's voice was pleading as Amber eyed him coldly.

He was wearing a different jacket I hadn't seen before. The forest green velvet had been replaced with black, and the vine embroidery was now roses and thorny branches.

"You expect us to believe you? How are we supposed to trust a suspicious stranger showing up on Samhain?" She replied icily.

"Please. I know Kyanie has taken refuge here; I want to protect her." He said earnestly.

Gardenia's usually friendly composure turned wary. "How do you know all of this?" She crossed her arms over her chest.

"If you just give me a chance to talk to her, I can explain everythin'." He pleaded: I had never heard him sound so despairing.

"Then explain," I said loudly and firmly, stepping into the entryway and his line of sight.

His shoulders slumped in relief.

My blood heated as a range of emotions ran through me.

"Can I please come in?" Pyter asked me, his emerald eyes looking at me longingly.

I crossed my arms and raised my eyebrows. "It's not up to me; you'll have to ask my lovely hosts." I smiled sweetly and wickedly.

Gardenia turned to him, not an inch of a smile on her face, and eyed him beneath her mask. Amber, however, removed her mask to show him a single eyebrow raised. Her crimson lips curved in a bloodthirsty smile while her hands toyed with her knife.

"May I please enter—."

"No, not like that. Get on your knees." I seethed, arms still crossed and chin high.

Without hesitation, Pyter dropped to the ground. On his knees, looking up at the witches, he brought his hands together and began to beg. "Please, oh mighty and powerful witches. Beautiful Daughters of the Wild. Please allow me to cross your threshold and explain myself. I promise you all I mean no harm." His voice cracked at the word promise.

I wonder if that has anything to do with the sincerity behind it....

For a moment, the two looked down on him with disdain, then shared a look and finally glanced at me.

"Did that suffice?" Amber asked.

I shrugged. "I suppose."

Pyter exhaled loudly and arose from the ground.

"Thank you." He said sincerely as he dipped his head down respectfully and entered the coven.

"Go sit on the stairs." I snapped.

With Pyter sitting on the bottom stair in the entryway, Amber, Gardenia, and I surrounded him, all of us with hands on our hips, eyeing him warily.

"Lovely home you ladies have here." He said charmingly, his alluring green eyes glowing in the candlelight as he took in the decorations. "I would've loved to be part of your festivities."

"Explain yourself." I said curtly, my lips pursed in vexation.

"Right, fair enough." Pyter sighed and shrugged. "Well, to start, I'd like to apologize for takin' ya to Shadowmere's cabin. It's been a few years since the last time I saw him, and I guess in that time, he's grown exceedingly more arrogant, aggressive, and possessive."

"Thanks for that. I don't *really* forgive you but go on." I said, removing my mask to cool down my flushed cheeks.

"So, after ya ran away, I was left alone with Shadowmere, and naturally, we did what any two raging men would do— we brawled." He chuckled lowly. "We'd gotten into wrestlin' matches before, but this time was different. After breakin' a couch and a vase in his study, we finally calmed down, and I appeased him enough to get back on his good side." He rolled his eyes. "Which, I might add, seemed entirely backward to me considerin' I'm thousands of years older than him and thus his superior...."

He started to trail off and then glanced up to see us completely unamused. Amber was still toying with her knife menacingly with a deadly straight face.

Pyter cleared his throat. "So I've spent the past few days infiltratin' his operation and convincin' him I was on his side and wanted to help with his, em, revenge."

"Revenge? On me?" I gawked.

He smiled weakly, cringing slightly. "Let's say that Shadowmere despises being bested by women. After ya got away, he was hellbent on huntin' you down and makin' you his personal Handmaiden."

My stomach dropped, and my icy composure fell away, replaced with blind, searing rage.

"And now here you are. Leading him right to me." I stared at him, willing daggers to come out of my eyes.

Pyter waved his hands. "No, please. I told him I was feelin' ill, so I locked my room and escaped out the window. They don't know I'm here, as far as my knowledge goes, but they will be soon. I came to warn ya, to help you all prepare."

"Why?" Asked Gardenia, her voice calm yet hostile.

"For Kyanie." Pyter turned to me, his eyes boring into my soul. "In all my years on Earth, I've never met a being like ya. Someone who cares so much, about so much, that she would let it consume her rather than live in blissful apathy. I'll admit I should have been honest about who I am and why I'm journeyin' to the Tree, but I wanted ya to trust me."

"So you lied to me? To get me to trust you?" I asked mockingly, my eyebrows raised as high as they would go.

Pyter cracked a smile. "Well, when ya put it like that." He cleared his throat again. "Right. Okay, I understand how it seems. But if I told ya I was a shapeshifter over ten thousand years old, you would have never come with me. You are *destined* to lift the Veil. Regardless of my agreement with the Solar Lord, I will always revert to my natural state— disorder." He shrugged before leaning onto his knees. "Which is why I'm here; to bring complete chaos to Shadowmere's plan and ego. I want to help ya fulfill your destiny. If you'll allow me." He exhaled and shifted back against the stairs.

I eyed him angrily, chewing on the inside of my lip and deliberating with my inner voice.

Either he's a compulsive liar, and showing up is part of Shadowmere's plan, or he's being sincere and wants to help. Considering everything that's happened between us….

"Now I can see those gears turnin' in your quick, inquisitive mind Kyanie. Let me add two things before ya make your decision."

He shifted. "Firstly, I've spent the last few days scopin' out these woods to find our best escape route. I mapped out a trail that leads to the main road with a bus stop that can take us straight into Olympic. Secondly, I'd like to remind ya that I wouldn't have even been able to *see* the coven if I truly had evil in my heart." He concluded with a smug smile, making me want to smack the look off his face.

I looked at Gardenia, whose mouth shrugged at the realization that her relative's wards would have indeed stopped him from entering if he were part of Shadowmere's revenge.

"How did you know that?" Amber interrupted, looking at him suspiciously.

"Most covens implement the same kind of wardin'," he shrugged. "It was also a lucky guess that you just confirmed to be true."

Amber snarled at his self-satisfied expression.

I don't want to put the coven in danger by waiting to find out if Pyter's warning is genuine, but I'm not sure if I'm letting a fox right into a hen house....

I inhaled deeply. "Here's what we're going to do. I'm going to lock you in my bedroom and have a meeting with the coven to decide how we will prepare for this attack if there is to be one."

Pyter clapped his hands together. "Splendid plan!"

His enthusiasm was very off-putting to me.

Amber seemed to sense my wariness or perhaps had her own trepidation, so she chimed in. "Allow me to show the prisoner to his cell; I have an extra pair of handcuffs that I think would fit him perfectly." She snarled while maintaining a saccharine smile.

"Lovely." I mimicked Amber's look of sweet death. Then I turned on my heels, linked my arm to Gardenia's, and sauntered away to rejoin the rest of the coven.

~*~

We gathered on the fourth floor, sitting around the pentacle in the ritual room and discussing what Pyter revealed.

"Why don't we hang him from a tree as a warning to those Guardian assholes? Like witchy Vlad the Impalers." Fiadh asked feistily.

"Vladimir the Impaler decapitated his victims and put their heads on stakes around his castle." Corrected Celeste in between drags before she shrugged and exhaled. "I suppose it's a less extreme but still fitting solution."

"That won't stop them," I said, shaking my head. "We need to *exterminate* them. Not just scare them away."

"Why don't you consult your scrying mirror for answers?" Alden, who sat on the outskirts of the circle and had hardly said a word since the meeting began, asked Gardenia.

I shot a look at spring-embodied, whose beautiful face was painted with worry, and her eyes lit up.

"Of course..." Gardenia muttered to herself.

Suddenly the door leading to the stone staircase and attic creaked open.

"Excuse me." Finrod poked his head into the room. "I apologize for intruding. I couldn't help but hear the mention of the Blessed Mirror. I believe there's something in my chambers that could help us."

Gardenia rose, tilting her head. "Why do you say that?"

"Well...when Headmistress Ruth, your ancestor, founded our coven, she put wards on the attic door so only sworn-in coven members and myself could enter." He tapped his tiny hands together nervously. "Then she hid a locked chest and its key somewhere in the

251

attic, using magick to hide its true form. She told me it should only be used for emergencies, and the only way to find it is by using the Blessed Mirror." He concluded, nose and whiskers twitching.

Immediately Gardenia shot up. "I need volunteers to help me bring the mirror upstairs. Quickly."

Within minutes, Gardenia, Fiadh, and Mar had hauled the mirror, which was much bigger than my memory recalled, up to the fourth floor. When they reached the top of the staircase, Amber, who had joined the meeting while the three witches were outside, helped them place the mirror on the back wall.

Stepping back to ensure it was centered with the pentacle, Amber turned to face the awaiting coven and clapped.

"Let's get scrying."

~*~

As if it were muscle memory for each of the witches, they prepared the ritual space with haste, then assumed their positions around the circle. Finrod and I stood respectfully to the side.

After removing the sheet covering the mirror, Gardenia took her seat at the top of the pentacle, directly in front of it. Around her, the witches cast a circle and opened communication beyond the Veil.

I watched Gardenia's warm brown eyes glaze over as she stared into the reflective glass. Her delicate hands raised to her sides as if they, too, were working to discern the chest's location.

A handful of moments had passed before her eyes fluttered back to reality, and she turned around to face the other witches.

"I know where it is."

Gardenia arose, pulling Amber up with her.

The remaining coven members closed the circle as I followed the two to the attic doorway. I stepped toward the small, dimly lit space but was immediately met with an unseen barrier.

"Sorry, kiddo, sworn-in coven members only," Amber said with a wink. "You'll have to guard the stairwell for us."

Upon my first glance, I could see a dozen taxidermy animals and several mannequins with blank expressions painted on their plastic faces. Suddenly the barrier separating us felt more like a shield.

A strange, macabre space indeed....

Gardenia headed straight to the back of the room, weaving between old furniture, paintings, and other unknown objects covered in dusty sheets, and stopped before a large trunk lying in front of a shelved wall with small wooden boxes.

Amber came to her side. "What are these?"

Gardenia slid out a box, respectfully pulling out a wooden wand and other small trinkets. "I've been in this attic dozens of times with my mother and grandmother, but I never truly appreciated these." She shook her head and smiled. "These hold the magick of every witch that has passed through our coven. Including my great-great-great-grandmother...." Her look turned solemn, puzzled even as she eyed the boxes belonging to her relatives. "If I can find that spell, these could help...." She muttered to herself.

Gently Amber put a hand on her shoulder. "Babe, not trying to rush your little moment here, but we need to focus. Midnight is approaching."

"Right." Gardenia shook her head and threw a braid over her shoulder. "Help me carry this trunk into the ritual room."

"And the key?" Amber asked with a single eyebrow raised after we set the bulky, yet surprisingly lightweight, trunk down.

Gardenia turned to Finrod somewhat breathlessly. "When I asked the mirror where it was, all I could see was you."

253

The brownie's ears turned attentive. "Me? Oh. Well, perhaps it's this." He pulled out the smooth jade necklace from inside his black dress tunic. "Do be careful with it. 'Twas a birthday present from Headmistress Ruth."

As he plopped it into Gardenia's outstretched hand, a brass skeleton key suddenly lay in her palm.

She hastily opened the trunk and unearthed a velvet jewelry box, a thick, leather-bound book, and a wax-sealed envelope. Gardenia opened the letter with her quick, nimble fingers and immediately started reading aloud.

"If you are reading this, it means the coven is in grave danger — what a shame. Luckily you will find the Witches' Enchiridion, which contains some of the most powerful, life-altering spells known to witch-kind. This book should not be taken lightly and should thus only be utilized in the direst of emergencies. You will also find amulets of protection to distribute amongst the coven. If you are my descendant, I pray that you protect this coven, and thus the future of the Daughters of the Wild, with your life.

— With magick and love, Headmistress Ruth."

As Gardenia read, Amber took it upon herself to rifle through the Enchiridion with eager eyes. At the same time, Mar opened the cobalt velvet box and began handing out protective amulets — polished black stones that hung on black cords.

Amber skimmed through the book, and a wicked smile spread across her lips. "I found what we need."

~*~

Various duties were given out in the coven. Juno, Alden, and Lea were tasked with gathering large branches to serve as wooden stakes surrounding the front of the house. Jude and Iris were sent to the observatory to watch for the oncoming invasion. While Jo, Eli, and

Isha went to the library to find a particular spell that Gardenia requested for backup.

On the other hand, I was sent to my room to pack my things. It was unclear whether I was leaving tonight or first thing in the morning. Regardless, as soon as I entered my chambers, all deliberating thoughts seemed to cease. Pyter was handcuffed to my writing desk by the window as Bella rested her head on his lap.

His eyes glinted, and his head perked up. "Welcome back." Pyter smiled cheekily. "Lovely view ya have of the forest." He said, nodding his head towards the window.

I crossed my arms, not saying a word.

Pyter heaved a sigh. "Look. I know I've completely broken your trust, and that's somethin' I'll probably never get back... but I genuinely want you to succeed. Even if it's not with me, I want you to ascend. Here," he motioned downwards to his chest, "there are two bus tickets to Olympic in my inner coat pocket. Take 'em."

Still, I said nothing as I eyed him warily and slowly made my way over, kneeling to his seated position. I undid the top pearly button on his jacket and hesitantly reached in, pausing as the warmth of his chest beneath his thin cotton undershirt met my fingers.

Pyter's shamrock gaze bore into my soul the second I dared to glance into his eyes— a look I had never seen before. One of longing, hazy desire as his gaze darted between my lips and eyes.

His lips were full and tempting, causing me to imagine how they would feel against my own without being a forcible show like the night at the bar.

"You have no idea how much I missed your presence." His throaty voice whispered. "From your face to your attitude, to your wild, untamable hair. You remind me of my favorite thing about humans...

free will." He breathed, leaning towards me.

The temptation sunk into nearly every fiber of my being, aching for the physical contact I had gone so long without. I leaned closer to Pyter while creeping my hand into his pocket until my hand was firmly around the tickets.

Our breath was almost one when I yanked the tickets out and pushed him back from me. "Thank Goddess for free will, huh?"

Before we could exchange another word, Iris's voice echoed from the observatory. Our guests were arriving.

~*~

Gardenia ordered everyone to stay inside, save for Amber, Celeste, Mar, and Fiadh— The Headmistresses of the Daughters of the Wild, my cloaked rescuers the night at Shadowmere's.

I hadn't realized their hierarchy, even in my days there, because each of the thirteen coven members seemed to have equally important roles. They were one cohesive unit, united under witchcraft.

Standing in the entryway and looking out the window with the bulk of the coven members, I fiddled with the black protective stone Mar gave me. Watching the five Headmistresses stand their ground on the lawn in their formalwear left deadly guilt clawing at my insides.

How can I let them fight this battle for me? I can't allow any of them to be hurt, let alone killed, *on my behalf.*

I chewed my lip nervously as a herd of shadows faced them.

Hot rage soon replaced my anxiety as the Handmaidens, including Adelaide, collared and leashed, came into view. Their satin dresses were soaked with rain that had only stopped minutes before their arrival and left nothing to the imagination.

"A little snake told you of our arrival, I see." Boomed Shadowmere's distinctive voice. "No need to fear, witches." He snarled the last word. "I have a bargain. Hand over Kyanie, and we will spare this coven…probably."

I could not see his face, though I imagined its jeering nature.

"We have no fear," Amber yelled, standing with her legs hip-width apart, a portrait of brave defiance. "And *you* shall be the ones begging to be spared."

Shadowmere and the eight other brutes, all wearing dark hoods, laughed heartily. Tauntingly. I noted three of them carrying jugs of gasoline, and my heart leapt into my throat.

"Stupid witch." Shadowmere's voice turned guttural. "Can you not count? You are outnumbered and overpowered."

"Are you sure about that?" Gardenia chimed in before clapping her hands briskly three times.

An undead, semi-transparent army arose at the sound of her claps from the forest surrounding the males.

"As witches, we are never alone in this reality," Gardenia spoke with poised confidence, like a true leader. "Our ancestors, those that have died for us to live, are always with us. Protecting us."

Again Shadowmere and his hooded brutes all laughed.

"You think ghosts can stop us?" He sneered, removing his dark hood to show his deadly charming face. "I will offer this one more time before I burn you all— hand over Kyanie, and your coven may be spared."

I suddenly found myself ripping open the front door.

"Stop!" I yelled, rushing down the porch stairs I was unsure if Shadowmere and his brutes could see. "I will go willingly if you release your Handmaidens to the coven."

"There you are." Shadowmere stepped forward, his near-purple eyes locked on me intensely. His mouth curved into a cruel smile as he cocked his head. "You're in no place to bargain, little girl. Either come with me or watch as I burn this coven and its members to the ground."

"Release the Handmaidens, and I will," I spoke defiantly, not breaking his gaze. "What's worse? Going home with the same boring Handmaidens you've had, being bested by me again? Or losing all three in exchange for me, who will gladly and willingly do anything you ask?" I raised my chin confidently, though my insides felt like uneasy mush.

I couldn't bring myself to look at the Headmistresses, whom I could feel were watching me in horror, especially as Shadowmere mulled over my request.

"I will join her as well," Gardenia said, stepping forward.

"Me too." Amber included, joining me at my side.

Shadowmere looked feline as he took in Amber and then Gardenia. "Fine. Having witch Handmaidens is a fantasy of mine." He snapped his fingers at the brutes holding the leashed women, and in response, they shoved them forward onto the muddy ground.

Immediately I was on the ground with them, helping them up until Celeste and Mar grabbed them, ensuring they were safe.

"Let's go, *sluts*." Shadowmere hissed.

I went to step forward, willingly giving up my quest for the overall good of the coven that saved my life when Amber and Gardenia looped their arms in mine.

"No." They spoke in unison as a blazing ring of fire surrounded us, outlining the perimeter of wooden stakes.

"Excuse me?" Shadowmere snarled. "What is this? Have you all prepared to burn to death on your own terms?"

Suddenly to my left, a cloaked brute took his last gasp of air as several undead witches flanked him and snapped his neck. Within seconds, two more Guardians collapsed to the ground in the same manner. Each held a jug of gasoline that the transparent females quickly relocated away from the growing fire.

Shadowmere and I both had similar shocked expressions as he turned back to the three of us, flames illuminating the rage in his eyes.

"How dare you." He roared. "You three are coming with me if it's the last thing I do…." He snapped at the remaining brutes, and they all lunged forward, unafraid of the ring of fire surrounding us.

"So mote it be," Amber crooned.

The second they stepped foot over the fire ring, as if struck by an invisible wall created by the wooden stakes, each figure froze. Shimmers of magick swirled around them, binding them to the stakes at their ankles as flames engulfed their long, billowing cloaks.

Shadowmere locked eyes with me. "You think this will stop me from getting what I want?"

To my horror, he transformed into a cloud of black smoke, with those familiar glowing red eyes and demonic smile. The dark mist only lingered for a second before it flew over the flaming ring.

In an instant, Amber shot me a look of knowing pain before pushing Gardenia and me to the side. The shadow engulfed her swiftly, swallowing her into nothingness and leaving no trace.

My arm, linked with hers, burned from the passing smoke.

"Amber!" Gardenia wailed as she instinctually lunged toward the remaining wisps. "AMBER!" The floral witch dropped to the mud, pure agony in all her features. She called her name several times, growing more despaired and shattered each time.

"Gardenia," I soothed while stroking the back of her head. "Gardenia, let's get you inside."

The shock had rendered me surprisingly calm. Though I knew my storm of rage would arrive when I had a moment of downtime to process what just happened.

Crackling from the burning, remaining Guardians and their screams of pain were a strange symphony of triumph.

At what cost had we triumphed? If at all? We had just lost one of the most powerful witches in the coven. Not to mention someone I had come to think of as an older sister....

Leaving as soon as possible is my priority. Shadowmere is still alive and now has Amber. The longer I wait here in the safety of the coven, the more I endanger the remaining witches along with my chance of ascension.

Gardenia wrapped her arms around me upon standing, trembling slightly.

"I will get her back. I don't know how... but I will. I will bring her back to you all. Promise." I said into Gardenia's shoulder, squeezing her with all my loving might.

The following hour was spent adjusting to an Amber-less coven. Most of the witches were either crying or visibly fuming as they discussed how to bring her home.

"How are we supposed to track down a shadow? Especially a Guardian-warlock-shadow?" Mar questioned. She was the only one whose face remained neutral upon hearing the news.

Trauma will do that to a person....

I ruminated, remembering the tragedies that summer-embodied had gone through and shared with me.

"I'm not sure. Maybe The Blessed Mirror has answers. Just...Just keep the faith that she'll come back. Okay? Believe it until it's a reality again." I spoke as confidently as possible.

I glanced at the Handmaidens. Juno had warmed blankets by the fire to wrap around their damp, freezing bodies, and color had returned to their cheeks.

"The Headmistresses said you can stay here as long as you'd like," I told Addie, moving to give her a loving embrace. "Please take care of yourself, and know that you'll always have a special place in my heart. No matter what, I love you."

"I love you too." Adelaide choked out between her tears. "Thank you for saving me... for risking your life. I'll always be in debt to you for that." She embraced me, then grabbed my hands. "Before you go... in case I don't see you again, I need to tell you something."

I cocked my head, asking gently. "What's up, Addie?"

"Pretty soon after Luke started driving us west, I told him about what you said at the cafe. He...," she licked her lips nervously, "he told me that it was him and my brother that reported Onyx to the local Guardians." She frowned deeply. "It turned my insides hearing that. I'm so sorry I didn't believe you."

Hot inner rage flashed in my belly, though I refused to fan the flames. At least not here, not when the coven was grieving.

"Thank you for telling me." I lifted my head, swallowing my last bit of anger and letting it fuel my quest. "It's okay, Addie. It's not your fault." I smiled sadly and motioned her toward me.

A wave of tears began building as I hugged her goodbye and finally turned to say farewell to the core witches that brought me back to life. I wiped my nose on the mint green sweater they had gifted me, cherishing the cozy, soft fabric woven with memories of magick.

The four remaining Headmistresses encompassed me in a warm, group embrace. The building wave of tears finally crashed on the shores of my face.

"We're honored to have been a part of your soul's journey, Kyanie." Gardenia stepped back to look at me. "We believe in you," Spring-embodied said with hope in her eyes. Her typically joyful expression had turned puffy and red, though the beauty in her spirit still shone through brightly.

"I don't know what to say or how to adequately thank you for what you did for me. Saving my dog and me, taking us both in as if we were one of you." I wiped a stray tear.

"Are you sure you don't want to leave Bella here?" Asked Fiadh, kneeling beside my canine, scratching her head and stomach.

My mouth thinned. "I'm sure. She deserves to get into the Ethereal Realm arguably more than I do."

I sighed and glanced at Pyter, whom I had begrudgingly agreed to accompany me out of fear of the rogue Shadowmere.

"Think Amber will mind if I take those handcuffs with us?"

"Not at all," Gardenia half-smiled. "I think she'd prefer it."

XXII. Trials

Along with the handcuffs, the coven supplied me with a knapsack full of everything I could ever need to complete my ascension journey.

They gave me an entirely new wardrobe with thermal, waterproof clothing and boots to help me with the Washington rainy season I was going into. In addition to new outdoor gear, considering mine was still in my truck parked at Shadowmere's, and enough trail mix and dried fruits to last me a month of camping.

Ignoring his pleas of innocence, I demanded that Pyter walked in front of me. With the handcuffs, he could only hold the paper map he had drawn.

Before leaving the coven, I consulted with Gardenia, who knew these woods better than anyone, to ensure that Pyter led us back into civilization as he promised. Her keen eyes deciphered the trail he had found and assured me that a bus stop was indeed on the main road right outside of it.

So the three of us walked in the dead of night, hardly speaking a word to each other besides Pyter's occasional warning of a hidden rock or root until we reached the bus stop.

Plopping down on the cracked wooden bench, I rummaged through my backpack in search of the detox Gardenia gave me.

"What is that?" Pyter asked with furrowed brows as I took a large swig of the gray-green liquid.

Grimacing slightly from the flavor, I jolted my head before replying. "The coven's healer made it to help cleanse Shadowmere's attachment to me. He's been plaguing me with nightmares and coming to me as a dark mist."

"Better to be plagued by a mist than rats or locusts."

I glared at him as he chuckled.

"And that won't do much against a warlock attachment." Pyter nodded at the bottle.

"A warlock? Is that why he can turn into smoke?"

"It is. Shadowmere heads a sect of Guardians that dabble in the occult. Secret clubs that partake in blood-magick rituals to receive all their wildest dreams and desires." He sucked in a breath as he continued his explanation, "These desires are more often than not linked to furtherin' the Trine of Power's scope. They're called '*warlocks*' because they are locked on war— war on the feminine."

I huffed angrily, feeling powerless in this cosmic battle between the divine masculine and feminine.

"That man, er warlock, is the closest thing to a real-life demon I've ever encountered. And *you*," I pointed angrily at his chest, "agreed to pawn me off to him as part of a deal with the Solar Lord." I crossed my arms and looked up at him.

"Look, I was never going to leave you there, Kyanie. You want to destroy the Machine, take down the Guardians, and end the Solar Lord's reign, right? Wouldn't it make sense to infiltrate the Trine of Power and learn about your enemy from the inside?"

"I suppose, but I could have done with a little heads-up," I answered sharply. "And now, all I've learned about my enemy is that I'm in way over my head."

"Right, well, I didn't want to scare ya."

"Yeah, imagine what would have happened if you had 'scared me' and we avoided this whole mess!" I snapped, raising my voice. "Because of you, not only do I have a *warlock* attached to me, but the

264

coven is missing a Headmistress." I exhaled angrily, "A Headmistress that is like a sister to me... is now a hostage of evil."

I put my head in my hands, looking at the ground dejectedly. *How will I ever fix this?*

Pyter sighed just before headlights came, casting the early morning darkness with bright, fluorescent beams. He turned his back on the oncoming bus and lifted his handcuffed wrists.

"What are we to do about this?"

"Stay behind me and keep your hands down in front of you." I arose and shrugged. "I still don't trust you enough to free you."

He laughed dryly. "Fair enough, I suppose."

As the bus stopped before us, I noted its number— 919.

We're nearing the ending, which is also the beginning, soon to be another ending. The cycles of life never cease to turn: dying and being reborn in a perpetual loop of existence.

The sleep deprivation had indeed caught up to me. Settling into the navy fabric seats, I leaned against the window to watch the first rays of dawn peeking through the trees, and my eyelids could no longer stay open.

~*~

I was home, surrounded by all my loved ones in my living room, as our fireplace blazed brightly. The air was warm, with spices wafting from the kitchen, and my heart felt so full that it would burst with love.

Suddenly a *WHOOSH* from the chimney extinguished the flames and made my family and friends vanish, leaving me alone in a strange, cold darkness. I began running, searching blindly for a way out and screaming for help into the void of my childhood home when those glowing red eyes found me.

265

The shadow, blacker than black, formed its jagged-toothed mouth and hissed. *"You will never be rid of me."*

My eyes shot open, and I clutched my chest. With no concept of what time it was besides that it was well after sunrise, the darkness I had fallen asleep in had been taken over by a gray, overcast day. Portions of darker, more ominous gray loomed on the horizon.

From across the aisle, Pyter looked at me with concern. "Did you have a nightmare?"

I nodded while stroking Bella, curled up in the seat directly beside me, calming myself more than her.

"Well, at least you woke up at the perfect time! Look out your window." He said kindly, nodding to my left.

As I turned, the massive trees surrounding us on both sides opened up just enough to reveal a wild, expansive ocean. The churning waves echoed in my veins, and I felt peace.

"Along this stretch of coast is the *'Tree of Life'*: a massive tree with exposed roots clutching onto the eroded edge with pure magick seeming to hold it up." He narrated.

I furrowed my brows. "That's not the Tree we're looking for?"

Pyter breathed a laugh out his nose. "No, it's not. Truthfully, I believe it's a distraction to hide the real magick nestled in the heart of Olympic."

I turned to the window, watching the blur of looming trees and rugged coastline with loving appreciation.

This Realm can truly be so beautiful and awe-inspiring. If only the majority of people cared enough to make our natural world as big of a priority as our modern-industrial-capitalistic one.

~*~

We got off the bus at its third park stop, directly north of

266

Mount Hope and the Tree of Fate, around midday.

I had agreed to un-cuffing Pyter for the sake of him going into the ranger station to get an official trail map. Meanwhile, Belladonna and I enjoyed a late breakfast of nuts and fruit for me and canned dog food for her.

He came out grinning, folding the glossy paper map into his coat pocket. "I have great news, ladies! Firstly, that very helpful man inside told me there are lean-tos scattered throughout the park, so we don't have to worry about building a shelter for the night." He clapped his freed hands together. "I've scoped out our travel route and believe we can reach the Tree tomorrow before dark."

I wanted to share in his zest for reaching the end goal of our journey together, but my emotions were a jumbled mess of nervousness, excitement, fear, and impatience.

Suddenly, the screech of a red-tailed hawk flying overhead broke me from my emotional haze. I paused to admire its display of aerial prowess.

"Great," I said flatly, arising from the stone wall where I was perched. "Let's get moving; we're losing daylight."

~*~

The forest was something I had never seen before. Giant, ancient trees and their branches dripping with pastel green moss draped overhead. Intricate protruding roots with equally as much rich shamrock moss carpeted most of the ground beneath our feet. Never-ending rows of ferns, some fully grown and others still tightly curled, waiting to explode with life, lined our path.

We had been walking well over an hour into the dense, vibrantly-alive forest when Bella began to slow down and limp. Veering off the trail, I crouched down and rested my bag on a tree stump to look for the bone-healing elixir Gardenia had given me.

"Let me carry her," Pyter said from behind me after I gave Bella several droppers full of medicine.

"I can't ask you to do that...."

"You're not. I'm offerin'." He replied firmly yet gently.

"Are you sure you —." I began before Pyter knelt beside Bella, lovingly petting her head as he scooped her up in his other arm and secured her over his shoulder.

"Positive." He said with a grin. "I needed a little extra *oomph* to turn this hike into a workout." He winked. "I want to look my very best for our ascension."

I couldn't help but crack a smile. "If you insist," I said, grabbing the coven's knapsack to lessen his load.

We continued hiking up the steep and rocky slope of Mount Hope, intermittently getting drizzles of rain until we finally reached the structure that would serve as our home for the night.

It was simple, made from dark wood with a raised floor, three walls, and an overhang that provided dry shelter as well as covered ground to build a fire in the stone pit.

Luckily the sun had only just begun its descent, so we wouldn't have to cook in the dark of nightfall. Regardless, I quickly removed both backpacks from my shoulders to gather food for our dinner as Pyter collected sticks for a fire. The unspoken bond we had shared picked up like we were never separated, and I soon remembered why my feelings of fondness had formed.

As a pot of instant rice and beans warmed over the small propane stove, I watched Pyter build the structure of a perfect campfire with focused precision. Then with a single match, his fire blazed to life and never faltered.

Noticing me watching, Pyter flicked his head to move some stray hairs, now glowing orange in the firelight, out of his eyes.

"Yes?" He smirked.

"You started the fire in the diner, didn't you?"

"I did. But only because you willed it so."

He sat up, leaning his elbows on his knees. "Your energy was like smoldering coals when I entered that diner. I have a way of amplifying the underlying energies in a person— all it took from me was intentionally willing your current desires to come true."

I blinked at him, still unclear about the scope of his powers.

"I want you to tell me the truth about you," I voiced, unwilling to acknowledge that I had, in fact, wished to burn *Hank's 'All You Can Eat, All the Time' Diner* to the ground.

Pyter's mouth thinned, and he nodded slowly. "I suppose I owe you that." He cleared his throat. "Roughly ten thousand years ago, my spirit was born from the primordial, cosmic chaos in the Void and the Earth Mother. I was among the first intelligent, sentient beings on the planet, alongside the Goddesses and several other nature deities. We all lived harmoniously, flowing with the Earth Mother's cycles for thousands of years. Even for a while after humans were created, until, of course, men manifested the Solar Lord."

He straightened, fidgeting with the top button of his jacket. "At first, he seemed to have good intentions. He promoted peace, eternal bliss, and all that, as long as one has a pure soul, clean of the sins of this Earthly existence. But I saw the ulterior motive behind his creation: a ploy for power and control."

He paused as he added more wooden fuel to the fire.

"Naturally, I was intrigued. Soon the Solar Lord came to me with a proposition— to cast away the Goddesses and split the Earth

269

into three Realms. The two of us would rule the Logical Earth Realm together, actin' as the most powerful forces in this human existence: love and fear. The masses would love and pray to him while fearing me, reinforcin' their devotional need for him. It was a perfect plan. Especially for someone such as myself, born entropy, I couldn't resist the offer to shake up life on Earth *so* drastically." He exhaled and looked at me for the first time since beginning his story.

"You… you're Lacius?" I asked calmly, though my heart thudded loudly in my chest.

"The one and only," he held up his hands in a half-hearted display of self, "but you may still call me Pyter if you'd prefer."

I nodded slowly, shrinking into myself while attempting to untangle my thoughts and feelings with my inner voice.

If I've been with a being of evil, why do I feel no fear? He's been a perfect gentleman to me, despite the stunt at the bar and Shadowmere…who he saved me from but is also an acquaintance of his… I should definitely *be scared, but I'm not… not even a little bit….*

"Are you truly evil then? If millions of people believe you are, does that make it so?"

Pyter let out a bitter laugh. "Other's perception of us holds no value unless we let it. Think of it like a Halloween costume— a facade of fear." He spoke with his hands like a businessman making a pitch.

"But people worship you as a being of sin and wickedness. That energy, the belief, is so potent, wouldn't it create the reality?" My eyes narrowed as Pyter's truth finally came to light.

"Dear, inquisitive Kyanie, everyone's reality is different. Perhaps a purely wicked version of myself is floatin' around the collective consciousness." He shrugged, "But, honestly, chaos brings about good as much as it does evil. Disorder, havoc, anarchy, change, it's all the same. So what is chaos if not the free will of the universe?"

He shot me a look, and madness flashed through his gaze. "The universe, the cosmos, the Earth, they're constantly movin', constantly evolvin'— humans are the ones striving for forced order. Human beings have such beautiful, innate free will, just as the Void wishes. And that free will grants the ability to choose good or evil, love or fear. The realest, *truest* evil is the power that aims, that *chooses*, to suppress spiritual evolution. Human ignorance— now *that* is true evil."

Pyter's gaze was transfixed by the flames as he continued.

"Truthfully, if I could go back in time, I would have flipped the switch on the Solar Lord and let my Goddesses continue their harmonic rule over the world. Instead of letting the Trine of Power dominate every aspect of reality."

I had been absentmindedly stirring our dinner as he spoke, completely enraptured with his voice and story.

"Now, here you are, helping a girl who wants to end his, and apparently your own, reign," I stated after a lull of silence. "We could *actually* end the Trine of Power's domination," I whispered earnestly.

Still watching the ever-growing fire with glazed eyes, he nodded. "Right, here I am, here we are. You, about to make your ascension into the Ethereal Realm. Me, likely to be rejected by the Veil and about to feel the Solar Lord's wrath for failing him....."

I tilted my head at him. "I don't understand. You just said you would do it all over, and yet you're still acting like his bitch-of-evil."

Pyter belly-laughed and threw his head back. "Bitch of evil... Hah!" His emerald eyes looked at me with adoration. "Dear Kyanie, I love ya."

My eyes widened, and my heartbeat jumped to my throat. "You... what?" I breathed nervously. "You don't even know me." I

271

gawked at him, unable to form words.

"Love defies all logical understandin' sometimes," He laughed upon seeing the disdain on my face. "After livin' in a car and tent with you for almost three weeks, I think I know ya." He winked. "You're a spit-fire woman with opinions as scathin' as your words can be. You love with such a fierce nature that anyone worthy of your heart must prove it tenfold. You've always felt different from your peers, like you were broken, but, in reality, you're a sane, awake person in a crazy, asleep world. Not to mention how naturally gorgeous you are, with your wild mane and hazel eyes as multi-faceted as existence itself…."

I felt my cheeks growing hot and held up a hand. "Okay, okay, I get it. Maybe you know me by now, but that doesn't change anything. Tomorrow we're reaching the Tree, and I'm ascending, leaving everything I've ever known."

As I said it, the words sunk into my chest, and I began to feel an aching for my mother, Rosemary, and Adelaide. To avoid crying, I turned my full attention to the well-stirred, cooked meal and announced that our dinner was ready.

Pyter sat down with a full plate of food on the slightly decayed log we used as a bench, then looked at me questioningly.

"Is there anything about this Realm that you'll miss?"

I sighed happily, eyes fixed on the flickering flames.

"Of course…," moments of bliss flashed through my mind, "the first sip of hot tea on a chilly morning, or the feeling of a crowd singing back to the musicians during a concert. Tasting rich, dark chocolate or biting into a particularly sweet and juicy piece of fruit…. Stargazing on clear summer nights and swimming naked in the ocean. Feeling the intimate touch of another….." I trailed off as my cheeks heated further, and my eyes caught Pyter's wicked grin.

"That's a lot to miss," He replied in a husky tone.

"Mhm," the warmth from my cheeks had traveled elsewhere, so I avoided his gaze, focusing solely on my meal.

We continued eating in silence by the fire as the night crept in, and a light rain pattered the wooden roof over us.

"What is it like in the Ethereal Realm? Do you know?" I asked after cleaning my plate of food entirely.

"All I've heard is that it's like a wish come true. Anything you can ever want or wish for is there, and all beings live together peacefully." Pyter replied after doing the same.

Suddenly a pack of coyotes sounded up the mountain, only a few hundred yards from us. I grabbed Bella's leash out of instinctual protection. Pyter, on the other hand, seemed to be unfazed by the nearby animals, so we fell back into that familiar, comfortable silence.

Taking my nightly swig of Gardenia's detox, I prayed the nightmares would cease so that I could get a restful sleep.

XXIII. Desire

Slipping into my dream state, I began having visuals of a fire. Unlike the other fires I had encountered thus far in my journey, this one was wholly unique.

People were worshipping it. Dancing, singing, and yowling around the blazing flames beneath an impossibly bright moon. All seemingly as bare and natural as the sleeping forest around them.

Most noticeable about the scene was a whimsical tune floating in the air. A shadowy figure sat on a stump on the other side of the flames, the source of the melody.

It pulled me, beckoned me, closer to the fire. A heat began building inside, starting at the apex of my thighs, the root of my being, then slithering up my spine.

It begged me: *"Go to the fire… Go to the fire…."*

The warmth had now spread through my entire body, and a primal sensation overcame me.

Suddenly my dream state coincided with reality. I opened my eyes to see Pyter sitting by the campfire, playing a small wooden pan flute. For a moment, I laid there and watched him. My eyebrows furrowed heavily as I tried to decipher if this was still a dream.

A quick pinch of my finger gave me my answer.

Sitting up slowly, I found my voice. "What are you doing?"

Pyter's eyes, which were closed as he played, opened calmly.

"I found this old toy of mine at Shadowmere's and couldn't resist giving it another go. Especially since this may be my last night on Earth." He set the instrument down carefully on his lap. "Sorry about that; I was hoping it wouldn't wake ya."

I shrugged, "Couldn't sleep anyway." Rubbing my icy hands together, I looked at the flames, "Can I join you?"

"Of course," Pyter replied with a devilish smile, cast scarlet in the fire's light. His fine velvet jacket, embroidered with thorny vines and bright red roses, glinted subtly from the flames.

I sat down and removed my socks, lifting my frigid toes to the warmth. Fixating on the radiating heat in front of me, I sighed.

"Can I be honest?"

"Always."

"I'm nervous, Pyter. What if this has all been for nothing? What if the Tree doesn't accept me and I don't ascend? Or worst, what if the Tree isn't even he—."

He held up his hand.

"Stop. Dear Kyanie, if ya drown yourself in the 'what ifs,' you'll never reach the surface." Pyter leaned as close to me as he could from the other side of the log. "Believe in yourself, Kya. You are *good*, and if you aren't worthy of ascendin', then I'm not sure who is."

I smiled bashfully. "Thank you." Tilting my head, I questioned, "Do you think you're worthy?"

Pyter spluttered, shaking his head while tending to the fire. "Truthfully, no." He shifted his focus to me, and the spinal serpent continued slithering up my core. "But with you, I feel like anything is possible. Even an undeservin' man like me could reach the heavens with a woman like ya by my side."

I blushed and cast my eyes down. "Can I be that good, though? In the last few years, I was a cold, untrusting person who broke the heart of the only lover I've ever had."

"Kyanie," He breathed my name as if it were his last. "You're giving up everything you've ever known for the chance to help

275

humanity see the truth. Perhaps grief broke you, causing you to break another, but you are selfless. On top of that, you are passionate, brave, loving, empathetic, and *unbelievably* sexy."

My heartbeat sped up and thrummed through every nerve in my body as our eyes locked on each other. Only the crackling fire, sporadic drops of rain, and undeniable tension hung between us.

After the lovers that brought me fleeting pleasure in my ploy to get over Adam, my previously high libido was extinguished. My heart's trauma snuffed out my underlying addiction to the euphoria of sexual ecstasy.

Though to feel another's passionate embrace was something I had been longing for in my last year of hollow, aching solitude. Now, desire was staring me dead on, and I could not look away.

If this were truly my last night in the Logical Realm, I would revel in all the earthly pleasures I could. If he's immortal, he must have had a lot of time to perfect his—.

As if he could read my mind, Pyter broke our prolonged silence, smirking. "Would you like me to play you a song?"

"Can I dance to it?" I replied, feeling brazen.

"I'd prefer if you did." He purred before licking and puckering his lips, drawing them towards his instrument.

I removed my oversized sweatshirt, feeling my nipples pique beneath the thin t-shirt as they met the chilly mountain air. Throwing it onto my sleeping bag, I quickly looked at Belladonna, resting peacefully in the corner.

At first, the tune was gentle and soothing.

I began by mindfully stretching my body. My hands reached to the heavens, elongating the sore muscles in my back, then I rotated my neck, relieving stored tension.

My hips started moving instinctually to the melody, deliberate and sensual. I closed my eyes and let the music take me over, releasing any shame or care about how I looked.

My hands trailed up my thighs, grasping at my hipbones as they made their way up my stomach. I wrapped my arms around my midsection, swaying slightly to the music, and felt such immense self-love that my smile was uncontrollable.

When I cracked open my eyes, Pyter's gaze was firmly focused on me. His eyes were hooded, and his expression was sultrier than I had ever seen.

The heat building in my core grew into a roaring fire.

I stepped closer to him, moving rhythmically and gracefully to the tune he was playing. Only an arm's reach away, I planted my bare feet firmly on the ground as his tempo shifted.

No longer gentle and soothing, his music became alluring and dark. The spinal serpent slithered along my back, moving my hips and chest fluidly, seductively. For I'm not sure how long, I moved in perfect tandem with the music Pyter played.

Tipping my head backward and exhaling loudly, I arched my back and raised my hands above my head once again. While writhing and dancing like the flames before me, the spinal serpent swallowed me whole, and arousal took me over.

Before giving it a second thought, I straddled Pyter's lap, throwing my hair behind me and exposing my neck. His instrument promptly vanished as he grabbed my waist with one hand and the back of my head with the other.

In a flash, his full lips were kissing my neck, trailing his tongue softly up to my earlobe, where he nibbled it gently.

A soft moan escaped my lips as the hand holding my head

grabbed a fistful of my hair, keeping me firmly in place.

"I've ached for the feelin' of your skin under my tongue since the moment I saw ya." He breathed into the nape of my neck, causing a cascade of goosebumps throughout my body.

My lips were parted, longing for his mouth on my own, when he adjusted me to look at him straight-on. I breathed deeply, unable to form words or thoughts as his emerald orbs looked into my soul.

"Goddess, you're beautiful...." He whispered huskily before our lips met in a passionate dance.

With him firmly holding my hair, I grabbed his face in my hands and dipped my tongue into his mouth. Teasing and swirling around his for several breaths, I broke away for a moment and gave him a sensual smile.

His hands had both moved to my waist, sliding down to cup my rear in one sly, cheeky maneuver. My internal fire had become all-consuming as I ground the peak of my thighs onto his lap and the growing bulge in his pants.

Our lips met once again, feverishly.

He roamed my body as if he were memorizing each curve. Meanwhile, I continued my relentless gyrations on his lap, our mouths refusing to separate, even for a second.

"I need you, Kyanie," Pyter broke away to breathe those words against my wanting lips. "Please, give yourself to me." He concluded by nibbling my ear again, eliciting a moan and more goosebumps.

The wetness between my legs was too much to bear as my lust left me in a trance-like state of pure longing. Who Pyter was didn't matter to me at that moment: Just *my* pleasure, *my* last moments of fleeting, ecstatic bliss.

"Okay," I said breathlessly with a dazed, flirtatious smile.

In an instant, Pyter arose, grabbed his blanket, and laid it on the ground between the campfire and our sleeping area.

He proceeded to scoop me up in his arms, my legs wrapping around his waist as my hands fell back onto his neck, my lips outlining his strong jawbone. Something overcame me as every second spent without his touch, his affection, now felt achingly cold.

Slowly and deliberately, Pyter lowered both of us, laying me on my back as he knelt above me. His eyes bore into me as he removed his jacket, one elegant button at a time.

I bit my lip as the flickering campfire cast a shadow on his dark-colored jeans, leaving little to my imagination. Instinctively, my hips moved upward, straining to make contact.

"My, my, someone's impatient...." He grinned wickedly before removing his plain white t-shirt, "I'll be taking my time with you."

As I ogled at the rippling, defined muscles of his shoulders, chest, and core, he slipped a finger under the waistband of my sweatpants and began pulling them down.

While he did so, he left a trail of butterfly kisses along my stomach, then my hips, and then down my legs as my skin was exposed to the nighttime air. He then wasted no time doing the same as he worked my t-shirt off my body, leaving me in only my panties beneath a sliver of moonlight.

His eyes widened, then turned feral, as he took in my above-average breasts that I had worked so hard to keep hidden beneath layers and oversized clothing.

My breathing deepened as Pyter's expert mouth met my nipples. He kissed, licked, and sucked every inch of my chest while his hands caressed my thighs and hips.

Just when I thought his delightful teasing would end and I would finally feel his length inside me, he lowered his head even further. Without hesitation, Pyter kissed me through my thin underwear, causing me to gasp, giggle, and squirm.

"That tickled a little bit." I smiled, chewing my lip.

"Perhaps I should remove the barrier then," he smirked and replied smoothly before he slid the last bit of my modesty to my ankles. He paused a moment to admire the dampness he had caused.

My breathing became shallow as I lay starkly bare amidst the mountainside elements. My breasts rose and fell quickly as anticipation nipped at each nerve in my being.

Pyter watched my every move, my every reaction, while his broad, rough hands never stopped their mindful roaming.

Suddenly, a single finger found its way to my opening. With control, he gently swiped from the top to the bottom of my wetness, then dipped into me slightly. He brought his finger, coated with my nectar, to his full lips and sucked with hungry delight.

"You're just as delicious as I knew you'd be," his smile was carnivorous as he lowered again, his mouth finding my delicate lips.

All of my past lovers paled in comparison to the pleasure I now felt. My moans were impossible to suppress as my deepest sexual frustration was finally released.

Pyter devoured me as if I were his proper last meal on Earth. His movements at first were slow and teasing, with his tongue tracing every part of my most intimate area. He kissed it as if it were my face, with his lips and tongue honing in on the spots I reacted to the most.

Shifting his focus to the apex of my thighs, he flicked the bundle of nerves with his tongue as one of his fingers fully entered me.

A deep, primal moan escaped my throat. His movement

quickened, and my climax was already approaching.

"Please," I panted, "I want to feel you. All of you." I grasped at his pants, clawing my way towards the button and zipper that were now my biggest obstacle.

Pyter smiled sinfully. "So mote it be," he purred, kneeling upright and unhurriedly removing his jeans.

I whimpered as he finally freed his manhood. His sheer length astounded me, though his girth had me squirming in suspense. My breathing was ragged as my eyes moved from his rock-hard member to his eyes, glazed over in primal arousal.

He moved so his face hovered over my own, and our intimate parts were mere inches away from meeting. Then he kissed me softly, innocently, several times on my mouth, cheeks, nose, and forehead.

"Please," I breathed onto his lips as he went to kiss me again.

Finally, he moved so that his warm, engorged tip was ever-so-slightly touching my tender lips.

While grinning wickedly, Pyter shifted his hips towards me, then back again, watching my reaction intently. He'd push further in each time, then retreat, leaving me aching.

His hands continued worshipping the rest of my body, maintaining my burning arousal and preparing me to take all of him. My squirming became relentless, my body begging for his every inch when he finally slid into the deepest regions of my core.

Our hips touched as we became one and our moans harmonized in the most beautiful, cosmic song of pleasure. Just like the zeroes and ones of numerology, we were the Void meeting creation.

For a moment, we were both still as I adjusted to the newfound, borderline-overwhelming feeling of being stretched to capacity.

Then his hips began their rhythm. Slow, steady, and deep.

I had become his place of worship, and he was rapt in prayer.

Nothing else had meaning in that moment of union. Nothing but pleasure and earthly delight.

My sighs and moans gave him all the information he needed as his tempo increased. No longer gentle and loving, our union had become animalistic. I clawed at his muscled back as he buried his face in my neck, kissing softly while our hips met with fevered passion.

"It's my turn," I whispered in his ear before licking it and then pushing him off, maneuvering so that he now lay on the blanket.

"I knew I'd coax your inner whore out of hiding," Pyter declared with hooded eyelids and a devilish smirk as he leaned back.

Kneeling before him, I grinned wickedly and bent down. In one swift lick, I tasted him from base to tip.

Pyter shot up, "None of that," he said breathlessly, "I need to feel you on me again. Please."

"So mote it be," I smiled cheekily, to which he did the same.

Straddling his midsection, I kissed his broad chest and muscled stomach while holding his throbbing erection firmly below my dripping opening. I took a deep, steadying breath as I admired the gorgeous male that laid under me. Then I sat down, feeling every inch fill me.

Gravity worked in my favor as new sensations began building deep within my core. My breathing and sounds of pleasure kept me tethered to this plane as my eyes rolled back and closed entirely.

I inhaled deeply, sensually drawing all my energy inward, and started grinding my hips into him. Quickening my pace as pleasure was building, Pyter sat up, deepening his manhood, grabbed my rear, and brought me closer to release.

The sensation deep within me had become a tidal wave, rearing to crash on my shores as his movement synced with mine.

"Pyter, I—" I attempted breathlessly to vocalize.

My eyelids blinked open, only to be met with spots of black in my vision as my climax conquered me. I moaned and partially screamed as an orgasm stimulated every nerve of my body. Tremors shot through my legs as my entire vessel buzzed in rapturous delight. Every inch of me felt pure bliss, and for a moment, between my fluttering eyelids, I swore the stars shone even brighter.

Still shaking, Pyter managed to stand while holding me by my rear, then moved to a nearby tree, never retreating from inside me.

My eyes opened widely as the rough bark met my naked back.

"I'm not done with you yet," he said huskily.

With my breathing still erratic and my body still trembling, Pyter dropped me further onto his shaft, with gravity now in his favor.

My voice had become a blend of moaning, whimpering, and screaming as he pushed me firmly against the bark while simultaneously establishing his rhythm.

Once again, his hips met mine, and he buried his face in the nape of my neck. His growls and grunts of pleasure were music to my ears as hedonism became my new way of life.

I heard his breathing shift and could feel his release nearing as another climax approached me. My hands, securely holding onto the back of his neck, moved his head out of my way. As he continued his thrusting, I licked from his collarbone up to his ear and nibbled it before wrapping my mouth around his lobe.

The soft, gentle action was enough to push him over the edge. His manhood throbbed inside me as his climax claimed him.

The feeling and sound of his release caused another toe-curling orgasm of my own as I howled in ecstasy. With the remainder of his strength, Pyter replaced my back on his blanket before collapsing beside me.

I had just begun catching my breath when the pack of coyotes sounded nearby, responding to my wild call.

A raspy laugh escaped my lips as euphoria settled into me.

"I hope I made your last night on Earth enjoyable." Pyter said with a tired, satisfied smile between breaths before wrapping his arms around me in a comforting embrace.

I looked at him and grinned, breathing a laugh of disbelief at the sultry vixen that had emerged from me that night. Evidently, my 'inner whore' that Pyter evoked had been yearning for deep release.

Now that she was satisfied, exhaustion melted into my body, easing my tense muscles. Turning so that I was facing the dwindling fire, my eyes closed, and undisturbed sleep finally came to me.

XXIV. Transformation

I awoke to the sound of heavy raindrops overhead and a loud squawk from a raven. The feel of blanket on my naked skin indicated that Pyter had covered me at some point in the night.

"*Kyanie... Wake up....*" He crooned lovingly from within my half-conscious state.

Coming to my senses, the events of last night swam through my mind, and I became increasingly aware of my lack of clothing.

Slowly I sat up, clutching my blanket tightly, and felt prickly heat on the side of my face I had been sleeping on. Quickly realizing my eye was also swollen shut, I touched my face and then felt the bumps of a familiar rash.

"*Shit!*" I blurted. "We must have come into contact with poison oak last night." Hanging my head in my hands, I felt shame creep up my backbone.

Bella, who was sitting beside Pyter by the morning campfire, approached me with loving, supportive licks.

"You still look beautiful to me, dear." Pyter looked at me, smiling weakly. "On the plus side, in the Ethereal Realm, all physical problems are left behind, so that won't be a problem once we ascend!"

"Why don't you have any rash?" I retorted.

"As an immortal, I'm unaffected by most things in the Logical Realm." He replied, shrugging.

I rolled my eyes at him and grabbed my best, warmest waterproof clothing from the coven. Slipping my under-layer on my torso, a burning sensation on my back caused me to pause. Jagged scratch marks from the tree now lined my spine and elicited soreness with each movement.

Though our night together was passionate and everything I had ached for recently, my mission would not be derailed.

I heaved a sigh.

All my Earthly ailments will be over soon.

It's time to start our final day of journeying.

~*~

After a filling breakfast of instant oats, peanut butter, and dried and fresh fruit, we began our perilous ascent up the mountainside.

It was utterly down-pouring the entire duration of our hike that day, the giant ancient trees doing hardly anything to prevent us from getting soaked to the bone.

The large, jagged boulders we occasionally had to climb up and over were drenched and slippery. Each footstep had me worrying that my old leather boots would give and send me rolling down the mountainside.

Not to mention the severe lack of sleep that undoubtedly took a toll on my mental and physical health. Every step upwards simultaneously sent fire down my legs and a throbbing up to my head.

Truly, I was miserable. So miserable I hardly spoke a word aloud, though my inner dialogue kept me occupied.

I can't believe he's been carrying Bella and hasn't complained about the extra weight. He was the one to question her coming in the first place, and now he has her secured to his back as if she were his child... I wonder if he has children. He must, right? He's thousands of years old, so he's got to have a lovechild somewhere on the planet....

I had been so consumed with my musings that I hadn't noticed Pyter stopped in front of me. Not until I collided with his back, losing my footing on the muddy ground.

My ankle rolled over a rock, irritating the injury I incurred during my downhill descent with Bella. Yelping in pain as I hit the ground, Pyter quickly set my canine down to offer me a hand up.

"Are you alright?"

"I'm fine. I just rolled my ankle," I replied while regaining my footing. "Why'd you stop?" Irritation exuded with each word.

"Because we're about to make the final ascension. We're reaching altitudes over six thousand feet in the air, so this rain might turn into sleet." He turned around to face me, and I noticed a rosiness on his cheeks and nose.

"Are you admiring how handsome I look in the forest?" He smirked after I had subconsciously smiled for precisely that reason.

"No." I quickly shook my head, refusing him the satisfaction. "Just smiling because we're almost done with this hike from hell," I said breathily, the thin air catching up to me.

"If you'd like to put on more layers, now's your chance." He said as he grabbed a granola bar from his pocket.

"Are you going to?"

"I wasn't planning on it." He shrugged. "I don't feel temperatures like mortals do."

How did I never notice how un-human he was?

"Gotcha," I replied before adding a flannel layer over my long sleeve and under my thin yet effective raincoat.

"After you, m'lady," Pyter prompted as he placed Bella back on his shoulders.

So we continued up… and up… and up until no peak loomed above, and clouds surrounded us. Though we were undoubtedly close to the top, I swore a massive shadow still towered over us.

Either we had hiked above the rain clouds, or it was indeed too cold and windy for it, but we were finally free of the precipitation. Though the bitter cold and thin air took some adjusting, being so close to the end, I no longer cared about the physical ailments plaguing me.

I was sore, damp, itchy, only able to see out one eye, limping slightly, and utterly chilled to my bones, but it would all be over soon— that was all that mattered.

Finally, we reached a point where the trail veered left and curved around the mountainside to arrive at the official summit. To the right, two massive boulders were split with another flat rock atop them: It appeared to be a stone gateway.

"Is this it? Are we here?" I excitedly asked, catching my breath and looking out from the mountainside. The view was an expansive array of green giants standing tall and proud on their land.

Thank you, ancient tree druids, for all you do to sustain life.

We had been hiking all day, and between the clouds overhead, the sun's descent began to peek through with golden brilliance.

"We are," Pyter stated, putting Bella down carefully by my side. "Would you like the honors of going first?" He dipped his head and motioned his hands towards the passage between rocks.

A smile beamed from inside my soul as I took Belladonna by the leash. Walking us slowly through, we came to a small, vibrant patch of moss with the most magnificent tree I had ever beheld. As I stood in front of it, I leaned to peer around behind— a waterfall cascaded magically from an unseen water source and created rainbows in the mist.

We had reached the Tree of Fate.

I dropped to my knees, eyes wide and my smile agape as I took in this ancient tree of magick. It appeared to be a yew, based on the curved warps in its trunk and far-reaching branches that squiggled outwards like octopus legs. At the base of its massively wide trunk, an opening so large I could stand inside beckoned me.

It was different from all other trees I had ever seen and, indeed, had energy radiating off it. For a split second here and there, I could also see an iridescent shimmer surrouncing it.

Unable to wait any longer, I tentatively stepped toward the Tree of Fate and placed my hand on the scaly bark. A wave of emotions flooded me, along with visions of a utopian world. Images flashed of trees as ancient and massive as this one covering the land. Animals, humans, and otherworldly creatures frolicked through rolling fields of multi-colored wildflowers and exotic flora.

"Welcome home...."

A deep, old voice sounded in my heac.

Tears immediately pricked the corner of my eyes.

Pyter had come up silently behind me, staying a respectful distance, leaving me to my moment with the Tree.

"Can ya feel the magical power emanatin' from it? It's intoxicatin', isn't it?" He breathed.

"I'm ready. I want to ascend." I said cefinitively, nodding.

"You're positive?"

I didn't tear my eyes away from the swirls in the bark, feeling such a resounding notion of coming home. "I am."

As I turned back to him, fully ready to center myself for ascension and cross over, I saw a sadness glaze over Pyter's eyes.

"Hey. Before we do this I want to tell you that...." I swallowed as Pyter looked at me with raised eyebrows. "That my gratitude and appreciation for you will never go away. If it wasn't for you... frankly, I have no idea what I would have done without you. You were the flint I needed to start a blazing fire in my soul, and if all goes accordingly, you are the reason I could be reunited with my family. For that... I have no words except thank you."

"You're welcome." Pyter smiled widely and took my hand, gently kissing its back. "It was my pleasure."

Deciding words weren't enough, I grabbed his face and kissed him. Slowly and passionately, our mouths met, and reality seemed to fade away. Who I was and who Pyter was no longer had significance; it was only the two of us as one for this moment in time.

When we broke away, he took my hand in his with a cocky smile on his charming face.

"Last chance to run away with me, Kyanie. I'll find a remote island where we can lounge on the beach, get boxes of books shipped to us, and enjoy some peace. Right here. In the Logical Realm." He planted a quick, loving kiss before whispering, "And I *definitely* wasn't kidding about wantin' to see ya in that barely there bikini."

I pulled back and then shook my head, laughing in disbelief.

"Are you joking? After all we've been through to get here? As wonderful as a tropical getaway sounds... No. I don't want that. I want to be floating on clouds, amongst the stars, with unicorns and fairies prancing around us in the Ethereal Realm." I reached up and touched his strong jaw, "Where I'm sure I can make this bikini dream of yours come true." My smile was near giddy as the words flowed out of me like the dreamy, shimmering waterfall nearby.

"Then so it shall be," Pyter said with a hint of melancholy before he kissed the back of my hand.

Together we sat inside the trunk, cross-legged with our knees touching. I closed my eyes and focused on my breath. Counting to six on my inhale and eight on my exhale, slowly but surely, my reeling mind quieted. I focused on my breath and the connection between myself, the icy breeze blowing on the mountainside, the magnificent trunk we were sitting in, and the Earth supporting us all. Then I began to gather all the love in my being into a concentrated, golden glowing ball in my chest.

I thought of my mother and how proud she would be to know I had made it. My father and brother and the possibility of being with them again soon. Rosemary and how badly I wanted to thank her for showing me 'The Original Religion' and changing my life. Adelaide and her freedom and safety for the remainder of her life in the Logical Realm. All the witches who taught me that magick doesn't just exist in the Ethereal— it's around and within me all the time, waiting for a clear intention to spark.

The warm, glowing energy concentrated in my chest slowly seeped into the rest of my body as I became one with the present moment. I continued breathing for several minutes, bathing in love, until my spirit was as pure as the snowcapped peak.

Feeling weightless, I opened my eyes, peeking from inside the tree trunk to see an unbelievable sunset. The once gray clouds were now puffs of celestial cotton candy while the sky was aglow with lilac purple, rich pink hues, and vibrant blood-orange. Combined with the altitude and us being almost entirely above the clouds, it did indeed feel as if we were going to the heavens.

We arose together and stood to the left of the Tree. Pyter's hand was in my right, and Bella's leash in my left while love and light oozed from every pore of my being.

An iridescent barrier shimmered before our eyes: the Veil.

I squeezed Pyter's hand, and he glanced down at me.

"Ready?" He asked.

"Ready." I nodded.

Smiling and taking one final, deep exhale, I stepped towards the waterfall, away from the Logical Realm.

My left foot, along with Bella, passed through the barrier with ease. A warm tingling spread throughout the parts of me that ascended, and I nearly laughed in response to the faint tickling sensation. The smell of milk and honey greeted my nostrils, and my smile widened further.

I'm ascending. Dad, Onyx, I'm coming....

Suddenly my right arm was yanked back as the Veil rejected Pyter, and time around us froze.

"Come on, push through." I pulled backward.

"You're too smart to genuinely believe that I'm comin' with ya," the corner of his mouth tugged upwards. "I'll never forget ya, dear Kyanie." He looked at me with fondness and ripped his hand free, causing me to fall back entirely and collide with a cold, foreign, shimmering ground.

I scrambled to my feet and smashed my fists into the iridescent barrier, screaming. "Pyter! Can you hear me?!"

As my vision adjusted, I lowered my hands and struggled to make sense of what I saw. Pyter, or Lacius, was in his true form, with massive antlers, glowing scarlet hair, goat legs, and large black wings.

Though the sight was jarring, watching him walk away with his antlered head hung low nearly brought tears to my eyes.

I had love for this... being. But my love for myself and my journey outweighed it tenfold.

Coming to terms with going our separate ways, I moved to turn away. At that moment, a massive, dark-winged beast briefly landed atop the stone gateway before snatching Pyter and disappearing below the clouds.

"PYTER!" My voice cracked along with my heart.

The pain of losing every man I had ever loved resurfaced. Suddenly I was brought back to the morning my mother sat me down to tell me my father and brother would not return from their trip that day or ever.

I was empty again; my chest sunken as I stared at the patch of moss surrounding the Tree of Fate. The familiar burn of tears brought me back into my body.

Pyter knew he wasn't coming with me. He knew he'd be leaving me, just like my father and brother did when they ascended instead of coming home to us. All of them did it... for me. It's all been for me, even if it hasn't felt that way.

Then it dawned on me— who I was and my purpose here— so I centered myself with three steady breaths. Consciously choosing to leave the pain from my past behind the other side of the Veil, I stood firm and tall, turning around to face a glittering rainbow bridge.

I took a single step, moving towards eternity and the fate that awaited me in the Ethereal Realm.

PART THREE:
SOLAR

XXV. Ascension

My first handful of steps on the rainbow bridge made me feel like I was learning to walk for the first time. Gravity was different in the Ethereal Realm, and I had to adjust to the floating sensation each time I lifted my foot off the glittering ground.

Belladonna, on the other hand, was gleeful— her paw was healed entirely, and she took to the weightless feeling with leaps and bounds. Every so often, she looked back at me, a broad smile on her muzzle and her tongue hanging happily.

My physical aches had subsided entirely. I could see out of both eyes; the poison oak reaction vanished without a trace.

In the distance, a colossal gate awaited us. As we approached it, I noted a familiar iridescent sheen, like the entire gate and surrounding fence were made of pearls. Millions of shining, incandescent pearls.

"Huh, I guess they weren't kidding about the 'pearly gates' thing...." I mumbled to Bella while we stood staring up at the seemingly impenetrable entrance.

Suddenly, the flapping of large, heavy wings tore me from my musings, and I turned around to see a broad-shouldered, dark-skinned man smiling softly at me as he landed.

His pure beauty stole the breath from my lungs. Swirling up his arms, neck and bald head were intricate golden tattoos that glinted in the light while massive white and brown speckled wings flanked his strong shoulders. Though he was only wearing a simple white linen shirt and olive-green cargo pants, his overall presence exuded that of a fierce, angelic warrior.

"Welcome, Kyanie Redferne." His deep voice rumbled, causing my heart to leap into my throat.

Still stunned by his appearance, I stammered, "Thank you…" then shook my head and chuckled nervously. "I mean…hi, er… who are you?"

Smooth Kya… really smooth….

He chuckled, revealing a mouthful of teeth so perfectly white they almost glowed. "My name is Calliel." He dipped his head down respectfully. "I am one of your Guardian Angels, here to help you transition into the Ethereal Realm."

Bella, who seemed to understand, jumped up on him excitedly, wagging her tail frenetically and looking at him adoringly.

Again, he chuckled softly and then bent down to her level. "I know. I'm excited to finally meet you too, Belladonna."

"You can communicate with her?" I gawked at them.

"Yes." He rose to his full height, well over a foot above me. "And soon you will too. Once I've finished giving you your Ethereal-orientation." Calliel flashed his dazzling smile, and I found myself smiling widely back at him.

"Okay, so… what now?" I peered back to the gates behind us, chewing my lip. "Is my family waiting? Do they know I'm here?"

Calliel nodded. "Yes, they know you've ascended. Though it's not just them that have been awaiting your arrival— the Cosmic Goddess is keen to speak with you."

My eyes widened. "The Goddess wants to speak with… me?"

He nodded again, smiling with amusement at my astonished expression. "To be fair, she meets with everyone that enters the Ethereal. Regardless, she's been waiting for you for quite some time."

"Are you taking me to meet with her now?" I faced the urge to fidget, though looking at the beautiful angel in front of me dissipated my nerves.

"Firstly, I'm going to show you to your home and give you a brief rundown of the Realm. The Cosmic Goddess is technically in her own Realm, the Aethers, with countless other Ascended Masters, above the one we're in now."

With every word he spoke, his rich brown eyes did not move from my own. As if he was peering into my very soul and could not look away— which was, unironically, how I felt.

"Then lead the way, angel. I don't know how much longer I can wait to see my family." I attempted to say it lightheartedly, but anxiety tinged my words with agitation.

"Patience is a virtue, you know," Calliel said with a smirk.

"A virtue I've never had," I replied, returning his expression.

"Maybe I'll teach you a thing or two about it then."

Concluding with another soft smile, Calliel led me to the pearly gates, stopping to check in with the winged creatures that were stoically guarding the entrance.

"Greetings. Kyanie Redferne has ascended with a pure heart and soul. Please allow us admittance inside." Calliel's deep voice commanded respect, and I stood a bit taller and prouder with him by my side.

The creatures, I now realized, were hippogriffs with large wings, eagle heads, and strong horse posteriors. They clacked and chittered in response.

Bella, surprisingly, did not bark or growl at the hybrid animals but instead seemed to respect and understand what they were saying.

"Thank you," Calliel answered with a solemn bow.

I mimicked his movement, and as soon as we were more than

an earshot away from the gates, I grabbed his muscled forearm, drawing his attention down to me.

"How can you understand what they were saying?"

"There is no barrier of language here. Once you've been fully accepted into the Realm by the Goddess, you too will be able to communicate and understand any language, human or otherwise, that you encounter."

The smile that spread across my mouth was uncontrollable.

"Wow…." I breathed in what Calliel had just said, along with the most spectacular civilization I had ever seen.

The rainbow bridge continued inside the gates, transforming into a major walkway where several smaller yet identical, shimmering roads branched off towards various shops and buildings.

Surrounding the infrastructure was a colorful, lush landscape with grass so green it glowed in the sunlight. Meanwhile, thriving, exotic flora brought vibrant hues to every corner and fostered a multitude of fauna, insect life, and elementals.

Not to mention all the other walks of life cheerfully going about their days in the Ethereal. There were many angels— winged humans who had ascended— as well as sparkling fairies and pixies fluttering in the air. Little gnomes and elves scurried on the ground, nymphs and druids blended in with the trees and flowers, and many other creatures I had never seen before strode around the bustling town. Some appeared outright alien, with large bulbous heads, blue to green skin, and large black eyes. In contrast, others were hybrids like the half-human, half-lion beings that walked around with their manes held high with pride.

I had indeed entered paradise. A paradise where beings of all shapes, sizes, and skin tones lived harmoniously with their environment. There was no longer an illusion of separation to divide, only love and peace ruled this existence.

Out of the corner of my eye, I could see Calliel watching me with a smile.

"What?" I asked, unable to stifle the joy that spread from deep in my soul.

"Nothing. I…" He shook his head. "I'm just happy you're finally here."

"You and me both," I replied before Bella barked, vocalizing that she, too, shared in our happiness.

"Would you like to see your accommodations?" Calliel asked, extending his hand out to me.

I nodded and held out my hand, nearly half the size of his, before he led me away from the epicenter of life in the Realm into a dense, enchanted forest.

As we walked, he explained to me how there was no leadership or hierarchy besides the Cosmic Goddess in the Realm. Everyone was equally as valued because there was an understanding of unity bonding all beings together. And because of that unity, there was hardly any conflict, let alone crime, to taint this paradise.

"Also," Calliel continued, holding back a branch to let me pass by. "Once you've been accepted, you can instantly manifest anything you could ever possibly want with your mind."

"So I really just think what I want into existence?" I asked joyfully, imagining the possibilities.

He nodded. "Mhm, anything you set your mind to."

We kept walking, passing by giant trees, along with actual giants and trolls, all draped with moss just like the ones I had seen on my journey to the Tree of Fate. Amongst the ancient, supernatural trees, where I should have been filled with amazement, a feeling of lack stirred in my midsection.

This past month all I thought of was ascending; now I've succeeded, so...why don't I feel satisfied? What am I missing?

~*~

"It's...perfect," I said as I beheld the quaint, Tudor-style cabin I could now call home.

It was deep within the magical forest and could only be accessed via a small wooden bridge over a flowing, glistening stream. Minus the abundance of magical creatures in the surrounding forest, my abode was well secluded from any other dwelling.

There was a small garden with differing shades of dahlias, my favorite flower, exclusively growing in it. It blossomed with life on the right side of the circular stone pathway that led up to the front door. Smoke billowed out of the stone chimney, which was set in the back center of the house.

I furrowed my brows at Calliel. "Is someone here?"

"No. Not that I'm aware of, at least. The Realm provides you with all your hopes and desires, delving deep into your subconscious to do so." He waved a hand at the cabin. "Apparently, it's your dream to live in a cottage alone in the woods." Calliel breathed a laugh out of his nose.

"I can't wait to see the inside," I said excitedly, patting my leg to draw Bella's attention, which was fixated on the magical life flying around us, back to me and our home.

Opening the front door with a beaming smile on my face, the first thing I saw was the roaring brick fireplace and two figures sitting beside it. Bella quickly ran inside to them, tail wagging excitedly.

"Welcome home, Honeybee." My father said warmly as he

turned to face me, his green eyes gazing into my heart. His hair was still the ragged mess of tawny brown that I fondly remembered resembled a bird's nest.

"Long time no see, kiddo," Onyx smirked beside him, his striking hazel eyes peeking out from his long, dark, hickory brown hair.

"Surprise," Calliel said with a weak smile as I shot him a look of pure disbelief.

At that moment, my knees gave out, shock making my muscles limp while a wave of emotions crashed onto me. I would have collapsed onto the hardwood floor had my angel not caught me on my way down.

Stabilizing me by gently, yet firmly, holding my shoulders, Calliel gave me a comforting squeeze. "I'll let you get settled and come back in the morning to bring you to the Goddess." He smiled softly at me and nodded respectfully to my family before departing.

Words seemed too difficult to form as I faced my father and brother for the first time in almost three years. I felt ecstatic, heart-wrenchingly sad, angry, and elated again.

"I… I missed you guys so much…so much that it broke me." I shook my head, tears welling up rapidly. "So much that it made me angry. Anger that ate away at who I was the entire time you were gone and…." I threw my hands up, "and now here you are." The two looked back at me with loving and slightly concerned eyes. "And honestly, I don't know how I feel." I ran my hands through my unruly hair. "All I know is how much I love you." I choked out, exhaling deeply before the tears fully erupted.

"My sweet little Honeybee, come here." My father cooed as he strode over to me with outstretched arms.

For I'm not sure how long, my father held me to his chest, and

I wept, and wept, and wept. Onyx had come up behind me, intermittently patting my frizzy hair and rubbing my back in slow, soothing circles.

"I'm so sorry, Kya. We wanted to tell you everything so badly, but—." My brother spoke gently.

"But you didn't," I interjected exasperatedly. "You just left mom and me to fend for ourselves." I wiped the tears away, feeling my lingering grief boil into something bitter.

They both looked down dejectedly.

"It was too dangerous…." My father began.

"Not too dangerous for both of you to pursue the truth." I spat, years' worth of resentment acidifying my words.

Onyx sighed. "You're right."

My father began to vigorously nod his head in agreement. "You're absolutely right."

"I know… I…" My mother's face popped into my head. "Goddess, what's going to happen to Mom?" Panic surged.

Onyx's mouth thinned. "We're not exactly sure at the moment…."

"What?!" I shouted. "How can you be so calm about this? We have to do something! We need to get her here!" I felt dizzy with anxiety, and a little bit of guilt, at the thought of my mother having to fend off Guardians alone.

"Please, Kyanie, calm down." My father soothed.

I instantly saw red.

"Don't you dare tell me to calm down. I went through absolute hell when you two vanished. I lost my sanity…." I shook my head angrily. "And now I'm a hypocrite for leaving behind someone I love more than anything. The woman who gave me life and kept me alive during my darkest days."

I felt nauseous and reached for the back of the padded fabric sofa, centered with the fireplace, to steady myself. Onyx came around and sat on the couch, looking at me with concerned, pleading eyes.

"Kya. Please." He reached for my hand, and I fought the urge to swat it away. "I know this is a lot to take in, but trust us— Mom is stronger and wiser than anyone gives her credit. She has a *plan*. She's the reason we left; she wanted to protect you because she always knew that you were destined for more than just a normal ascension."

My father came around and sat next to Onyx, reaching for my other hand. "It's true, Honeybee. Your mother taught me about the Old Ways in the first place: But it was a different time back then." He sighed. "It was not as fatally dangerous to stray from the Trine of Power's norms as it is now."

I snatched my hands back, crossing them over my heart.

"I think I need to be alone," I whispered, unable to look either of them in the eye. They both just watched me for a moment, then shared a look and arose from the sofa.

"Don't forget how much we love you, Kyanie," Onyx said as he walked towards the door.

"We watched over you every single day…." My father added, still gazing at me, longing for me to look back.

My emotions overwhelmed me. Unable to cipher through them, I needed solitude.

"I love you guys, too," I responded, slowly shutting the door behind them. "I just need some time to myself." Before they could get another word in, I closed and locked the door with a click.

For a handful of breaths, I stood with my back against the wooden entryway, taking in the space that was wholly, totally my own.

To the left of the fireplace was an aptly stocked kitchen, with slate-gray marble countertops and sea-foam green painted cabinets. A round wooden table was tucked into a small breakfast nook, complete with massive windows similar to the coven's dining area, towards the front of the house.

To the right of the fireplace and sitting room was a single closed door adjacent to the entryway and an archway leading to a flight of stairs in the back corner. Investigating the closed door, I passed by Bella, who had taken up a spot on the couch as soon as my father and brother evacuated their cushions.

Though still a jumbled mess of emotions, I was filled with childlike delight and wonder when I saw my bathroom. It was ocean-themed— with white tiles on the floor and inside the shower that resembled scales. A teal-colored, wave-patterned curtain wrapped around the shower and clawfoot tub, long and wide enough to fit two real-life mermaids. Pastel purple and green accented towels, which complemented the aquamarine walls, flanked a pearly white sink that ended in a tail on the ground. While in the corner, an iridescent clamshell lamp cast the room in a dreamy glow.

I put my hand on my heart and beamed. "This Realm wants me to live my childhood dream of being a mermaid."

Excitement filled my chest as I made my way up the stairs to my assumed bedroom. I was met with double doors, curved at the top to fit faultlessly in the arched door-frame, before opening them and beholding my new and improved den.

Immediately to my right was a plush bed for Bella and an orange knit rug, with a large swirl in the center, in front of it. Beside them sat the four-poster canopy bed of my dreams.

White gossamer fabric was tied with a bow to the wooden

posts at each corner, while a cloud-like comforter with an additional blanket, uncannily similar to the colorful hand-knit one made by my grandmother, draped over the bed.

My eyes burned as I saw my bed facing a stained glass window, nearly an exact replica of the one in my father's studio. The only difference was a cluster of four silhouettes sitting on a blanket surrounded by the hillside of wildflowers. Walking up to the window, I touched it tentatively, half convinced that my hand would pass through this illusion.

I can't believe this is real. This is my home now, and it's everything I could have ever wished for....

Turning to the end of the room, my jaw dropped as I noticed arguably the best part of my new living accommodation. Precisely parallel with the curved double doors was a pair of french-style glass doors that led out to a balcony filled with vining plants and flowers.

Heading toward it, I passed a large, ornate vanity on my left, with several framed pictures of all my loved ones.

Wasting no time opening the doors and stepping onto my stone balcony, I took in the spectacular view. In addition to the expansive surrounding forest, a shimmering waterfall cascaded down a majestic mountaintop in the distance.

Leaning against the stone rails, I took a deep breath in, savoring the smell of clean, fresh nature as if it had just rained.

Bella had found her way up the stairs and to my side, nudging me with her nose to indicate she was there. I gave her a half-smile and bent down to scratch behind her ears with my fingernails.

"My baby girl... Here we are, finally reunited with our family in the Ethereal Realm, in the forest cottage of my dreams. Yet... my joy and excitement only feel surface level."

Her mismatched eyes bore into mine.

"I agree. I need to sort out my inner health...."

Through her gaze, I knew what she was telling me I needed for an emotional reset.

~*~

Indulging my water-based-hedonism, I soaked in my magnificent clawfoot until the light disappeared and my stomach began booming with hunger.

Even while taking the most magical, blissful bath of my life, I still feel unsatisfied. Perhaps the only thing to quench this unending thirst is to end the Trine of Power's reign once and for all. I paused my inner monologue to dunk under the water once more before exiting. *Though as long as I keep searching, striving, and wanting for more, I'll never feel truly fulfilled.....*

I concluded my musings as the last bit of water drained. After drying myself off with a soft towel, I looked to the back of the door where a plush robe, identical to the one Mar had lent me, was waiting.

I could get used to this.

Rejoicing internally, I slipped the comforting garment around my shoulders, reveling that it was perfectly warmed by some unseen, cosmic energy. I slid on a pair of overly-fluffy slippers before meandering into the kitchen for a well-overdue meal.

After making grilled cheese and tomato soup and then feeding Bella an extravagant cut of steak, my warm, full belly beckoned me to rest. Eating my mother's and my favorite comfort meal brought me a sense of familiarity and security that subdued my nervous system.

I tied my still-damp hair into a loose braid, then went about my nighttime routine before heading to my room and slipping on a silk nightdress from my infinite wardrobe options.

With Bella already curled up and sleeping in her bed, I untied each ribbon and climbed into my new bed, encompassing myself in the sheer fabric. As tired as my body and eyelids were, I could not get comfortable, regardless of my heavily blanketed cocoon, because of the never-ending stream of thoughts.

Is Pyter dead? He must be… But wait, he's immortal, so maybe not? What was that creature, and what did it want with him? Who would he become if that creature killed his physical body? Will he have to find a new human body to inhabit? What would that entail… Agh, I don't even want to know….

I turned over, sighing in agitation.

I can't believe my mother was the driving force in the 'tragedy'… which I can hardly call a tragedy anymore; it's more of a… I don't know… a misunderstanding? No… That doesn't seem right….

I tossed and turned once more.

My mother… Please, Goddesses above and below, let her be okay….

As if the Goddesses heard my plea, my mind silenced, and my muscles sunk deeper into the soft mattress for a night of uninterrupted, nightmare-less sleep.

~*~

I initially awoke from a beam of sunlight hitting the edge of my bed, reflecting the bright white comforter onto my sleeping eyelids. Then a symphony of birds, more beautiful and enchanting than I had ever heard, caused me to peek open my eyes.

The morning sun shone through the balcony glass doors and the stained glass, casting my room in a kaleidoscope of colors. It amazed me that this dreamy morning scene was a product of my life's worst heartaches.

Where would I be now if I had just accepted my father and brother's deaths and moved on with my life? Would I be one of those complacent souls lost in the tides of the Trine of Power's ocean?

Suddenly, a series of brisk knocks on the front door broke me from my daze. Bella was up the second I stuck my foot out of the canopy, and after wrapping myself in my beloved plush robe, we headed down the stairs, stepping in sync.

I opened the door, expecting to see my brother or father or perhaps Calliel to bring me to the Goddess like he said. Instead, a woman of golden blonde hair, with two thin braids framing the sides of her breathtakingly-regal face, was smiling at me. Her heavenly blue eyes and a shimmering golden diadem with a glowing amber stone in the center left me awestruck.

"I'm so happy to finally meet you, Kyanie!" She promptly pulled me into her arms. "I'm Freyja, your Matron Goddess that's watched over you all your mortal life."

XXVI. Wisdom

"I've got to tell you, Kya...can I call you Kya?" I nodded. "You've been the talk of the Realm," Freyja said as she dripped a heaping spoonful of honey into her tea, stirring it in mindfully.

She was accompanied by two long-maned, orange-and-ivory striped cats who flanked the sides of her flowing white dress. They wore golden collars that matched the glinting accessories on her forehead, neck, and waist.

Sitting opposite the goddess and her felines in my quaint breakfast nook, I finished swallowing a delectable bite of the chocolate-covered waffles made by Freyja.

"Why?" I asked, wiping my mouth with a napkin. "I can't be the only person to ascend with the goal of lifting the Veil."

"You are." She raised her eyebrows, smiling coyly. "In fact, you've stirred up quite a controversy around here. Some beings are in full support of you, calling you brave and fearless for fighting for the freedom of all life on Earth. Others are more concerned with how life in the Ethereal will change if you succeed."

"I... I'm not trying to change life in the Ethereal Realm, though. I just want people on Earth to be aware of the truth." I replied with knit, worried eyebrows.

"I know that. Trust me, I do." Freyja took a long sip of tea. "But have you not thought about the consequences of your actions? I mean, Kya... come on... you would be altering the course of human history forever. There will be serious aftershocks that echo throughout all three Realms."

I hadn't really thought of much besides reuniting with my

father and brother, then having my revenge on the Trine of Power. Truthfully, the details of the latter, and the ripples that would be sent outwards from it, had not crossed my mind.

Pursing my lips, I worked on how to respond to the intimidatingly beautiful goddess. She sat across from me, eyeing me carefully while toying with the largest amber jewel on her thick golden necklace.

Two short, forceful knocks came from the door before Calliel tentatively poked his head in. Bella shot up from under my seat and greeted him gleefully in the doorway.

"Kyanie? Are you awake yet?" He asked, petting my canine's head just before he noticed us in the nook. As he stepped into the room, Calliel straightened to his full height and bowed.

"Goddess Freyja, I was unaware you were coming." His deep voice said respectfully. He tightly tucked his ivory wings in, attempting to shrink his enormous humanoid-bird-of-prey silhouette, which barely fit inside my quaint cottage.

Her face was as feline as her companions while she took in the sight of my Guardian Angel.

"I enjoy the element of surprise." She shrugged, smirking. "And my, oh my, what a lovely surprise you are."

"You are too kind." Calliel looked bashfully down at the ground. "Your reputation of beauty has preceded you."

"Well, you know...." She gracefully swatted a slender hand at him, "Being a goddess of love and war makes me pretty infamous." Freyja threw a long golden lock of hair over her shoulder.

"I thought Aphrodite was the goddess of love."

My inner voice said aloud unintentionally.

Freyja practically snarled.

She took a deep breath before drawing her attention to me. "There are a handful of goddesses of love, stemming from different geographic locations and cultures." Sipping her tea with irritated, raised eyebrows, she added. "Those pompous deities in the Greek pantheon have seeped so deeply into the human psyche, they're nearly as bad as the Solar Lord when it comes to the erasure of other belief systems." She huffed before concluding. "Though they're not, obviously, and I should include that Aphrodite is actually a close friend of mine— we understand each other and the throes of being constantly lusted after."

"I see," I said quietly, feeling small in her divine presence.

"So Kyanie…" Calliel cleared his throat and turned to me. "Are you ready to meet the Cosmic Goddess?" Though his question caused my heart to leap into my throat, seeing his gentle smile eased my growing nerves.

Before I could respond, Freyja rose from her chair and wrapped her falcon-feather cloak around her shoulders.

"Well, I suppose I should see myself out." She snapped her long fingers to her felines. "I'll see you both again soon."

She winked at Calliel as she floated by him out the door.

I watched in amazement from the breakfast nook as her small cats turned into mighty feline beasts, pulling Freyja and her ornate, golden chariot into the sky.

"So, Calliel, how do we get to the Aethers?" I asked, closing my front door behind us, leaving Bella safely in our new home, much to her dismay.

"You can call me Cal if you want." He replied, putting his hands on his hips as his wings breathed open in the fresh air.

I half-smiled. "Okay, Cal, how do we get to the Aethers?"

"How are you with flying?" Cal smirked.

My eyes widened. "Flying as in…."

"As in, I would hold you while I fly us up."

"You can't just us manifest there?" I asked.

He shook his head. "Not into the Aethers, no. There are timeless, impenetrable wards to protect the Goddess and the other Ascended Masters residing there."

I chewed the inside of my lip.

"And my other option would be?"

A single, hearty laugh erupted from Cal.

"I'm not sure if there is one."

He held out his hand while his enormous white speckled wings surrounded us effortlessly. "All you need to do is trust me."

I swallowed the biting remark about my deep, longstanding trust issues and took his hand.

He wrapped both of his arms firmly around my torso.

"Is this okay?" Cal asked.

I nodded, feeling my nerves take hold of my voice and render me mute. Cal's wings flapped without another word, causing a small tornado of dirt where we were standing, and we took to the skies.

Heights never bothered me, likely from my childhood spent hiding out in treetops pretending I was a bird. I'd had countless dreams of flying throughout my lifetime— my soul aching for the weightless feeling of air rushing beneath me, giving me the sensation of being utterly unstoppable and free.

Soaring through the air with Cal immediately put me into those dreamscapes, especially considering the views beneath us. I had never seen a landscape so vibrant and bursting with life while also being such a diverse, eclectic mix of ecosystems.

There were countless rolling green hills filled with blooming wildflowers and flittering pollinators initially surrounding the hustle-and-bustle of Ethereal life. In another region, there was a wet, colorful rainforest with waterfalls and white-tipped rivers winding between dense tropical trees. Across from it, where we had taken off, was an expansive temperate forest that housed infinite secrets of magick and cosmic mischief within its richly green flora. While encompassing all life in the Ethereal were white-sand beaches, with waves of shimmering starlight breaching the shores rather than ocean water.

As we continued flying north, up towards a looming, pearly castle on a cloud, a starkly-white mountain range with snowcapped peaks came into view.

"Is that why I couldn't make the journey to the Aethers on foot?" I shouted to Cal over the whooshing air.

"That and the million ice-covered steps you would have had to climb to reach it," Cal answered, leaning into my ear.

The proximity of his breath on my neck, alongside the thin, brisk air, gave me chills. Suddenly, the thick turtleneck sweater and fleece-lined pants I wore were no longer a sufficient barrier.

We neared the pearly structure, and I soon realized it was not just a single castle on a cloud but a settlement of grand buildings.

"Welcome to the Aethers," Cal said as we landed, and he released me from his hold, stretching his arms and wings happily.

The two of us were standing in a cobblestone town square surrounded by ornate pillars. Encompassing it all was a pristine, sparkling river resembling molten stars with merpeople swimming around playfully within the shimmering liquid.

Divine beings, most so beautiful that I could hardly look at them without gawking, strode around the center with palpable power exuding from them.

The buildings all seemed to be made from the same ivory marble stone, giving the feeling of unity and togetherness regardless of how vastly different all the deities were that resided there.

Facing the tallest structure, I noted a symbol on the ground of a large circle with two crescent moons on the sides. My recurring dream of three moons came into my consciousness, and I found myself mesmerized by the emblem.

"That's the mark of the Goddess," Cal said beside me, following my intent gaze to the ground.

I tilted my head to the side curiously.

"Come." Cal nudged me gently forward with an outstretched wing. "She's expecting you."

~*~

The Goddess's chambers were atop a hillside with pillars instead of walls, overlooking the Aethers like a watchful mother bird. Its stone floors, along with the few pieces of furniture, were encrusted with pearls and other shimmering jewels, portraying simple elegance rather than a gaudy display of wealth.

As we fully entered the throne room, I was surprised to see three females seated at the head.

The woman in the center was dark-skinned, with a shaved head, several silver bands going up her long neck. Her intricately patterned robes were bursting with rich, colorful hues.

To her left was a fair-skinned, auburn-haired female with crisp blue eyes. She wore a shamrock green dress, with gold embroidery flowing up the arms and chest, that hugged her shapely figure perfectly. Amazingly, a small flame flickered above her head, seeming to come out of her fire-colored hair.

315

Lastly, to the right, was a wrinkled, tan-skinned elder woman with long gray hair, wrapped in a knit sky-blue shawl draped over her simple, long black dress. Even more remarkable than the mystical flame above the fair-skinned woman were the eight spindly legs that grew from the elder's back.

"Welcome, Kyanie Redferne." They spoke in unison.

I bowed my head, unsure of the proper etiquette when addressing such powerful, divine beings.

"Hello," I said nervously, toying with the bottom of my sweater. "I thought I was only meeting one Goddess."

"We are three in one, the cyclicality of all life. We are one, just as all of life is one. Together we are the Cosmic Goddess." They replied.

"The mother." Said the one in the center.

"The maiden." Said the one on her left.

"And the crone." Said the elder.

"Though we can unify into one if that would make you more comfortable." They spoke in unison before joining hands and transforming into a massive, green goddess whose head narrowly avoided the tall ceilings.

I stared up at them with my jaw hanging. "Whichever you prefer is fine with me," I answered, smiling meekly. In an instant, they were separated once more, each sitting on their respective thrones.

"I am Songi. Mother of all humans and protector of the feminine." Spoke the goddess in the center with her chin high, regal confidence in her features, and strength oozing from her.

"I am Brigid. Maiden of creation and bestower of fertility." Said the flame-holding goddess on the left, smiling playfully.

"I am Kokyangwuti. Grandmother of life and weaver of fates." Croaked the spider-woman, eyeing me intensely.

316

I bowed once more. "I'm honored to meet you all."

"Likewise, Kyanie." Spoke Kokyangwuti.

"We have long awaited your arrival." Said Songi, smiling kindly. "Your fate has been of our utmost concern."

"Yeah, I've been on the edge of my throne watching your ascension journey." Smirked Brigid.

"Please tell us, what do you plan on doing now that you've ascended?" Asked Songi, putting her elbow on the side of her throne and resting her head on her hand.

"I…uh…" I stammered, regretting my lack of preparation for this. "I'm not sure, to be honest." I took a deep breath and willed my hands to stop fidgeting. "I'm most concerned with my mother on Earth at the moment."

"We can take you to our Globe Room so you check on her if you'd like." Said Brigid sweetly.

"But first, we'd like to learn more about your plan to dismantle the Veil." Came Kokyangwuti's wise, stern voice.

"Truthfully, I don't have a plan. I was hoping you guys could give me some direction… Or maybe some helpful information?" I smiled weakly once more.

"I see." Said Songi, raising her head up. "You may peruse the Library of Eternal Wisdom to search for the answers you seek. We are not allowed to conspire with you on these matters— it would break the Treaty that the Three Divine Rulers set in place."

"Treaty?" I questioned.

"When the Veil was created, the Solar Lord thought it was best to immortalize our agreement in a physical book he named the Treaty of Separation." Spoke the crone solemnly. "When we all signed it, we, the Goddesses, were condemning ourselves to be bound to our respective Realms and forbidden to meddle in the affairs on Earth."

"Where can I find it?"

Brigid scoffed. "You can't. The Solar Lord keeps it under his strict protection. His entire scope of power stems from that book so he rarely lets it out of his sight."

"Enough," Songi said firmly, holding up a slender hand. "I'm sorry, Kyanie, but we cannot discuss this further. You may seek the answers in our Library, but we cannot directly help you anymore."

"Then why did you ask me what my plan was if not to help me?" My inner voice slipped out.

Brigid raised her eyebrows. "To make sure you weren't going to do anything *stupid* that would jeopardize the fate of us and our Realm." She snapped.

My lips thinned, and my cheeks grew hot with embarrassment. "I'm sorry." I squeaked, bowing my head down.

"No need to be sorry, child," Kokyangwuti reassured me gently. "We just want you to exercise caution— the feat you are attempting is not for the faint of heart or weak of soul, so you should be fully aware of the dangers at hand."

A strong gust of wind bellowed through the throne room, and in the blink of an eye, a majestic dragon sat at the feet of the Cosmic Goddess. It was a mighty beast with a long, serpentine body covered in orange, white, and gold feathers, shimmering with the iridescence I had become accustomed to in this Realm. Its enormous feathered wings, if outstretched fully, could touch from one end of the room to the other.

"It is time for your initiation into the Ethereal Realm, Kyanie Redferne." Came Songi's firm yet gentle voice. "I now ask that your Guardian Angel, Calliel Oakford, step forward as a witness."

Truthfully, I had nearly forgotten he was there. He stood in a corner by the entryway and kept a respectful distance, until he joined me at my side at the Cosmic Goddess's orders.

He towered over me, his height, as well as his wingspan, casting me in a small shadow. Though I hardly knew who he was, simply being in his presence felt like a wave of peace and serenity crashing on the shores of my soul.

"Do you, Calliel Oakford, solemnly swear that Kyanie Redferne has ascended with pure heart and soul and thus deserves the Universal Flame and the power that comes with it?" Songi asked.

"I do." Came Cal's deep voice.

A chill, like a jolt of electricity, traveled up my back.

"Do you, Kyanie Redferne, solemnly swear that your intentions are pure and true, and you thus deserve the Universal Flame and the power that comes with it?" Asked Kokyangwuti's wise, old voice.

"I do," I responded, raising my chin.

"Then, by the power vested in us, the Cosmic Goddess, we accept you fully into the Ethereal Realm. Lumeriarcis may now bestow the light of oneness upon you— the Universal Flame." Said Brigid, the flame above her head growing as if an unseen force was fanning it.

Cal stepped off to the side as the dragon Lumeriarcis flapped its mighty wings and began flying in circles around me. The speed and force of the winged beast caused a vortex of air to swirl around me as I was enclosed in a coil of feathers and scales.

Fear of the unknown began to bubble in my gut, though I quickly banished it with unconditional love and trust.

I am love. I am love. I am love.

Lumeriarcis had successfully coiled its serpentine body around me. Leaving only an inch of room between myself and its feathered tail, its head perfectly aligned over mine.

As I looked up, locking in on its glowing yellow eyes, it opened its jaws and breathed golden-white flames onto me. I instinctively opened my mouth to scream, but no sound came out, and no burning pain plagued my body. Rather than the searing pain of blistering flesh, a warm, comforting sensation began at the base of my spine, traveling to the top of my head.

It felt like I was dying and being reborn in the same instance. Losing hold of who I was, transforming into cosmic nothingness, so that I could be renewed of universal oneness.

I was no longer Kyanie Redferne, the girl who had lost half her family and her mind; I was everything. I felt one-in-the-same as the Cosmic Goddess, as her dragon that enclosed me with heavenly winds, as the flowing starlit river that surrounded us in the Aethers.

Everything was one, and I was no exception anymore.

Lumeriarcis eventually uncoiled, flapping its feathered wings away from me and seating itself again at the base of the Goddess's throne.

I was filled with such ecstatic bliss I couldn't do anything but beam at the Cosmic Goddess, who was, in turn, smiling back at me lovingly. Standing in the throne room, I felt more myself than ever before. I stood taller and stronger— with the power of all creation supporting me.

"Welcome to the Ethereal Realm, Kyanie. We hope you use the gift of the Universal Flame bestowed upon you with the utmost respect." Spoke Songi.

"As a traditional welcoming gift, we allow the granting of a single wish," Kokyangwuti said with a knowing smile.

"What is it that you desire?" Asked Brigid, eyeing me curiously.

I sucked in my cheeks as I weighed my options.

All I truly wanted was for my mother to be with us in the Ethereal, for my family to be fully reunited. But, deep down, I knew that that would not be allowed, for no one can skip their unique ascension journey.

"I wish for my brother and father to accompany me to the Library of Eternal Wisdom," I answered confidently.

"Then so mote it be." They spoke in unison.

XXVII. Power

"I don't think you realize how big of a deal it is that the Cosmic Goddess granted you access to this place," Onyx said, staring up at the structure. The library looked more like a medieval castle, complete with a moat and drawstring bridge.

"It's true, Honeybee." Chimed my father. "Usually, they only allow Ascended Masters the privilege of learning, well, every secret and fantastical mystery known to man."

"Well, I'm honored," I replied.

Immediately after my wish, the two had been blipped into the throne room. As badly as I wanted to immediately apologize for being so curt, I didn't want to do so in front of Cal and the Cosmic Goddess.

"Before we go in, I wanted to, er, say something to you both." They turned to me with wondering eyes. "I wanted to say that I'm sorry for getting so upset the other night and I forgive you guys for leaving. I know you were endangered and didn't have much choice...." They waited intently for me to finish. "I just want you both to know that I forgive you and love you with my entire being," I concluded.

Jasper shook his head lovingly and took me in his arms.

"Thank you for your forgiveness." He said after kissing the top of my head and squeezing me tightly.

I had almost forgotten how therapeutic his hugs were.

"If I had known you would have gone so crazy, I would have left you hints. Like a little scavenger hunt from the beyond." Onyx smirked as he patted my shoulder.

I smiled back at them. Memories of my hollow, aching heart and the bitter root of anger in my gut drifted further away from my consciousness to be replaced with glowing, unconditional love.

~*~

Stepping inside the library felt like we were entering a place of worship. The impossibly tall glass ceiling illuminated an open floor plan showcasing all five floors of never-ending shelves stuffed with sacred and ancient texts. In the center of the impressive library was an iron spiral staircase with thin metal walkways leading off to each floor. As I beheld it, I fondly remembered the coven and prayed they were all safe and healthy.

We were immediately greeted by a female gnome whose short stature was hidden behind the large receptionist desk where she worked diligently. If not for her scarlet hair, I would have missed her entirely as her tan skin and simple brown dress blended in with the dimly lit background like a chameleon on tree bark.

Her pointed ears perked up at the sight of us humans tentatively entering this holy, priceless building.

"Welcome! My name is Qinlee; I am the head librarian here. Can I help you find something in particular?" Her chipper voice questioned.

I cleared my throat and stepped forward. "I was granted permission to come here by the Cosmic Goddess to research...er... the Veil and how the Solar Lord created it."

"Hmmm." Qinlee tapped her chin with a petite finger. "I recommend going to the top floor where we keep all our most ancient texts on the primordial order, the Old Ways, and the Realms." She hopped down off her chair and disappeared briefly behind the desk.

"Follow me." The gnome led us up the winding staircase. As we reached the top floor, I took in the expansive collection of all the knowledge in the universe surrounding us.

"Excuse me, miss." Onyx approached Qinlee with a charming smile. "Would this floor be the best to find books on how to obliterate the Guardians of the Order?"

Qinlee cocked her head at him before whistling loudly. Three more female gnomes with varying, brightly colored hair appeared instantaneously.

"Reywynn, could you please show this young human to the second floor and help him find texts on the Order?" Qinlee spoke to a violet-haired gnome wearing a black jumpsuit.

Reywynn nodded and took my brother's hand, fully extending her arm to reach it, before leading him back down the iron staircase.

"Alenia and Lillia, could you please help me pull books on the Three Divine Rulers and the Veil for these humans?" She asked the other two gnomes, one with bright blue hair and the other bubblegum pink, both wearing dreamy white dresses.

The blue-haired gnome, who I later learned was Alenia, quickly sorted through the shelves, pulling out books and tossing them onto a cart that magically followed behind her.

Instead of following suit, Lillia stuck beside me, waiting until we were a reasonable distance from the others before speaking.

"Is it true you are attempting to destroy the Veil and unmask the Solar Lord?" The pink-haired gnome whispered to me while maintaining focus on the shelves in front of her.

My eyes shot to her. "Where did you hear that?"

Lillia smirked. "It's all anyone can talk about around here." She pulled a book almost as large as herself off the shelf. "When you live in paradise, there isn't much gossip to entertain the masses." Her slate-gray eyes slid to me. "Especially not gossip involving a mortal girl altering the Realms."

"Is this a fool's mission?" I asked earnestly.

"If you believe it is." Lillia turned back to the shelved books. "Your intention is what matters more than anything else. If you believe you're changing this existence for the greater good, even if it's a fool's mission, so it shall be."

~*~

After collecting a stack of books nearly as tall as my lanky father, we stood around a simple wooden table, deciding what text to dive into first.

"I suppose I'll just start at the top," I said, reaching for the highest book before I sat down and started reading.

Qinlee, Alenia, and Lillia all burst out in a fit of laughter.

"Oh, how cute she still reads books like a human!" Alenia squeaked in between giggles.

I laughed in response. "What do you mean? You can't possibly be telling me that you have books about everything in the conceivable universe and beyond, but you don't actually read them?" Confusion contorted my face.

Still tittering softly, Qinlee took the book from my hand.

"In the Ethereal, manifesting a desired outcome happens instantaneously. Because of that, all you need to do to absorb the information in a book is open to the first page, focus your mind on believing you've read it, and then flip to the end."

The gnome demonstrated and then declared. "This text focuses solely on the Dark Goddess, Inanna, and the betrayal that cast her down into the Basal Realm where she was bound to spend eternity, overseeing the dead."

"I've been in this Realm for years, and I never knew…. To think of all the reading I could have gotten done." My father mused to himself.

I caught his eye, and we shared a beaming smile before diving into our towering pile of sacred texts.

~*~

My brain was actually throbbing by the time the natural light was fading from the glass ceiling. The 'truth' I had been scouring for was nonexistent— there is no singular truth besides the essence of life being love. That's it. Humans have complicated this truth and foolishly tried to understand everything logically when, in reality, we have no *idea* of the span of this existence and never will.

As I closed the final book from our pile, I took a deep breath and mentally recounted all the truths I had uncovered.

Before the Solar Lord created the Veil and separated the Realms, Earth looked just like the Ethereal Realm. Pristine nature, happy and healthy beings of all species, and an overly peaceful existence where harmony and love were at the forefront.

Humans worked in tune with the cycles of nature. Anything and everything they could possibly need was supplied by the Earth Mother, and they all coexisted peacefully regardless of skin tone or cultural background. No wars plagued the lands, and no Machine dominated existence.

There was an innate understanding of energy and how the intent belief in something creates an entity to match that energy— which is how the Solar Lord came to be. Man had become jealous of the Goddesses that ruled their existence and began to internalize their misogyny. This fueled the creation of a male God who would support their domination of the Earth Mother.

It didn't take long for sects of Solar Lord worshippers to transform into more Guardians of the Order. All violently forcing their beliefs on a multitude of indigenous civilizations across the world. The Old Ways were almost entirely erased in only a few thousand years. Through pillaging and burning libraries and pagan societies, the Guardians separated humans from their Earth-based beliefs and created a world based on power and greed.

Humans and magical beings no longer coincide harmoniously on their fantastical, living home planet, loving and supporting one another without caring about monetary gain.

No longer were humans aware that they were made of the same divine, magical energy as the gods and goddesses they prayed to. That we are, in fact, the Void experiencing itself through the lens of a human.

No longer was there an all-encompassing understanding of the non-dualistic nature of our reality. Everything was separated into black and white, right and wrong, and good and evil. The universal oneness humanity once knew was gone, along with the Goddesses and their respective dragon companions, known as the Dragons of Duality.

The Cosmic Goddess's dragon, Lumeriarcis, was a bringer of light and creativity to mankind, inspiring the greatest philosophers, artists, scientists, and infamous geniuses of history. While the Dark Goddess's companion, Maliandha, was a bringer of the dark subconscious and man's most primal drives— love, fear, war, sex, power, and desire.

Lumeriarcis represented the structure of cosmic creation, and Maliandha, the Void where we all came from and will return to someday. Once again, like the zeroes and ones of numerology taught to me by my father's old professor.

Before they were bound to the Basal and Ethereal Realms, the dragons swirled around each other, Lumeriarcis in the skies and

Maliandha in the oceans, as humanity evolved. A dance of light and darkness, feminine and masculine, action and emotion, creation and destruction. They were two separate beings, two opposing energies, yet one entity— together, they were everything.

After they were banished from the Logical Realm with their Goddesses, the entire cosmic order was disrupted, and the opposing feminine and masculine energies were thrown out of balance.

As man forgot about the Goddesses and how magical the Earth once was, it became easier for a new dominating, patriarchal system to take its place. In the Solar Lord's world, masculine energy entailed power and control, while feminine energy was powerless and weak. Female sexual freedom and autonomy were stripped away and replaced with pious servitude.

Those still wild, believing in the Old Ways, became the biggest threat to their growing Order. Hence the reason for the witch hunts and hundreds, if not thousands, of years of imperial colonization that set out to destroy any differing 'savage' beliefs. These atrocities strengthened the masses' faith in their Solar Lord and his oppressive Guardians, paving the way for the Machine to dominate and degrade.

It became clear to me what would have to happen for the Veil to be lifted: The Three Divine Rulers would need to be reunited to restore the cosmic balance of feminine and masculine energies. How exactly that would lead to the Veil being destroyed and the truth being set free, I still wasn't entirely sure.

All I knew was that knowledge indeed was power. As long as humanity remained unaware of the systematic manipulation ruling society with a not-so-subtle iron fist, then there was no hope of saving the Earth from the Trine of Power.

Sitting with my elbows on the table, hands holding up my

head, it felt like the universe's weight fell onto my shoulders. I glanced at my father, who was still combing the shelves, hoping to absorb as much wisdom as possible.

Onyx made his way back up to us, a forlorn look in his eyes indicating the discouraging information he found in his studies of the Guardians of the Order.

He pulled out the chair across from me.

"How's it going up here, little sis?" He asked, plopping down onto the wooden seat.

I heaved a sigh and looked at him.

"Oh, you know… just feeling the weight of all three Realms and their rulers on my back." I twisted my mouth dejectedly. "How about you?"

Onyx sputtered a breath. "Oh, you know… just feeling totally helpless in the face of misogynistic tyranny."

"Are you worried about Amber?"

He nodded solemnly. "Yes…and no. She's so fearless and strong. I know she can hold her own against that Guardian prick, but… I do worry."

"She'll be okay." I nodded back at him reassuringly. "We're going to get her back…" I reached for his hand and squeezed. "Don't worry too much."

Suddenly Qinlee appeared beside us, her three companions standing behind her.

"Excuse me. We're closing soon, so I'm afraid you'll have to wrap up your studies." Qinlee said politely.

"It's okay. We were finishing up anyway." I smiled slightly.

My father snapped shut his final book and joined us.

"Phew, does my brain feel heavy!" He put his hands on his

hips. "It's funny, you know, even after absorbing over a hundred sacred texts, I'm still so acutely aware that I'll never know everything…And that's perhaps some of the wisest knowledge I can pass on."

Onyx and I smiled at our father, neither wanting to disrupt the energy of happiness he was radiating for our bleak study finds.

As the group of gnomes dissipated to their library duties, Lillia quietly moved to my side.

"Psst. Kyanie." She tugged on the bottom of my sweater. "I want to help you. Let me be an ally for you. Or just a friend here in the Ethereal." The pink-haired gnome implored.

"Lillia…" I shook my head. "I don't want to endanger you…."

"Oh, please. I'm immortal and… to be truthful… I am not a gnome. I'm a shapeshifter." She smirked, gray eyes glinting with mischief. "I could be anything you need me to be."

I smiled, nodding my head side to side as I took in her offer.

"Just don't forget about me, okay? If you ever need me, all you need to do is think of me, and I'll be with you."

I dipped my head kindly. "Thank you, Lillia. I'll remember you. I promise."

With that, the little creature slunk into the growing shadows of the library, and I was left facing my brother and father.

They looked at me with wondering eyes.

"So what now?" Onyx asked, rising from his chair.

A grin spread across my face. "Well, there is something I learned about that I'm dying to explore."

~*~

My father, Onyx, and I stood on one of the numerous Ethereal beaches as the sun began to dip below the horizon and deep purple hues filled the sky.

"How exactly did you guys discover your spirit animals? And what are they? The text I absorbed on the subject said each person is different." I asked while taking a cross-legged position on the sand.

Onyx grinned widely, looking slightly smug in the dusk lighting. "Well, Amber and I discovered our animals together during our mushroom trip on the beach." He shrugged, still smiling. "We're both ravens."

A knowing stirred inside me.

I turned to my father. "And you?"

He sputtered a sigh. "It was so long ago... Before I even really knew what a 'spirit animal' was. I was on a hunting trip with my father and was tucked in a bush when a fox walked by me. I was camouflaged as best as possible, yet somehow it saw me, and we looked into each other's eyes and souls for a few breaths. At that moment, I realized we were not so different from the animals we share a home planet with, and the fox has stuck with me since."

"So... it was you two visiting me in the Logical Realm. At home, on the road, at the coven....." I spoke slowly.

They both nodded.

"Nearly every day," My father said as he gazed at me lovingly.

"A part of me always knew...." I smiled and then moved my head as if shaking away cobwebs from the past. "Anyway... I want to find my spirit animal. I learned a visualization technique to help— quieting my mind and recalling any memories I have of profound experiences with an animal. If that doesn't work, I just have to sit with a still mind and imagine myself encountering it."

I heaved a sigh.

"Good luck, kiddo. I bet it'll be as badass as you are." Onyx nudged my shoulder playfully.

I concentrated on my breath. Counting my inhales, counting my exhales, until finally, I felt still and calm, mind, body, and soul.

The first memory that came to mind was a summer I spent working as a camp counselor a few towns over.

We had taken the campers down to a beach, a quaint shore where the bay met land. Most of the children were either playing field games or hunting for crabs in the jagged rocks along the coast. I sat with five campers on a picnic blanket, facing the water and tanning myself while teaching them how to weave friendship bracelets.

"There's something in the water!" Shouted a boy.

"I think it's a sea turtle— we have to go see it; they're my favorite animal!" Yelled the boy's younger brother.

I looked at the water and saw something thrashing and moving toward the shore.

"Okay, but we need to be quiet so the other campers don't come and scare it away," I said in a hushed tone, smiling at the small group of children around me.

We snuck down to the shore and looked around to see where the unknown creature had washed up.

"I found it! It's a hawk!" Hollered the older boy.

"What?" I replied in disbelief as I went to where he was standing, facing a large rock that jutted out of the shallow water.

There in the water, getting tossed against the rock by the waves, was a red-tailed hawk.

I ordered the kids to stand back and get to the shore. This was a wild bird of prey with razor-sharp claws and beak— a major liability for a camp full of young children.

The helpless bird was trying to get onto the rock to dry off its non-waterproof wings, no doubt exhausted from swimming from Goddess-knows where. I saw no other option but to help the bird onto the stone. As gently as possible, while telling the hawk what I was doing and why, I lifted it up.

It perched and did not fly away.

By that point, word had gotten out, and the camp director was informed, leading to animal control being called.

Even as we waited for the hawk to be officially rescued, with me sitting on the rock next to it, no more than a foot away from the deadly predator, it did not move.

"It was likely attacked by a murder of crows over the water and fell in." Said the female animal control officer, who gently put the bird in a net. "It must have swum quite a distance to wind up here. Poor thing was so physically exhausted; that's why it let you get close."

As I watched the truck drive away, I felt deep down that there was more of a reason for this bird to cross my path. Of all the shores on the east coast, and of all the days and times for it to happen, that hawk fell into the ocean at precisely the right time for me to be the one to rescue it.

From that day on, hawks followed me. Whether through artwork and literature, or literal hawks that flew above me wherever I went, they were always close by. Its aerial nature and keenly perceptive vision were traits I admired each time the bird crossed my path.

"A red-tailed hawk," I said aloud to my father and brother, keeping my eyes closed.

Though it felt like something was missing, so I returned to focusing on my breath, once again quieting my mind.

Visuals of a dense forest with only one path forward came to me. Walking down the path, I found a cave at its end. Its mouth was wide and inviting, despite how dark and ominous it may have seemed on the surface.

Inside the cave was a small fire, casting the stone walls in a flickering, orange glow, while a massive black wolf slept beside it. As I approached the animal, its bright yellow eyes shot open, a slight snarl and low growl coming from its partially opened mouth.

Feeling no fear, I crouched down to its level, extending my hand so the predator could become accustomed to my scent. The way it hardly sniffed me before licking my palm indicated that the animal was already familiar to me.

I sat on the cave's dirt floor by the fire, with one hand burrowed into its coarse, black fur, mindfully scratching the scruff behind its head. Though it was just a visualization, it felt so real, and in that moment, I felt more safe and content than I had ever been.

A fire on one side of me and a dark beast on the other.

Here I truly saw it— my ferocious, fiery self.

"And a wolf. A black wolf." I breathed, opening my eyes.

Onyx raised his eyebrows. "Two spirit animals, huh? You couldn't decide?"

I smiled assuredly. "One of air, one of land. I didn't have to decide between the two because I am more than one. I am the Earth and the sky and everything in between."

My brother offered to fly me home with the enormous raven wings he could conjure with a single thought. I declined but requested that he teach me how to grow my wings and fly the next day. He agreed cheerily.

My father offered to walk me home, reminding me of the simple things from our past that brought us both such joy. I declined but invited him to join Bella and me for dinner the following evening. He accepted happily.

After I was left alone on the beach, I set my mind to focus on manifesting myself back to my home.

"Think what you want into existence."

I am home. I am home. I am home.

Opening my eyes, I faced my quaint wooden cottage. The lights were on inside, not as I had left them.

I recognized Freyja's golden chariot parked outside. Though now, there was also a majestic white horse and a darker-colored chariot with a great-horned owl sitting on the bow and two black horses flanking it. Additionally, a white and pink carriage with two enormous swans resting beside it and a slate-gray chariot bejeweled with iridescent stones were all situated outside my home.

Cracking open my front door, I was met with loud music and women chatting, some laughing. Freyja and the other unknown females were sitting around my breakfast nook with multiple bottles of glowing liquid and a platter of fruits and cheeses.

"Uh, hi," I cleared my throat as all the breathtakingly beautiful women looked at me, "what's going on?"

"I believe you humans call it a 'slumber party,'" answered Freyja with a smirk.

XXVIII. Divinity

"I hope you don't mind the surprise; I came here to check on Bella. She was so excited to have company that it inspired me to introduce you to some of my favorite beings in the Ethereal." Freyja said, beaming as I took my seat at the table.

Belladonna was beside me as soon as I returned home. Remembering that I had been officially accepted into this Realm, I talked to her, hoping she would speak back.

"Were you lonely, baby girl?"

"Yes, and so were you." She replied to me mentally before licking my dangling hand.

Freyja cleared her throat. "Kyanie, I'd like you to meet my closest friends in this Realm— Rhiannon, Athena, Artemis, and Aphrodite." She introduced her companions, pointing to each one as she said their names.

Whether intentionally or not, I squared my shoulders and lifted my chin.

"So lovely to meet you." Cooed Rhiannon, her golden hair and ivory-golden dress moving fluidly as she extended her hand from the chair next to mine. Incredibly, three doves perched on her shoulders and head, unmoving even as she delicately shook my hand.

"We've heard so much about you." Spoke Athena before dipping her head down in greeting, a simple golden circlet inlaid with rubies glowing from the embers of the roaring fire. The red liquid she swirled in her crystal chalice was only a shade darker than the velvet gown she donned.

"Most of it good," Aphrodite said, a half-smile tugging

mischievously at her rose-colored lips. Her pink chiffon dress dipped into a deep v-shape neckline and matched the bubbly rosé she was sipping flirtatiously.

I wasn't sure what to say in the presence of these powerful, divine females. Everything felt too human and mediocre.

"Most of it?" I cringed.

"Don't pay her any mind." Tutted Artemis, adjusting the crescent moon crown atop her silver-haired head. "She just likes to stir the pot." She wore a long, bell-sleeved dress beautifully woven with dark blue and black hues. Her gown nearly camouflaged with the night-scape seen through the window behind her, if not for the glinting silver jewelry adorning her neck and waist.

"What?" Protested Aphrodite. "I'm only telling the truth." She moved a lock of strawberry-blonde hair behind her ear and crossed her arms over her ample chest.

"She already knows the truth, so drop it," Athena replied sternly. "This is a celebration." She smiled warmly at me.

I smiled back. "What are we celebrating?"

"Your acceptance into the Ethereal, obviously!" Beamed Freyja, standing beside me and pouring me a glass of shimmering liquid.

"Oh, I don't really drink," I said to Freyja.

My night with Pyter at the bar has firmly closed that door shut.

"I know, dear. This is the Nectar of the Cosmos— it doesn't have any alcohol but will undoubtedly make you feel euphoric."

I took a small sip of the fizzing, sparkling drink and immediately tasted the sweet hints of berries and honey.

"When Freyja invited us all here, none of us could pass up the opportunity to meet and congratulate you." Declared Rhiannon

337

kindly. "You remind us of ourselves — fearless and unapologetically yourself. Despite all odds, you've grown into a strong, independent, divine female, just like us."

"I don't know how independent I can claim to be with my hundred or so lovers." Muttered Aphrodite into her chalice.

Artemis gave her a swift nudge with her elbow and snickered when she almost spilled her drink.

"*Wench*," Aphrodite said irritatingly before flashing a cheeky smile to Artemis.

I chuckled softly. "So, is this a common thing for people who Ascend? They get to have a slumber party with a bunch of goddesses?"

Freyja and Rhiannon both laughed heartily while the other three chuckled softly.

"No, silly girl, because you did not have a 'standard' ascension by any means… and I think you know that your soul's work is not done," Freyja replied, looking at me knowingly.

"Is this about the Veil?"

"It's so much more than the Veil." Interjected Rhiannon. "Truthfully, we enjoy being separated from the Logical Realm because, well, humans have become terrifying and destructive. Best to keep them all separated from us." She began toying with the end of one of her golden curls.

"This is about helping you restore the balance," Freyja spoke with a serious tone I had not yet heard from the Goddess.

"It wasn't just the Dark and Cosmic Goddesses that suffered when the Treaty of Separation was created," Athena said after taking a single bite of fruit and a quick sip.

"Humans stopped believing in the deities they once adored.

They stopped caring about anything outside the Solar Lord's norms because it was easier that way." Artemis spoke while collecting a pile of cheese slices and pieces of fruit atop her plate.

"We became a thing of the past," Athena added.

"What's so great about being a goddess if hardly anyone prays to you, ya know?" Chimed in Aphrodite.

"We want to help you." Artemis began after biting into a particularly juicy strawberry. "We want to see the Trine of Power, especially those bastard Guardians of the Order, suffer just as the collective feminine has. To feel the pain and helplessness they've inflicted these past four thousand years."

"Though it's not just the feminine— men are suffering too. They're lost, stumbling blindly through darkness inflicted by the hyper-masculine plague ravishing the Logical Realm. They suppress their emotions, their innate feminine energy connecting them to the Goddesses and the divine until it takes root as anger, resentment, and womb-envy." Athena interjected wisely.

"Ironically, their aggression is increasing while their testosterone drops. Feelings of inadequacy are channeled into rage and violent overcompensation. All because they lack the feminine, the softness that Goddesses allow us to have." Artemis added, her words and face perfectly stoic.

"Poor lost men." Aphrodite shrugged her mouth. "But imagine how it feels to go from having hundreds of thousands of people pray to you daily to a meager few hundred." She scoffed.

Artemis leaned back against the window and began aiming a grape at the goddess of love's voluminous hair.

"Wait, Arty, let me finish!" She held up her delicate hand.

The goddess of the hunt slowly lowered her ammunition.

"Without humanity praying to me, er us, our powers have been weakened. I can hardly make anyone fall in love anymore. Most of the prayers I receive go unanswered because I just don't have the energy to spare." Aphrodite's full lips pouted dejectedly.

"It's true," Athena said sadly. "Even in the face of humanity's seemingly never-ending wars, no one prays to goddesses of war... just the Solar Lord." Her lip curled.

As the other goddesses conversed, sharing their stories, I watched Artemis slip two pieces of cheese to the black and gray hunting dogs beneath the table.

"Why do they get table scraps, and I don't?" Bella asked as she stared at me with her sad, puppy dog eyes. I gave in almost immediately, dropping a block of cheddar on the floor for her to happily snack on.

"Anyway!" Rhiannon said cheerily, clapping her hands together. "Enough talk about war and politics; this is supposed to be a happy evening! For celebrating and basking in our feminine energy but more importantly to remind you...," she reached for my hand, "that you are just as divine as all of us."

"Thank you. Truly from the bottom of my heart. I didn't even realize how badly I needed to be surrounded by other women like this." I said, smiling, motioning to the women who encased me in a circle of powerful female energy.

"No need to thank us. Though it is appreciated." Said Freyja, who had taken the seat on my other side. "We're here to be young and wild with you for the evening." Her smile dazzled the fire-lit room.

"Let us toast," Athena said, raising her chalice and chin.

The other goddesses and I mimicked her.

"To the reclamation of the wild, divine feminine energy that stirs within all of us." The goddess of wisdom grinned.

"To the feminine!" Aphrodite announced as we clinked our glasses, her smile wide and genuine.

"*To the feminine!*" The goddesses and I repeated.

~*~

After we polished off several bottles of intoxicating beverages, gossiped, and shared raunchy stories, Aphrodite put on a record and insisted we have a dance party. My tight living space felt impossibly roomier as the goddesses and I twirled, swayed, and giggled amongst one another, relishing in beautiful, fluid energy.

Following our ecstatic dance circle, Artemis suggested we play a game called 'Womanhunt.' It was an outdoor version of hide and seek that had lost its enjoyment after multiple rounds of Artemis winning each time, hiding amongst the trees like a stealthy feline. By the last game, in which the goddess of the hunt volunteered to be the seeker, she found everyone in under five minutes and was finally declared the 'Ultimate Womanhunt Champion.'

We concluded our evening stargazing in a newly-manifested garden on the side of my cottage. The goddesses helped me design it so the center lined up with an opening in the trees, leaving a perfect view of the heavens above.

The night sky I had seen in the Logical Realm was nothing compared to the infinite stars and galaxies that dazzled into eternity before our eyes. Clusters of multicolored stars, some of which I learned were distant, foreign planets, sparkled with crystalline brilliance and left me speechless.

Additionally, encircling us on the ground and in the surrounding forest were bioluminescent mushrooms, magically glowing hues of green, blue and purple.

As the goddesses and I lay on a woven picnic blanket, I was so full of peace, joy, and childlike wonderment that I hardly knew how to handle it. Soaking in the starlight above us and relaxing to the sounds of the babbling stream stirred something in my soul. My spirit felt complete and vast, yet so light and breezy that it was as if I could float into the cosmos like a feather in the wind.

By the time we were all ready for bed, I could hardly keep my eyes open. Freyja had created a guest house adjacent to my cottage where the goddesses could sleep without cramming into my small living room.

Though I did not want to stop the festivities, I finally bid all the goddesses a good night and sleepily moseyed into my cozy home, alone.

~*~

The sound of chatter and clinking dishes awoke me the following day. It was shocking how refreshed I felt upon opening my eyes, even after having almost an entire bottle of the Nectar of the Cosmos to myself.

Since time wasn't linear in the Ethereal like in the Logical Realm, as I had learned in my studies and from the goddesses, I had no concept of how much I had slept. Regardless, I assumed it was late into the morning as Bella was no longer in my room and had likely given up on trying to wake me to feed her.

Reaching the bottom of the stairs, I first noticed Bella tucked in on the couch between Artemis's two dark hounds. Secondly, was Calliel surrounded by the goddesses in my breakfast nook. In front of them sat a box of partially eaten baked goods.

All the goddesses wore casual, loose-fitting clothes, a stark contrast to the ornate outfits they had on the previous night.

Bella, as well as Cal, perked up at the sight of me.

"Morning!" My angel said cheerily, his smile lighting me up internally. "I brought you some tea and pastries from my favorite bakery."

"Morning," I replied groggily with a smile before sliding into the empty chair across from him. "That's so sweet." I continued, eyeing the flaky, golden pastries. "Did you get anything for yourself?" I asked, picking up a fruit danish.

"Just a coffee. But Aphrodite took it when she answered the door and thanked me for the offering." He chuckled. "Apparently, she needs it more than I do."

"Well, what kind of freak prefers tea over coffee? No offense, Kya." Aphrodite bantered, her strawberry blonde hair bobbing in a messy knot atop her head. "But if you had coffee in the house, I would have just made that."

"Oh please…" Muttered Artemis. "You could have manifested an entire river of coffee if you wanted."

Aphrodite smiled cheekily. "Fine. You're right. I guess I couldn't pass up the offering from such a fine specimen."

"It wasn't an offering…." Cal mumbled.

I snickered, locking eyes with him.

"So, what brings you over?" I asked.

"Onyx told me he was giving you flying lessons this morning, and I wanted to help."

"You're friends with my brother?"

He nodded. "We ascended around the same time and found things in common."

"Such as?" I implored, my eyebrows raised.

The goddesses all sat sipping their teas and picking at their food, watching our interaction as if it were their morning entertainment.

"Music, art, and…er…watching over you." He looked at me nervously, reading my reaction.

Slight discomfort stirred in my gut.

How much did they see?

"Well! I suppose it's time we headed out." Rhiannon said from the other side of the table, arising from her chair.

"Right. Yes. So many important goddess duties we must attend to." Freyja added, smiling at me.

"Last night was so much fun." Aphrodite swatted my shoulder as she breezed past me. "We have to do this again."

"Take care, Kya." Artemis began as she stood up and then leaned into my ear. "Let me know if he tries any funny business." She whispered before throwing Cal a wary glance.

"Don't hesitate to reach out to us again," Athena said, holding my hand tenderly. "You have our full support, no matter what."

As all the females funneled out my front door, my cottage felt increasingly empty, lacking the exuberant life brought to me by the goddesses.

"Did you have a good night?" Asked Cal, smirking.

I breathed a laugh. "I did. Truthfully, I had more fun last night than I have in the last two years combined."

"Well, let's keep that momentum of fun going!" Onyx said from the doorway, smirking at me. "It's time to fly."

~*~

We had found an open, expansive field within walking distance of my cottage for me to practice flying.

Conjuring my wings with sheer mind-power proved no issue,

344

though adjusting to the new weight on my back certainly took some getting used to. The two spent the most time going through core-strengthening exercises until it felt like my abdomen would split.

"Can we at least try to get me in the air?" I asked between breaths after another excruciating round of crunches.

"If you feel like you're ready," Cal replied smoothly.

I stood up before swiftly conjuring my wings; the wings of a red-tailed hawk.

"Excellent! Now, stretch your wing muscles to get a feel for them on your back." Cal cheered as I followed his instruction.

"I'm impressed, little sis. It took me over a week before I could grow my wings to their full size and figure out my balance." Onyx said from his seated position in the grass before arising.

"Guess I'm just a quick learner," I nodded, smiling smugly at my older brother.

"Now, flap them a few times to stir up an air current," Onyx said as he demonstrated. "Then, when you feel the gust is strong enough, jump up and flap as forcefully as you can."

With that, my brother took to the skies.

Cal glanced at me. "You got that?"

"Mhm," I said, my face knit with concentration.

Standing hip-width apart, I drew all my strength into my core. With a few steadying breaths, I flapped my wings to create a small tornado around me. I jumped, though my feet fell back onto the ground. After a handful of tries and a single, loud scream of annoyance, I was finally airborne.

I had been waiting for that moment of airy freedom all my life. Dipping and swooping between clouds, it felt as if flying was something I was always made to do.

Fits of giggles and occasional tears of joy came from deep within me as the wind breathed beneath my wings.

I glanced at Cal, protectively flying beside me, as Onyx took the lead. His golden tattoos glinted in the sunlight as he flapped steadily. I had never seen my angel from this angle, seen his broad white speckled wings from the side as he flew.

A flash image hit me with such force it felt as if I had been struck by something in the sky.

Cal looked back at me; without thinking, I faltered my wing movement and began to free-fall. In a split second, I was wrapped in Cal's arms, his face warped with concern and confusion.

"What happ—." He began with worry in his voice, his wingbeats never faltering.

"You were the owl I saw in my dreams… and in the desert," I stated rather than asked.

He nodded, returning his gaze back to the sky ahead of him. "I told you I watched over you. To ensure your ascension."

"Well, I've ascended. So why are you still watching me?" I questioned, eyeing him intently.

Before answering, Cal landed us back in the take-off field.

"The truth is a long story for another time." Cal exhaled. "In short though, because my soul never wants to be separated from yours again. I've waited years for our paths to cross."

My heart thumped loudly in my chest, whether from the adrenaline or Cal's revelation, I wasn't sure.

Onyx landed beside us in a current of dust and pollen.

"It's nearing dinner time." He nodded toward the descending sun. "Want me to go pick up Dad?"

I chuckled to myself over the notion that he meant literally picking him up and flying him over to my cottage, then nodded in confirmation.

After Onyx took to the skies once more, I turned back to Cal. "Care to join us for a family dinner?"

His glowing smile warmed me from the inside.

In contrast to the night before, strong, divine masculine energy encompassed me that evening. I basked in the presence of my favorite men, feeling wholly, totally protected, and safe.

~*~

For the first time since being in the Ethereal, I dreamt. I was surrounded by darkness, with only a flicker of blue flame in the distance to stand out against the all-encompassing black.

"Come home, Kyanie! Come home!"

My mother's voice echoed within the darkness.

"Come home."

Her voice clanged through my head as I shot up in bed.

There was only one thing on my mind.

Hastily getting dressed in jeans and a loose-fitting flannel, I made sure to put the black protective stone given to me by the coven around my neck. Then, after grabbing an apple for the skies, I grew my wings and headed towards the Aethers.

I bowed, entering the throne room of the Cosmic Goddess. "May I use your Globe Room to check on my mother?" I asked with worry lacing each word.

"Of course." They replied in unison, bowing back at me.

"I'll show you there," Brigid said, arising from her throne. "There are a few things I must review before you use it."

The maiden-goddess led me down a hallway to the left where, at the very end, we entered through a pair of double doors. The Globe

Room was aptly named for the massive, realistic model of Earth taking up the entire area.

Roughly two dozen guardian angels filled in the empty space, all consumed with whatever, or whoever, they were watching over. I smiled at a trio of angels who were avidly monitoring down below with the enthusiasm of spectators at a sporting event.

Sadly, my grin quickly faded, and my heart grew heavy.

Unlike the globes I had encountered through my education in the Logical Realm, depicting a beautiful blue and green sphere, this model planet was shrouded in a gray fog.

From our view in the Aethers, it was obvious that the Earth was being demolished and devoured by the Machine. Numerous gargantuan factories, spread across multiple continents and nations, pumped out hot, gray smog while dumping sludge into the once-blue oceans. Mountains of trash— filled with single-use plastic and styrofoam, outdated electronic devices, fast fashion, bottles, cans, food wrappers, and more— overflowed from plentiful landfills.

No wonder everyone is so depressed and angry... Look at how we've treated our own Mother....

Shaking off my anger at the desecration of our Earth Mother, I asked Brigid how to check in on my hometown.

"Concentrate on where you're trying to go by focusing on the area on the globe. Then close your eyes and imagine your spirit animal there. When you open them, you should see what you're looking for."

After following her instructions and reopening my eyes, I faced the image of my childhood home's front door broken and ajar.

As my hawk-self entered my entirely ransacked home, a deep sense of dread began building over the discovery that my mother was nowhere to be found. I proceeded to survey my hometown— checking the botanical garden, the cafe, and Rosemary's house, all empty and lifeless.

Guilt and despair clawed at my midsection as I dropped to my knees and buried my face in my hands. My breathing hitched.

How can I possibly think of saving the Earth from the Guardians and the Machine if I can't even protect those I love most from them?

At that moment, I felt all hope drain from my heart.

Hope. Hope. Hope.

The word rang through my consciousness.

I've lost....

Slowly an all-knowing calmness spread. I arose, piecing together a puzzle I didn't even know I was conjoining to show me the bigger picture.

Unsure she could see what I could, I whipped my head to Brigid, the maiden-goddess looking back at me, concerned.

"How can I get to the Basal Realm?"

XXIX. Descension

After seriously warning me of the dangers and implications of traveling to the Basal Realm, the Cosmic Goddess reluctantly told me about the Well of Dreams.

"Now, accessing the Well can be done anywhere in the Ethereal." Songi began, rising from her throne. Brigid, at that moment, snapped her fingers, causing a spark and a small piece of paper to appear in her hand, which she then passed to Songi.

"Here is the rhyme to guide your visualization." I moved to unfold the note, though Songi's gentle hand stopped me. "When it comes time to descend, go to a place you won't be disturbed. Trace a circle on the ground and visualize a stone well in its place. Then follow the rhyme." She nodded solemnly.

"The only being who has successfully traveled between the Realms is Persephone. She spends half her year with us in the Aethers and the other half with her lover, Hades, in the Abyss." Kokyangwuti included informatively.

"Unfortunately, she cannot accompany you as she is there already until the Spring Equinox," Songi added.

"Can my family come with me?" I asked hopefully.

"If that would put you better at ease." Brigid chimed in. "Darkness can be harder to tackle alone. But they'll have to visualize and follow the rhyme individually, just as you will."

Kokyangwuti arose from her throne, holding a carved wooden staff to steady her as she approached. Her spider legs stretched and twitched behind her as she walked.

"You'll need to be prepared. Go home and fetch a relic from

the past— you must hold memories of life to enter the Gates." She croaked, guiding me out of the throne room. The crone-goddess wrapped a strong arm around my shoulders as we stood in the entryway, overlooking the bustling life in the Aethers.

"You've done excellent, child. Aligned with your soul's purpose in perfect, divine timing." Her mouth and eyes smiled.

I looked at her, her deep wrinkles showing thousands of years of existence and wisdom in a single expression.

"Now is the time for your journey into darkness. A journey that hardly any human takes upon themselves willingly." She held my shoulder with loving tenderness. "Though it may be difficult and uncomfortable, journeying into the darkness now will illuminate your path ahead."

Her blackish-brown eyes bore into my soul, and I knew she could see the entirety of my life woven before her eyes like a silken spiderweb. I had so many questions for her, the weaver of fates.

"Why me?" I finally asked.

Kokyangwuti smiled. "Why any of us? In truth, we are all just the Void painted in different pictures, hoping to live through every possible range of the human experience." She took a deep sigh before continuing. "But you… I believe you are the Void reaching its breaking point with humanity. You have taken on the burdens of the Earth into your own mortal hands because, well, it seemed no one else would." She squeezed my shoulder firmly before concluding. "You ask why, and yet I think you know. Because you *care*. You care about life other than your own. You hope and believe in a better future for the Earth; nowadays, that is the most courageous act of bravery I could think of."

~*~

I had yet to learn where Calliel lived. He never mentioned it nor invited me to see, so as I closed my eyes and willed myself to be where he was, I put blind trust in the cosmos.

As I opened them, a quaint cottage, no bigger than mine, was in front of me. It was a simple structure with white, paneled wood and dark brown trimming set on one of the numerous, pristine beaches.

A wind chime made from driftwood and seashells clinked and swayed in the misty star-ocean breeze. Bella sat dutifully by my side, looking up at me with wondering eyes.

Knock. Knock. Knock.

I took a step back from the blue wooden door.

Cal opened it, wearing a smock covered in paint, with various colors staining his hands. He smiled at me, clearly enthused.

"What a wonderful surprise." His smile widened as did his doorway while he motioned me in and then stooped down to greet Bella. "Welcome to my humble abode, ladies."

I stood in the doorway, peeking in on the bright, expansive windows and ongoing artworks in the background. "I would love to, but I'm actually leaving. Today." My lips thinned as I saw his expression drop.

"Leaving?" His eyebrows drew together sadly.

"I'm going to the Basal Realm. I believe my mother is there." I heaved a sigh. "I was wondering if you could take care of Bella while I'm gone? She really likes you, and I trust you…It'll be like part of me is still with you." I smiled weakly.

He grabbed my hand. "Let me come with you."

I shook my head. "I need to see my family back together."

"And I can't come with you all?" He asked.

Shaking my head again, I looked at him, and a fresh heartache began to form. "Please. Take care of Bella." I squeezed his hand as hard as I could. "I promise I'll come back to you guys."

"If this is what you want, I'll support you in any way I can." Cal nodded solemnly, his expression turning stoic.

I knelt before my canine and patted her lovingly, tears forming. "I'm sorry you can't come with me, baby girl. Really I am. I just can't risk something happening to you." I cooed to her, thoroughly scratching her ears.

"I'm tough! Let me come! Think of everything we've been through together. If I could survive falling down a hill with you, I can certainly survive descending! Please, please, please don't leave me." She licked the back of my hand feverishly, eyeing me imploringly.

Saying goodbye to her always hurt, but this was a new ache. The type of ache that I wasn't sure would have an end. Before I allowed myself to release the tears building, I arose and sighed sadly.

"Cal will take such good care of you. I know it. And I promise I'll come back for you." I kissed her head, scratching her ears a final time. "I love you so much, Belladonna, my baby girl and best friend." I couldn't elongate my pain any longer, so before either had the chance to protest, I handed Cal her leash and turned away.

Unfurling my wings, I gave him a final reassuring smile. I took to the skies, refusing to look back where I knew my canine was sadly watching my departure.

~*~

"To enter the Well of Dreams,
your soul must be stark
Fully prepared, it seems,
to face the Dark.
Your inner eye,
that can truly see,

353

must look through the lie,
of what could be.
Go deep within;
face your worst fear.
Your descent can then begin,
but only if you spare a tear."

I recited the rhyme for the third time to my brother and father.

"Okay, so first, we visualize the stone well here," my father began as he traced a circle in the dirt. "Then, we open our spirit up to our worst fear and release it through our tears." He put his hands on his hips, "Not too bad!"

Onyx sighed, "I think it'll be much easier said than done."

"Still, how *thrilling*!" My father said excitedly, fixing his glasses and bag strap as we all stood around the dirt circle. "We will be the only beings besides the Goddess Persephone who has traveled through all three Realms!"

His unyielding optimism was a trait of his I severely missed.

"Maybe wait until we've reached the Basal Realm before celebrating, Pops," Onyx replied, tightening his grip on his guitar case.

"You couldn't have picked a more travel-friendly relic from the past?" I asked, eyeing the bulky hardshell case.

He shrugged defensively. "You told me to bring a memory from life." He held up his guitar. "This instrument *was* my life."

I rolled my eyes and smirked lovingly at my brother.

My father breathed a laugh. "Oh, how I missed seeing you two together." He inhaled deeply, then placed his hands on his hips.

"Are you both ready?" We nodded.

"I'm more than ready," I added, raising my chin and ensuring there wasn't an ounce of hesitation in my voice. My recent experience with Shadowmere's attachment left me unafraid of any nightmare scenario my spirit dug up. Tears were also my second language, so I felt fully prepared to make my descent. Especially if that meant reuniting my family once and for all.

"Then let's not waste another moment!" My father exclaimed.

~*~

Since we were in the Ethereal, creating a reality only required concentrated thought. All we had to do was sit cross-legged around the hand-drawn circle that would soon become a stone well and internally say, *'Let my worst fear become a reality.'*

I began to quiet my mind, concentrating solely on my breathing. A breeze whispered through the trees surrounding us in the grassy field where I'd been taught how to fly.

Inhale. Exhale. Inhale. Exhale. Inhale. Exhale.

Let my worst fear become a reality.

Within my mind's eye, a hazy, low-lit image began forming.

I stood before a large wooden door reinforced with iron bolts.

Cold metal stung my hand as I turned the knob.

I was at the top of a curved stone stairwell, with the faintest glow from below illuminating the descent. The rancid smell of death assaulted my nostrils just before a blood-curdling scream met my ears, sending a shiver down my spine.

Though every fiber in my being anxiously protested, I made my way down. With each step, the air grew colder and damper, while the putrid smell only intensified.

Crack. Scream. Crack.

Sounds of torture echoed against the stone.

My heartbeat thrummed at the pace of a hummingbird's

wings as I reached the last step.

At first, all I saw was the enormous silhouette of a hooded figure, too preoccupied with their victim to notice me. As they shifted, their movements focused yet brutish, I caught a glimpse of the poor, screaming soul, and my blood turned cold.

My mother was bound to a chair; the rags she wore showcased the gauntness in her features and the open wounds on her bare skin. Her gray-speckled hair hung limply in front of her face.

Thwack. The hooded figure sounded his whip before lashing my mother's bare chest. *Crack.* Her screams of pain resounded in my chest and broke my beating heart as I stood on the outskirts of the damp space.

Suddenly, her eyes shot to me.

"How could you leave me?" She cried before the hooded figure stuffed her mouth with a dirty cloth.

I began screaming, begging them to stop and take me instead. All I heard in reply was diabolical laughter that seemed to sound from all corners of the dungeon. "Please! I'll do anything to save her… Please!" I shrieked.

"Anything?" A disembodied voice said evilly as tears stung the corners of my eyes. The hooded figure turned slowly to face me, showing only glowing red eyes and a mouth full of pointed teeth.

In a blink, my father and brother were also in the dungeon. Instead of being the focal point of torture, they were chained to the walls and looked as lifeless as the stone that encased us.

"What would you sacrifice to save them?"

The helplessness I felt seeing my family drained of their life force in the most brutal ways was too much for my heart to bear.

"You think you're going to save your family, to bring them back together,

when really you're bringing them to their doom." The voice hissed.

Anxiety pulsed through every nerve as fear overtook me.

'Must look through the lie of what could be....'

Fear is only real if I believe in it; if I feed into it.

"You're wrong." I held up my chin defiantly in the face of evil.

"Are you sure about that, little girl?" The voice mocked.

The hooded figure cracked its whip with resounding force before lashing all three of my family members. Each of their pain-filled screams sounded so real, so lifelike.

I covered my ears and yelled, "This is not the truth! This is not reality!" My eyes grew misty as several more lashings echoed in the small space. "I release my fear because fear is not real," I repeatedly whispered, my watery eyes shut tightly. *"Fear is not real. Only love. Only love. Only love...."*

A single tear broke free and fell softly down my face.

In that instant, I became aware of the soft grass beneath me and the tear that dripped down my chin into it. Opening my eyes, I saw my father and brother standing around the Well of Dreams.

"Are you okay, Honeybee?" My father immediately stooped down to check on me. His eyes were slightly red and puffy, indicating that he had successfully gone through the visualization.

I sniffled once and arose. "Mhm." Breathing in deeply to recenter my being, I stood over the seemingly bottomless stone well. "What did you guys see?" I asked, eyeing Onyx, who could hardly look at me without pain in his features.

My brother's lips thinned. "I saw the night Shadowmere attacked the coven. Only this time, he didn't just take Amber...," he paused, struggling for words. "He got you too." The anguish in his eyes was enough to tell me how the rest of this story went, "And there was nothing I could ever do to get you back."

I chewed my lip as the thought of Amber being Shadowmere's personal Handmaiden sunk in my heart. "We'll get her back, trust me," I assured him and myself. "What about you, Dad?"

A seriousness flashed in our father's eyes before he waved his hand dismissively, "No need to wallow in the fear." He gestured toward the Well of Dreams, "Shall we?"

Onyx and I shared a glance and nodded in unison.

Jasper swung his body over the stone so that he was sitting with his legs dangling over the black opening. He turned back to my brother and me, gave a thumbs up and a broad, goofy smile, then fell face forward into the dark.

Onyx copied our father's action and then reached his open hand out to me. "Together?" He asked with a tinge of loving remorse.

I nodded and grabbed his hand as we sat on the edge. Deep fear of the unknown crept in as I peered into the darkness we would be free-falling into. Nervousness buzzed through my veins, and as if he could sense my hesitation, my brother pushed off the stone encasing, pulling me down to the Basal Realm with him.

Though we did not stay conjoined for long. The descent was cold and disorienting, twisting and turning my body like I was the puppet of an unseen force.

At first, there was a crisp, bitter wind whipping around me.

Then, in the pitch darkness, my body collided with a frigid body of water. Panic struck me as the biting cold sensation seeped into my every nerve. I had no sense of up or down and was no longer in charge of my own body, while the force continued pulling me as if I was water being sucked down the drain of a bathtub.

There came a point I felt as if I would drown. I had been

submerged for so long I could no longer hold my breath and found myself on the verge of opening my mouth, relinquishing my life into the hands of fate.

Suddenly I broke free from the water, crashing through an invisible barrier onto a cave's cold, stone floor. Soaked and chilled to my core, I lay on the ground, catching my breath, and felt my impact injuries begin to burn and ache. The groaning and mumbling of my family caused me to stir.

"Is everyone okay?" I asked hoarsely as I sat up.

My father was also upright, rubbing his eyes with one hand and holding his glasses with the other. "I'm certainly in one piece." He grimaced as he arose from his seat on the ground.

Onyx was sprawled across his guitar case, unmoving.

"I can't tell if this broke my fall or made it worse." He muttered, still facedown, with his wet, dark hair hanging limply.

After wringing out the excess water from my mane, I pulled up my pant leg to see if the fall had broken skin which, miraculously, it did not. Then I stood up and went to Onyx, kicking him lightly to make him stir. He lifted his head to see my outstretched hand, offering to pull him to his feet, which he accepted.

"Kids! You've got to see this!" My father hollered, motioning us over to him enthusiastically.

We staggered over to where the cave widened and a spectacular collection of crystals glittered above our heads and flanked our sides. All around us were sparkling gems of rich purple and blue hues, some so dark, yet shiny, they looked like black glass.

"I want them all," Onyx said with wide eyes that reflected the shimmering geodes surrounding us.

"I second that." I breathed.

As enticing and magical as the crystal cave, a blue light emanating from a tunnel at the far end of it beckoned me. I slowly wandered toward the glow until I could make out the source of light— a massive iron gate with blue flames seeping from every inch of it.

Approaching it, with my family following behind, I saw a woman standing at the threshold, holding a wooden staff and wearing a dark cloak. Three tall, skinny black dogs surrounded her, guarding the iron gate. She was turned to the side, with only long white hair visible beneath her hooded figure.

"Hello. Is this the entrance to the Basal Realm?" I asked the woman. As I did, she turned to face us directly, and I was both amazed and perplexed by her appearance. One side of her face was that of an elderly woman, while the other side was perfectly youthful and supple.

"It is. Have you brought your Offering of Life in exchange for entering?" She held out a wrinkled, shriveled hand as she smiled a wicked, wisened smile.

I reached into my bag and pulled out the pocket knife.

Thanks, Rosemary. Hopefully, we will leave this memory of life behind forever. Good riddance, Bastards of the Order; your reign is coming to an end.

Placing the sheathed knife into the crone's hand, she winced slightly as she beheld the weapon.

"Guardians." She hissed under her breath.

"Are you Hecate?" My father interjected suddenly.

The woman lifted her gaze from the sheath she was examining to look deeply at him. "I am. How do you know of me, mortal man?"

"We've come from the Ethereal. The Cosmic Goddess granted us access to the Library of Eternal Wisdom, where I learned about you and the Dark Goddess." He replied respectfully.

Hecate raised her hooded head, looking at all of us peculiarly before landing her gaze on me. "You are Kyanie Redferne." She stated rather than asking before her mouth widened knowingly. "The Dark Goddess Inanna is waiting for you."

The flaming iron gates opened on cue as she waved for me to go in. Onyx was only a step behind me as I hesitantly entered through the blue-hot threshold.

"No." Hecate snapped, holding her staff out to prevent Onyx or my father from entering with me. "Only one at a time."

"We can't let her go into the Basal Realm alone." Pleaded my father, looking at her with a lifetime's worth of regret in his eyes. "Please let us go with her."

"No," Hecate repeated. "She will not be alone. I will be with her until she has been delivered to The Abyss"

"It's okay." I soothed from across the threshold. "I'll be okay," I assured them, but mostly myself, while standing beside the glowing blue flames that radiated cold rather than heat.

Hecate was soon next to me, leading me to a black wooden rowboat with a single blue lantern lighting the bow. One of her canines accompanied us, the other two staying at their guard posts.

"Welcome to the River of Memories." She croaked as she boarded, motioning for me to do the same. "Please keep your arms and legs inside as we travel."

I sat uncomfortably on the thin wooden bench in the center of the boat just as the crone untethered us and pushed us off from the cave's shore. Dark silence surrounded us, with only the occasional sound of lapping water to break up the void of cold nothingness.

At first, all I could make out were damp stone cave walls and stalactites dripping down from the ceiling. Though as we progressed, terrifying, eye-less faces began appearing in the shadows, then in the water around us. They coiled and spread throughout the darkness, watching us like vultures over a roadside carcass.

I felt a thousand eyes on me but could see none except those of Hecate's canine, who remained focused on me as we journeyed down the river. Nonetheless, my stomach began to turn with anxiety, and my heartbeat accelerated.

"You abandoned your dog, you selfish, heartless owner, just like you were abandoned by your family. You are so unlovable and emotional— that's why they left you. You are a burden just like your canine, who will be waiting for you for eternity." A chilling voice whispered in my ear, causing me to swat the air as if it were a mosquito attempting to suck my blood.

"Your mother is gone. Dead. Your brother and father will soon be as well. You've fallen right into Shadowmere's trap to finally capture you. To beat you down into submission until you've given up on all your hopes and dreams, relinquishing your soul to the Trine of Power." Another voice continued, causing panic to spread through me at the mention of Shadowmere.

I covered my ears and closed my eyes, willing the voices to leave me alone as fright trembled through my body.

It's not real. Fear isn't real.

"You are killing yourself for the sake of a human race that couldn't care less if you were alive or dead. You've lost all those who loved you, and for what? To be a hero? You are no hero. You are a sad, lost little girl who can't find her way in the darkness." A voice spat directly into my brain, utterly unaffected by the hands covering my ears.

I squeezed my eyes shut tighter and bit down on my lip.

"You are pathetic. You are worthless. You are nothing."

"ENOUGH!" I screamed, throwing my hands down to my side and opening my eyes to only see Hecate sitting calmly at the bow, watching the winding river in front of us.

She turned her head back, her youthful side primarily facing me. "Pay no mind to the voices, girl. They only wish to implant fear and doubt in you."

Suddenly we rounded a corner and, in an inlet on the river, sat a stone fortress with iron bars separating us from whatever was on the other side. As we floated by it, I noted cells filled with strange, demonic-looking creatures. They gnashed their crooked teeth at us, some growling and snarling, others more of a hissing shadow.

The fortress continued along the river for some time, with the beasts of darkness stalking us through their cells until we finally reached the end. A steep waterfall that dropped off into complete blackness signified the completion of our journey downriver.

However, the final cell held a man. His tan arms and legs were chained to a rock, and his long, unkempt black hair sat sadly atop his head. Most jarring about him was a brown thread that sealed his lips together. We looked at each other for a moment, his glossy eyes locking onto me with familiarity brewing in his gaze.

Hecate tethered our boat to a post directly outside the man's cell. "We've reached the end." She said definitively. "Now, step out and remove your clothing."

"What?" I balked back at her.

"If you wish to reach The Abyss and the Dark Goddess, you must arrive as she did— naked and vulnerable to the unknown," Hecate answered calmly.

I swallowed nervously and glanced at the male chained nearby, who watched me with a closed smile on his weathered face.

"There's no other way?" I asked meekly, stepping onto the rocky edge of the waterfall.

Hecate simply shook her head.

You are safe. Nothing can hurt you. You are safe.

I unbuttoned my flannel, exposing my breasts to the cold air before sliding my leggings and undergarments down to my ankles. Spreading my hair across my shoulders, then crossing my arms across my chest, I felt no less exposed.

"And the necklace," Hecate pointed to the protective black stone corded on my neck. I hesitated and looked at her pleadingly. She sighed. "Nothing is ever truly lost. It will come back to you in one form or another."

I nodded and added it to my mound of earthly possessions.

"Wonderful," Hecate said as she gathered the pile and then threw it over the drop-off. "Are you ready?" She smiled at me warmly, dissolving my anxiety.

"I believe so." I smiled back at her bravely.

Without another word, Hecate took a step closer to me and promptly pushed me off the edge into nothingness.

An initial scream escaped at the start of my final descent, though as the frigid air whipped at my face and hair, I could hardly open my mouth to make a sound. Tears stung my eyes as I continued falling down, down, and down into complete blackness until there was an opening of light.

Within seconds of seeing it, I fell through the opening and crashed into another body of cold water. Had these been normal circumstances, the impact alone would have killed me, but instead, an unseen force seemed to ease my landing.

When my head surfaced, gasping for air, I saw a lavish castle in front of me. Surrounding it were numerous torches of blue flame, while the castle's interior was lit with a comforting orange glow. The flickers of light reflected the crystal walls of the massive underground dwelling, continuing the spectacular cave we had initially fallen into.

I began swimming to the shore and felt vibrations from loud, rhythmic music and distant chatter and laughter. There were festivities underway in the castle.

Emerging naked, soaked, and freezing, I wrapped my arms around myself and started toward the only source of life I could see. Though I could hear voices, there were no other beings in sight.

Making my way up the torch-lit stairs, I took in the carvings within the stone railway. Stars of differing shapes and sizes, varying phases of the moon, and intricate swirls littered my ascent. Finally, I stood in front of the castle's enormous double doors, made of the same carved stone as the staircase, and hesitated before knocking.

The moment my knocks sounded, the party hushed. Footsteps drew closer, causing me to tighten my arms around my chest and the top of my thighs. The doors were ripped open, and a devastatingly-gorgeous woman beamed back at me. A woman whose violet eyes, jet-black hair, and eight-pointed star crown were all too familiar.

"Welcome, Kyanie!" Her voice was deep and sultry, though excitement tinged it with vibrato. "Don't be shy. Let me see you, my child." She swept her arms between us, her long-sleeved black velvet gown draping effortlessly off her curvy body. Against my inner wishes, I lowered my hands and willed myself to raise my chin as I stood before her in all my glory.

"*Absolutely divine.*" She whispered lovingly before handing me a purple satin robe to cover myself.

After tying the smooth ribbon around my waist and securing the robe, I was able to find my voice again. "You are the Dark Goddess, Inanna, aren't you?"

Her smile was dazzling and sinful. "Was it my breathtaking

beauty or crown that gave me away?"

"Both," I smirked back at her.

She guffawed, throwing her head back. "Correct answer. I knew I liked you." Inanna turned to the side, waving her hand inwards as an invitation. "Please. Come enjoy the festivities."

I stepped over the threshold. "What are you celebrating?" The entryway we stood in was decorated with golden candles, evergreen boughs, colorful paintings, and an ornate rug of deep purples and blues to cover the stone floor.

She threw her arms up dramatically. "The Longest Day of Darkness, of course!"

"You mean the winter solstice?" I asked, eyebrows knit.

Inanna rolled her eyes. "Yes, I believe that's what they call it in the Logical Realm."

"How is that... I only ascended four days ago. How did more than a month already go by?" I questioned.

She sighed as if the topic bored her. "Ah, yes. Time operates differently across the Realms. I believe roughly twelve days go by in the Logical Realm while only one passes here and in the Ethereal."

I quickly did the math in my head before responding. "So every two hours that pass in the other Realms is an entire day that goes by on Earth?"

"Mhm," Inanna responded, clearly disinterested. "Enough talk about numbers," she waved a long-nailed hand, "would you like to see your mother?"

XXX. Love

Inanna led me through her lavish castle, avoiding the party per my request, into the guest wing. As we ascended a third set of stairs, passing by another collection of beautiful paintings and alluring statues, the energy of the Dark Goddess's abode transfixed me.

"Your home is beautiful, Inanna. I had no idea this was what the Basal Realm was like." I said dreamily, staring at a painting of lilies floating on a moonlit river.

"Thank you." She turned to me, smiling proudly. "I think I've made the most of my damnation." She faced the lily painting, "And truthfully, I've worked quite hard to keep my underworld-haven one of the best-kept secrets in the Realms."

"Can you tell me what happened to you?" I questioned, yearning for the whole truth of life before the Veil— the Old Ways.

She sighed exasperatedly. "I'll save my story for after the festivities. I'd like to enjoy this evening without being reminded of the betrayal that cost me everything I loved."

Inanna turned away from the painting, leading us to a closed wooden door with a large iron handle. "I'll leave you to your family reunion." She touched my shoulder gently before gliding away.

Opening the door, my mother was sitting at an ornate, black vanity, styling her unruly locks. At that moment, everything I had been through and everything I was working towards no longer mattered.

She turned to me only a second before I collided with her back, pulling her into the most ferocious hug I could muster. Sobs of sheer solace and pure joy erupted from me as she wrapped her arms around my shoulders.

"My brave, warrior daughter." My mother kissed the side of my forehead. "I missed you so." She whispered as tears began falling from the warm brown eyes I had longed to see again.

"I thought… I lost you." Staggered breaths broke my words, "I thought I lost everything."

"My love, my child," she took my face in her strong, slender hands, *"Nothing is ever lost."* She wiped my tears, then winked.

There was so much I yearned to share— what I'd learned and how I'd grown since leaving our home. But, like the Dark Goddess, only the air of celebration filled my lungs that evening.

~*~

By the time my mother and I joined the party, both of us wearing black velvet gowns, my father and brother had separately arrived as naked and unsure as I had.

As soon as the two saw us descending the massive staircase into the entryway, I could practically see the relief sweep through them. I fought the urge to laugh, returning a genuine grin instead. My mother, always thinking ahead and preparing, left her chambers with towels and dark velvet clothes for my father and brother. That simple action ensured the most time possible together as a family.

The party was jovial and lively, a shocking atmosphere for the underworld I had feared entering. We danced and socialized, my father being especially keen to introduce himself to Persephone now that they 'had so much in common.'

Onyx stood by him for that introduction, eager to meet and converse with Hades, a close consort of the Dark Goddess. My brother had hoped to gain his under-worldly advice on his *'Revenge & Rescue'* plan to get Amber back and assassinate Shadowmere in the process.

Being surrounded by an eclectic mix of dark beings— mostly

human souls that passed on without ascending, as well as deities of the dead— was surprisingly enlightening. A refreshing blend of gentle understanding yet blunt truthfulness fueled each interaction.

Perhaps facing death and our shadow is the most peaceful path to tread.

My mother and I found ourselves in deep conversation with Kali, a blue-skinned goddess with four arms and a long, forked tongue. Despite her unnerving appearance and stories of death, destruction, and change, her presence brought comfort in a way only a mother's energy could.

"Nothing dies; it simply changes form. Change is the only constant. Remember that." Kali concluded as she bid us farewell for the evening. "Oh, and if you ever need help tearing the Guardians of the Order apart, one by one, you know who to call upon. I'd love to have their heads." She smiled, bearing pointed, razor-sharp teeth.

Finally, the festivities began to wind down, and only a handful of guests lingered in the magnificent hall.

"You know what I just realized?" I asked as we sat by a roaring fireplace, which produced heat, unlike the blue flames we had encountered outside the castle's walls.

"What?" My brother replied, shifting in his cushioned seat and moving his plate piled high with food to a nearby table.

"Tomorrow will be Christmas in the Logical Realm," I replied, a joy from deep inside spread into a wide smile.

"This calls for a toast!" My father said jubilantly, one hand wrapped firmly around my mother's and the other holding up his crystal chalice. "To family, blessings, and love."

"To love." Onyx and I said in unison, looking at each other as if we would never risk our family being separated again.

~*~

The morning after the solstice celebration, my family and I gathered, once again, around the roaring fireplace in the grand hall of Inanna's castle. I had told her in the evening that I wanted to surprise them with a traditional Christmas tree. She corrected me, calling it a Yule tree, and happily obliged.

The four of us sat around the tree, decorated with dried oranges, cranberries, pinecones, and magically lit blue-flame candles. We had no presents to open, no way to get swept up in consumerism, and it made no difference: Our greatest gift was granted the previous night.

Inanna also provided a decadent Yule breakfast for us, complete with eggs, seasoned potatoes, crispy bacon, buttery toast, and fluffy pancakes. Despite being in the underworld, the food was some of the best I had ever eaten.

"Man, am I glad I'm not with you in spirit-animal form anymore." Onyx knocked our shoulders together before we sat down with full plates.

"I definitely felt you with me, even if I didn't know it was you cawing obnoxiously." I smiled, nudging him back.

Reaching across the coffee table to where my parents were sitting in identical armchairs, hands locked on one another, I pat my father's crossed knee.

"I felt you there too." I leaned back, smirking knowingly. "And thanks for darting behind that garden shed."

My father beamed back at me. "You've always been so keenly perceptive, Honeybee. Nothing gets by you." He winked.

"She must have inherited that from me." My mother added playfully, throwing Jasper a cheeky grin.

"Absolutely." My father kissed the back of her hand, looking at her like she was the finest masterpiece he'd ever seen.

"Do you guys remember the Christmas that we almost burnt the house down?" Onyx asked, chuckling softly.

I threw my head back as a guffaw erupted from me. "How could any of us forget our stockings catching on fire from a game of charades gone terribly wrong?"

Both of my parents joined in our laughter.

"As terrifying as it was to watch you throw your little sister off your back and into the mantle, I had to appreciate your commitment to literally becoming a 'catapult.'" My mother said, shaking her head while smiling fondly.

We were then interrupted by clicking heels on stone floors as two terrifyingly gorgeous women entered. Both had long, dark hair, though one had cobalt highlights resembling a raven's coat, while the other had tints of burgundy. The blue-tinted one wore what looked like battle armor sewed into a corset, with tight black pants showing off incredibly muscular legs. The other donned a flowing chiffon gown cinched at the waist and exceptionally revealing around her chest.

"Sorry to intrude." Purred the burgundy-haired woman.

"The Dark Goddess is requesting your presence, Kyanie." Spoke the raven-esque female formally.

"She'd like a chat with you." Nodded her companion.

"Can it wait?" I asked hesitantly, looking around at my family, wanting nothing more than to spend the day with them.

Shocked by my response, the blue-haired one quickly retorted. "We would not have come to retrieve you if it could."

~*~

After I begrudgingly bid my family farewell, the two females led me down several flights of stairs and through numerous winding passageways. Only the occasional flicker of a wall-mounted candle lit the way, giving me the feeling that I was deep within a dark, complex labyrinth.

They promptly introduced themselves to me— Morrigan was the warrior-like female with cobalt hair, and Lilith was her sultry counterpart.

"How did you two meet the Dark Goddess?" I asked curiously, watching their backs as we walked.

Morrigan turned around to answer me. "She summoned us."

"How?" I tilted my head.

"She prayed to the Void." Interjected Lilith, looking over her shoulder at me. "After being betrayed and condemned to the Basal Realm, she prayed and performed rituals incessantly to receive companionship." She turned forward as she continued. "Inanna is the greatest sorceress in creation— it was through her pain that she created magick and witchcraft."

"So she's like the Mother of Witches?" I questioned.

"More like the Goddess of Goddesses." Morrigan corrected before we rounded another corner and faced a set of wooden doors inlaid with sparkling crystal gems.

I could feel the ancient power exuding behind the closed doors and subconsciously fixed my purple satin set of clothes provided by Inanna herself.

"Don't be nervous," Lilith whispered, smiling, as she opened the way into the Dark Goddess's throne room.

I was immediately awe-struck by the dazzling chamber. The walls and floors were made of a glassy black stone with millions of tiny, sparkling gems embedded within, creating an ambiance like the night sky. Additionally, thousands of candles and large clusters of crystals embellished the space, decorating the path to the Dark Goddess herself, who was a sight to behold.

Draped over her throne in a relaxed position, Inanna wore a rich purple gown made of the same fine velvet as her gown the evening before. Though this time, her sleeves were sheer and showcased arms of intricate, swirling black ink. Her dress hung fluidly as her legs kicked playfully over the side of her jewel-encrusted throne.

Despite her casual nature, two massive, black lionesses flanked the Goddess and immediately put me on alert as they warily watched me enter her chambers.

Swinging her legs around so that she was sitting forward, she exuberantly opened her arms to me. "Welcome!" She snapped her fingers, and a chair encrusted with gems appeared in front of her. "Please, come sit. I've been *dying* to speak with you."

Her smile was so enchanting that the nerves of approaching her, along with her deadly felines, dissipated. Morrigan and Lilith strode behind me as I took my seat, then they respectively sat on the outer sides of Inanna and her lionesses.

"Dark Goddess—." I began.

"Please, call me Inanna. Or even Ina if you'd like."

"Okay, Ina," I said, smiling timidly, "I wanted to thank you for bringing my mother here and keeping her safe." I bowed in gratitude. "I don't know what I would have done if something had happened."

She smiled graciously. "You are very welcome. Though, in the spirit of being transparent, I must tell you my ulterior motives for your descension."

I furrowed my brows. "Oh?"

Ina sighed dramatically. "Besides saving the woman who prayed to me daily and created you, my Child of Destiny, I desperately needed to get you here. To tell you the whole truth." She raised her eyebrows, a sly smile on her lips. "About everything."

I swallowed, my heartbeat picking up as I could feel the truth bubbling to the surface, about to break free.

"Please. Please tell me. Tell me everything." I replied breathlessly, finding myself on the edge of my gem-covered seat.

"I suppose I should start at my beginning." She threw a jet-black lock of hair over her tan shoulder and straightened her silver, star-crown. "As you already know, I was the first sentient being on Earth for thousands of years until my sister Goddess was created." She sighed ruefully. "The thousands of years the two of us lived on Earth together were the best years of my existence— even after humans were created. They were excellent stewards of our Earth Mother, living their lives in tune with her wishes, not forcibly dominating their will over her."

Inanna paused, rapping her nails on her armrest.

"Unfortunately, humans' creation of the Solar Lord was their ultimate demise. They began seeking outside of themselves for the answers that lay dormant within their very DNA, within their *souls*. They put all their faith and power into their Solar Lord, ignoring that they were made of the same divine matter as their ruler. This, in turn, created a power-hungry system of control."

She huffed, vexation building in her features.

"There came the point when the Solar Lord realized that the mere existence of us Goddesses threatened his growing world-order— so he hatched his plan to create the Treaty of Separation." She barred her teeth. "You may wonder why I would ever agree to condemn myself to a life of darkness."

I nodded, enraptured by her story.

"In short, I didn't." Her face turned feral, anger growing in her violet eyes. "You see, I had quite a few lovers during my time on Earth. One, in particular, truly captured my heart. We were so similar — hedonistic and wild— I felt I had finally met my male equal. He treated me like the Goddess I am, worshipping me, telling me sweet nothings at all times of day, and doing nearly anything I asked of him."

She closed her eyes as if she could see her old lover standing before her. "It was because of him that I chose to go to the Basal Realm. Because he claimed we could rule the Realm together, in ecstasy and love away from the affairs of humans and the Solar Lord, I gave up my existence above ground." She opened her eyes, the anger now a roaring fire in her gaze. "Leaving behind my sister was the hardest thing I ever did." Ina shook her head slowly. "But I did it for the one I loved."

"Where is he now?" I implored.

She tutted. "I'll get to that. Don't you worry." Taking a long, deep breath, she continued. "He claimed he could not make the initial descent with me because he was not as divine as I. So I descended to the pit of the Earth, completely and utterly alone." She breathed a laugh. "Not to mention that I was stripped of all my Earthly matters, rendering me as naked and vulnerable as a newborn.

"For days, I sat in the center of what is now my beautiful castle, praying to the Void. I begged for answers, clarity, anything really to help me escape the darkness that swallowed me whole." She smiled proudly. "Luckily, my magick stayed with me on my descent, and I soon honed my skills to become the greatest sorceress in existence. A High Priestess of the Void— alchemizing my pain into a creation I could call my own." Ina glanced at the two females, watching and listening with love and adoration in their eyes.

"In time, through my rituals, I learned the truth about my old lover. He was not a simple, kind mortal man as I thought he was. He was an ancient being, nearly as old as my sister Goddess and I, that could shape-shift at will. The Solar Lord, aware of my… promiscuous ways, called upon him to make me fall in love. To attempt to distract and weaken me."

Ina smiled threateningly. "What the Solar Lord didn't realize was that love did not weaken me. Not even the devastating heartache that came after I found out the truth. No. That pain *transformed* me; it gave me purpose." She leaned back, looking aloof yet still emitting immense power. "When I learned of my betrayal and felt that I was reduced to nothing, I found that I was *everything*."

She held up her arms, showcasing the elaborate throne room we sat in. "I decided to make the best of my new reality. As the ruler of the underworld, I separated spirits of the dead from demons and forces of evil that prowled these caverns. In addition to my pets, I allow some dark beings access to the Logical Realm to stir up trouble and release my pent-up anger at the Solar Lord. This leaves me to my underground haven of peace in the Abyss amongst the innocent dead who did not attain ascension."

Ina then motioned to the two other females. "Once I had established my Realm, I continued praying to the Void to bring me the sisterhood I grieved and ached for." She smiled warmly. "Through their help, I captured my old lover in the Logical Realm, then condemned and bound him to rot in a jail cell amongst the demons for eternity." Rolling her eyes, she added. "Unfortunately, however, that little trickster had already made a deal with the Solar Lord. So, though I had captured his physical body, his soul was still free to roam the

Earth and take the form of any weak or lost soul he could find."

I blinked back at her, my jaw open, as I began to see.

"Pyter, er,… Lacius is the lover that betrayed you?" I stuttered in disbelief.

"Technically, yes." She grimaced, shrugging. "Though he was *much* more handsome when I loved him." A cheeky smile spread across her lips, "And my gods, was he a hell of a lover."

My cheeks flushed.

Does she know of my last night on Earth…?

"I don't understand… Lacius is supposed to be this being of evil, so why did he help me?"

"Ah, you see, he's not truly evil. As terrible as he was for betraying me and working with the Solar Lord, his intentions are never to bring upon evil. Though that is who he has been painted to be by the Trine of Power, he is, at his deepest core, a bringer of chaos — entropy embodied." She spoke matter-of-factly.

"I believe he's grown bored of watching the Earth Mother be destroyed for the sake of greed that's as temporary and fleeting as human life itself. He yearns to see humanity as wild and free-willed as possible, which is hard to accomplish under the strict, anti-pleasure reign of the Trine of Power. Lacius helped you because he wants the Treaty destroyed and humanity freed just as badly as you."

"How can it be destroyed, though?" I questioned, leaning toward her eagerly.

"I'm glad you asked." Ina grinned slyly. "This is exactly where you come in, my child." She snapped her fingers, and immediately a dark-scaled, winged beast flew into the chambers, in front of the black lionesses, before comfortably settling at the feet of the Dark Goddess.

I smiled, realizing the dragon before me.

377

"I believe you met my beautiful pet's brother in the Aethers," Ina said like a proud mother. Stroking the dark blue and purple scales shimmering with iridescence in the light, she continued. "This is Maliandha."

Whereas Lumeriarcis was feathered, with pointed, angular features, Maliandha was smooth with wispy tendrils flowing along its head and down its back.

I bowed my head respectfully to the mighty dragon.

"You have a rare opportunity here, Kyanie, to be touched not only by the Universal Flame but also the Eternal Fire." Ina continued, still stroking her beast lovingly. "I have waited thousands of years for a being brave enough to stand up to tyranny. Someone to fight for the freedom of all beings in this multi-realm existence." She tore her eyes away from Maliandha to look at me fiercely.

"To free me," she breathed.

"Wait, but won't you helping me lift the Veil violate the Treaty of Separation?"

Ina leaned forward, her inner fire glinting in her eyes.

"Fuck the Treaty."

I smirked, raising my chin. "What do you need from me?"

"Everything." Ina laughed drily. "And we don't have much time to spare."

The Dark Goddess nodded to her female companions. "I've gone over my plan extensively with Morrigan and Lilith, and they will tell you more details as we prepare to act."

"Why don't we have much time?" I asked, concerned.

"In the fine print of the Treaty of Separation, the Solar Lord, cunning and all-knowing as he is, included a vital clause. By the end of the year 2030, if humanity had complacently accepted the state of their reality, the Treaty would become immortalized and irreversible."

My heart dropped as I realized the mathematical implications of what she had just said. "So I essentially have twelve hours to destroy the Treaty, or everything I've fought for has been in vain?" I asked, feeling stunned and overwhelmed.

Ina smiled weakly. "Yes."

I breathed a nervous laugh. "Oh, so no pressure or anything."

The Dark Goddess chuckled in response. "Don't worry, though. I've prepared for this. All I need from you right now is a way to reach my sister in the Aethers."

Feeling the divine pressure of the situation, I was about to ask how, when a particular pink-haired gnome popped into my head then immediately appeared in front of us.

"Yes!" Lillia exclaimed excitedly. "I knew you would think of me when the time was right." She looked around enthusiastically at the crystal-embellished throne room. "Wow, there isn't a single book in the Library that talks about how lovely it is down here." Seeming to remember where she was and whom she was standing before, the gnome straightened, then bowed. "Dark Goddess Inanna."

Ina looked at the pink-haired creature with amusement in her eyes. "Could you deliver a letter to my sister for me?"

Lillia raised her petite chin and saluted the Dark Goddess seriously. "It would be my honor."

XXXI. *Loss*

"You're leaving?" My father asked despairingly.

"I have to." I nodded solemnly.

"Can't the Dark Goddess do her own bidding and let you enjoy this well-deserved time with your family?" Added Onyx with annoyance and concern dancing on his face.

I shook my head. "That's the problem— time is fleeting, and we're running out of it before there's nothing to be done to save humanity from the Trine of Power and its Treaty of Separation."

"*Screw* humanity!" Onyx exclaimed, standing up from the cushioned couch I had left him on. "Humans are selfish and greedy. They would never, and *have* never, done anything to end the Trine's tyranny, so why are you risking your life to show them the truth?"

I sighed and ran my fingers through my hair. "It's not just the humans I'm trying to free. It's the Earth Mother. It's the Dark Goddess. It's the suppressed and oppressed energy of the divine feminine that needs me to care. That needs *someone* to care about anything other than themselves or their immediate loved ones." I replied gravely.

My mother stood calmly and walked over to where I was standing, taking me in her arms without saying a word. "I love you so much, my child." When she pulled away, she had tears running down her face. "My grandmother would tell my sisters and me tales about a fearless human who would someday face the Trine of Power with unflinching courage and bring back the Old Ways." She squeezed my shoulders. "Part of me always believed that Child of Destiny was you, my brave-hearted Kyanie."

"Child of Destiny or not," my father joined us, wrapping both of us in a comforting hug in his long, lanky arms. "From the Aethers to the Abyss, our love has never faltered for you, Honeybee. It only grows stronger with each breath we take." He took a step back, his green eyes looking into mine deeply.

I smiled sadly at my parents. "Hey, how did you visit me in the mirror? I thought you could only visit the Logical Realm in spirit-animal form."

"Truthfully, I just willed it so — I really, *really*, willed it so." My father breathed a laugh through his nose, gazing at me with adoration. "Have I ever told you why I call you my Honeybee?"

I shook my head, smiling at him curiously.

"Honeybees bring such sweetness to life. They cultivate honey from nature, working tirelessly to do so. Yet they also sting— dying as martyrs for their queen. Their collective mindset always strives for the good of the hive." My father grabbed my hand gently, "When you were a baby, you were the sweetest little girl. Though soon into infancy, I saw your ability to sting in the face of injustice… even if that just involved your brother stealing your toys." He chuckled, concluding, "You've always cared about the good of the hive, the good of our family, above all else."

'Dying as martyrs…for the good of the hive'….

My smile turned weak as the gravity of my fate loomed over me. I tightened my arms around my family, holding them closely as my heart grew heavy.

"You guys are just letting her leave?" Onyx asked dejectedly, throwing his hands up in irritation from an arm's length away.

"What's the saying… *'If you love something, set it free.'*" My mother whispered lovingly into my hair, hugging me tightly.

I looked out from my parents' embrace to see Onyx slump his shoulders in defeat. "I guess you're right." He sighed and glumly joined our family hug. "I thought saying goodbye to you once was hard, but this...." He shook his head, burying it deeper into our entwined arms. "You better come out of this alive, or I'll be pissed."

I laughed nervously. "I'll do my best to stay alive for you, big brother." Giving one last squeeze to my family, I concluded. "For all of you."

Suddenly my heart ached as my inner voice philosophized. *Love and heartache are two sides of the same force. You cannot love deeply without accepting that pain will accompany it. Love, and the grief we feel over the loss of it, is ugly; it's painful and dark,* Ina's face came to the forefront of my mind, *but that's also what makes it beautiful.*

~*~

Morrigan and Lilith had come to retrieve me shortly after my final embrace with my family, emphasizing the time pertinence of the situation. They denied my request to go to my chambers to freshen up before we left, saying that the Dark Goddess had attire for me to wear that would be more appropriate.

"So, what exactly is the plan?" I asked as the two hurriedly walked me to Inanna's personal chambers.

"We will travel on Maliandha to the Spring of Soul atop Mount Hope. There we will call forth all Divine Rulers," Morrigan informed me.

"Spring of Soul?" I replied confusedly.

I just traversed Mount Hope… how did I miss a Spring of Soul?

"The Spring of Soul is what feeds the River of Memories. It runs from the Aethers to the Abyss, encompassing the Veil and Basal Realm." Explained Morrigan without glancing back.

Lilith turned back to me. "You see," she began as if sharing hot gossip, "when Inanna went down into the Basal Realm, the Cosmic Goddess was so stricken by grief she sat atop Mount Hope and sobbed. She cried for weeks, eventually creating a cascading river that flowed into her sister's domain. That way, at least she could be with her in some form." She half-smiled before we all abruptly stopped outside a partially-opened door.

"Ina?" Morrigan asked, knocking on the door lightly and causing it to open further. In an instant, Ina ripped open the door, standing in dark, flattering armor resembling her dragon's scales.

"Are we ready, my bad bitches?" She asked, cheekily smiling.

"Could we make one quick stop on the way?" I asked after Ina handed me a set of armor identical to hers.

The Dark Goddess shrugged. "I suppose."

~*~

Standing outside the prisoner's cell, with the Dark Goddess and her companions impatiently waiting a respectful distance away, I struggled to find all the words I wanted to say.

"Pyter?"

The prisoner lifted his head to look at me, and I knew it was indeed him in his gaze.

In the blink of an eye, the dark-haired, mortal Lacius transformed into a ragged-looking Pyter. He was still chained and bound, though his mouth was not sewn shut as the prisoner's was.

"Why are you here?" I questioned, eyeing him cautiously.

"Turns out, the Solar Lord has a bit of a vengeful side. After I failed to stop you a second time, our bargain was broken, and my soul was turned over to the Basal Realm for all eternity." He spoke with an aloofness that severely contrasted his captured state.

With my arms crossed over my chest, I pressed on.

"So how does your whole shape-shifting thing work?"

"Oh, how I've missed your inquisitive brain...." He smirked smugly upon seeing my irritated expression. "I can shift into any life-form that I have personally slain."

My heart leapt into my throat.

I can't believe I went on a cross-country road trip with an immortal, shape-shifting serial killer... and I actually caught feelings for them....

"So if you are truly Lacius, then who is Pyter?"

He sighed amusedly, "Do you get frequent headaches from spending so much time inside your brain, dissecting everything and everyone around you?"

I puckered my lips in irritation. "Do you get frequent mouth sores from all the shit that comes out of your lips?"

Lacius cracked a crooked smile and laughed drily. "Years ago, while traveling through the Irish countryside, I needed a new mortal host when I came across a wealthy, corrupt tavern owner with a bit of a gambling problem." His devious expression widened, "It's impossible for me to turn down a game of cards, especially when the poor lad wagered his body and soul for the chance of obtaining a never-emptying gold pouch."

He shrugged before continuing, "I tried warning him, sharing my wisdom that life is the roll of the dice, anticipating the result only for them to fly off the table, never to be seen again. Nonetheless, he was blinded by avarice...." He trailed off. "To answer your question, dear Kyanie, Pyter was a venal, dishonest human who unsuccessfully attempted to cheat to beat me." He leaned forward as far as his chains would allow. "His greed and arrogance led to his demise. Wouldn't you agree he brought it upon himself?"

"Perhaps, but what of Inanna, whose demise was entirely unprovoked and unwarranted?"

He took in my wary stare and then glanced at the Dark Goddess. "So you've learned my secret."

I chewed my inner lip and raised my chin.

"I have. Are you sorry for it?"

Lacius appeared amused. "Does it matter?"

Irritated by his response, I snapped back. "Yes. It does. Have you ever even apologized to The Dark Goddess?"

I saw Inanna perk her head up from the corner of my eye.

"She never gave me a chance! How was I supposed to say anything with a mouth sewn shut?" His weak defense was met with unyielding un-amusement.

He sighed and shook his head.

"Then do it. Now." I said sharply, crossing my arms.

"Inanna. My Goddess. My Empress of Love." Lacius began theatrically.

"Cut the fluff!" She yelled back, still standing a reasonable distance away from his cell.

"Fine." He put up his chained hands. "I'm sorry."

"Sorry for what?" I implored.

"I'm sorry for betraying you," Lacius said, looking at Ina longingly. "Satisfied?" He asked me.

"No, I want you to apologize for betraying her and the divine feminine itself. Because of *you* and *your* bargain with the Solar Lord, the Treaty was created in the first place. Because of *you*, the entire cosmic order was disrupted."

"Dear Kyanie, you want me to apologize for being myself? Disorder is who I am." He replied smoothly.

"I don't care who or what you think you are— show some damn accountability for your actions. Stop being a coward that hides behind anarchy to avoid feeling remorse for the pain and suffering you've caused." I spat, feeling my face heat with anger.

Taken back, Lacius looked at me with raised eyebrows before shrugging his mouth and responding. "I'm sorry... for everything."

"Don't look at me. Look at her." I pointed fiercely to the Dark Goddess, watching our interaction with a sly smile on her lips.

Lacius sighed before shifting back into the form she once knew and loved. Now, as the prisoner, he morphed a single finger into a long, sharp claw, then cut through the dirty twine that bound his lips.

"Inanna. I'm deeply, truly sorry for the suffering I caused you and the ongoing suffering I've caused the feminine." His voice was coarse and groggy after thousands of years as a mute prisoner.

Despite his damnation, Lacius's face was still ruggedly handsome, with a strong jaw-bone and full lips. Even from a distance, I could tell his eyes were the only thing that remained the same— a kaleidoscope of green that a lover could get lost in for hours.

However, suddenly his eyes turned sharp and cunning.

"Though, let's not forget how you had your revenge on me, dear Inanna. How you made sure karma came for me with unforgiving brutality." He snarled, baring two rows of yellowing teeth.

My eyebrows knit together, I turned back to the Dark Goddess. "What revenge?"

She opened her mouth to elaborate before Lacius interjected.

"Oh, did she glaze over the part in her story where my wife and child were murdered?" Lacius asked sarcastically.

"Your what...." I breathed in disbelief.

"By the time she had grown powerful enough to retrieve my

body, to condemn me to the underworld, I had moved on. I had fallen in love with a beautiful maiden while traveling near the equator, and she soon fell pregnant with my first son. We led a simple life in a small shack on the edge of a rainforest." Lacius paused, throwing Inanna a resentful look. "One night, I was awoken by the most terrible growls outside our home. I told my wife to stay inside and guard the baby, so I could go out and shift into something to protect us."

He shook his head forlornly with a flare of dramatization . "I had no idea of Inanna's power to transfigure— she had changed my wife and child into jaguars, and the roaring was, in fact, their cries for help. I shifted into a monstrous demon with razor-sharp claws to take down the beasts that I thought were threatening my family, killing them both with a single swipe." He sighed deeply. "It wasn't until I witnessed the imposter wife and child morph into creatures of darkness that I saw their mutilated bodies. Then, I was dragged and chained here by demons to live out my condemnation with their flesh and blood still fresh on my clothing."

"I had no idea...I...." Words had wholly failed me.

"Save your pity, dear Kyanie. I've come to terms with my karma." Lacius shifted, his chains clanking on the stone ground.

"Is that all true?" I turned to Inanna, a look of horror surely painted on my face.

The Dark Goddess sighed, "What can I say? Loss and grief are monsters of their own accord." She shrugged, "I think that was reasonable retribution after my life was ripped away, and the Earth I knew and loved was destroyed as a *joke*." Ina hurled the last word as if it were poison on her tongue.

I raised my eyebrows, then furrowed them as I swallowed.

"What do you mean?"

"Oh, did he glaze over that tiny detail?" She replied mockingly, crossing her arms before a single eyebrow raised with deadly calm. "How he 'jokingly' suggested that the Goddesses had enough time to reign."

"Well, technically, all I did was say to the Solar Lord, *'Can you imagine what Earth would be like if the Goddesses no longer ruled?'*. He was the one that took that idea and ran with it."

Words failed me as a range of emotions flooded my senses— disgust, rage, regret.

I shared my most intimate energy with the sole cause of the Treaty of Separation. I gave myself willingly to the being that betrayed the Dark Goddess and gave the Solar Lord his master plan… Sleeping with the enemy in this context doesn't feel like it did any good in this cosmic war….

I moved closer to the cell as Lacius looked at me longingly.

Spitting on the ground in front of him, I scowled. "You deserve to rot here for eternity."

"If it's any consolation," he glanced between the Goddess and me, remorse burning in his gaze, "I did truly love you both. You wild, free women." He concluded, smirking.

"We're not free," I replied, turning to join the other females sitting on Maliandha, half-submerged in the inky black water of the River of Memories. "Not until all of humanity is truly free."

~*~

"I'm so angry, Ina," I said as fresh rage burned through me.

"Good," she turned over her shoulder, "Anger is sacred. Anger is your emotional body telling you that injustice has been done and you will not stand for it."

388

XXXII. Unity

Inanna, Morrigan, Lilith, and I rode atop Maliandha's back, holding each other firmly, up the River of Memories, dipping in and out of the water like one long, magical dolphin. We traveled along the river in darkness for quite some time until a break in the crystal cave walls opened to the sky.

As soon as the sunlight hit the dark, iridescent scales of Maliandha, Inanna, whom I was clutching tightly around the waist, took a joy-filled breath.

"How I missed the sky." She said dreamily to herself. Though unable to see her face, I could feel how deeply she was smiling at the sun, the clouds, and the birds flying past us.

The air was crisp with winter while the sun shone down radiantly, basking us in its warm rays of light. Despite the slight warmth from the sun, I was eternally thankful for the dragon-scale armor Inanna gave me, which blocked out the biting air.

We continued soaring through the water, gliding through a large lake shortly after breaching the day-lit surface. Eventually, we faced a mountain so tall that the peak was hidden amongst the clouds.

The surrounding alpine valley was glistening with fresh snow and buzzing with life. Birds darted between towering evergreen trees; elk combed the vegetation for berries and looked at us with wide eyes as we flew by their herd. Meanwhile, a single, massive grizzly bear lumbered a reasonable distance away, hunting for its next meal.

"Do you see the Tree?" Ina turned around, smiling broadly. "We've arrived at Mount Hope, darling."

Whether it was the direction we came from, my perspective

now being on dragon-back, or the fact that I had attained ascension and descension, but my view was unrecognizable.

The mountain I had climbed, and eventually ascended from, was a measly hill compared to the behemoth that jutted out of the Earth before me. I spotted the Tree of Fate, its broad limbs reaching out to me as we flew past the mossy patch that held me in my last moments in the Logical Realm.

Maliandha did not falter as we made our way up the steep waterfall, mist mixing with the sunlight to cast us in rainbows, eventually passing through the Veil effortlessly. I relished the scent of milk and honey before we finally reached the summit.

Our aquatic dragon waded in the Spring of Soul, a pool of crystalline-blue water that was surprisingly warm for being atop an icy mountaintop, as we took in a jarring sight.

"What in the—." Ina breathed as she slowly stepped off Maliandha, standing knee-deep in the clear water, staring at a large, modern-looking mansion.

The architecture was bland and minimalistic, with an overly boxy silhouette and large, square windows. More noticeable were the over one-hundred stone stairs lining the walk up to the white building, lifting it off the ground and up towards the Aethers.

The Dark Goddess shook her head vigorously, walking to the shore with focused, angry strides. "How could someone build here?" She whipped around to the three of us standing hesitantly beside Maliandha. "Did any of you know of this?" She snapped.

"No, Inanna. It was my understanding that this mountain was sacred and protected." Morrigan replied seriously, frowning slightly at the ugly, ivory structure that shaded us in its large, angular shadow.

Inanna closed her eyes and took several deep breaths before

speaking again. "Well. No use getting riled up over more blatant disrespect and utterly disgusting use of resources… Come join me, my sisters, and let us cast a circle," Ina said definitively, waving us over to her on the shoreline.

I stood by as the females prepared their summoning ritual. Lilith drew a large circle on the sandy shore with her finger. Meanwhile, Morrigan removed several items— a small cauldron, a large black feather, a bundle of dried herbs, matches, one white candle, and one black candle— from the pack she had strapped to her. The three females stepped into the center and turned to me as they began joining hands.

"Come join us, Kyanie," Lilith said sweetly.

"Yes, please, we need all the energy we can get." Ina chimed in, smiling warmly and waving me into the circle.

Unable to argue with a Goddess or her equally powerful companions, I complied.

Morrigan lit the two candles on opposite sides of our circle. Then Lilith lit the bundle of herbs, fanning it with the black feather so the smoke swirled around us all, then placing it in the cauldron, still smoldering.

"From the earth we are born into, to the water that sustains life. From the fire that fuels our spirit, to the air that breathes through our lungs. Oh, great and all-knowing Void from which we came and will return to, hear our prayer. Bring my sister here, reunite her with me and help us restore balance." Inanna spoke ritualistically, her eyes closed and face turned upwards to the sky.

"Cosmic Goddess, appear now!" The females said in unison.

Suddenly a rumble of thunder, accompanied by a simultaneous lightning bolt, struck the mountaintop.

The Cosmic Goddess arrived, all three holding firmly onto

Lumeriarcis on an ornate, golden saddle as the mighty, winged beast flapped its wings gracefully into landing. Inanna looked as if she would leap from the circle, then, clearly remembering the ritual underway, took a calming breath and concluded.

"Thank you, thank you, thank you. I am eternally grateful for the spark of life gifted to me by the ever-present Void." Ina took the smoking herbs and waved them in a counter-clockwise circle as Morrigan blew out the candles she had lit. *"I close this ritual with a heart full of love and gratitude."*

The Dark Goddess broke free from the circle as soon as the last words left her mouth. She ran over to her sister like a child reuniting with a dear friend. The Cosmic Goddess, in return, smiled widely and let out a laugh of disbelief as they collided with Inanna in a loving force.

"I missed you all so much," Ina whispered, buried in Brigid's fire-red hair, before stepping back to look at all three of her sisters. "Did you get my letter? Did you ensure a trustworthy Ascended Master to watch over the Ethereal? How are you? How have you been? I have so many questions."

Several tears fell from the Dark Goddess's violet eyes.

"We're good. Very good." Songi answered kindly, looking at her sister lovingly. "As you can tell by this ever and over-flowing spring, we missed you dreadfully as well."

"The gnome delivered your letter with haste and volunteered herself as the temporary head of the Ethereal, taking the form of a giant pink angel," Brigid added, breathing a laugh through her nose. "I had to admire the little being's confidence, but alas… We allowed the Greek pantheon their time to supervise."

"I see you've made the most of your time in darkness," Kokyangwuti spoke slowly, gazing intensely at Inanna and the web of her life. "Morrigan," she bowed, "Lilith," she bowed again, "Thank you for saving our sister from the pits of loneliness."

Ina's companions, along with myself, joined the Goddesses' reunion several strides away from the shore.

"With all due respect," Morrigan began, bowing back at the crone-goddess. "It was not us that did that, but her." She nodded to Inanna. "Without her alchemizing the pain of heartache, we would not be here."

"We owe her everything," Lilith added.

Ina swatted at her two sister companions. "Oh, stop. You know what they say... *In the greatest times of darkness, one can finally find their own inner light.*"

I cocked my head curiously. "Who says that?"

"You know, I think it's probably an original that the Solar Lord ripped off as his own," Ina laughed cheekily, tapping her chin.

I chuckled, as did Ina's companions.

"It is nice to find humor in times of uncertainty," Kokyangwuti spoke wisely, moving her gaze to me. "Miss Kyanie, are you prepared to meet the Solar Lord?"

I swallowed my nerves, not allowing anxiety to bubble over.

"I am," I said with as much stable courage as possible.

"Excellent because he is certainly prepared to meet you." She replied, her gaze unmoving. "I have never been able to see or sense his life force but here, on this mountaintop... He is near, that is for certain."

Inanna moved to grab my hand. "Remember— we will perform our prayer, summoning the Solar Lord here, and you will take it from there." Her eyes scanned my face, searching for an ounce of trepidation.

"A prayer? I thought we were performing a ritual, a magick spell of sorts?" I questioned.

"Prayers...spells... they're the same thing, really. Saying any words with intention, with consciousness supporting it... It creates something. A *belief*. And a belief in something is just as real as the thing itself." Ina held her arms out to the spring and mountain surrounding us. "Faith. Hope. These are things that are not as tangible as, say power, yet the belief in them is just as strong and real as the densest metal on Earth. My sister wept here for weeks, clinging to the faint hope that we would be reunited again." Ina grinned at her goddess sisters, "And here we are."

I hope I can do this... No... I believe *that I can do this.*

"Kyanie," Songi interjected. "I want to be certain you're aware of the implications of lifting the Veil."

I nodded, looking at the mother goddess intently.

"With the Veil gone, humans will be able to fully see the otherworldly beings they've unknowingly shared the planet with. How they react to said beings is unclear." She raised her chin, a look of worry flashing across her face. "The other Realms will also become visible to humans and, once again, their reaction to learning of the Ethereal and Basal Realms is uncertain."

"I don't want to endanger you, Cosmic Goddess. And I certainly don't want to endanger your entire Realm." I chewed on my lip and glanced at Inanna, who looked at me as if I were truly the one she had been waiting for since her descension. "But I accept these implications. For the sake of the Earth Mother, for the Dark Goddess... I must set the truth free even if it's the last thing I do."

Songi sighed. "Then so mote it be."

Brigid clapped her hands together. "I, for one, am ready for some change." She looked across the spring, out to the Logical Realm. "I believe in a greater future for humanity on Earth. We all should because, well, believing in the opposite will be all of our damnations."

The fate of Earth, as well as these Divine Rulers, began to weigh heavily on my shoulders.

"I suppose it's time we call our brother here, eh?" Inanna asked all of us females, raising her eyebrows questioningly.

Nodding, my heart thudded loudly.

"Together?" The Dark Goddess asked the Cosmic Goddess, unconditional love radiating from her gaze.

An image of my brother reaching his hand to me atop the Well of Dreams flashed in my mind. I closed my misty eyes before taking a calming breath.

We made our way over to the ring in the sand. Stepping into it, then, upon seeing how small it was now that our group had doubled, Inanna retraced a larger circle to encompass us all.

Morrigan once again lit the black and white candles before Lilith relit the herb bundle, dipping into both flames, then floated around us in a whirl of sweet, pungent smoke.

"We call upon the elements — earth, water, fire, and air — to aid in our ritual. Oh, great and all-seeing Void from which we came and will return to, hear our prayer. Summon the Solar Lord to us, reunite the Three Divine Rulers and help us restore balance."

A great gust of wind blew through the mountaintop, whipping my already windswept, frizzy hair around my face.

"Solar Lord, appear now!"

As suddenly as Lumeriarcis and the Cosmic Goddess appeared, the mansion's doors flew open, and three men strode out, making their way menacingly down the stone steps.

Though they were far from the shore where we were still standing in ritual, I could make out the male on the left as clear as day — Shadowmere. He looked downright blood-thirsty upon spotting me.

In contrast to Shadowmere's black hair and dark purple satin suit, the center male wore a loosely fitting, gold-and-white robe with long white hair and a beard to match.

All three males proudly wore their emblem— a twelve-pointed sun with a bisected X. I was facing the Trine of Power.

"Long time no see, sisters." The center male bellowed, attempting to be friendly yet smiling arrogantly.

The Solar Lord.

The other male, whom I had a strange, distant recollection of, donned a black suit with an angular face highlighted by his lack of head and facial hair. As the three males approached, I noticed a faint green hue on the unknown man's lumpy skin. Small horns protruded from his forehead, and, even more terrifying, he displayed a mouthful of tiny, needle-like teeth.

Ina quickly closed the circle before she stepped out, strong and defined in her movements, towards the men. I, along with the other divine females, did not move from the circle.

"Thank you for joining us, fellas." She said with a slightly mocking tone. "I believe this meeting is long overdue."

The Solar Lord laughed heartily. "I believe this meeting could have been entirely avoided if Lacius had succeeded in deceiving and manipulating a woman, just *one* more time." He jeered, smiling at his companions, who sniggered in response.

Ina sucked in her cheeks, likely fighting her snarky remark with agitation. Watching the Divine Rulers' interaction and the Solar Lord's mocking nature relit the fire in me that had begun to smolder months ago.

"Have you brought the Treaty of Separation?" I blurted.

The males and the divine females around me stared, startled by my abrasive bluntness.

"Ah, yes. Miss Redferne. I've heard much of you as of late." The Solar Lord smiled, though it did not reach his eyes. "Come to me, my child. Let me look at you."

I made no movement. "You can see me fine from where you are," I replied, raising my chin defiantly.

Shadowmere muttered something under his breath, and I caught his predatory stare.

The Solar Lord chuckled softly. "Just as insubordinate as you led me to believe." He whispered to Shadowmere, though it was loud enough for me to hear.

"Now, Miss Redferne, to answer your question. Yes. I do have the Treaty. Enki, show her." He motioned to the green-skinned male, who took a hefty black leather book from his coat and held it up. "Though I hope we chat a little before getting into all of the serious nitty-gritty." The Solar Lord smiled patronizingly.

XXXIII. Destiny

"What would you like to discuss, brother?" Songi asked, stepping in front of myself and the other females, all of us still standing safely within the ritual circle.

"Well, I feel as if I've been made out to be the bad guy throughout the Realms. I want to get my story straight before the Veil is lifted. If it can actually be done, that is." He replied pompously, looking down his nose at me as if I were a foolish child.

"Let's hear it," I spoke bravely, subconsciously crossing my arms over my chest to protect my energy.

The Solar Lord snickered, and Shadowmere's lip curled.

"All those years ago, man created me out of love and desire for a male leader to support their conquests. At the time, I had no intention of severing the Realms or casting aside the Goddesses. I just love being loved." The Solar Lord began, making slow, steady movements down the stairs towards us. "I wanted to rule the Earth alongside my divine sisters." He smiled at the Dark and Cosmic Goddesses, though they did not return his expression. "I wanted us to rule every aspect of human existence together.

"It wasn't until the men who manifested me declared that the feminine was inherently weak that I did what was best for me and my reign. They refused to bow down to anything and everything female, so I made some changes, thanks to a suggestion from a dear companion." He spoke smugly, watching both me and Ina scowl.

"As the numbers of men who believed in me grew, so did their unending desire for resources and power. What kind of Divine Ruler would I be to deny my loyal subjects what they want? They believed I created the Earth for them to use and exploit as they wished. They spread their belief in me, above all else, across the world." Greedy power flashed in his eyes, and I grimaced in angry disgust.

"It left me no choice but to remove the Goddesses and create the Treaty of Separation to properly cement my place as the true ruler of man." He lifted his head triumphantly. "Afterwards, my Guardians of the Order, originally chosen by me and born from human domination, did my dirty work on Earth, destroying the Old Ways. Meanwhile, the Machine, a byproduct of the Order born from human greed, amassed wealth to sustain my power and control."

Anger burned in my veins, and I bit my tongue.

"For the past four thousand years, man and I have had a mutually-beneficial relationship. I allow humans to do as they see fit, using my name to accomplish their global conquest goals. In turn, all they have to do is pray for forgiveness and stay devoutly loyal to me. Then, I absolve their earthly sins and help them attain ascension… or at least let them believe it."

The Solar Lord smirked and lifted his chin. "As you know, sweet little Kyanie, the belief in something is enough to make it real. Now imagine thousands, millions, of people believing… that sort of power can be insurmountable."

He fixed the golden tassels hanging on the front of his robe. "So, clearly, I am not evil, and I am not a villain. I simply have masses of adoring fans, er, subjects." He cleared his throat. "Humans, who love me, and I them. They believe me to be a righteous, loving, forgiving Lord, and to those who pray to me, that is precisely what I am! I come in many faces, in many names. I am just as multifaceted as the mortals that worship me. They are my children, and I will never abandon them as their Goddesses did."

I simply could not, and would not, be quiet any longer.

"Their Goddesses did *not* abandon them," I yelled, angrier than I intended. "They were tricked into a life separate from the Earth that they stewarded for hundreds of thousands of years. Until some jealous men created you out of the twisted belief that a male god was the true giver of life when, as biology shows, that is a gift given solely to the female."

I stepped out of the circle, suddenly feeling very vulnerable. Inanna, as if she could sense it, moved to my side.

The Solar Lord tutted. "Anger does no good for a woman. Please, Miss Redferne, calm down."

I laughed in response, seeing red.

"No," I replied, smiling, with a surely crazed look in my eyes. "No, I will not calm down. You say anger does no good for a woman — what about assault? Or domestic abuse? Or the inability to have bodily autonomy, to be sovereign beings instead of breeding livestock? Anger is *exactly* what women need right now because it is our suppressed rage that will no longer be silenced. We," I motioned to the Goddesses behind me, "will no longer be silenced."

I exhaled, regaining my composure. "I have some questions for you, Solar Lord."

The Lord waved a bored hand at me. "Go on."

"Where did Lacius fit into your plans?"

The patriarch smiled pretentiously. "I needed the energy of evil and fear on my side to help humans see that I was the bringer of love and faith. To see that I would protect them from the evils of the world." He replied heroically.

"If he's so important to your reign, why did you send him to me? I'm just an insignificant mortal."

400

"Because you, dear Kyanie, are a Child of Destiny." The Solar Lord answered. "I knew there would come a day when some human would be brazen enough to question the status quo— and who I would need to call upon if that day came. Once my Guardians got word of your eye opening, I sent Lacius, or Pyter as you knew him, to throw you off your life path." He smiled smugly, seeing the angry, contorted look on my face. "Just as I used him to mislead the Dark Goddess into damnation."

The Solar Lord continued moving towards me, closing the distance between us with each long, dominant stride.

"You see, I prefer to stay on top. So, as an omnipotent and omnipresent being, I've thought out all the possible outcomes." He cleared his throat as he began. "On the one hand, if Lacius had gone through with our initial plan and left you to Shadowmere, we're only a few days away from the Treaty being immortalized. This would have allowed me to easily continue my complete domination of the Earth."

The Solar Lord shrugged casually as he continued. "After you escaped, I offered him the option to *attempt* ascending with you to gain his freedom from Inanna's imprisonment. In this *highly* unlikely case, he would have brought chaos to the Ethereal and begun my expansion there, for me." He smirked patronizingly, "Though I knew he'd never pass through the Veil, so I prepared for the only other outcome— your ascension *alone*. In this scenario, where your persistence pays off, and you're actually able to lift the Veil, my Trine of Power will be free to expand into all three Realms."

He lifted both hands as he concluded. "So here we are, Kyanie Redferne, atop Mount Hope's true peak, with the fate of the Veil in question." The Solar Lord continued his self-satisfied expression until he was only an arm's length from me. "Truthfully, I'm indifferent to your little quest. Whether or not you succeed, I still have my loyal Guardians and the Machine," he motioned to the two males behind him, "To continue my reign."

"Your reign won't go on when humans see the truth." I finally found my voice, though it wavered.

The patriarch laughed coldly. "You really think that will change anything? How many humans have you met in your lifetime, foolish girl?" My mouth pressed into a narrow line. "And how many cared enough to change their lifestyles from the convenient norms of society to make a difference?"

He pressed on, "You are the first and *only* mortal that has actually done something." Snickering, he mocked, "Isn't that enough indication of humanity's likely reaction to the Veil being lifted?"

I opened my mouth to protest.

"Additionally," The Solar Lord straightened, holding up a firm hand to cut off anything I had to say. "I now have great plans in store. I foresee an all-inclusive luxury resort within the Ethereal," he glanced to the Cosmic Goddess. "An impenetrable jail within the Basal," he looked to Ina, who bared her teeth, "And even a global spring-water company based right here on Mount Hope."

The Solar Lord motioned to the Spring of Soul. "I mean, imagine how much profit we could amass from bottling and selling the very tears of the Cosmic Goddess. To sell people soul-filled water in a bottle with the hope of attaining enlightenment."

I exhaled in disbelief, my anger officially transforming into blinding rage. "What is it all for?! Is there no end to your conquests? No rock, river, or creature that is free from your never-ending desire to consume, to amass wealth, all at the expense of the feminine?" I spat.

"I suppose the end would be once we simply run out of

resources." The Solar Lord answered smugly as if he weren't referencing the complete and utter devastation of the planet.

Confusion and doubt flooded my brain. In all scenarios, the Solar Lord would still win. The Trine of Power would still dominate the human experience, the Earth Mother, the feminine, regardless of whether the truth was out.

And yet… something stirred in me.

Hope.

Hope— it left me in pieces as I clung to its last thread.

Hope destroyed me and gave me life in the same breath: Now, it felt like a beacon of light.

Hope that humans will wake up once the truth is out. That humans will forsake their greedy, power-hungry ways to help us return to our original ways of living. That creativity and femininity would be cherished and celebrated rather than condemned and suppressed. Hope that the ways of the Goddess and living in harmony with the Earth and our fellow humans would respell reality.

I glanced at Inanna, who also appeared to have doubts brewing in her mind.

"So if I were to destroy the Treaty, would you step down from ruling alone and allow all Three Divine Rulers to reign together?" I questioned, choosing my words carefully.

"Well, if I relinquish the Treaty, I will not just willingly give away my power. So I have a bargain for you, Miss Redferne. If the Veil is lifted, I will appoint Shadowmere as my ruling head on Earth while I stay comfortably away from the affairs of man in my mansion here." He waved to the obnoxious white building.

"And…." I said, feeling there was more to this bargain.

"And, for the sake of equality or feminism, whatever you want to call it, Shadowmere will take a queen to be his counterpart as King of the Earth." The Solar Lord concluded.

My lips thinned again, and I glanced at Shadowmere, looking at me like a prideful predator who had finally captured its prey.

"Will Amber be your Queen?" I questioned.

Shadowmere smiled, causing my stomach to churn. "Of course not. She is my Handmaiden; she is not worthy of being my ruling Queen of Earth."

He broke my gaze to glance at the females behind me.

"What of the Goddesses?" I questioned.

The Solar Lord shrugged indifferently. "They will be free to do as they see fit once the Veil is lifted off their Realms."

Again I looked to Inanna, whose eyebrows were tight with worry, then the Cosmic Goddess, looking equally as unsettled.

Either I turn back now, letting the Solar Lord continue to rule and hide the truth of our multi-realm existence...Or I go through with the plan, lift the Veil, and allow complete anarchy to ensue...

I chewed the inside of my lip as I deliberated with my inner voice. Unsure if I would accept the Solar Lord's bargain or walk away, knowing the truth and not sharing it with the rest of humanity.

"I'd like to say something," I said, squaring my shoulders and keeping my chin high as the Solar Lord motioned for me to elaborate. "You clearly think very highly of yourself. You assume that man has a never-ending loyalty to you and the patriarchal society we've all been forced to endure for the past four thousand years."

I stepped forward, lifting my chin as high as it would go.

"But I think you overlook that the ways of the Goddess— the ways of living in peace with one another, not competing and fighting for power or wealth— are deep within our blood, our bones. Deep inside, we know where we came from. Where we will return to. The Void of nothing, yet everything, of masculine and feminine in one."

The Solar Lord retreated a step.

"You seem to underestimate the feminine. You've been led to believe, by the angry, power-driven males that created you, that 'feminine' is inherently less than when it is blatantly untrue. You've thrived in a world of human discord that would rather destroy any differing beliefs than see that they're all the same. That everything in this existence is one."

I dared to point an angry finger at the chest of the Solar Lord.

"You are no Lord of mine. It has been in your name that man has done the unthinkable. Guardians have used your name to make the unjustifiable justified. Nearly every war on earth has been fought for *you*. Nearly every genocide of indigenous peoples, of witches, of queers, of people with beliefs more attuned to the Earth than your patriarchy, has been done for *you*. Millions of people have died in the name of what is *'holy.'*" I felt hot tears well up.

"When in reality, it is us that is holy. Everything created by the Void and nurtured by the Earth Mother is holy, is divine." Shaking my head angrily, I continued. "Life in the Logical Realm, before it was such, was so mystically, magically beautiful. Humans were equally sexual flesh as they were conscious spirit in one."

I turned back to Ina, who was watching me proudly. "The dark feminine was once a thing of mystery, reverence, and magick. Then it became evil, sinister, and the subject of male hatred.

"You were fully aware that the first cultures on Earth worshiped the female form, the life-giver. So you set out to erase this history because you *knew* that you'd never have the power of the female. Womb-envy blended seamlessly into your egotistical belief system until it became the norm for males to be superior, just as you are over humanity. So you and your men worked tirelessly, ingraining life-fearing denial of the female energy that flows through us all to repress our innate bisexual nature. Your only option was to annihilate the Old Ways because, if you hadn't, you would be seen as the fraud you are."

I laughed drily. "Our very own home planet has been subject to an infinite variety of violence and murders, just as the human female has been beaten and killed by the hands of angry men. You allowed your Guardians to plunder, rape, and desecrate all things feminine. From our Earth Mother to any woman whose rights have been stripped away by the patriarchy. You allowed the Machine to be created and continue the vile desecration of our planet because it served you, your chosen men in power, and all other compliant humans who benefit from a society based on masculine domination."

Exhaling angrily, I threw a glare at the green-skinned male.

"That evil, all-consuming Machine pumps out multinational corporations and their accompanying pollution like a candy dispenser. Our reality is slowly being swallowed by this robotic, technological monster, leaving humans as ignorant, entitled brats hopelessly addicted to conveniences. All of it, just to keep people numbed and distracted."

I composed myself, drawing my anger inward.

"You are not a Lord of love and peace. No. In fact, far from it. You are a Lord of war and destruction. You've turned our beautiful Earth Mother into a degenerate wasteland of material goods, a global network of greedy, power-hungry institutions, and death machines, all stemming from you and your *bullshit* word. You've created a world where things are mechanized and monetized until the last drop of soul is squeezed out for profit maximization."

I scowled angrily, wanting to throw as much verbal poison as possible at the head of all that was wrong with society.

"So I accept your bargain, Solar Lord. Because I believe that once the truth is out, the divine feminine will finally get the momentum needed to break free from the shackles of oppression put in place by you. To return to the original ways of humanity, of three-hundred thousand years of Earth-Mother-based-existence, before you and your evil Order took power."

I smiled like a lunatic. "Your reign ends today. The society you've created and its facade of holiness will crumble alongside the Treaty. I hope you're ready to watch your hyper-masculine reality fall to the feminine, indigenous, and queer because *we* are rising."

The Solar Lord's smug look vanished, and he stared back at me with utter disdain. For a moment, he looked as if he would retort, then instead snapped his fingers to the green-skinned man.

"Enki, give her the Treaty." He finally said, not breaking his gaze from my defiant face.

Enki shared in his master's disgust as he begrudgingly handed me the leather-bound Treaty of Separation. Its dark cover was littered with foreign symbols I could scarcely decipher.

"You have no *idea* what you'll be doing if you lift the Veil." The Solar Lord said through gritted teeth. "Best of luck to you, Miss Redferne. I believe you'll need it." He flashed a final wrathful grimace as the Treaty was placed in my readied palms.

Holding the book in my hands, I felt power seep through the cover. Taking a steadying breath, I turned back to Inanna, still looking at me with raised, knit eyebrows. She nodded somberly to me and took the Treaty from me, knowing she had extensively reviewed the plan before our arrival.

I slowly walked back to the Cosmic Goddess, who bowed to me as solemnly. Standing in front of Songi and Brigid, I removed the top layer of dragon-scale armor from my chest, arms, and legs. All the while, my chain stayed high and proud.

"Your bravery will never be forgotten." Kokyangwuti croaked as I moved past her, removing the long sleeve thermal shirt I donned underneath the protective coverings given to me by Ina.

Now facing the Dark Goddess, who had been one step behind me the entire time, and her companions, I slipped my fleece-lined leggings to my ankles and stepped out of them. The frigid mountain air meeting my bare skin shocked my system and made the final part of my underdressing the hardest by far.

"We will always remember what you've done for us," Morrigan said, taking a knee as I removed my undergarments.

Once again, I found myself standing completely bare in front of the Dark Goddess. No shame or modesty crept up my spine. Not even as I admired the pouch of fat that sat atop my hips, the stretch marks that lined my upper thighs and breasts, or the layer of dark, fine hair that covered my forearms, legs, armpits, and pelvis.

All the 'imperfections' I despised were now simply a part of me. Unsure of how much longer I'd have in this flawed human body, I sent every ounce of self-love I had into each fiber of my unique, perfectly-imperfect being.

"Thank you," she whispered as she replaced the Treaty of Separation in my hands then placed a corded necklace with a rough black gem around my head. It was nearly identical to the one given to me by the coven, though rather than polished and smooth, this one was jagged and raw. As if she had harvested the gem herself before leaving her crystal-cavern-castle.

I smiled at Inanna, and when she returned my expression, her eyes glistened with assurance.

Making confident strides into the water, I braved my destiny. My heartbeat thrummed in my ears with every splashing step toward the epicenter of the Spring.

My spirit broke the day I lost my family. Now, my heart and soul finally feel whole again, and I'm giving it all away. I took a moment to soak up every last drop of my senses: the smell of fresh alpine air and the feel of the crisp breeze on my bare, rosy skin, the expansive blue-gray sky littered with cirrostratus clouds, and the endless sea of evergreen trees. *This life is a gift,* I thought as tears pricked the corners of my eyes, *A beautiful blessing from the Void, from the Earth Mother.* My lip quivered as I sucked in a breath, not allowing a single more tear to fall down my face. *Thank you for my life; I hope I lived it well— despite my last few years of being a depressed asshole.* I smiled sadly to myself and the Void. *And thank you for letting me see my family together again.*

Finally standing centered in Spring of Soul with the Treaty of Separation in hand, I defiantly faced the Trine of Power once more. The goddesses stood on the shore, holding hands in unified support and silently, subtly sending me prayers of success.

The Solar Lord, clearly repulsed by my naked state, scoffed.

Shadowmere, evidently aroused, snarled hungrily.

Enki, who had shown little to no emotion thus far, sneered.

I looked each in the eye, obstinately displaying my nudity and the power held in my natural female form. Clutching the book firmly, I took one more final, deep breath and raised my chin and voice.

"I call upon the elements— earth of the north, fire of the south, wind of the east, and water of the west." I raised my left hand, pointing towards the cardinal directions as I named them. *"Oh great and all-seeing Void from*

which we came and will return to, hear my prayer. Allow me to be basked in the Universal Flame and the Eternal Fire to break the binding of this Treaty. Use my life force to create a new life for humanity."

A fierce wind bellowed across the Spring. *"I believe in a better future, oh great Void, please, help me reveal the truth for all humanity to see. Destroy the Treaty of Separation; destroy the Veil— so mote it be!*"

Maliandha began to swirl within the water, creating a whirlpool around my feet. At the same time, Lumeriarcis took to the skies above me. The two started their cosmic dance— one in the air, one on the earth, one of fire, one of water— encasing me in a whirling tornado of snow-speckled air and crisp blue water.

The Treaty started glowing a green hue that brightened with each turn of the Dragons of Dualism. An icy-hot sensation started in my hands, moving through my arms and the rest of my body. I focused on my breathing, though I found difficulty centering.

Above me, Lumeriarcis unhinged its jaw and showered me in the divine, golden energy of the Universal Flame. At the same time, Maliandha began spewing a burning-cold blue flame, the Eternal Fire, from the crystalline water.

I felt equally scorching hot as I did numbingly cold.

My vision began to blur before I saw Shadowmere lunge for the Cosmic Goddess, snatching Brigid in one quick movement. The two disappeared in a cloud of familiar black smoke. Her sisters cried in agony before Kokyangwuti collapsed into Songi's readied arms.

I wanted to stop, to save the maiden-goddess from the vile head of the Guardians, but it was too late. My body was no longer my own, and I could not move, no matter how hard I willed it. Still fully engulfed in both flames, my rage finally reached its peak.

The anger I felt— over the desecration and disrespect of our

Earth Mother, the oppression and exploitation of female labor and energy, the blatant massacres conducted in the name of a holy man who cared more about staying in power than actually helping the humans that prayed to him— it all came to this. I'd had enough.

Suddenly, my heart center cracked as I opened my mouth, and a primal yell erupted from my throat. Just like the red kettle that started it all, I screamed.

I screamed as if my voice were representing the pain of the entire divine feminine. As if thousands of years of female persecution had been built up to this moment. I screamed with the force of millions of angry, battered, beaten, scared, hungry, helpless women and innocent, lost souls.

Radiant emerald energy began to emerge from my chest, and images of my hawk and wolf spirit, both surrounding and supporting me, came into view. Slowly, the two morphed together, taking the form of a magnificent dragon.

Its body was bright chartreuse and ivory, with strong, feathered wings poking out from its side and wispy iridescent tendrils lining its spine. As its serpentine body caught the sun's rays, I saw every color on the spectrum shimmer in each scale.

For a moment, it looked at me, its hazel eyes an eery mirror of my own, and familiarity brewed between us. Then it opened its jaw and showered the Treaty of Separation, as well as myself, in a blazing fire. Combined with the Dragons of Dualism's unrelenting flames, burning pain now shot through every nerve of my vessel.

The ground shook, and the sky rippled— the Veil was lifted.

Within seconds, the leather-bound book had disintegrated along with any and all of my remaining energy. Pain was replaced with a terrifying lack of feeling as my body lost all sensations.

As soon as the Treaty's ashes blew away in the icy mountain breeze, Lacius, in his true, macabre form, appeared. He pounced on the Solar Lord, and the two tussled as if they had been waiting thousands of years to hash out their differences.

All of the goddesses I had encountered in the Ethereal Realm also materialized, consoling the Cosmic Goddess, especially Kokyangwuti, who could no longer stand alone. Each of the divine females looked at me, horrified concern painted on their faces.

The green dragon from my heart flapped its mighty wings far above the other two dragons and me. It let out an earth-shattering roar as my heartbeat slowed and my vision wholly failed me. At that moment, a single, strong pulse throbbed in my stomach.

I collapsed into the Spring of Soul with only my hearing left.

"NOT YET! SHE CAN'T DIE! NOT YET!" Inanna screamed before several splashes sounded in the water around me.

The Dark Goddess had prepared me for this; she had told me not to fear death or the "ultimate surrender," as she called it. Truthfully, I was never scared of it— especially not after seeing the Realms, which were as timeless and immortal as our souls. Letting go of my life and releasing myself into the hands of the cosmos, I trusted wholeheartedly that this was not the end.

Suddenly, every heartache, moment of laughter, tear, every *thing* I experienced in my brief twenty years of living flooded my mind's eye. And I felt bliss; I felt complete. Thoughts of my family, my dog, my friends, my witch family, and everyone who impacted my journey amalgamated as one and filled my slowed heart.

A calm, peacefulness flowed through me as a new voice began whispering. *"I am the Way and the Life. I am the Nothing and the Everything. I am Death, and I am Birth. Come home to me, my Child of Destiny."*

The voice, both male and female, spoke with a gentle knowing, and I indeed felt no fear. Not even as the last of my life force slipped away.

"From the Aethers to the Abyss, our love never faltered."

My father's voice echoed, causing my heart to forcefully beat just one more time. In my last conscious moment, I felt only pure love.

I did not want to die but accepted it graciously.

From the Void in which we came and will return to.

EPILOGUE

I had accepted my fate and the death brought upon myself in my quest to lift the Veil and save our Earth Mother, to save the divine feminine as a whole.

Now, I felt weightless. Free of my physical body and free to roam the liminal space I found myself in.

My soul had left my body atop Mount Hope and was now traveling through a place in time that felt like pure love, pure consciousness. A warm, white glow was all around me, encasing me in a cosmic cloud.

No longer Kyanie Redferne; that name felt foreign to me. I was no longer anything, bringing me a joy I had never known.

In the distance, there was a black hole, its gravitational force slowly drawing me closer and closer. And yet, another energy seemed to be pulling me away.

I was in the middle of a cosmic stalemate, about to be sucked into true oblivion, while another energy refused to let me go.

"NOT YET…NOT YET…."

I could still hear the Dark Goddess's screams.

Perhaps it wasn't my time, or perhaps it was.

Unattached to either outcome, I fully released my spirit into the universe's hands.

"NOT YET!"

A final voice sounded as I was yanked away from the black hole, back into the midst of cosmic consciousness.

ACKNOWLEDGEMENTS

The amount of love and gratitude I have for each soul that's impacted my spiritual journey would fill the pages of this book and then some.

To my parents, Trip and Susan: your unending support and love during this time have been my greatest foundation. If not for the safe, loving environment you created in my childhood home, "The Red Kettle" would not exist. You have both taught me so many invaluable lessons throughout my life, and words can never justly thank you for everything you've done for me. Thank you, I love you.

To my other family members, all my aunts, uncles, and cousins: thank you for your love and support. Special thank you to Aunt Abbie: you've gone above and beyond to show acceptance of who I am as a spiritual being, and I can't thank you enough for that.

To my womb-mate, life partner, editor, manager, sweet cheese-good time boy, Megan-Rose-Rouge: Oh man, do I love ya. Once again, words cannot describe all you've helped me through. From healing through nearly every romantic relationship I've had, to helping me brainstorm and talk out the plot of this book, your insight and advice are unmatched. You were the first person I told about the premise of my first book many summers ago on a back deck in the Cape. Your excited intrigue gave me my first boost of writing confidence. Since then, your never-ending support and encouragement have been the backbone that's kept me aligned. Truthfully, I could write an entire book on the lessons we've learned together and the memories of tear-filled laughter we've shared, but I'll cut it short. I love you so goddamn much, and I cannot wait to legally bind our houses to ensure a smooth global-matriarchal takeover.

To my editor, illustrator, O.G. wifey, avid book-lover, and nearly life-long friend, Phoebe: hey dude, isn't it crazy that I'm thanking you in my acknowledgments? I've been almost as excited to write my gratitude for you here as I am to publish my brainchild. Having you as a friend, not to mention a professional writing asset, has been one of the greatest blessings in my life. For as long as I can remember, you have always been 100% authentically you and no one else. Honestly, you're one of the coolest people I know. From romping around the world on spontaneous travel trips to building an entire chicken coop during quarantine, you are one of a kind. The inspiration you've given me, through your unapologetic, authentic nature and incredibly helpful creative insights, has been infinitely valuable to me. Never stop reading, dancing, singing, traveling, farming, cooking, or simply being the way only you can do. I love you so so so SO much and can't thank you enough for your help in actualizing my life goals.

To my wife, best friend, personal 5-star chef, girl boss, Trixie to my Katya (and vice versa), soul mate, Emma: thank you for transferring into our hell of a high school and saving me from the worst years of my life. I have no idea who or what I'd be like if we hadn't become friends. You are one of the strongest, smartest, bravest (look at you conquering your fear of heights one hike at a time!), most beautiful people I know, and I'm so grateful to have you in my life. Your blunt truthfulness keeps me checked in reality, and I can always count on you to tell me how it is. Though we can go days, weeks, or even months not talking, I know that when I see you again, it will be as if no time has passed. I hope you always remember how much I love and appreciate you, my wonderfully cynical, sarcastic, witty girl-boss-bad-bitch.

To my old roommate, best friend, si-star, favorite Virgo with a Leo stellium, Princessa Alexandria: meeting you sent me on a trajectory towards my destiny. You taught me what it means to be a witch, but not just any witch, an unafraid, bold witch who knows how to take up space and not be sorry for it. From the moment I met you in EEC 101, and you guessed I was a Gemini (after astutely seeing my bracelet labeling me as such), your magick has radiated off of you. You are so undeniably unique; you are meant for such big, beautiful things in your lifetime, and I'm honored to be a part of it. I can't wait for the day we've cultivated a land of our own for our children to romp, play and learn about nature together — a dream come true. Thank you for opening my eye to my inner witch through your authentic, magical way of being. I love you. I love you. I love you.

To my first spiritual teacher Angela Potts-Mang'andah: I am eternally grateful for your' Writing for Wellness' classes taught after yoga. It was there you introduced 'A Course in Miracles' and the concept that all our choices can be reduced to either love or fear. From that point on, my spiritual journey fully took off. You taught me how to process my emotions, set personal goals, and care for my soul. Not to mention the misconceptions surrounding natural home births, which permanently altered my feelings about hospital births. Your radical and often humorous approach to life will stay with me forever. Though it's been years since I saw you (at Sweet Cakes with baby Justine), I always wish you well and send you my love and eternal gratitude.

To my most important professional writing asset, Kathy Bizzoco: I've thanked you numerous times but can't do it enough. I submitted my questions to Green Frog Publishing almost a year ago and never would have dreamed that I would actually be creating my own publishing house. Through your honest advice and encouragement, I was able to start Moonstruck Ink. Since its inception, my life goals have become all the more apparent. Not only am I meant to be an author, but as the CEO of my own publishing house, I can uplift and share the voices of authors who may be drowned out by mainstream publishers. Your insight from decades in the profession has saved me thousands of dollars and fully empowered me as an independent writer. Thank you so much for your advice as well as your dark-satirical sense of humor that combined inspired the addition of my 'Desire' chapter.

To Ani Paparigian: I can hardly put into words how thankful I am that you took me in as your live-in nanny at a time when I needed community so badly. You will always be my older witch sister to me since we've definitely been through the whole sisterhood thing in a few lifetimes. You showed me how to live a life I create rather than falling into the old ways of colonization and patriarchy. You are the raddest, baddest, most creative, ingenious woman I know: I pray that Amber exudes the best qualities about you. I love you so and am dying for the day we reunite — 'we' including Tai, Scrumpy, and my dear Penelope.

There are so many people to thank, and though I wish I could write sincere, heartfelt paragraphs for everyone, I will try (try being the keyword) to keep it concise from here on.

To Lillia Dellagrotta: you will forever be one of the most unique souls I've ever met in my lifetime. Part of me is still convinced that you fell from the stars as some beautiful alien-hybrid sent here on Earth to equally care for children as well as cause chaos. I'm still mentally planning for our matching star tattoos, so let me know when I should come to NYC to get them. I love you to the stars and beyond.

To Grace Pruneau: you will forever and always be my sister. Though not related by blood, our souls are inexplicably linked together, and no matter what, I will have such a fierce love for you.

To Bridie Keefe: you may not remember it, but one night during my freshman year of college, we walked through the campus. During that nighttime walk and conversation, the concept for The Red Kettle formed. Thank you for being that initial creative spark. I love and miss you always, and can't wait to (hopefully) publish your first book someday!

To Libby Meeks and Savannah Bennett: thank you for being my original coven. You both have taught me what it means to stand tall and proud in my witchdom and look hot while doing it. No matter how far we roam, our coven will always beat strongly in my heart. I love you both so much.

To Olivia Musto, my little Gemini shnookums: thank you for being there for our sporadic FaceTime dates and for listening to a handful of these chapters as I worked on them. I can't wait for the day my audiobook is complete, so you can listen to my story in its entirety. I love you!!!

To Sarah Griffin: thank you for being such a consistent, supportive friend. Our game nights with Jeb (if you're reading this, hi, thank you, and love you!) and the gang always recenter me and remind me to not take life too seriously. I love you, my favorite librarian.

To Briana Pacheco: thank you for being the funniest, wittiest, kindest, and most sincere friend. The deep, meaningful conversations we held while utterly stoned at IHOP will always bring me joy. You are one of the baddest in the game, with your soul just as gorgeous as your external appearance. I love you so much!

To Riley Ayn: thank you for creating the Rage Release

Embodiment Practice that lit a fire of inspiration under my ass for the finale of this book. I love you and our penpal voice messages, girlie!

In addition to these beautiful souls, I'd like to thank each of these people (in no particular order) for impacting my life in some way or another: Jude Weinstein, Jebediah Fontaine, Hannah Tremblay, Lily Gelinas, Kayla MacEachearn, Tyler Kumes, Rosy Bell, Alec Mauk, Jordan D'Orazio, Sebastian Trabucco, Katherine Boustany, Mika Rayne, Diego Rivas, Dosia, Drew Hannigan, Sam Tompkins, Gabe Kolovos, Kali Ruoff, Parz, Jo Rapisarda, Lori Callahan, Simona Trandafir, and anyone else I didn't specifically name but know & love!

Lastly, I'd like to thank Sarah J. Maas for her series 'A Court of Thorns and Roses.' Though you may never read this acknowledgment, I cannot thank you enough for relighting my love of reading. Your magnetic, intoxicating style of story-telling sucked me into a magical Fae world as Feyre, and to this day, won't let me go. I have never felt a love for a book series like I do for ACOTAR. If the world loves my written word even *half* as much as I love yours, then I will consider myself a smashing success.

If you, the reader, have come this far drinking every last syllable of 'The Red Kettle,' then honestly, I thank you from the depths of my soul. I hope the rest of my life is spent toiling over these silly written words, impacting at least one person through my stories.

Until we meet again, I am eternally grateful for the spark of creative life given to me by the Great Cosmic Mother. To her, above *all* else, I thank.

'Green Glass Door' Preview

Flapping my hawk wings steadily while keeping a tight arm around the weight on my hip, I surveyed the Ethereal Realm. Wine and the Nectar of the Cosmos flowed freely from fountains, intoxicating all who divulged in a sip. Deities, gods, and goddesses now walked around glowing a golden hue. Since the Veil had been dismantled, their divine powers had only increased as the number of human worshippers did as well.

Finally landing on the eastern beach where I had left my canine soulmate and Guardian Angel, my heart pounded.

What will Cal think of me now? Perhaps he hates me for abandoning him and Belladonna to lift the Veil. I started toward his blue-painted door. *Or maybe he's grateful he had Bella with him and will be even more thankful upon seeing I've returned for her… and hopefully him as well….*

Swallowing the nerve-induced lump in my throat, I knocked. Bella's immediate *WOOF* elicited a wide, heart-filled grin from me. Within seconds of her barking alert, Calliel opened his door.

"Kyanie! You're back!" His facial expression shifted from surprise to joy to confusion. "Who is this?"

Begonia B. Joan is a Rhode Island native whose debut published work is *The Red Kettle: Tree of Fate Chronicles Book One*. She is a magick practitioner, artist, yogi, nature lover, and feminist. Begonia is the founder and CEO of *Moonstruck Ink*, an independent publishing house that aims to spread authentic, uplifting written works.

Moonstruck Ink Publishing, LLC
moonstruckink.com
begoniajoan@moonstruckink.com
@begoniajoan & @moonstruckink
on Instagram

www.ingramcontent.com/pod-product-compliance
Lightning Source LLC
Chambersburg PA
CBHW020501260626
47156CB00006B/1821